A smart, scrappy teacher is called upon by her traditional Mexican-American grandmother to help a relative in Mexico escape the clutches of a dangerous cartel. Reluctantly, she agrees, but in coming to her grandmother's aid, she needs the help of The Hated One, an ex-fiancé who broke her heart years before. Together, they must devise a plan to rescue her desperate, long-lost cousin and her cousin's child. To do so, Dina Salazar must enter the dreaded turf of the Zetas, a ruthless Mexican drug cartel. Such a mission is not for the faint of heart!

This book is a work of fiction. Names, characters, places, and incidents either are products of the author's imagination or are used fictitiously. Any resemblance to actual events or locales or persons, living or dead, is entirely coincidental.

Saving La Familia
Copyright © 2021 Donna Del Oro
ISBN: 978-1-4874-3260-7
Cover art by Martine Jardin

Published by eXtasy Books Inc

Look for us online at:
www.eXtasybooks.com

Saving La Familia

By

Donna Del Oro

DEDICATION

I dedicate this novel to my oldest and dearest friend, Connie Villalovas, and her family. We shared many laughs together, some heartaches and occasionally a little wise advice. I'll always remember her and her friendship.

CHAPTER ONE

Grandma Gómez—"Life is like an artichoke. It takes a lot of peeling to get to the heart of things."

How did I, in three short months, get to the heart of my Mexican-American family? It wasn't easy, believe me. Especially since I was the family's *desgraciada*. The disgraced one. Ever since I turned eighteen and had my legal name changed from Dolores—which means aches and pains in Spanish—to Dina. My namesake, Grandma Dolores Gómez, refused to speak to me or acknowledge my existence for about a year after the name change. Before that, I was simply the family brat and rebel. The know-it-all.

But you see, Grandma *was* the heart of the matter. And the big, dark secrets she kept closed up in her heart all got exposed in those tumultuous months. And before I could blink and realize what was happening, I was roped into a scheme to rescue cousins I never knew I had out of the deadly clutches of a Mexican drug cartel. Why was I chosen, you ask? Me, Dina Salazar, the *desgraciada*? A single schoolteacher with a long line of loser-boyfriends? How did I end up looking up the barrel of a cartel commando's automatic weapon? Come along with me and I'll tell you.

It took five years—six, counting my teaching credential—to work my way through college and, oh yeah, I lost my fiancé along the way—according to Mama and *Abuelita*, my *only* chance at happiness. Their idea of happiness meant you married young, spent the next twenty years changing diapers, cooking and cleaning for a man you seldom saw because he was working two or three jobs to pay for all the mouths you'd brought into the world . . .

¡Gracias a Dios!

Horrors, in my opinion.

That was the world they knew, anyway, and they didn't have the imagination to picture me in another, I suppose. I had another vision of the world. And myself. After all, I was Dina Salazar, not Dolores — the rambunctious little girl I used to be, saddled with what I thought to be a horrible name and all it implied. I was certain my family considered me the smirky smartass, the brazen wise-ass. No matter what, I was going to scratch and crawl my way into the American middle class, and if I lost whatever family status I had or whatever love came along, so be it.

After all, according to them, I had *una cabeza dura*. Hard-headed. And they were right.

My self-imposed exile from the family home in Salinas was easier to bear because I'd never really felt accepted by my mother and grandmother. Or my sisters. But there it was. I was forging my own path in uncharted waters. If I was sometimes a little frightened, I tried not to show it.

It was during one of these periods of self-imposed exile that a phone call from home changed everything.

I was sitting, drinking my favorite macchiato, chilling out and slogging my way through that day's student papers. After reading a condensed, sixth-grade version of *The Iliad* and watching a *History Channel* documentary on the Trojan War, I had assigned my thirty students at Lincoln Elementary an opinion essay entitled *Why the Trojan War Was Fought*.

I couldn't help but chuckle over one kid's thesis statement. "The Trojan War was fought because Helen was more beautiful than Britney Spears and had a better body, too, and because Paris stole her away from her mean Greek husband, Menelaus."

All the power struggles between the various Greek kings, Agamemnon's excuse to unite these warring factions under his leadership, and Troy seen as the gateway to the riches of Turkey—that entire lecture of mine had been lost on some of my students.

Oh well, sex always sells, especially when the twelve-year-olds you're teaching are thrumming with newly released, pulsing hormones. My students were at the stage when everything in the world at large was beginning to translate itself into a sexually charged experience. Talk about a slanted view of the world! Although I had to admit that slanted view also applied to most of the college men I'd met. But these poor pre-teens were no more interested in the politics of Ancient Greece than I was in the current rap music scene.

Ah, but how I loved my job! What more could I say? I was doing what I had set out to do more than ten years ago and loving every interesting, challenging day of it. Teaching kids was something I was meant to do. It was my destiny.

A destiny that Mama and my *abuelita*, of course, never took seriously. Not that I had much contact with them anymore. I was too busy making my way in the world.

"Aren't there any men teaching at your school?" *Mamá* asked me the last time I made the mistake of going home. I think she regarded a profession occupied by mostly women as somehow the equivalent of a well-paid babysitting service.

"I don't like that Huge," Grandma'd said, mispronouncing my current boyfriend, Hugh Goss's name—intentionally, I thought. "He acts too uppity." Mama had concurred, probably meaning that I was acting uppity as well.

Grandma just didn't like the ones who acted superior to her little clan, and I'm afraid the one time I brought Hugh home—over six months ago when I first started dating him—

he acted like a *gabacho*—asshole. This was my brother Roberto's assessment of him, anyway. I thought his adding *chingado* was over the top and totally unwarranted. Nevertheless, Hugh had made the mistake of calling Roberto's old, low-riding *Lincoln* a mob mobile. My sharp jabbing Hugh in the side was just met with a confused look, accomplishing nothing.

Poor Roberto. He was happy to barely make it out of high school with a GED, his skills with cars and anything mechanical fulfilling his *raison d'etre*. Parents were relieved, *Abuelita* was pleased, and everything was right with the world.

My cell phone chirped the Indiana Jones theme. I put my school papers down and dug the phone out of my purse.

"Dina, good news." It was my sister, Pet, probably calling from her hair salon.

"Don't tell me, you got Roberto to move out." My ding-a-ling, ex-con brother—served a year in juvie for stealing the hitch off an SUV—had moved with Pet and her husband, Juan Pablo, and their two kids into their rental home so that he could save up for an apartment. He was working again with my eldest brother, Frankie, and Pop in the tile business, fixing cars on the side, and we all hoped, staying out of trouble this time.

"Huh, no. Not yet, but working on it. Good news is I'm *not* pregnant. I don't want to be, not until we own a house . . .and even then, I don't think I want any more. Is that so terrible of me?"

"For chrissakes, Pet, why should it be terrible to be satisfied with two? Don't you have your hands full with one business, one husband, two kids and two dogs? Oh, make it three kids now with Roberto. How could you manage with another baby to buy stuff for and take care of?"

"Oh, good. I thought I was being selfish by not wanting any more, but I guess not. I'm being practical, right? And practical is good. I have to think American, like you. Not let *Mamá* and *Abuelita* influence me. They want me to have five, at least. So how are things with you and Hugh, *hermanita*? Still seeing him?"

Pet, two years my senior, wanted to weasel some secret or juicy tidbit of gossip out of me but I wasn't in the mood.

"Okay, I guess." I mentally shrugged. Six years ago when The Hated One and I broke up, I dated no one for a very long time.

Then, when I couldn't stand the celibacy one day longer, I made an effort to date again. The results of which have been a lamentable string of boyfriends over the past three years. The one before Hugh lasted two months. Hugh seemed to be different, though, but I was on my sixth month with him, and already, the bloom was off the rose.

I had no idea why.

Or maybe I was the girlfriend that the guys all got tired of. I chewed on that unwelcomed thought for a full two seconds. Then spat it out. Naahh!

"Just okay?" Pet probed. "Not moving further towards marriage or anything like that?"

"No, I'd like to be able to tell you that Hugh is the love of my life, and we're deliriously happy, but it's just not so."

Many thought Hugh was quite a catch. Tall and handsome in a thin, lanky-hair, geeky way, he was a Deputy District Attorney for Santa Clara County. Since the nineteen-eighties, known to the outside world as Silicon Valley, the hub of computerized America, the center of information tech, the location of the Apple mothership. Where the most geeks on the planet lived. So all things considered, I couldn't help but feel dating him was stepping up in the world, like getting a big salary increase or winning a free trip to *Disneyland*.

I was waiting and hoping something inside me would open and flood me with warm emotion and certitude that *this was the one*, but it hadn't. I suspected he'd been waiting for the same thing, too.

Pet was quiet on the line.

"Know any single guys who might just manage to rock my world?" I joked. "Oh, and they have to play golf, be employed, be kind to children and animals. And not substance abusers or smokers. Or chew with their mouths open. Most of all, they have to play golf."

"Guess you have your priorities straight, *chica*. You want a shallow relationship, not anything deep, huh," Pet chuckled.

"Guess so," I concurred flippantly, "deep is too scary."

After all, the opposite sex was scary.

Heck, anything deeper than a fling with any one of them was like *Fatal Attraction*. I had an instantaneous vision of a knife piercing my heart, blood spewing out geyser-like, a looney-bin boyfriend raging with jealousy hunting me to the ends of the earth.

I was creeping myself out. Pet sighed audibly.

"'Fraid I don't know anyone who meets your terribly . . .uh, high standards. There *is* someone, but he doesn't play golf. You wouldn't consider *him* an honest man though others probably would."

Huh? I had no clue.

"Jeez Louise, I'm not going to say his name. You made me promise not to mention him again, and I've stuck to that promise, that silly, childish promise."

The Hated One. My eyes narrowed to slits. My blood ran cold.

"Yeah, well, I'm a silly, childish kinda person. And you just now mentioned *him*, so you broke your promise, Pet."

"Well, too bad. He's divorced now. Has been for some time."

"Ha, probably cheated on his wife. That topic is closed for discussion, anyway. Always will be."

I'd overheard Grandma tell Mama about The Hated One's divorce years ago. That he'd divorced the girl he'd gotten pregnant while still engaged to me was further proof he was a lying, cheating SOB. There should be an MTA website for SOBs like Rick Ramos.

Men To Avoid. Like the plague.

"Well, too bad about Hugh. I kinda liked him. He's smart, and he makes a lot of money. There are worse qualities you could find in a husband."

I was astonished to hear Pet say that. I thought my family thoroughly disliked him. He was an uppity Anglo who didn't fit in. I suppose Pop liked him well enough, though, but my easygoing sweetheart of a father liked everybody.

Pop was impressed when I told him that Hugh was a graduate of *Stanford Law School* and belonged to the *Triple-9 Society*, a group whose IQs were in the 99.9 percentile. A fact which Hugh never let me forget. When Hugh also announced his membership in *Mensa*, Pop thought it was a food co-op, like *Costco*, and he wanted to know if the produce was any good. That made Hugh shut up. He thought Pop was making fun of him.

"Want another, Dina? It'll be on the house," Manny called out from behind the espresso machine.

"You talked me into it," I called back. I covered my cell phone and looked back at my favorite hangout's barista. "Can't say no to a free one."

"One condition. You have to go out with me Friday night."

"Aha," I said, smiling wryly, "why is there a catch these days to every gracious offer?" I turned back to my phone. "Sorry, Pet. Some guy just asked me out."

"You in *Starbucks* again? I might've known. Do you go out with guys you meet at a coffee store?"

"'Cause it's the only way I'll get you to say yes," Manny hollered above the din of the clamoring customers that had just entered the front door. Thankfully, I was spared from our usual banter and teasing repartee.

"Well, Pet, I have to find them where I can. The only male teacher at school is married, and the other guy is my boss — the new vice-prince. I don't do bars or singles groups. They're like an advertisement that you're . . .desperate, which I'm not. Or if I was, I'd sooner have root-canal surgery than admit it. So where, pray tell, am I supposed to meet them? Other than the golf course."

I could hear my sister puff audibly over the phone. No doubt she was sitting in one of her customer's chairs, smoking a cigarette — to keep her weight down — and fingering her dark, curly hair.

"Beats me, maybe hardware stores. Roberto said he picked up a girl in one last week."

"Which department, where they keep the loose screws?"

"Ha, ha, smartass. Hey, I'm calling about something else, too. Dina, something strange's going on over at *Mamá's.* I dropped off Lucy this morning, and *Abuelita* was crying up a storm. Imagine that, hardnosed Grandma crying!"

I couldn't call up such a vision. *La Bruja?* It would be like picturing Darth Vader crying.

"So, what's up? Did *Abuelita* lose her broomstick?"

Pet clucked her tongue just before giggling. "You're sooo bad, *chica.* No, I'm serious, girl. She was sitting at the table, her head in her arms, just sobbing. Little Lucy started crying, too, she got so scared. They were speaking Spanish, so I only caught a few words. Something about family — *hijo, nieta,* Juárez, *mafufo* — strange word, isn't it? What do you think, Dina? They wouldn't tell me anything but before I left, Grandma made a phone call to Mexico. To her sister, I think."

"*Mafufo, mafufo,*" I murmured. Spanish was my minor in college, so I was the bilingual dictionary for my siblings whenever Mama wouldn't or couldn't translate. It came to me. "It's an old Mexican word for marijuana, I think. Juárez is a city in the state of Chihuahua, Mexico. *Hijo* is son, of course. *Nieta* is granddaughter. Grandma has no sons, just *Mamá* and *Tita* Carmen. All her granddaughters are here in California. You, Connie, me. If Grandma hasn't disowned me, that is."

"No, *Tita* Carmen in Amarillo has got two sons and a daughter in Texas, somewhere. Maybe she's talking about her. I don't think she lives in Amarillo anymore. She moved with her husband somewhere . . .our cousin. We met her that time she and her husband came out to California. Y'know, Dolores García. Yep, she got stuck with Dolores, too."

"Poor girl. Well, it's none of my business. Grandma sure doesn't want me butting in. I'm not exactly her favorite person, y'know. If you find out anything, let me know. Just curious. Don't know why *Mamá* wouldn't tell you. That's strange."

"*Abuelita's* got a big secret, something bad, that's what I think. I also think you should come home more often. Just because they didn't like Hugh doesn't mean *you* have to stay away. I miss you. Pop misses you. *Mamá* and *Abuelita*, too . . .in their own way."

"Yeah, right — "

"Gotta go. My next client just walked in."

"Hey, I'm glad . . .things worked out in your favor this time. Y'know, that you're not pregnant. Try the Pill, *m'ija*."

"I do, have been. Jeez, what do you think? Juan Pablo and I aren't stupid, y'know, just because we didn't go to college like you. I just got busy and lost track one month."

Her defensive, hurt tone came across loud and clear, making me feel guilty for my careless remark.

"Hey, I wasn't implying anything — just an off-the-cuff thing to say. Sorry," I apologized, feeling bad. I knew around my family, I had to go out of my way to look and sound humble, had to suppress my big mouth.

"Come home this weekend, Dina. We'll talk some more. Haven't seen you in ages. You're not avoiding us, are you? Please, don't abandon us. Gotta go. Bye."

Smiling to myself, for Pet had made that last plea jokingly in her usual melodramatic way, we rang off, and I went back to my students' papers. We were okay again, thank goodness. I had to mentally smack my forehead and remind myself to watch my sarcasm around members of my family, especially the ones I truly liked. They'd interpret it as disrespectful and arrogant, an attitude not to be tolerated in a blue-collar Latino family.

Another reason why I seldom went home. It was difficult to curb my true nature. Know what I mean?

Pet's conversation lingered in my mind for a few minutes, though, especially hearing about *Abuelita*'s apparently upsetting news from her daughter, Carmen, in Texas? So why call Mexico? Grandma Gómez didn't fritter away money—she was as tight-fisted as a retired boxer with her Social Security check. A call to Mexico wasn't cheap.

Oh well, I thought. Probably a relative in Mexico is asking for more money. Gringo relations in the US were always good to hit up for a couple hundred or so each month. I knew Mama had sent money over the years to *Abuelita*'s sister and some cousins in Chihuahua. They couldn't help me through college, but they could send Pop's hard-earned money to Mexico. What a family!

I mentally harrumphed and started concentrating in earnest on my students' papers. Minutes passed. Three more essays and I'd treat myself to another tall cup—mmm, yummy—of nonfat caramel macchiato, finish the pile and then go home.

Home was my aunt Flora's three-bedroom, two-bath, custom-built ranch house in the Rose Garden area west of the

Alameda, a tree-shaded boulevard that connected the old mission town of Santa Clara to the metropolitan downtown of San Jose. The Alameda neighborhood was the oldest, toniest enclave of San Jose — the old gentrified heart of Silicon Valley. Much to my delight, the *Egyptian Rosicrucian Museum* was nearby.

"Dina Salazar?"

I looked up and blinked a few times, pulling myself away from those clever, persevering ancient Greeks. I immediately recognized Mariana di Matteo, a fellow-teacher friend of mine whom I had lost touch with when she hopped school districts. Last thing I'd heard, she was teaching at a high school in Palo Alto.

"Mariana! You look great! Come, sit down. Let's catch up."

With alacrity, she took a seat across the table and effused pleasure and eager surprise. Her surprise could not have been greater than mine, for it was apparent she had lost a lot of weight. Her attractive face was no longer plumped out by extra poundage and was now strikingly contoured.

"I know what you're thinking," she gushed happily, "God, has she lost a ton! And you're right. It took me three years to lose it all, but I did, I'm proud to say. Had to change my whole lifestyle to do it, though, but it paid off."

I noticed as I gushed back my congratulations and other pleasantries that Mariana was wearing black-spandex tights, an oversized t-shirt spotted with sweat, and running shoes. She was clearly on her way from a jog, for there was a fine sheen of perspiration on her face and arms and her body emanated warm sweat and a hint of citrusy perfume.

"Hope you don't mind. I just ran my five-mile loop. Been sweating gallons."

I shook my head. A memory surfaced — a time when Rick and I used to jog together around the San Jose State University campus neighborhood. We had a three-mile loop. I could

11

never do more. Rick would run the same loop twice while I waited and sat at the curb, panting for breath. We'd run three or four times a week and then later shower together . . .

Don't go there, I swiftly admonished myself, clicking off that memory. All thoughts of The Hated One were strictly *prohibido*.

"You look so different," I said, "so . . .healthy and happy."

Mariana's glossy, black hair was straightened, pulled back into a high, long ponytail. Her pretty complexion, a cafe-au-lait brown, was set off by a red-hued lip gloss and matching nail polish. I remembered that she spoke fluent French, which was her major, had minored in Spanish, and had spent her childhood on one of the Caribbean islands—Martinique, I think. Her father was an Italian businessman, her mother an island travel agent. She was a couple of years older than me, if I recall correctly.

I got the summary of Mariana's weight-loss diet and exercise regimen, which I pretended to listen to with exaggerated interest, feeling a little guilty. I had regained twenty of those twenty-five pounds I'd lost in *my previous life* and, though no longer willowy, I was a firm size ten and, at five-eight, I have to admit, content enough with my body shape. I'd never make the cover of *Vogue* or even *Latina*, but who the hell cared!

"When was the last time we talked?" I wondered aloud. "I know, the EdTech class at State."

Educational technology had been a dreaded requirement, dragged out a semester, and a total waste of time for most of us who were all a bit geeky to start with. After all, we lived in Silicon Valley. You absorbed the techie stuff by osmosis.

"Yes, that's it," Mariana concurred. "It's been four years now. I just got tenured in my new district. Where're you teaching, Dina?"

"Same place as before," I replied, "Lincoln Elementary, sixth grade. It's just four miles from here, so there's no real commute. Love the kids, my coworkers. We need more parent involvement, more money, but what else is new?" After a pause and a glance down at her left hand, I went on, "Don't tell me, is this an engagement ring? C'mon, Mariana, spill the beans."

With unsuppressed excitement, she brought me up to speed, telling me how she met her fiancé, where he worked, what he was like, and so on. All the while, I wished I could be as enthusiastic when it invariably came time to tell her about my boyfriend. Still, I was happy for her.

"Joel and I just moved into the condo complex behind us."

Starbucks was one of several upscale stores and cafes that fronted a recently constructed, four-story condominium complex along the Alameda, one of the revitalization projects on this venerable boulevard.

"We've only been in a month. I'm still decorating, having fun picking colors and buying new furniture."

"What's the complex like? Pool, clubhouse?" I inquired.

Part of me wanted my own place instead of a room and bath in Aunt Flora's house, with kitchen and TV privileges, of course. The sad truth was, I was still paying off student loans, I had bought a modestly priced car that my parents claimed cost more than their house, and I loved to travel in the summer. Two months before, I'd come back from a tour of Spain and Portugal.

"All that, yes, and tennis courts, gym, lots of trees, a management company that actually comes out and fixes things. It's expensive to own anything in this valley, let alone a two-bedroom condo in a fantastic complex, but it's been worth it."

"How much, if you don't mind my asking?"

"Six-hundred-fifty."

When my eyes bulged, she went on, smiling ruefully.

"I know, I know, but what can you do?"

Six-hundred-fifty thousand for a two-bedroom condo! I

knew Aunt Flora had paid eighty-thousand for her home thirty years ago, her lovely, custom brick-ranch with garden and garden shed, patio, sunroom, built-in spa, and a two-car garage. In a great neighborhood shaded by tall, mature trees.

"Oh well, it can only go up," I said encouragingly.

"Let's hope so"—she laughed and held up crossed fingers—"let's hope our luck holds and the Big One never hits in our lifetime."

These days, anyone who spent a small fortune on real estate in this valley always crossed their fingers. It was like playing Russian roulette with Mother Nature. Instead of Middle Eastern terrorists, we had the San Andreas and the Loma Prieta earthquake faults striking terror in our hearts.

"Speaking of luck, I ran into an old friend of yours in my complex. He's lived there almost two years, he said, moved in right after it was completed, so he bought his condo when they were selling for four-seventy-five. Got a good deal. He's already made a hundred thousand. His is ground-floor, too."

Mariana's non-sequitur had me confused. "What old friend?" I asked, instantly wary as I drained my last mouthful of macchiato.

"Rick Ramos. I ran into him in the gym sometime last week—"

She faltered when she saw how my face had dropped like a sack of potatoes. I felt like my skin had blanched snow-white. The blood drained so quickly from my face. All of a sudden, the caramel macchiato running down my esophagus met the bile coming up, making me queasy. I swallowed carefully, willing myself not to throw up. After a couple of seconds of fierce concentration and I was able to squeeze down the bile.

"Are you okay?" Mariana asked, looking concerned. "Dina, I knew you'd broken it off, but I thought from the way he talked, you were still friends," Mariana explained, her voice sounding stricken with apology.

"What do you mean, the way he talked?" With superhuman effort, I kept my voice steady.

I ventured a half-smile of bravado. Leaning back in my chair, I folded my arms over my chest and adopted what I hoped was a nonchalant pose.

"Well, when I said, *Aren't you Rick Ramos?* he said, yeah, he was, and he remembered meeting me at your place—when you and I were cramming for that Spanish literature exam our senior year. What a memory he has! I'd completely forgotten about that. Anyway, he said he'd lost touch with you after you broke up with him."

I nearly laughed out loud when I heard that. He made it sound like a whimsical decision on my part. What a *cabrón!* He was the one who, in a fit of jealousy, had gone to a party, hooked up with that Hernández slut, and gotten her pregnant.

Yet, repressing my cynical laughter, I kept still, immobile and smiling like a goofy Buddha on meds.

"And then he got married, had a daughter who, by the way, lives with him. He didn't say why he has full-time custody of the child. Anyway, he's divorced. Wonder what happened." Mariana paused, frowning. "You don't know any of this, Dina?"

"No," I said calmly, the fake, frozen smile making my facial muscles begin to twitch, "I don't. Well, I heard he was divorced, but I haven't seen or spoken to him in almost six years."

Appearing hesitant, Mariana took a sip of her coffee drink before continuing.

"If I'm treading on toes here, please say so, Dina."

"Not at all. I'm just stunned to hear he lives so near."

"Anyway, this is what he told me last week. He divorced his wife—I don't know when—and got custody of the little girl. She's in kindergarten and a real cutie-pie, from what he says. When he learned I was teaching, he said that the little girl has learning problems and wanted to know what he could do to help her. I told him that I taught high school and this was not my area of expertise. I told him you were an elementary teacher, he should ask you. I let it go at that—"

She broke off when she heard me gasp. Actually, I was so rattled, I could barely speak. I'd long since concluded Rick Ramos was a heartless bastard, and if I'd been a medieval knight, I would've gladly run him in with my sword, then drawn and quartered him.

Nevertheless, learning that he had full custody of his and Anita the Slut's child and that the child had problems put a new wrinkle in things. I felt a little less bloodthirsty—not sympathetic, mind you—just a tiny bit less hateful.

"I wonder, how does he know a lot about you, Dina, if you haven't stayed in touch?" Mariana shook her head. "He knows that you're living with your aunt and teaching sixth grade, and he knows about your boyfriend. A prosecuting attorney, I think he said. We were running on treadmills, so we were both panting like crazy. Some things he said I didn't catch."

God almighty, I thought, what was Rick Ramos doing, nosing into my life? And why, for Pete's sake? How could he know all these things about me when I hadn't laid eyes on him, let alone exchanged a word with him in all this time?

Then, of course, it hit me. I felt like a dunce. Surely, Mama had brought Mrs. Ramos's sister—who still lived in Salinas—abreast of my comings-and-goings, and the gossip must have traveled along the Salinas-to-San Jose grapevine. I could almost hear the crackling of electrical lines as phone calls relayed the news. Dina Salazar finally got another steady boyfriend. Imagine that miracle!

I should've been rejoicing, hoping that Rick Ramos was

picturing me doing the hot, sweaty, horizontal Salsa with another man. One with a professional job and a big salary.

"Yeah, I've got a boyfriend. His name is Hugh Goss. He's a deputy DA for Santa Clara County."

Boasting wasn't a sin, just a character flaw, and I had plenty of those.

"He's handsome, graduated *Stanford Law*," I added.

That was all I cared to say on that subject, for I couldn't find the enthusiasm, in all truth, to say more. Suddenly, like a precipitous drop in blood sugar, I felt drained of emotion. I didn't have the energy or spirit for lying or exaggerating.

"Hugh Goss? I think I've seen him in the papers. Isn't he supposed to take over when District Attorney Sal Ochoa retires next year? Or run for the office? The reason I know, I'm a news junkie. I read the paper every day, from cover to cover."

She actually said that with a sigh of embarrassment, like she'd just confessed her addiction to cocaine.

I nodded. "He just launched his campaign. He's got Congressman Velásquez's endorsement." I wanted to change the subject, but instead of talking shop or just feigning an errand somewhere, I sat there, riveted, unable to leave. I couldn't believe I was about to utter the next words.

"Tell me more about Rick Ramos."

Mariana looked a little baffled but gamely returned to reporting her encounter with Rick.

"He looks good. Not that his face doesn't show he's had personal problems, but he still looks like a cross between Benjamin Bratt and that other guy you see on TV a lot—what's his name? Whatever—"

There were so many Latino actors on television these days that I had no clue whom she was referring to, so I shrugged. Bratt—yes, in some ways. The dimples and the sensitive, mocking mouth. Benicio Del Toro, his husky voice.

"Has he changed much since our college days?" I asked, wishing I'd bite my tongue and let matters lie. I swear there was a masochistic streak in me a mile long. Why else would I want to find out about a lying bastard who threw me over for a conniving lowlife who wouldn't know a Cervantes from a Gabriel García Márquez?

"He's still got the bod, maybe a little heavier. He looks great though tired-looking...and, I don't know, kind of weary. He says his work takes up all his time."

I could imagine. *Ramos Roofing* and *Ramos Construction, Inc* signs could be seen all over San Jose, wherever space in this overcrowded valley could be found to squeeze in more commercial and residential buildings. From what I'd heard, the economy was reviving, and business for the Ramos family apparently was thriving.

"Who takes care of his daughter?"

"His mother, he says, and his youngest sister helps. She's in high school?"

"Probably María Teresa," I replied. "She'd be sixteen by now."

A fragment of memory surfaced. The girl, at about ten, showing me one of her schoolbooks, asking me for help one day when I was at Rick's house. I tutored her for two months one summer.

She wore two long pigtails in the traditional fashion. All the Ramos girls were brought up strictly and modestly, and I had sometimes suspected I was looked upon as an anomaly, a threat to their old-fashioned values, the kind of woman the Ramos elders wouldn't want their only son to marry. Huh! So he ends up marrying the skanky Anita Hernández.

"His girlfriend was there, working out with him. At least, I think she was his girlfriend."

Like a punch to the solar plexus, I found myself short of breath. I closed my eyes, feeling a bit woozy while pretending the need to rub my eyes. As if eye fatigue had suddenly caught up with me.

Well, of course, he would have a girlfriend!

What was I thinking?

"Oh, that's nice," I murmured vaguely, clumsily shuffling the stack of student papers back in the manila folder in which I had filed them. "Rick Ramos never had trouble getting girls."

I stood up to leave. Inspiration struck me as my old friend, a little, red-caped devil, danced on my shoulder. *Diablito*, Grandma Gómez used to call it. As a child, I wondered why I could never see it, but she could.

"Next time you see Rick Ramos, tell him I'm engaged to Hugh Goss, and we're getting married in Italy next summer after he's elected District Attorney."

"That's wonderful, Dina," Mariana gushed, believing me even though she sneaked a quick look at my left hand, third finger.

It was bare, of course, but hey, not everybody wore an engagement ring to work.

Didn't women butchers and potters leave theirs off? Oh hell, who was I kidding? Mariana was kind enough to ignore my naked ring finger, anyway.

"So, do you think your fiancé will win the election?"

"So far," I said, feeling a trifle guilty for lying, "Hugh's running unopposed, and he has endorsements from all over, including the local Latino Political Caucus and the Democratic Party chapter."

Thanks to me, I thought, at least concerning the Latino Political Caucus. I was the one who introduced Hugh to Héctor Velásquez, one of the founders of the local Latino Political Caucus. One summer during college, I'd worked for Velásquez as one of his assistants. As long as Hugh Goss was seen with me, he was projecting a bias in favor of the Hispanic population, a large voting bloc in this valley. Congressman Velásquez was impressed enough to issue a tentative endorsement.

Perhaps our relationship was based on pure politics, I mused uneasily. Maybe Pet was right. I wanted shallow relationships. It was true that Hugh's and my relationship was so shallow, it wouldn't float a rubber ducky.

So why did I continue to see him? That question, and the fact that I was increasingly becoming disenchanted with the man, was the issue I hadn't yet wanted to deal with.

Mariana watched me as I gathered my things.

"Listen, Dina, why don't you and Hugh come to our housewarming at the end of this month? It's an Oktoberfest with a German theme and lots of beer. Simple, fun and it won't break the bank. It'll be at our condo and poolside. People can swim if the weather's still warm. I'll send you an invitation."

"I'd like to . . ." There was no way I was going if Rick was going to be there. But, of course, it would be rude to say so. And so I added another white lie to the one I'd just told Mariana. "I'll definitely come. In case you don't have my phone number . . ." I entered my contact information into her cell phone. She smiled and did the same to my phone.

What did Grandma Gómez once say to me, that I told enough little white lies to frost a wedding cake?

My friend appeared very pleased and, going a step further, took a card out of her wallet. It held the address and phone number of her high school in Palo Alto. I took it and thanked her, wishing I had a professional card to give her. Business/ social cards in Silicon Valley were *de rigueur*, as the French say.

"It's okay if I invite Rick? It'll be like a reunion of old university friends."

"It sure will," I said brightly, cringing inside. "Listen,

Mariana, it's been wonderful talking to you. I have to run, but I'll see you soon."

I stuffed my cell phone in my tote bag. "I'd love to come to your party, and I'll definitely bring Hugh. Gotta run. It's later than I thought."

When I slung my purse over my shoulder, ready to leave, she tapped my left hand with a manicured, red-polished forefinger. I patiently looked down at her, knowing that her curiosity would not let it go.

"Dina, are you sure it's okay for me to invite Rick Ramos? He's such a sweetheart of a guy, but your reaction was . . .kind of strange."

Yeah, he was a sweetheart all right. 'Til he drove a semi over your heart and crushed it. I sighed. The bald-faced truth was always difficult. The lie was always easier.

"It's not a problem. Really, I haven't thought of him in years."

"Well, I just thought . . .I know you two used to have a real hot thing going."

"More like hot and cold. Now ancient history. Don't worry about it. We've moved on."

We said our goodbyes and parted on a cheery note. Outside in the parking lot, I noticed my hands were shaking. I looked up at the condo complex behind the row of stores.

Damn! So close, it was frightening. To think, The Hated One was living there with his daughter. His and the skank's daughter. Within two miles of Aunt Flora's house. My sanctuary.

The back of my neck shivered, and my stomach revolted again. I squeezed my eyes shut for a second and swallowed hard.

Despite my attempts to calm down, that macchiato sent sour juices back up, making me gag a little. I opened my eyes and glanced over the store's roof at the towering complex

behind the strip mall.
  Damn! Way too close for comfort.

CHAPTER TWO

Actually, I wasn't in uncharted waters. I had my role model, Aunt Flora.

My father's youngest sister was the epitome of cleverness both in and out of her home. She'd designed and constructed her life like a brilliant architect. At her firm, she was the paragon of a practical businesswoman. I know because I'd seen her in action. She had twelve employees in her accounting firm, including a receptionist, three executive assistants and eight CPAs. Her offices were in an old, restored, converted Spanish-style mansion on the Alameda.

Flora Salazar was the prototype, the original one in Pop's family, and the only one with a college degree—besides yours truly. Accounting was her passion. Although living with her for five years now, I'd learned about her other passions as well. She called herself a bean-counter, a numbers-cruncher. In reality, she was an astute businesswoman whose clients were among the most successful, if not largest, of the valley's computer tech, software and biotech companies.

Each of her eight accountants handled at least ten to twenty clients while she oversaw, managed and validated the entire operation. She gave personal, face-to-face attention to her clients' CFOs and vice-presidents and every day held court over business lunches that would last up to three hours.

This was why she preferred small dinners prepared by her niece, *yo-mismo*, the live-in chef. My hobby was cooking, and Aunt Flora's kitchen was as well-stocked as a Cordon Bleu's chef. She had every type of pot, pan, appliance and utensil, although it was a blue moon in a leap year when she touched any of them.

Our unique arrangement was that I'd buy groceries and cook dinner on certain evenings and tidy up—though there was little to tidy up with a biweekly cleaning service—in exchange for free board. I had my own bedroom, the guest bathroom and the living room with its entertainment center. Since I was a homebody and she was the social butterfly, I often served as the caretaker of her property when she was away—nearly every weekend—visiting one of her numerous relatives in the big Salazar clan.

"I stopped and got some mushrooms and a can of artichoke hearts," I told her as soon as she walked in the door at six-thirty. "I'll make a veggie frittata to go with a small Cobb salad. How does it sound?"

"Sounds fine," she called out, disappearing into her bedroom suite.

She'd looked tired and a little low, but, truth be told, my aunt at forty-nine had more energy and stamina than I had at half that age. Pop had finally revealed her true age to me one day though I never let on I knew. For outside the family, she told everyone she was thirty-nine. She was young in her thinking and unconventional. And passionate about nearly everything.

And she loved to keep up on topical issues, always urging me to think about La Raza, the UFW, the Mexica Movement and concerns of Hispanic people in general. My family had been too busy surviving to get involved with La Raza, and I was too busy assimilating to take the Mexica Movement seriously. Their banner always left me puzzled. "We are not Latinos. We are not Hispanics. We are not Mexicans. We are *Indios*."

Well, I didn't feel like an *India*. Ethnically, I was half Mexican-American and half Spanish-American. I felt American first and foremost. And struggling to get a toehold in the American middle class.

In the morning, over the newspaper, she'd notice an article. "Dina, did you know that twenty-four percent of Latinos in California are optimistic that they'll be able to afford to buy a house, compared to only seventeen percent of non-Latinos, specifically whites. Isn't that interesting? Why do you suppose we're more optimistic than they are? Especially when only twelve percent of Bay Area residents of any race or nationality can actually qualify for a home loan."

I shrugged and told her I'd think about it — which I did. Later that day, I returned with an answer.

"Two possibilities, I think, Flora. We Latinos are either more self-deluded. Not a happy thought." I made a rueful face. "Or we believe more fiercely in the American Dream — whether we achieve it or not."

She agreed with me that the second answer was probably the correct one. After all, weren't we living it? Especially Flora.

From habit, I checked the magnetically-held calendar on the fridge. Today was Wednesday, which was *Steve night*. As I said, my aunt was passionate about a lot of things, including men. She loved them, and they loved her. Steve was Aunt Flora's personal trainer/lover, and they had twice to three times a week *workouts* in her large bedroom suite, which usually continued to some muscle-relaxing in the backyard spa. Occasionally, Steve would join us for a low-cal dinner before their *workout*.

Grandma Gómez had hinted once that Flora was a lesbian because she'd never married, but I knew she wasn't. I'd walked in on her one time, doing the horizontal nasties with some guy. It was one of her personal trainers in a long string of them that I caught her with that time. I was a college student at the time.

One Friday night with Rick Ramos, I'd driven my old, dilapidated Honda from San Jose State U over to Flora's. She'd given me her house key and was supposed to have already taken off for Lake Tahoe to visit Uncle Ralph. Rick and I were going to use the guest bedroom—I hadn't moved in with her yet—for a sexy sleepover, and I'd assumed the night light in her bedroom was on for security reasons. I suppose I'd been so excited, so much in love and looking forward to having Rick all to myself for the weekend that I didn't notice anyone's car at the curb, and I didn't check the garage for Flora's *Mercedes.*

Pleased to be able to show Rick my aunt's lovely, custom home, we quietly moved from room to room, flicking on and off the lights, murmuring sweet nothings to each other, stealing little kisses that we knew would lead up to the big event in the guest room. I eased open the door to Flora's suite, wanting Rick to see how beautifully decorated it was.

There, on a blue-foam workout mat, were Flora and her then-personal trainer in all their pink-and-tanned nakedness. He was pumping in and out of her to a rhythmic counting—*one-yes! Two-yes! Three-yes!* My aunt was simultaneously doing what the current Steve would call *glute crunches.* Exultantly, she'd been squeezing her buttocks with each thrust, her legs encircling the trainer's hips for balance.

They'd been so engrossed in their *glute crunches,* and we'd been so quiet in our shock, Flora and her trainer hadn't noticed us. Later, in the guest bedroom, Rick and I tried to duplicate this highly pleasurable form of muscle toning, but our giggles kept distracting us from its true purpose.

Damn! There I go again, I scolded myself. Gotta squash those memories once and for all. The Hated One was history. I had to fall in love with somebody. That'd do it.

Busy at the stove, I barely noticed when Flora entered the kitchen. Her long chestnut-brown hair was gathered back and tied in a high, long ponytail. Her work makeup, pantsuit, and jewelry were replaced with freshly scrubbed skin, a black tank top, gray warm-up pants, and simple gold-hoop earrings. My aunt could often convince any casual observer that her age was under forty, maybe even thirty-five. No one believed that she was edging fifty. I think she told Steve she was in her late thirties. In any event, I thought she was exceptionally pretty. She and my father shared the tall, slim builds and high cheekbones of their Spanish heritage.

"The salad looks yummy, Dina girl. I'll skip the frittata, and Steve called to say he's already eaten, so don't make a large one . . .unless you're famished, of course."

She leaned over the Cobb salad, picked out a piece of lettuce leaf, and popped it into her mouth. Next came a bite of ham, turkey, bacon chip and little balls of blue cheese in little finger-pickings.

"No wonder you stay so slim, Flora," I said, eliminating the family title because she'd asked me to years ago. I believe she wanted to give people the impression that we were sisters instead of aunt and niece.

"The older I get, the harder I have to work at it," she groused, mocking an expression of self-pity by curling her lower lip over her upper one.

Some of the traits I liked most were her animated expressions, her expressive speech and her sense of humor, often self-deprecating.

Still, I sometimes found myself envying her ability to juggle a pressure-cooker job with its long hours and a fairly active social life. Compared to Flora Salazar, I was a reclusive hermit and a prude. A twenty-eight-year-old prude! How sick was that!

"Tomorrow night, will you be eating out with Porter? Before going dancing?"

"Oh yes, every Tuesday and Thursday as usual. Tomorrow

night we learn the Argentinean Tango—not the American version, mind you, which has very simple steps by comparison. The Argentinean will be challenging . . .and oohh soo hot."

My aunt mounted the stool at the high pub table she used in the kitchen and took a sip of the white zinfandel I'd already poured into crystal goblets.

"Hmm, good, Dina. Fruity, but not too sweet. You're so talented at picking the right wine with the food you cook. As I was saying, tomorrow night will be challenging and rigorous and sexy, so tonight Steve'll have to whip me into shape."

She winked at me as I turned to her and smiled slyly. Flora was her own woman, lived by her own rules and brooked no criticism or disapproval. I admired that kind of independent thinking and nonconformist approach to life. I knew Flora's lifestyle scandalized my mother and Grandma Gómez. Living with her made me guilty by association. They just knew she was corrupting poor little me!

Monday nights were occasionally open when Steve was occupied elsewhere, so the two of us would eat in and maybe watch a video. Either that or she hadn't yet found a steady Monday guy.

"Where to this weekend?" I asked her, turning off the burner and letting the mushroom-artichoke frittata cool and congeal. I went over to sit at the table and clicked goblets with her. "*Salud,*" I added.

"*Salud,* Dina . . .*y amor, dinero, y el tiempo para disfrutarlos.*" Health, love, money and the time to enjoy it all. An old Spanish toast.

I rarely heard Aunt Flora speak Spanish, but I knew she was nearly fluent. Occasionally, when she'd drunk a little too much wine, she spoke about the year she spent in Spain when she was in her early twenties. Pop said she'd almost married a Spaniard while there, and the Salazar family was concerned that she'd never return to the States. But something happened, she never married the man, and a month later, she returned and went back to college to finish her degree.

"San Francisco to see Linda and Joe. What about you, Dina? Any hot plans with *Huge*?" she asked, mispronouncing Hugh's name the way my grandmother had. It'd been *Abuelita's* way of ridiculing my choice of boyfriend.

I smiled, albeit wanly, at our private joke. Upon meeting Hugh Goss for the first time, Grandma Gómez kept calling him *Huge*. So now, for laughs, we sometimes referred to him that way. Flora, however, meant it as a double-entendre about the size of his manhood. His *pito*. Believe me, it wasn't huge.

"Maybe," I replied ambiguously. "He's supposed to call later tonight so we can make plans. He mentioned golf on Saturday and a working luncheon on Sunday, something having to do with the police officers' union. He's scheduled to give a speech on police and prosecutors working with the Latino community. Since he's been dating me, Flora, he thinks he's an authority on Latino culture and demographics." I gave a short laugh. "The privileged boy from Connecticut whose father paid his way through seven years of *Stanford* has never lived it, though."

"You've got to give the boy credit for doing his homework," she said wryly. "Are you enjoying his, uh, research so far?"

I shot her a thin smile. If only she knew how empty sex with Hugh made me feel. I always felt like, after collapsing over me, he was mentally checking off—climaxed, good. Next—tell her how pretty she is. After that—set up a date for next Friday.

"Y'know," I began, fingering the stem of my goblet, "sometimes I think he's merely using me. Other times, I think I'm using him. Y'know, for the theater and fancy restaurants."

I said this with about as much enthusiasm as if I'd

announced a weight gain of twenty pounds. Sighing, I added, "Mutual exploitation."

"*Querida*," Flora murmured, her voice evincing a nuance of compassion along with the term of endearment, "would you marry him if he asked you?" When she saw me shake my head, she went on.

"Well, then, you use each other until someone better comes along. Someone who really turns you on. Men and women do it all the time. It's called dating. I've been doing it all my life. So what else is new?" She paused, a piece of ham caught between her thumb and forefinger. "What's wrong? You seem so . . .down, so out of spirits."

I blinked, immediately reverting to cover-up mode. I'd learned from my mother never to show one's emotional weakness, for then someone pounced and criticized or scolded you. Or worse, mocked you. I knew from whom she learned that! We seemed to be a generational cycle of repressed, angry females.

"Nothing, just y'know . . ." I sighed. "My period's due soon."

Did I actually believe such lame acting would fool Aunt Flora? She was such a keen detector of bullshit. She could have been an undercover cop.

"Dina." Her gentle command was issued with such authority, I felt like a PFC ordered to reveal battalion secrets to a three-star general. "It's not about Hugh, is it?"

I took a sip of wine, stalling a bit, wondering how much I should tell her. Then I realized with a jolt that I wasn't speaking to Mama or *Abuelita*, but a woman who would not judge or criticize.

"I ran into an old friend I'd lost touch with . . .at *Starbucks*. She lives in that condo complex on the Alameda. The one called Villa Florentine. The one that looks like a Tuscan village."

I filled in the rest about the party invitation, Mariana chatting with Rick Ramos in the complex's gym, his current single status and custody of his daughter, his new girlfriend. After I finished, I looked away, unwilling for her to see the tears welling behind my eyes.

"Well, I knew this all along."

"Knew what?" My head whipped back so fast, I cricked my neck.

"Do you recall you told us all never to mention his name again? Well, I took you at your word. Yes, I've heard about him from your father, from Perpetua, whose salon is like a news gazette of gossip. Let's see, where else?"

I stared at her, transfixed, while she tapped one cinnamon-lacquered nail against one of her front teeth. "Oh yes, he's also one of my clients, and I had lunch with him and his father on Monday."

"Omigod," was all I could mutter.

"You didn't forbid the rest of the family to see Rick or do business with him," she said matter-of-factly, "did you? If you did, I must've missed that family memo. For all intents and purposes, what your friend reported is true. I really don't know about a girlfriend, but my impression is that he has little time for anyone else."

"Anyone else?"

"Other than his daughter, Angelina." Her dark, perfectly sculpted eyebrows arched. "You know he has custody of her, don't you?"

I nodded. "I suppose you've seen her, too."

"A photo. Cute little girl. Big brown eyes like her father, and that same slightly dimpled chin. Anyway, they're new clients, and I'm happy to be able to work with them. I've always liked Rick and his father. Even though speaking with the father taxes my Castilian Spanish. Mr. Ramos speaks a fast Mexican, but Rick is always there to translate when necessary, so it's not really a hindrance. They've expanded into general construction and have done very well."

There were a hundred questions I longed to ask Flora about Rick and his father, their family business, Rick's situation with his child's custody.

Stubbornly, I sat there, refusing to yield to my inflamed curiosity. I'd been with The Hated One for three years, engaged for one of those. It seemed a lot of time to spend with one man—for me, anyway. But those years had convinced me I'd found The One. At least, I thought so at the time.

No, I could not open that door even a smidgen because I knew what would happen if I did. The floodgate would burst open, and all the old, scary emotions would come surging back, drowning me.

"Just say the word, Dina, and I'll tell you all I know."

I sat there in silence. Stubborn, yes, but mostly afraid.

Flora raised the goblet to her lips, pursed her pretty mouth, waiting for me to make a decision.

"No," I said firmly, shaking my head, "I don't want to know."

"If you say so," Flora said, pausing to take a sip, "here's to passion, whether inspired by love or hate. Certainly keeps life interesting." She delicately picked up another salad morsel. "You're better off not knowing and not caring. A woman should never drink from the same well twice—I think that's how it goes. Especially if the well makes her sick." She shot me a mournful smile, then stared off into space as if she were thinking of someone or of another time in her life. Not for the first time, I wondered about the man who'd broken her heart.

"Know what I mean? He's poison, Dina. Like so many men. Handsome but entitled. Charming but selfish. They promise the world, but all the while, they're conning you. I saw what that *pendejo* did to you. As a business client, it's a different story, Dina. He's acceptable. But romantically—"

She grimly shook her head. "Don't go there again."

I jumped in to reassure her. "I won't. Believe me, I won't. Schedule me for a lobotomy if I even mention his name again."

I clicked my goblet against hers, then pointedly handed her a plate and utensils and indicated the salad servers in the wooden bowl. She grinned, and we changed subjects.

Our conversation meandered about while I poked at my salad and sipped more white zin. The mushroom-artichoke frittata remained in its *Teflon* pan, ignored, hardening and drying like yesterday's leftovers.

"Hey, babes!" Steve greeted us after a startling rap at the kitchen bay window, where my aunt and I sat. We practically fell off our stools.

The breezeway separating the garage from the house led into two places — to the laundry room and to the back walkway, which curved around to the patio, kitchen and attached sunroom. For some unfathomable reason, Steve preferred that route to the more conventional one, the front door. I think it made him feel like his relationship with Flora was more permanent. In the five years that I'd lived with my brilliant, mercurial aunt, she'd had as many personal trainers. Romance, for her, had a shelf life of about twelve to fourteen months. I think Steve was on month number ten.

When Flora unlocked and opened the sunroom's French doors, Steve bounded in and enveloped her in a passionate embrace. I looked away, a trifle embarrassed, although this was his usual greeting.

"How are my pretty *muchachas* this fine October evening?"

That was about the extent of Steve's Spanish. That and *más cervezas*, perhaps.

With great aplomb, nevertheless, he accepted my forced smile and "Hi." Flora patted him on the cheek indulgently, the gesture making me wonder if she was going to pat his head next. He reminded me of a yellow Labrador we used to have when I was a child.

He trotted into the kitchen, gave me a peck on the cheek — at least he didn't lick me — while he cupped the crown of my head. Was his increasingly big-brotherly behavior an attempt to ingratiate himself with my aunt? Did he entertain aspirations of marrying her and grabbing hold of some of her *ass*ets? Or was he content enough to grab hold of her ass and forget her bank account?

I admonished myself for being so suspicious and distrustful. Not to mention cynical. Steve, in all fairness, seemed to be of a sub-species of Homo Sapiens that were perennial boys, narcissistic, fun-loving and covetous of their toys.

Steve, for one, owned a new model *Porsche Carrera*, a two-year-old *Hummer* and a five-year-old *Jeep Cherokee*. Though how he afforded them on his personal trainer's salary escaped me. I suspected that he wasn't home, knitting ski hats, the other evenings of the week when he wasn't with Flora. The *g*-word was never used, of course, but in my mind, I'd labeled him Georgio, the gigolo.

"Giorg — uh, Steve, there's a frittata on the stove and salad here," I said, indicating the pan first, then the big wooden bowl on the table.

"Help yourself, big guy, and pull up a stool," Flora cooed at him.

My aunt and I exchanged knowing smiles as the man took a plate and began to spoon up half the frittata. It was amazing how easily Flora slipped into her *mistress* persona.

"No, take it all, please," I urged. "I've lost my appetite." I shot Flora an accusatory glance, and she frowned back.

"I hope, not on account of me." Steve chuckled, spooning up the rest.

"No, no," I replied, all sincerity now. "Flora and I were talking about an old flame of mine. One that's been extinguished for years."

With a full plate, Steve joined us. His muscular build dwarfed the small table. In his mid-thirties, he had a buzz cut of what appeared to be dyed blond hair, a round, clean-shaven baby face, intense green eyes, and a tanned, buff physique. He was a couple of inches taller than my aunt's five-nine, not overly bulked up, but every muscle on his fat-free body was well-defined. He was wearing a black t-shirt, black *Adidas* running pants and black sneakers. No doubt, a black thong underneath those pants. A smug, good-looking guy who was accustomed to turning women's heads.

My suspicious mind couldn't help but wonder if he took steroids or some kind of medication, whose side-effect made him oversexed. He was too young for *Viagra,* but these days, who knew? Whatever . . . he made my aunt happy. Or, at least, satisfied and amused.

"Old flame? Why should that make you lose your appetite? I got lots of old flames, and none of 'em make me lose my appetite."

Steve glanced at Flora, his green eyes twinkling mischievously while she poured him a glass of wine.

"Oh, really? How many old flames?" she teased, stroking his male ego.

"Enough," was his light, terse reply, grinning from ear-to-ear.

Enough to buy you three overpriced gas guzzlers and a mountain-view condo overlooking a golf course, I thought.

"Am I your three-hundredth flame?" Flora chided, continuing to administer ego massage.

"Hell no, sweetheart. Haven't been around the block that many times."

"Am I your favorite, *mi amor*?" she asked coquettishly.

"Absolutely."

Thus began their little mindless, seductive ritual, which I

knew would build to a fulfilling cardiovascular workout in Flora's boudoir. Steve wouldn't leave until late that night.

Forgetting the question he'd asked me about my old flame, Steve started to wolf down the frittata, recharging the physical batteries needed for tonight's exercises. Meanwhile, he tossed lascivious looks at my aunt, who — may God strike me dead if I'm lying — preened before him on her stool like some colorful female bird in heat.

Feeling truly nauseated at this point, I excused myself, put my plate and fork in the sink, the goblet on the counter, murmured a cursory, "Off to grade papers," and fled the kitchen.

Inside my room, I changed clothes, kept on my panties, and pulled an oversized night shirt over my head. My little refuge. It was a large bedroom by older ranch-house standards — 15 x 17. There was space for a double-size sleigh bed, two matching cherry wood nightstands, a matching double-dresser with mirror, a comfy upholstered chair, my computer desk and an office chair. It was all my own furniture, which I had just paid off on the installment plan. I'd always yearned to afford to buy my own bedroom set, choose the style I liked, and decorate in my preferred colors of hunter green, purple and ivory.

In my little refuge, I felt relaxed and at peace with the world. Most days, at least.

Not tonight.

Tonight I was bothered by a whirl of self-searching questions. Was I truly envious of Flora's easy, unencumbered relationships with men? I'd been feeling neglected of late by Hugh, ever since his campaign for DA had begun in full earnest.

But was it his unavailability, which rankled me? Or was it our emotional distance when we were together? Even when making love, I'd felt the lack of intimacy with him. Like the body was there but not the heart or the mind.

I took a look at myself in the double-dresser's mirror. A

hard, dispassionate look. I was nearly twenty-nine, perhaps a little more sophisticated in my appearance, but I hadn't morphed into an alien creature. Even though, at times, I felt alien to myself.

Dina Louisa Salazar, what are you doing? What do you really want? Who the hell are you, anyway? That I did not know myself very well was a hard-to-digest revelation.

There I was, a taller than average, somewhat trim, fairly well-educated Latina with a pretty enough face, shoulder-length, wavy, dark auburn hair and steady hazel eyes that were capable every now and then of penetrating insight into others, if not myself.

I could be friendly, amiable, even upbeat at times. But I knew I could also be stubborn, resentful, mischievous, and a host of other not-so-sterling adjectives. I told little white lies regularly, especially to my mother and grandmother. And, thanks to my older brothers, I could curse at times, if sufficiently provoked, like a longshoreman. In English and Spanish.

I didn't smoke—have you ever seen the black lung of a smoker in a jar of formaldehyde?—rarely drank, and my only drug of choice was caffeine. Yeah! If this made me prudish, then so be it. I was serially monogamous—no promiscuity for me, thanks, although at times, I felt guilty about my casual relationships. I cared about my students deeply and worked hard for them. I loved my family despite their foolishness and foibles, and I knew they—well, most of them—loved me despite all of mine.

Beyond that, I was like a missing link—a mystery. What did I really want from life? Was I a twenty-eight-year-old Latina prude looking for a husband to complete her life? Or was I a modern, American career woman like Flora, content with casual relationships that led to nowhere?

As if searching for clues to the mystery of me, I surveyed

my cozy sanctuary, and my gaze settled on the hand-tooled, Mexican-style, dark-brown leather briefcase I took to school every day. To and from, it went like a faithful servant, carrying student papers, my lesson-plan notebook, tests to grade. The one that The Hated One gave me as a college-graduation gift. A bittersweet, farewell-forever gesture.

It served as a constant reminder that life and love were not perfect, that people disappointed you—no, stomped on your heart. Not because they were vicious and cruel, necessarily, but because they were human and made mistakes—terrible, long-lasting mistakes.

It reminded me of how flawed I was, that I could not forgive or trust ever again. But stubbornly, perversely, I could never toss that briefcase away. I wondered why.

Maybe it was like my own personal Medal of Honor. For courage and survival in the battlefield of love.

Yes, that was it! I had survived, even triumphed, on the battlefield of love.

On impulse, I picked up my cell phone and dialed Hugh's cell number. His message service answered.

"Hugh, Dina. I'm really tired tonight. Think I'm coming down with something. I'm sacking out early tonight. Don't bother calling later. I'll be asleep. Talk to you tomorrow."

I hesitated, not feeling up to adding another lie to the string of lies I'd just relayed. Self-contemplation was sure exhausting.

After a few minutes of further contemplation, I called home.

Pop answered with a gruff, "Yah?"

"Pop, are you okay?"

"Dina, it's been a long time. I was expecting a call from Frankie. Whatcha doing, *m'ija*?"

"Just called to see if everyone was all right. You okay, Pop?"

"Yeah, just tired. Gotta go in for tests, my doctor says."

He explained about some shortness of breath, extreme weariness and cramps in his chest, back and arms. That he laid tile for a living, bent over on his knees for hours at a stretch—it was no wonder he had aches and pains. Funny, I thought Pop was doing just the office work and bidding these days and Frankie, Roberto and Juan Pablo were doing the setting and laying.

"You gotta take it easy, Pop. Don't work too hard. You're in your sixties, you know."

I heard him chuckle. "Frank's got me sitting at a desk all day. How much easier can I take it? I just help out if they need me. Don't worry about me, pretty girl. I'm a tough old Spaniard."

"Pop, what's going on with *Abuelita*? Pet thinks something terrible's happened."

"Bad news from Mexico, Dina." Pop was silent for several seconds. "I don't know how to tell you this. I've known your grandmother for over forty years, and she's kept this a secret all this time. From your mother, too. I think she was ashamed."

To say that my attention was riveted would be an understatement. "What secret?"

"Your mother's twin brother, Roberto Martínez Carrillo, just died. In Ciudad Juárez."

Huh? My mother didn't have any brothers. Only her sister, Carmen, in Amarillo, Texas.

"Carlota, your grandmother's sister in Chihuahua, thinks he was murdered. There's no proof, from what your grandmother was told. She said they were waiting to hear from one of Grandma's nephews in Ciudad Juárez, I think. Your mother sent some money, that's all I know. For the funeral wreath."

Huh? I shook myself mentally, feeling left behind in this

unraveling story. Mama had a twin brother?

"Pop, why didn't we know about this Mexican uncle? *Mamá's* twin brother? Why would Grandma keep him a secret all these years? My mother didn't know she had a brother? How can that be?" I was stupefied. None of this made any sense.

I could hear Pop sighing audibly over the phone. He sounded so tired. God, how I wished I could be there for him. Pop had been my only defender when I was a child.

"Your mother didn't know, thought he'd died when he was a baby. Your grandmother knew he was alive, she wrote to him—her son—over the years, but he never wrote back. He was angry that he'd been abandoned, I suppose. Your mother's been closemouthed about this, I think, because she's still in shock. I mean, just finding out that you've got a brother and he's just died. How would you feel? At the same time, she doesn't want to upset your grandmother even more, y'know?"

Abandoned? *Abuelita* abandoned a child in Mexico when she immigrated to Texas all those years ago? What was it, over sixty years ago? How could she do such a thing? And *she* criticized *me* for being a rebel and following my own path?

And Grandma's married name was Martinez? Who knew? She'd always gone by Gomez.

"It's a long story, Dina. You should come home this weekend. Grandma's going to talk to the family after Mass on Sunday. You'll find out more then. It's a sad business, sad story. I almost can't believe it myself."

This weekend? I hadn't been home in six months, was still fuming over the fiasco of my last visit.

"C'mon, pumpkin, I know you're mad at us. Because we didn't care for your boyfriend . . ."

I sighed. The truth always hurts. "That's okay, Pop. I'm over it. So was this man who just died, this Roberto Martínez

Carrillo, the person Grandma's been sending money to all these years?"

I thought they were distant cousins, thrice removed, for all I knew about them — the relatives Grandma had been helping to support. Once a year, they'd send a photo at Christmas to let everyone know they were still alive, still needy. One of them hand-painted ceramics for a living and sometimes mailed a package of *cerámica primitiva* to the family. Grandma Gómez would display the items like they were *Lenox* china.

"No, Dina. That's Carlota, Grandma's sister in Chihuahua, the one who's an invalid and widowed. The one who sends those ceramic bowls and animals she paints. Your mother's brother, your uncle — this Roberto Martínez — was a very wealthy man."

Wealth in our family? I must've heard wrong.

"If he was rich, why wasn't he sending *us* money? At least, to Grandma? She's had to count pennies all her life. Didn't she used to work in the artichoke fields in Salinas?"

"Yeah, she's had a hard life. First in Texas, then here in California. That's how he — this Roberto Martínez — got revenge against your grandmother, pumpkin. He didn't write, didn't send money to her, his own mother. He was a hard man if you ask me. This Martínez was the head of the Juárez drug cartel. Maybe one reason she didn't want to use his name when she came to the US. And now he's been murdered. At least, that's what Carlota thinks. Isn't that the damnedest thing you've ever heard?"

¡Ay, caramba! You bet it is.

"Come home, little girl. As soon as you can."

CHAPTER THREE

"Juan, you can help me set the pace today, okay?" I said in Spanish.

"Yeah, can I, Miss Salazar?" the boy replied eagerly.

"Sure, you're a good runner. If I slow down to check on the kids behind us, you keep going. You show them how to run in a relaxed, measured way. So they can last the full mile."

Juan nodded in earnest. He was one of the four special ed kids in my sixth-grade class, the son of poor but hardworking Mexicans — undocumented nationals, I suspected. The school didn't ask, and neither did I. As long as he had a local address and adults as his emergency contacts, Juan was good to go. He was developmentally challenged in reading and struggling to learn English but was very sharp in math, a sweet kid with a round face and big brown eyes.

The Lincoln All-Stars were born three years ago. The idea started as a result of my serving detention. Or rather my having to supervise those serving detention after school on Tuesdays and Thursdays. Neither the miscreants under my supervision nor I wanted to spend that time in the classroom, glaring at each other or staring at the wall clock, so I, like a sadistic track coach, began a jogging regimen.

We began by doing a quarter-mile lap around the school's perimeter. After weeks of complaints and feigned injuries by these classroom cutups, I increased it to two laps, then three, and now four — a perfect mile. When these nine through twelve-year-old kids, most of them with excessive energy to burn anyway, realized they could actually jog a full mile without collapsing from cardiac arrest, Miss Salazar's detention punishment became a kind of status symbol of achievement.

Go figure!

Now, on this October Thursday, I was in the vanguard of a crowd of fifty-odd kids, fourth to sixth graders, who were determined to earn their seventy-two stars on the huge Lincoln All-Star chart posted in the glass-enclosed bulletin board by the administration office. The chart featured the participating kids' photos, names and accumulated stars. Anyone earning over sixty stars got an ice cream party in June. The diligent, persevering ones who earned the full seventy-two stars were rewarded with the ice cream party and lots of cool gifts before they left for summer vacation. All paid for by yours truly.

Who knew my idea for getting out of detention duty would bloom into an after-school fitness program? And cost me the equivalent of a week at *Club Med*?

Today I'd worn a short-sleeved, V-neck t-shirt with my usual dressy jeans — which meant they weren't faded, stained or torn — and running shoes. I'd banana-clipped my hair up for the occasion and had brought a bottle of water, another status symbol all the kids glommed onto.

If a kid forgot his water bottle, the school supplied one. That the bottles were refilled each week from the school water fountain and stored in the cafeteria kitchen fridge made no difference. The kids saw their *MTV* and celebrity models sporting them, saw me drawing from one, and Bingo! These water bottles were more popular than the latest designer sneakers. By three-oh-five PM, all the kids were lining up at the starting line, bottles in hand.

We rounded the far end of the school by the baseball/soccer field on our first lap before I let Juan lead the way. He puffed out his chest like I'd asked him to carry the Olympic torch into the Athens stadium, and he did a great job of maintaining a steady, relaxed pace.

My thoughts kept returning to last night's phone conversation with Pop. I still couldn't believe it. I had a drug lord uncle in Mexico that I never knew about. Now he's dead. Maybe murdered. Grandma Gómez had abandoned him when she left Mexico.

Why would she do that?

She'd always said she was raised in Amarillo, Texas. Why would she lie? To prevent us from spilling the beans, so to speak, which might lead to her possible deportation? So that meant Grandma Gómez was born and raised in Mexico. Not Amarillo, Texas.

And if this Mexican-born uncle was my mother's twin, then Mama was born in Mexico, too.

I stopped in my tracks. Kids flowed past me.

Grandma and Mama were here illegally.

Did my mother know before that she wasn't officially an American citizen? Had Pop known he'd married an illegal?

Crap!

I thought of Rick Ramos and his undocumented father. How very secretive and circumspect they'd been with me until they'd gotten to know me. And could trust me.

Good grief, did *Abuelita* think we kids would tell on her and our mother? Report them to the INS? *La Migra?*

Shit! Was that why Grandma seemed so critical and distrustful of me? I was so American that she feared I'd report them? I pushed these disturbing thoughts from my mind and punched the numbers of Hugh's cell phone. His answering service came on, naturally.

"Hugh, Dina here. Have to go home to Salinas this weekend. Call me tonight, okay?"

Or not, I thought. That taken care of, I pocketed the phone and then dropped back to see how Pete Gravinsky was doing.

From the special day class, Pete was a nine-year-old boy from Ukraine who was a wheelchair user. A bright kid with good English skills, he'd wanted to take part in the Lincoln All-Stars, and so I let him stay on the sidewalk that circled the school as long as he had a companion who'd watch over him. His fifth-grade sister was his companion today, and between wheeling himself and her assistance, Pete was bringing up the rear group.

"How's it going, Pete?" I asked, jogging in place on the sidewalk until they caught up to me.

"Great, Miss Salazar. See my gloves? They're special gloves for wheeling myself. My father said he would buy me a special chair, like the ones people use in the *Special Olympics*."

"Terrific! You'll be able to go much faster with a racing chair. Hey, you stay in the back here and let me know if anybody drops out and tries to cut through the school, okay?"

"We'll tell ya, Miss Salazar," his older sister proudly crowed. "We won't let anyone cheat."

"I have no doubt," I assured the two Gravinsky siblings.

I glanced behind me. Another teacher, a good friend of mine, Lisa Luna, was at the very end of the jogging crowd of kids. She gave me a thumbs-up and smiled. I returned the gesture.

At the starting line, a volunteer parent was marking the backs of the kids' hands with a quick lap-mark in erasable-red as they crossed the starting line after each lap. Four marks on your hand, and you got a star. She also kept an eye out for possible cheaters, although that turned out not to be necessary, for the kids happily reported on anyone taking a shortcut through the school campus.

I took off so I could catch up to the front. For two days, I'd been dying to tell Lisa the shocking news about my family. More than anything, I wanted to share it with someone—couldn't with Hugh, for sure. I didn't know if a deputy DA was obliged or mandated by law to report suspected illegals, but I wasn't going to take any chances. Until I learned more details, I hesitated to tell Aunt Flora, also.

I finished one lap with Pete and his sister, having decided to wait and tell Lisa when I knew more. Panting a little, I approached the starting line by the faculty parking lot and gave a thumbs-up to the volunteer parent, who was sitting on a cafeteria folding chair marking kids' hands. Then I jogged in place and took a sip of water.

"Drink some water, Pete," I said. We paused for a moment while Pete and his sister, Katrina, drew from their water bottles.

"Miss Salazar, that car has been there ever since the school bell rang. There's a man inside it," Katrina said.

I looked over to where she was pointing. A late-model, red *Ford Explorer* was parked across the street, but I couldn't see the driver due to the sun's reflection off the window.

"Could be a parent waiting for one of the kids."

"I don't think so, Miss Salazar."

"Why not?"

"I've never seen it before, and I know all the cars that come to the school."

"You do?"

We passed the starting line and were approaching the left rear-end side of the SUV. I still couldn't see the driver, but I spotted a flash of dark hair. There was a customized license plate, but I couldn't read it from our distance.

Katrina's blond ponytail bobbed as she glanced at the SUV, then looked back at me. "The reason I know, I stand here and wait for my father to pick me up every day, and he's always late, so I see every parent's car."

"Yeah," Pete chimed in, "there's a man in that car. He's just looking at us kids. Do you think he's a bad man, a kidnapper, Miss Salazar?"

"Well, let's keep jogging, and if he's still there on our next lap around, I'll call the police."

Pete and his sister looked bug-eyed at me. "Yeah, yeah, call the police," they chimed excitedly.

One lap later and the red *Ford Explorer* was still there. I began to get concerned, so I pulled my cell phone out of my jeans pocket and dialed 911. The Gravinsky kids watched me in awe as I reported a suspicious red *Ford SUV* parked across the street from the front entrance of our school. I identified myself, gave the name of our school and its location.

By the time we rounded the baseball/soccer field the second time and approached the school's front, a black-and-white was parked behind the SUV, and a uniformed cop was speaking to the driver. Because of the shift in the sun, I was just beginning to get a glimpse of the man's face. We were drawing abreast of the school entrance. Now I had a better look at the driver.

Shit, shit, shit! I thought in horror. The driver was pointing at me. A moment later, the uniformed cop walked over to me as I stood beside Pete and Katrina. Soon we were encircled by a group of about twenty kids, all curious.

"You're Dina Salazar? You're a teacher here?" the cop inquired. He was a muscular, curly-haired guy in his mid to late twenties. More than cute. He was *gor*-geous.

"Yes, I am," I answered, the dutiful citizen, always ready and willing to cooperate with law enforcement. Especially an officer of the law who filled out his gray uniform as nicely as this one did.

"The driver of that red *Ford* claims he's a friend of yours. He claims he's waiting for you to finish this, this . . .whatever it is so he can talk to you."

"We're the Lincoln All-Stars jogging team," Pete informed the policeman eagerly.

The cop looked down at Pete in his wheelchair, smiled at

him, then surveyed the sweating kids, some drinking water, some just staring at his uniform, badge, holster and gun.

"What did the man say his name was?" I asked politely, glancing over at the dark-haired driver of the red *Ford*. I knew who it was, and I was already angry at him. No, furious! Who did he think he was, stalking me like some pervert?

The cop glanced down at his notebook. "Inricky Raymos," he says. "Do you know this man? Is he a friend of yours?"

For a split second, I considered telling the truth. But if I did that, I'd actually have to talk to Rick Ramos, The Hated One, and I couldn't bring myself to do that. Not here. Not now.

So I broke the law and lied to the police. "No, sorry. Don't know that name."

The cop slapped shut his little notebook and narrowed his eyes. Oh, oh, I thought. Was Rick going to get arrested? Was I going to be arrested once they discovered I'd lied?

"Thanks. I'll get his license and get rid of him. If you see him again around this school, you call me."

The cop handed me his card, and I thanked him.

"C'mon, kids, back to our laps," I called out cheerfully.

We resumed jogging, Pete alternating wheeling and Katrina pushing. Juan was finishing another lap and joined us. All four of us stared, our necks craned back, while the cop took down information in his little book and said a few more words to the driver. I could just imagine how offended the proud Rick Ramos was as the red *Explorer*, with the customized license plate *Ramos Inc* took off down the street. I watched the SUV turn the corner, and a moment later, after the cop checked his computer, the black-and-white rolled off behind it.

Well, goody! I'd just given the finger, finesse-style, to The Hated One. In all truth, I felt wonderful!

Vengeance felt great!

While I continued jogging next to Pete and Katrina, Juan,

leading the pack, surged on ahead on their last lap. My conscience belatedly began to niggle me, making me feel a little guilty, even ashamed of myself. Revenge against a hated enemy was always sweet, but I was sure I'd broken at least one law by lying to the cop. I could see myself being handcuffed and slammed into some jail as a felon. Wasn't lying to cops a felony? *Dios*, I prayed. Would I lose my credential over this? My career? My pension?

More than that, I was immensely curious. What in the hell would Rick Ramos have to say to me after all these years? Not that I cared a gnat's eyelash, of course.

Guilt is a strange thing for me. It seems to dissipate like our morning coastal-mountain fog over the Santa Clara Valley, quickly enough when something hot and appealing looms ahead to distract me. Like my daily *Starbucks* fix. Now the valley was called Silicon Valley by the world, but the same morning fog still prevailed. Many things had changed, but not that fog.

I hadn't switched *Starbucks* stores, having determined that I wasn't going to let some old boyfriend who just happened to live nearby push me out of my favorite after-school hangout.

So an hour later found me waving to Manny behind the espresso machine and plopping down into one of the cushiony armchairs surrounding a low pinewood table. Reloaded gift card in hand, I left my things on the table and went to order my usual coffee drink. A grande-nonfat-caramel-macchiato. No, today I made that a venti. After all, I'd jogged a full mile! Gotta replenish those electrolytes. Or whatever was in my body that sweated out.

Ah, revenge was so sweet. Too bad the cute cop didn't haul Rick's sorry ass off to jail right then and there. Maybe he'd get slapped with a fine, at least. Maybe he'd have to pick up highway litter for the next month. Or go to stalkers' rehab clinic.

I chuckled to myself while a new girl took my card, scanned it, and Manny immediately began preparing my drink. Not missing a beat, he morphed into man-on-the-prowl, and we began our usual banter. What about a date Friday night? Naw, can't, got a boyfriend.

Actually, not really, but I didn't tell Manny that the bloom was off the rose. My romance with Mr. Future DA was more like a wilted, brown gardenia. No longer sweet or pretty, it was starting to stink, meaning it was time to move on. Exclusivity with Hugh Goss meant neglect, I'd already concluded. And too many lonely nights.

Still, Manny was cute in a nerdy, long-haired way, but he was at least five years younger than I. From the wry twinkle in his blue eyes, however, I could tell the flirtatious barista had been around the block a few times.

I settled back into my soft, cushy chair, sipped and just stared into the ether, my mind gliding along as if it were a freed bird. Sure, a tiny part of me still felt a twinge of guilt that I'd gotten Rick Ramos in trouble with the law, but for the most part, I felt liberated. Exultant with revenge.

So why did he want to talk to me? Then I remembered what Mariana had said about his daughter having learning problems, and she'd told him she couldn't help because that was not her expertise, that he should ask me, the elementary school teacher.

I sat up straight. So he needed help, and he thought of me. So why come to me of all people? Someone who hated him? Surely, his daughter's kindergarten teacher could offer advice, could test the little girl. I wasn't a Special Ed teacher, but, of course, I'd taken developmental-learning classes as part of the credential program.

My free-as-a-bird mind hit a window and crashed to earth.

Disheartened, I sipped my macchiato. I was feeling pensive, like somehow, in some way, my carefully organized little life was about to fragment into chaotic pieces.

Large male knuckles rapped hard on the table. I jumped.

"A damn childish thing to do, Dina Salazar."

I looked up at Rick Ramos scowling at me. Without another word, he sat down in the upholstered club chair opposite mine. For a long moment, I couldn't speak. We sat there, glaring at each other like the enemies we were. Finally, I found my voice.

"You followed me! Of all the sneaky things."

"Mariana said you came here after work—damn childish thing!"

"Maybe so, but I don't like the way you try to talk to people. You scared me and some of my kids."

"Aw, come on, you don't scare easily. Besides, what's my alternative when you don't return my phone calls? That cop thought I was a damn pedophile, spying on kids and picking out my next victim. He even followed me all the way to San Carlos Boulevard. When I veered off for the Alameda, he finally took off. But he's got me and my license in his database."

He pounded his fist on the table. It was so loud, it made me jump.

"If I get a visit from vice or whatever department handles these things, so help me, Dina, I'm going to damn well force you to fess up. I won't have anything like this on any fuckin' police computer. What if I wanted a government contract, and they do a damn background check? And there it is, some readout that says I was stopped for ogling kids. A suspected sex offender. This could cost my company a helluva lot of money. I won't fuckin' have it."

I sat there, indifferent to the blast of his tirade.

Well, three damns and two fuckin's! For Rick Ramos—the Rick I used to know, the former polite and well-mannered altar boy — that was like giving the finger to Christ on the Crucifix at St. Mary's Church. I looked back at him and met his anger full in the face.

"Well, tough shit," I muttered, glaring back at him.

In spite of his fury, he looked . . .nice. More than nice. Gorgeous in a dark, Latino way. His chest was heaving, and his full mouth was thinned to a taut line, but he was brimming with testosterone. His favorite outfit used to be short-sleeved black t-shirts and black jeans. His wardrobe had improved a notch. The red and blue plaid dress shirt sported a crimson tie at the collar, the cuffs of his long sleeves held together with silver Southwest-style cufflinks. Instead of dusty jeans, a black leather belt held up navy blue dress slacks on his narrow hips.

My throat felt dry and swollen, my heart began skipping in the usual way it always did whenever he was near. I'd forgotten how that felt. Could I hear my *diablito* chirping somewhere in my subconscious, laughing at my sudden fear?

Still, there was no way I was going to apologize. Not now. Not ever. If I had to straighten things out with the police, I would, but apologize to Rick — ha! He'd have to pry off my fingernails before I'd do that.

"I'll call that cop — I've got his card. I'll tell him I finally remembered you. Don't get your jockey shorts in a twist. Or have you switched to briefs? And what do you mean, phone calls?"

"Do you ever check your voice mail?" His dark eyes narrowed menacingly, as if daring me to lie.

"Not lately," I replied, bristling at his tone of voice. When his sonorous voice turned deep, I knew he was repressing a bucket load of anger.

Time to go on the offensive.

"How did you get my cell phone number?" A heartbeat later. "Mariana?"

He nodded and snorted. "How else?"

Dripping with sarcasm, I said, "You used to be charming, Rick. Now you're simply rude. What happened? Does marriage disagree with you?"

If I incited him to leave, then this confrontation would never have to take place. Some part of me knew it was bound to happen sooner or later, but I dreaded it. We lived in the same city of one million or so people, so I never thought I'd have to come face-to-face with him ever again. My heart was pounding so loudly, I thought he surely must hear it.

"Charming, huh? I used to be young and stupid, too. What happened? Goddamned life happened, that's what."

He took a deep breath and then, appearing to expend his anger, exhaled in one long breath, shuddering to a sudden stop. Tension seemed to seep from his shoulders as he slumped forward over his knees. He braced his elbows on the table and looked down for a moment.

I studied him, sitting there and trying to regain control. There were a few creases in his forehead, a sunken, pinched look around his luminous brown eyes, but other than those telltale signs of fatigue or worry, he looked the same. Just older and maybe a bit battered. There were smaller changes in his appearance.

His face and hands were a little tanned but not as much as when he used to work outside in roofing all year long. The ponytail was gone, replaced by a nice, shorter cut, highlighting his thick, wavy dark hair. He was clean-shaven, and I thought I could detect a new fragrance about him. Had old-school Rick finally switched from *Old Spice* to *Polo*?

It was difficult to tell, but he appeared a little thicker in the chest. I'd guess he was maybe twenty pounds heavier than the last time I'd seen him. Of course, back then, we'd both lost weight in those depressing months after The Big Confession. When he'd finally confessed to sleeping with Anita

Hernández the summer I'd been in DC, working for Congressman Velásquez. I hadn't found out until after Christmas that he'd gotten her pregnant. All those months, he'd lied to me, pretended all was well. We'd planned a June wedding. Then it was like, sorry, gotta marry her instead.

He looked up at me, his face still pinched with emotion. Staring at me, he leaned back in the club chair and crossed his legs. What did he think he was doing, settling in for a nice, little chat with a long-lost friend?

Now, in place of cowboy boots, he wore black loafers and navy-blue socks. Rick Ramos, the casually-but-smartly dressed businessman. And as handsome and sexy as the last time I saw him in his father's classic *'57 Bel Air*. No, even more so.

Damn him! Another testament to the old adage that life was not fair. He should've gotten belly fat or grown an ugly, overgrown mustache and mullet, both of which I disliked. No, as luck would have it, he was still a man who made girls' heads turn as he entered a room. Even now, a couple of women standing in line at the order desk began eyeing him and smiling. I tried not to sigh with defeat.

I began to gather up my stuff and stand.

"Dina, please stay. I need to talk to you."

I don't know why but I sat back down.

Here I was, in jeans and a sweaty t-shirt, my hair a mess of tangles in a huge banana clip. My face was devoid of makeup, and my underarms probably smelled. Great!

I looked at his left hand, ring finger. No ring.

No, but he had a girlfriend.

"Look, I don't want to fight," he said, an edge still in his voice, "but you're still a wiseass. Guess you haven't changed." Still, a muscle in his cheek twitched, and he almost smiled.

Now that hurt. He used to call me a *wiseass* when he was

kissing me, among other more endearing things like *querida* and *baby girl*. I'd always taken it as a compliment, but the way he said it just now was no compliment.

"No, you're wrong. I've changed a lot." I continued to give him a look that could kill. In return, he gave me a narrowed-eye, speculative appraisal. Up and down my body. Back to my face.

Maybe he hated me as much as I hated him. Hmmm, now that was a new concept. So why seek me out?

He looked pointedly at the Mexican-style briefcase on the pinewood table. The one he'd given me. Then he smiled slightly. Good thing it wasn't a smug smile or I'd have thrown the thing at him.

I frowned. Time to cut to the chase and get this over with.

"So you need professional advice?" He looked at me quizzically. "About your daughter?"

His gaze flickered away, then came back.

He nodded.

"Angelina just started kindergarten, but the school didn't want to take her this year. She just turned five, and she's behind all the rest of the kids. Way behind."

"In what way?"

As long as we kept our conversation on a professional level, I felt I was safe. Yeah, Dina, you can handle this. I coaxed myself like some demented cheerleader. *Just keep it professional – yeah, Dina!* I actually felt my shoulders relax a little.

"She's very quiet, seldom speaks. My sister, Esther, tells me her hand-eye coordination is like a three- or four-year-old. She has trouble doing simple puzzles. Y'know, those wooden puzzles for little kids? She can't connect the shapes to the spaces."

"Do you have an idea what has caused her to be developmentally delayed?"

"The pediatrician says it's because she was exposed to drugs before she was born. Dina, she's a cocaine baby."

I blinked a few times while his gaze on me was unfaltering.

"Jeez. Did you know?"

"I suspected, but I was so busy at work, building the business, y'know . . .and when I tried to get Anita to stop the drugs, for the sake of the baby 'n all, she just blew me off."

I didn't want to hear about his life with Anita, so I closed that route of questioning.

"I heard from Mariana and my aunt that you've got full custody of your daughter."

"Yeah. My mother, my sister, María Teresa—they help me out. My sister, Esther. You probably heard that my parents moved here from Salinas. They live nearby, off San Carlos. It hasn't been easy, but it's better for Angelina to have no contact with her mother. If you can call her that. She gave her birth, but that's all the mothering she's ever given her."

I swallowed back a snide I told you so. In truth, I was shocked. Way back then, Anita was a known slut but a drug addict? Since when? Did Rick play a role in her turning to drugs? That was hard to believe! Straight-as-an-arrow Rick Ramos?

"How long have you had custody of her?"

"Two years now. I tried to get it sooner, but the court— whenever I went to court, Anita would agree to rehab, and the court would deny it. Anita had that social worker so snowed. It was a joke. As soon as I dropped it, she'd slide right back, just wanted the child-support money. Angelina had a really difficult time of it for about a year after I moved out. I didn't know at the time—none of us did—how bad it got."

Rick paused and shook his head. He cleared his throat. I thought he even teared up a bit. It was difficult to tell, for he looked away, and by the time he resumed his level gaze at me, he'd gotten control of himself.

"When Child Protective Services threatened to put Angelina in a foster home, I got a lawyer and applied for full custody again. This time the court actually listened to me. Anita had gone off the deep end by then, and so she didn't put up a fight. She was into her cokehead boyfriends by then."

"Jeez," I muttered. Not very helpful, I know, but I was so stunned. Why hadn't I heard this from my family? Surely they'd learned about Rick's mess of a marriage. I bet Pet knew — oh, that's right, I remembered. I'd left the room every time the Ramos family was mentioned.

Now it was time to ask the dreaded question.

"How long were you and Anita married?" Something flickered behind his eyes — guilt, perhaps?

"Almost two years," he said, looking directly at me.

Uh-hmmm, just as I thought. He'd cheated on me, his fiancée. Maybe he cheated on his wife, which drove her — never a moral giant, herself — to drugs.

"Dina, she was taking dope when I married her. I just didn't know it," he added as if reading my thoughts.

"Is your daughter okay now?" I went back to the main topic, refusing to listen to any possible lies from Rick Ramos about his marriage.

Who knows? Maybe they'd fallen hard for each other and tried to make the marriage work. Maybe he'd loved Anita all along, and his engagement to me was merely a sham, something to please his traditionalist parents. Her pregnancy gave him the excuse he needed to break off with me and marry her!

Knowing men, I thought anything was possible.

Yep, my heart was hard and cynical, but can you blame me?

Rick nodded. "Physically, Angelina's great. She has several surrogate mothers now, and they all love her. That's what's important. She attends a school close to my parents' house, so my mother can pick her up after school. I drop her off in the morning on my way to work. In fact, I should go get her. It's"—he checked his watch—"nearly five."

But he didn't budge from his chair. He wiped a knuckle across his sensuous mouth, a habitual gesture that used to make me hot. Once upon a time . . .

"If you can recommend something, a tutor, a book . . ." he trailed off as his gaze dropped.

I struggled for a moment between my impulse to kick him in the crotch—what nerve he had to even ask for my help—and my desire to behave in a civilized manner. After all, if one doesn't care, one shouldn't over-react.

Should one?

I was impervious to his good looks and charm, was I not?

"Does your daughter know the alphabet? Her colors? Can she count up to twenty? Can she print her name? Does she recognize simple words in print, like dog and cat?"

To every question, Rick nodded.

"Doesn't sound like she's retarded or learning impaired," I said, "maybe just a little delayed in some areas. If that's the case, one-on-one remediation should help her catch up to her peers. Let her keep practicing with those puzzles. Toss a rubber ball, play catch."

He gave me a steady, serious look, his big brown eyes shiny. He took a deep breath and exhaled audibly.

"God, I hope you're right. I feel so bad for her, y'know. I feel responsible. She comes home crying because she can't read like the other kids. Chrissakes, they're kindergarteners, and most of them can read already! Really simple books, of course, but—she's bilingual, too. In an English-only school, that doesn't seem to count for anything."

I continued in my professional teacher's voice, "Thanks to *Baby Einstein,* preschool, *Sesame Street,* and very aggressive parenting, kindergarteners today are advanced." I considered the little girl's bilingual household. "Y'know, the Spanish might be a little bit of a hindrance now, but later it'll be an enormous advantage."

He shot me a slight grin and nodded. We were on the same page there. Rick was a true bilingual, slipping back and forth from English to Spanish as easily as slipping out of sneakers into loafers.

God, he was good-looking. I had to admit it. But now, in a different way. A manly way. The man before me had been through a crucible, and it showed on his face, his demeanor. Yet, he stirred something in me. Resentment. Sympathy. Fear. And so much more.

Damn! This was not good.

I wondered if he realized I hadn't addressed him by name during our conversation.

"Dina, you probably think I'm disrespecting you by showing up like this and asking for help. It's been a long time."

"Yep, but you always were a nervy guy," I said, not adding that gutsiness was one of the things I'd always liked about him. That got a full-blown, crooked smile out of him, transforming him into the handsome, cocky guy I used to know.

Rick Ramos was a mystery. I wondered if I ever really knew him when we were together as college students. I'd known and explored nearly every inch of his body but did I really know him, his mind, his soul? And what had his marriage to Anita really been like? What did it do to his heart?

Was his heart as hard and callused as mine?

I didn't think I wanted to know.

Our gazes locked in a long, hard stare until I broke it, looking down to pick up my macchiato for another sip.

Ay, no, *chica*, don't fall into this trap again, I warned myself. Remember what Aunt Flora said—he's poison. The top of my skull tingled with fear, a clear warning that I needed to bring this little impromptu reunion to a close.

Lord, how I wished he'd pick his nose or fart out loud so I could get royally turned off. No, not Rick Ramos, ever the suave one. Somehow, he always knew how to behave and look, given any situation. Part of his innate charisma and charm, I suppose, and the way he was raised. The Ramoses. As poor as they were — or used to be, that is — they were all a class act. Traditional, religious, hard-working Mexican-Americans. They must've been appalled by the kind of mother Anita turned out to be.

Despite the problems he'd had, Rick didn't look the worse for it, however. He was a great-looking guy who'd look sexy in a torn tank top, his shoulders bare and biceps bulging with effort, grease all over his hands and face. I'd seen him like that once or twice when he was in the midst of helping his father restore that old *'57 Bel Air.*

Which sudden vision, dammit, made me think of other steamier nights in that *Bel Air.* I wondered suddenly, out of the blue, how long it would take me these days to get Rick Ramos whipped up into a hot frenzy. It used to be, only a certain half-lidded look I'd shoot his way, and he'd be into shallow breathing. His big hands would slide up and down his thighs like they were on fire, and minutes later, they were usually all over me. Those days, when our passion took hold of us, we made love like there was no tomorrow.

Like that day, that moment was for us alone.

And we were at the center of the Universe, our hearts overflowing, about to burst with love and passion.

Unbidden, my gaze flicked down to his crotch, then away. Forbidden territory. Forever lost, like an Egyptian city buried under three thousand years of sand.

Crap! Don't even think it, I scolded myself.

I still had a ton of questions about his life with Anita, but some sane, self-preserving part of me knew better than to raise them. Stick to helping the little girl, whose innocence in this whole mess was indisputable. Do something good for the Ramos family, I told myself. Do something noble and unselfish. Never mind that you'd be helping the ex-fiancé who dumped you and married someone else. The shit! The *pendejo*!

I sighed inwardly. He was still The Hated One.

"Tell you what, I'll ask the special ed teacher at school, see if there are educational tools you can buy and learning exercises you and your mother or sisters can do with your daughter."

He nodded, a kind of light seeming to spark in his eyes.

"Thanks."

"You should speak with the special ed teacher at your daughter's school. Try to get her tested. Find out exactly what her learning disabilities are."

He whipped a business card and a pen out of the inner pocket of his sports jacket he'd slung over the back of his chair. He wrote on the back and handed the card to me.

"My cell phone. Call me anytime, day or night."

There was a time when we used to talk on the phone three or four times a day. Just checking in with each other to say a few words, to give a word of encouragement or love. Or to tell each other a joke we'd just heard. In those days, struggling to get through college, we needed to feed each other encouragement and jokes. We used to connect in lots of ways.

There was the proverbial pregnant pause as I took the card and stuffed it into my jeans pocket. I could sense he was waiting for an opening to bring up other topics. The air around us fairly vibrated with unspoken questions and answers. Things better left unspoken, as far as I was concerned.

"Okay, I have to go. Lots of grading to do. Get her tested. That's my advice." I took a last swig of coffee and stood up.

I grabbed my purse and briefcase and practically ran to the front door of the store. Incited by my *diablito*, I called out to Manny, "See you tomorrow night. Meet you here at seven, okay?"

A surprised Manny behind the espresso machine looked like he was going to drop his pitcher of milk. I waved at him, pretending I was looking forward to our date. Rick was right behind me, and I wanted him to hear.

What did I hope to accomplish by that little display of juvenile deception? Maybe nothing, but it still felt good.

Rick opened the door for me. Always the gentleman he was. I don't think I ever opened a door, car or otherwise, in the three years we were together. I used to call him Sir Galahad.

"So you're not with Hugh Goss anymore?"

I'd forgotten how he knew about Hugh and me. But, of course, the Salinas-to-San Jose grapevine. Pet or Mama told one of the Ramos cousins, who relayed the message to one of Rick's close family members. I'd estimate it would take less than 24 hours to spread any newsworthy item. More reliable than the US postal service.

And there was Mariana, his condo complex neighbor. Jeez-Louise, what had I told her to tell Rick about Hugh and me?

I mentally searched for a suitable answer to his unexpected query. "We're still dating, but I've started seeing other men."

I let it go at that. It was really none of his business.

Rick dogged my footsteps until I got to my car, a two-year-old *VW Jetta*. Not a cool, sexy car but one I could afford on my teacher's salary, which appeared to be plateauing out at $85,000, give or take some change. For Silicon Valley, that meant you qualified for food stamps and subsidized housing.

Rick stepped in front of me after I unlocked my car electronically and opened the driver's door for me. I shouldn't have been surprised, but I was.

"Uh-huh, still Sir Galahad."

"Yeah"—he chuckled—"some habits never die." His voice suddenly changed, deepened. "Dina, I—there's so much—"

No, we're not going there, Mister Ramos. I jumped in and tossed my stuff on the passenger's bucket seat.

"I'll be in touch," I said abruptly and slammed the door shut.

He barely had time to step out of the way as I backed up. I didn't wave goodbye as I sped out of the parking lot. There would be no tripping through the tulips down memory lane with Rick Ramos.

No way, Jose!

As I drove home, my mind was awhirl. Maybe I had no native ability to find the right man. After all, I'd lost Rick Ramos to a woman far less worthy than I—a cokehead, no less! I was going on twenty-nine and about to discard another boyfriend who, I was sure, didn't love me. Whatever I had going with Hugh Goss was like flat cola. No fizzle or sizzle.

I was on the verge of tears again! Behaving like a Jane Austen virgin, all aflutter for Lord Charming's promising glance and benevolent lies! Thoroughly disgusting!

For the second time in as many days! Not at all like me, the family rebel, the born skeptic, the family brat. The one who'd played gas station by putting the water hose in the family car's gas tank. My parents and siblings had stories about my childhood that'd strike terror in your heart. I'd grown up with two older brothers and two older sisters, had grown a skin as thick as a rhino's from all the complaints and criticism. For a young woman, I was about as cynical about life and love as you could get. So, what man loves a cynic?

What a hell of a week this was turning out to be!

Finding out Grandma abandoned a child—my uncle—in Mexico! That he'd been a rich drug lord, and now he was dead. Possibly murdered! That Grandma and Mama might be illegal, that they could be deported even! That Pop was apparently ill. It would have to be serious for him to beckon me home to Salinas so urgently.

Thinking of Grandma Gomez, I slipped into Spanish. *¡Qué pinche semana!* What a miserable week!

Chapter Four

Grandma Gómez—"Cutting short a mule's ears doesn't make him a horse."

"And forgive us our trespasses as we forgive those who trespass against us. And lead us not unto temptation . . ."

I was murmuring The Lord's Prayer under my breath with the rest of the congregation and the parish priest.

"But deliver us from evil, amen," *Abuelita* intoned in Spanish, glancing at me significantly from under her headscarf.

I ignored what Grandma was implying, that I was succumbing to evil by associating with men like Hugh Goss. Selfish men who put themselves and their careers first. She knew I'd slept with him, had done the horizontal tango with a man I was not even engaged to. How she knew this, I had no idea, but *I* knew that *she* knew. Believe me, that was enough. I was still a *desgraciada*.

That I'd ever be able to gain Grandma's love or acceptance was, I figured, as elusive as the proverbial horizon. I'd arrived in time Sunday morning to attend Mass with Mama, Pop and Grandma Gómez, having spent Saturday sleeping late, shopping at the Outlets and spending the night with an old college friend in Gilroy, which was about halfway between San Jose and Salinas. In other words, I was doing a damn fine job avoiding all the problems at home.

Believe it or not, I found our family church comforting.

65

Maybe it was the heavy miasma of incense and the tinkling of the altar bells. The painted glass windows depicting scenes from The Signs of the Cross, through which shafts of light always lent an ethereal, almost mysterious air. I don't know. Vague, sensual memories from childhood were sometimes very comforting.

I didn't like praying next to Grandma Gómez, however. She was dressed in mourning black from head to toe, and she hadn't said a word to me, merely nodded. I think she was incapable of showing affection except to babies, and as I pondered her sour ways during Mass, I wondered whether her life in Mexico and her decision to desert her husband and abandon her son had anything to do with it. I knew that she'd met and married Pablo Gómez, my grandfather — rather, step-grandfather — in Texas before moving to California. At the time, was she still married to this Martinez guy? The drug lord? Did she ever divorce him?

Oh well, I figured the whole story would eventually come out later in the day. All my siblings were coming for their usual Sunday visit, a nearly weekly tradition I'd avoided for over six months.

I looked up as a shaft of sunlight pierced the stained-glass window behind the altar and landed on the gold chalice, like a spotlight on a rock star's headpiece. Yeah, I know how cliche that sounds but in truth, it did something to my brain. My self-pity and loss of confidence after my face-to-face with The Hated One were beginning to bore me. I shook off the blues like a ratty old jacket and took a realistic, more optimistic stock of myself.

I was healthy and intelligent. And there was always the glimmer of hope that I'd fall in love again and that love might actually be returned. Couldn't one moment in life change one's destiny? So there was hope for me. Wasn't there?

Or was I so damaged, like Grandma Gómez, that I'd be

permanently scarred and embittered for the rest of my life?

Well, one thing was crystal clear. Hugh Goss was a mule, and I longed for a horse. Better yet, a stallion. Or else, why bother? Why settle for hand-me-downs and second-best, like Aunt Flora? All for the sake of cluttering your social calendar? Fuck that!

If I couldn't find myself a stallion, I'd go it alone. I'd be celibate, like a Catholic nun. A heartbeat or two later . . .nope, I don't think so. But I would choose very carefully next time. There would be room in my stall for *only* a stallion.

All this, I shared silently in my prayers, suddenly feeling too humble to ask for Their help. I sincerely doubted that God cared a fig whether I found true love or not. They had more important issues to deal with, like the war in the Middle East, famines in Russia and civil wars in Africa. I was positive that Dina Salazar's love life was way down on Their priority list, somewhere near stamping out crabgrass and ridding mankind of cellulite.

Back at my parents' house, I evaded questions about Hugh Goss and gave Pop a wheel of *Manchego* cheese I'd bought at a Spanish-import store in San Jose. I started to help Grandma prepare several large casserole pans of chicken enchiladas. Meanwhile, Mama made toast and scrambled eggs.

Which was strange. She usually made *Migas* on Sundays because it was Pop's favorite breakfast dish. *Migas* was a Spanish dish made of chorizo, garlic and fried dough. Guaranteed to coat the insides of your arteries with lots of stone-hard plaque that you'd have to take a pickaxe to.

Although everyone was a little quiet, I put on a rather chipper attitude and tried to fend off Pop's worried looks and incessant probings. I knew I looked like death warmed over. Kinda sickly and puffy-eyed. At my friend's house in Gilroy, I'd spent the night tossing and turning. I think I was dreading returning home.

Grandma gave me a pointed look. "What did you say *Huge* was doing today?"

"He's writing a speech for a group of Chicano business-men."

Perplexed looks. Why would anyone pass up a chance to congregate with the entire Gomez clan?

"Is he coming to your father's retirement party?" *Mamá* asked.

That was in six months. On Pop's sixty-eighth birthday. A big affair with all the uncles, aunts and cousins.

"'Fraid not."

"Is he coming to your birthday party?" That was in two weeks. Another big gathering of the Gomez clan. Pop's Sala-zar family were throwing me another party at one of the Spanish restaurants in San Jose.

"Probably not. Uh, why aren't we having *Migas*?" I often tried deflection in such uncomfortable moments.

Frowns and one big not-very-feminine snort from Grandma Gómez, followed by low mutterings in Spanish. To-day *Abuelita* had her long, mink-dyed hair in a braided chi-gnon. I noticed she'd let her mustache grow back—Pet was the family's beauty consultant and waxing specialist—and, for a beat, I wondered if I should suggest another waxing job at Pet's salon.

Nope, not a good idea. Let Mama handle such delicate mat-ters of vanity and grooming. Or lack thereof.

For the hundredth time, I tried to see proof of our common DNA—Grandma Gómez and I—and couldn't. My own grandmother and yet she seemed like a stranger. A woman who abandons her child, leaves her husband and country. How could I ever understand a woman like that?

"Your father's on a diet," Mama said, frowning. "We have to cut out fatty foods."

"So we're having enchiladas in creamy poblano sauce?" I

asked, incredulous. They'd never talked about dieting in their lives.

Mama looked heavily at Pop, who was sitting at the kitchen table, drinking coffee laden with cream and sugar.

"Tell her, Frank."

"Tell me what?" I looked at Pop, then Mama and Grandma. Now what, I thought. Another secret in this family? They were piling up like old, discarded tires.

Pop sighed. "The tests came back. I've got an artery in my leg that's clogged up and two near my heart. Gotta have surgery."

"An arterial scrub? Oh, Pop!" I went over to him, bent over his thick salt-and-pepper thatch, and kissed his forehead. Then I hugged him tightly, and he hugged me back.

"Oh, Pop, I'm so sorry. When? When is the surgery scheduled?"

"In one or two weeks. Doctor MacDonald over at *Kaiser Hospital* said he's going to get me in as soon as he can." With stoicism, he merely shrugged and sipped his coffee. "You don't worry about me, pumpkin. You've got enough on your mind with your students."

"Pop—*Mamá*, you've got to let me know. I'll take off work and come down."

I sat down next to him and really looked at him. His usually tanned skin was a little pale and jaundiced-looking. There were dark smudges under his eyes, and he'd lost weight. His long-sleeved cotton shirt seemed to hang from bony shoulders. Even his hair, normally so thick and lustrous, seemed dull and lank. My father was seriously ill, and all these months I'd stayed away because . . .well, for lots of reasons. None of which seemed to make any sense right now.

"How's that fellow of yours, that Hugh Goss?" Pop asked, apparently needing to change the subject.

"He's, uh, okay, Pop. We're dating other people. Y'know,

exploring our options."

His reaction was hooded but mild. "Hmm, I just don't want my little girl to end up like my sister, Flora. Going from man to man, like being in a cafeteria line. Picking here, picking there. Sampling this one, then that one. What kind of life is that for a woman?"

I smiled and touched his hand. "Pop, nowadays a girl has to kiss a lot of frogs before she finds her prince. Even then, sometimes the prince turns back into a frog."

Guess who I was referring to.

"So long as it's just kissing, I suppose it's okay." Pop glanced over at Mama and Grandma, who were naturally all ears. "You don't want to catch something that'll make you sick." He smiled tentatively and grasped my hand. His grip was strong, which was reassuring. "Young women nowadays expect too much from a man. You expect, uh, Prince Charming."

I smiled and shrugged. "Don't think he exists, Pop. Only in fairy tales."

Pop shook his head and made a rueful half-grin at me.

"Women expect a man to be perfect, to satisfy all their needs. Life's not like that, pumpkin. Men aren't perfect, and women aren't, either. What they need is true love and devotion. That isn't sexy or exciting, maybe, but it's real. You can find that in real life, but you can't find fantasies in real life."

Wow, I'd never heard Pop lecture on love before. I was fascinated.

His dark blue eyes settled on his coffee as he frowned. His own grandparents had immigrated to the US from the north of Spain, Galicia, once settled by the ancient Celts. The Galicians still played their bagpipes, like the Scots.

"Flora is my sister, and I admire her success in business, but she . . ." He hesitated to put his disapproval into words, I knew that. To him, it would seem disloyal. "She is too easy with men. And dishonest. She gives herself away but has no feelings for the men she gives herself to."

Huh, I wondered how Pop'd learned about Flora's many affairs, but I guess her siblings talked among themselves.

"Pop, it's not easy being a single woman. It's hard finding the right one to marry. It's hard learning to trust a man completely."

"I just don't want you to be influenced too much by her. She thinks differently. I don't want you to end up—" He broke off as Mama served him breakfast, scooping up eggs from her skillet.

"I feel the same way, *m'ija*," Mama said. "When did you and that Hugh decide to break up?"

"We haven't exactly broken up," I began, stalling a little as I tried on various versions. The truth, half-truth, lie, little white lie . . . That I hadn't really spoken to Hugh about this was irrelevant. "We're just expanding our horizons. Seeing other people but remaining friends. Still dating now and then. I ran into Rick Ramos the other day, by the way."

Mama almost dropped the skillet she was holding as I nonchalantly sipped my black coffee. I was hoping, of course, that slipping in the second tidbit would supersede the first, being a little more pleasant topic of conversation for my parents. They were still on very friendly terms with the Ramoses, the ones still in Salinas, anyway.

"Who did you run into?" she asked, pretending a hearing loss all of a sudden.

It was difficult keeping a straight face, I'll have to confess. Mama was so transparent. Not so Grandma Gómez, wearing an apron over her usual blouse and stretch pants but now all in black. She made no pretense. Instead, she made a hurried sign-of-the-cross. What that was for, I hadn't the foggiest. Was she thanking God I'd broken up with *Huge* or praying I hadn't whipped out a shotgun and peppered Rick with a vengeful blast when I ran into him?

"Ricky Ramos," I tried again. "As it turns out, he doesn't live far from Aunt Flora's, and we ran into each other at a *Starbucks* after school one day."

I decided to forego mentioning the incident about calling the cops to my school and getting Rick into trouble with the law. Which reminded me — I had to call that cute, young cop and set things straight, and then hope he didn't arrest me for lying under oath. Wait a minute, I wasn't under oath, was I? I was standing on the sidewalk and hadn't raised my right hand. Oh, good!

"His little girl might be DD. Developmentally delayed. He asked for my help, so I told him to get her tested."

"What do you mean, Dolores," Grandma asked in Spanish, "she has DD? Is that like polio? *Dios la bendiga.*"

Grandma Gómez remembered things like polio? I began to wonder just how old she really was.

"No, *Abuelita. Significa que . . .*" I began to reply in Spanish, then switched back to English. "It means developmentally de-layed. She is slower at learning certain motor, spatial and ver-bal skills than other children her age. At least that's what Rick thinks."

"*Pobrecita*," Grandma muttered and crossed herself again.

Mama looked at me steadily, going back to the stove.

"So why did Ricky Ramos talk to *you* about his daughter's problems?"

What, like I'm not an elementary school teacher and am clueless about such things? What did my mother think went into preparing to teach children — learning how to print on a blackboard and wiping kids' noses?

I shrugged. "Don't know. He could've spoken to the little girl's teacher, who would've recommended what I did. His daughter needs special testing. If she's developmentally de-layed, she'll need special learning strategies to help her catch up."

"Like special methods of learning?" Grandma asked.

"Yes," I replied. "There are proven strategies that do work. Each child is unique, though. The DD term is a general one, for lots of kids with learning deficiencies, from severe deficiencies, such as Down's Syndrome, kids with cerebral palsy, mild to severe mental retardation, to mild deficiencies, like you'd find in drug babies . . ."

My mother's hand paused at her mouth.

"Is Ricky's daughter a . . .a drug baby? María Ramos hinted at something like that when she was down here visiting her sister, Hortensia. She had us over for coffee one time, and she was talking about the little girl and all the problems Ricky had with the mother. That . . .*puta.*"

Mama and Grandma looked at each other and nodded.

"*Qué lástima, m'ija,*" Grandma said to Mama. They exchanged significant looks, then went back to their kitchen work.

Silence followed. I began to suspect that I was missing out on something. That they knew more than they let on.

Grandma took the ends of her apron and dabbed her eyes. "*Las drogas* do terrible things to people," she muttered in Spanish, "the people who use them. But also the people who make and sell them. *Los tráficos.* I know."

That got my total attention. Grandma was hinting at her own life, and all of a sudden, I was curious again about her story. I looked at Pop, who slowly shook his head. He placed a forefinger over his mouth. Telling me to stay quiet. *Abuelita* would tell her story in her own good time.

Suddenly, Grandma Gómez let the apron go and sniffed loudly. She flipped over a tortilla on the casserole pan and, without even glancing at me, said, "That Huge was not for you, Dolores. He was a *testarudo. Un mulo.*"

A mule, a man without much worth. At least, I think that's

what she meant.

Dios, but Grandma Gómez didn't miss a thing! She had the instincts and senses of a bloodhound. I ignored the fact that she'd addressed me by my old name and said nothing in response. For once, Mama did not add her usual string of dismissive and belittling remarks, like—why did you choose him in the first place?

So, until Frank, Isabel, and the kids showed up—and later, Roberto, Pet, Juan Pablo and their kids—I relayed to Mama and Grandma Gómez all that I knew about DD children and their hardships in school. There was even a glint of respect in their eyes by the time I had to break off the conversation to greet the other members of my family.

And I kept my mouth shut about this drug-lord uncle of mine in Mexico. I think Grandma wanted to tell her story only once, and so she wanted everyone there.

We had an early dinner of enchiladas, refried beans and tossed green salad. Well, at least one dish was fat-free. Poor Pop! Was he ever going to succeed on any kind of diet in this household? I think not.

My sister, Connie, and her nitwit husband, Jesús, hadn't come. They'd recently had twin girls and had moved to San Jose. Jesús supposedly had some job prospects though I hadn't been told what they were. It strained my imagination trying to figure out what those job prospects could be. Just as well, they weren't here. I had a feeling the family meeting was going to be a somber one. Goofy Jesús couldn't be serious about anything.

Frankie's oldest daughter, a pretty fourteen-year-old, ushered the older kids into the den to watch a Disney video while Pet's baby slept on Grandma's bed. The adults gathered around the kitchen table, pulling up random chairs. I sat on an ottoman next to Pop, his right hand raised, holding a goblet of *cava*, a kind of Spanish sparkling wine, which he sipped from silently, solemnly. My hands folded around his left arm, my head propped against his thin shoulder. I was worn out and still faced a two-hour drive back up north but let me tell you, wild horses couldn't have dragged me away from that table.

Mama sat at the opposite end of the table next to Grandma. They both clutched embroidered handkerchiefs, and their faces were drawn and pale. Pet glanced at me, her big brown eyes already tearing up, but it was Mama who spoke up firmly, her generous lips set in a thin line.

"*Abuelita*'s going to tell her story in Spanish, and I'll translate. Dina, you can jump in and help if I get stuck."

Mama looked at me, and I nodded. Being called to the stage, so to speak, made me feel a little proud of my language skills.

No one said a word while Grandma began to speak. Her voice was soft and sad as she stared at the handkerchief in her shaking hands. It dawned on me how difficult this must be for her to tell this story. She'd lived it and suffered through it, but she must've felt like she had an obligation to tell us, her closest family members. I actually felt sorry for her.

"I was not born in Amarillo, *Tejas*. I was born and grew up in a village called Delicias in the state of Chihuahua." She paused while Mama dutifully translated. I noticed her Spanish was simple, like that of a child. Her story was taking her back to her childhood.

"My parents were poor farmers who grew maguey plants and made them into *mezcal*. That is like tequila. Their name was Carrillo. Anyway, when I was fifteen, they persuaded me to marry a well-to-do farmer who lived north of the city of Chihuahua. He had a large farm near *El Sueco,* and his family was well-known in the area and very important people. The man's father was an old friend of Pancho Villa, the revolutionary. They were active in *El Partido de la Revolución*

Mexicana. I married this man, Ernesto Martínez Cárdenas. Two years later, I gave birth to twins, a boy and a girl."

Grandma paused and flashed a quivering smile at Mama, who dabbed at her eyes with her handkerchief. I glanced up at Pop. He was staring at his wife with concern in his eyes.

"As time passed, I realized why my husband's crops were making so much money. He was growing *mafufo—*" Even Mama wasn't sure how to translate this word, so I filled in.

"Marijuana," I supplied. A few pairs of eyebrows raised.

Grandma continued. "And then later, I learned he was smuggling this drug across the border into El Paso. There the desire for this drug was strong, and the *norteamericanos* had plenty of money. He did not care who the drug corrupted or destroyed. He said it was not his problem. He was a *tráfico.* That was his *negocio,* his business. As his wealth grew, his power grew, and whatever he desired, he got. Women, cars, guns, more powerful drugs from South America. Power and respect. The *campesinos* were afraid of him. So were the *federales.* With a single word, he had people killed."

When Grandma said this, announced her husband's infidelities and cruelties, she straightened in her chair as if she were finding the backbone to continue.

"His bad temper became worse, and he grew cruel, even to me. He beat me and controlled every part of my life. I knew I had to leave. My brother, Tito, had married and moved to El Paso, then to Amarillo. I pretended I had to visit him to help his wife with her baby, and so Martínez Cárdenas let me go. But I could take only one of my children. It was his way of making sure I returned. I thought my daughter would have a difficult time surviving in that house, but a son would be strong . . .so I took Conchita."

By now, Mama was weeping softly and couldn't speak, so I took over the translation. Pet went over to Mama and hugged her shoulders. Frank, Isabel, Roberto, Pet, and Juan

Pablo were all misty-eyed. I seemed to be the only one, besides Pop, with dry eyes. When Pet and Mama calmed down a bit, Grandma continued, looking at me to translate. I cleared my throat and waited for her.

"I had a visitor's visa, but I stayed. It was the most difficult thing I've ever done, leaving my son, little Roberto. Leaving him with that monster, but there were servants, and we had a *niñera*—a nursemaid—an older woman who was very good with babies. I hoped that little Roberto would be fine until I could find a way to get him out of Mexico. Martínez Cárdenas was furious, of course, and I later learned he told my son that I—and his sister—had died in a car crash in *Tejas*. In time he remarried—he secretly divorced me on the grounds of desertion. Of course, no one in Mexico questioned his decision."

Grandma sighed deeply. I paused, suddenly feeling teary despite my fascination with this unfolding melodrama.

"I found a job in Amarillo cleaning houses, and then I met your grandfather, Pablo Gómez, had your *tita* Carmen, and much later after your mother was grown, we came here to California to be near Conchita and Frank and all of you. I have lived here in California twenty-two years."

The man we'd called *Papá* Gómez was actually our step-grandfather. He died when I was fourteen.

"All these years, I thought of my son and prayed for him. I even went to an immigration attorney, a *Mexicano*, to see if I could get him here, but I was told it would be impossible. I was here illegally and had no rights. Martínez Cárdenas must have destroyed all the letters and cards I sent, and so I thought my son was lost to me forever."

Grandma sighed deeply and sniffed into her handkerchief. I waited for her to regain her composure. Pop patted my hand as though to praise me for my translation. He knew little Spanish but had encouraged me over the years to improve my fluency.

"My sister in Chihuahua, the one with rheumatoid arthritis so bad that she is an invalid, kept track of Roberto as well as she could. He grew up to become a handsome man, but unfortunately, he was expected to continue in the family business. He did, and Roberto became el jefe when the small traficantes joined together to make one large cartel. My sister told me this."

Grandma cleared her throat, and with a handkerchief, she withdrew from the cuff of her long-sleeved blouse, wiped her eyes.

"Then, many years later, here in Salinas, I received a letter from his daughter, Teresa. The daughter of my son, Roberto. Roberto had married a Val Verde woman, a woman of great beauty, I am told. My sister's son, Jaime, had met her—my granddaughter Teresa—in Ciudad de Juárez and had given her our address. She was shocked to learn that she had a family in California and Texas—a grandmother, aunts and uncles, and cousins. We have been corresponding ever since. Our correspondence started two years ago. However, I cannot send letters directly to her. I must send them to Carlota first, whose son, Jaime, then meets Teresa secretly in Juárez and passes them on to her. It was from Teresa that I learned of my son's death. She went to Juárez to buy burial clothes and called Carlota from there. Jaime says she has bodyguards and is watched closely. Her mother, this Val Verde woman—"

Grandma halted in her narrative, her face crumbling in horror or shame. I couldn't tell. Everyone at the table waited with abated breath as she calmed herself enough to go on.

"Teresa's mother, the Val Verde woman, was killed at the same time as her husband, my son Roberto."

"How were they killed, *Abuelita*?" Pet asked.

By now, Grandma Gomez had dissolved into tears of grief. Yet, she forced herself to continue, my mother's arm around her shoulders encouraging her to finish her story.

"They were ambushed on the road and were shot to death, the chauffeur, too. They think a pickup truck full of men from another cartel stopped their car and killed them in cold blood."

Murmurings around the table rose and fell, some shocked, some saddened, a few quiet in their horror. As a testimony to my grandmother's fortitude and determination, she continued on.

"Teresa, Roberto's daughter, is in her late twenties. Dolores's age, I think." Grandma shot me an impenetrable look while several at the table turned to stare at me. What, as if I had played a role in any of this?

"Teresa is married to her father's accountant," she went on, "a man by the name of Vargas. Anyway, her father—my son, Roberto Martinez Carrillo—was buried yesterday at the hacienda. Along with Teresa's mother. *Pobrecita*, Teresa."

While Grandma held the handkerchief to her face and I finished the tail end of the translation, she pulled two small photographs out of her apron pocket. We passed them around, and when they got to me, I studied them. One, a sepia-toned photo, yellowed and frayed with age, showed a small, dark-haired boy of about two or three. It was difficult to see his features, for his face was in shadows. He was standing in front of a high, white-stucco wall. His daughter, Teresa, must've found this one in an album.

The second photo was colored and must have been taken relatively recently. Grandma's son, our *tío*, was now a mature man in his late fifties. His hair was thick and dark, his face resembling my brother Roberto's, perhaps not so strangely. He was dressed in a dark suit and tie and seemed to be standing in front of the same stucco wall. However, in this photo, there was a black *Mercedes* sedan next to him. Evidently, Teresa had taken it, perhaps with the sole purpose of sending it to Grandma.

"*Abuelita*, did our *tío* know that his daughter—our cousin, Teresa—was in touch with you?" I asked in Spanish.

Grandma shook her head. "Teresa said she tried to ask him once about me, but he forbade her to ever mention my name again. From what she wrote, my son was not a man one defied. He had become like his father . . .very hard and ruthless. Nevertheless, he gave his daughter her middle name. Dolores. So he did this in memory of me. Teresa Dolores Martinez Val Verde."

My siblings all looked confused, what with all the names tossed around like so much confetti. Even I was a little overwhelmed by all the new information. While I translated that last exchange, Grandma got up and quietly went to her room. Mama started to get up, too, but Pop waved her down.

"Let her alone, Concha. She's a brave woman and very proud. It took a lot from her to tell you this"—Pop looked around the table at the somber faces—"because she's been ashamed of her past, ashamed of leaving her son. Now that he's gone, she felt she had to honor him by telling you her story. And his story. What little we know of it. What little we still know of him, this Roberto Martinez."

We all nodded glumly. Even my hopefully reformed, ex-con brother, Roberto—named after our drug lord uncle in Mexico—sat still, jokeless, his gaze glued again to the photos of the uncle we never knew. His namesake and a man he looked like but never knew existed until now. I wondered how he felt being named after an uncle that none of us ever knew. A Mexican drug lord, for crying-out-loud.

I wondered about my Mexican cousin, Teresa. No, Teresa Dolores. Guess she never changed her name. I suddenly felt silly and a little ashamed for changing mine. Was it really so bad?

Dolores—aches and pains. Hell, yeah!

Most of all, I wondered about *Abuelita*. How it must have

felt being married to such a violent man as Martínez Cárdenas. How it must have felt having a son who grew up to take his father's place in the Juárez Cartel. A son she could never know. A son she could never save.

We sat around the table in silence for a long, long time.

CHAPTER FIVE

An hour later, while the little kids went outside to play a game of pop-up softball with Roberto and Juan Pablo, Frank and his wife, Isabel, took me into the living room. Pop was lying down, resting, in the back bedroom, and we could hear Mama tinkering in the kitchen and talking to Pet.

"Hey, *dolor de culo*." Frankie nudged me, calling me by my childhood nickname, which meant *pain in the ass* in Spanish. It was also a play on my former name, Dolores.

My eldest brother, auburn-haired like me and tall like Pop, smiled and handed me a tall glass of chilled *cava*. We looked like we needed straight shots of whiskey or vodka, but Pop never kept in stock hard alcohol. The *cava* would do for the time being. We sat on the red-velveteen sofa. The lithograph on the wall behind me — the one I'd given Mama and Pop last Christmas — pictured a Goya-like scene of bucolic peasants in the square of a sleepy, sun-drenched Mexican town. It had replaced the bullfighter on black velvet that'd always made me cringe.

I think I was still in shock from Grandma Gómez's story. My mind lingered in Mexico, in that totally different world of a drug lord's wealth and power. In Grandma's sad flight to the US and losing her son for all time.

And now he was dead. At the age of sixty-two, for that was how old Mom was, and they were fraternal twins, according to Grandma. It seemed too young an age to die. Since his cause of death was so brutal and violent, no one at the table had pursued this line of questioning. I had let it go, too. We'd all read and heard TV reports of Mexican cartel violence, after all. There were many more questions in my mind, but I was letting them go for now. Pop didn't want any of us to bother Grandma Gómez, who had remained in her room the remainder of the afternoon.

Frankie's wife, Isabel, a pretty, chubby woman with thick, lovely black hair worn in a long, upswept ponytail, sat beside me with their fourth child, fourteen-month-old Tomas. The little boy was asleep. I murmured how adorable he was and touched his little bare foot.

When Grandma left Mexico, her son was just a little older than little Tomas. So again, I wondered what kind of desperation it took for her to flee with her baby daughter and leave behind a baby boy in the clutches of a violent, powerful man. The thought sent shivers down the nape of my neck.

I found myself wondering—well, for one nanosecond—if I'd ever become a mother. Or even if I wanted the responsibility of another human being 24/7, even one who weighed little more than a baguette of sourdough bread. Would my children turn out to be rebels and rascals, like me? Little *dolorcitos de culo*?

"He's the last," Frank said.

"How's that, Pancho? You giving up sex?" I teased. Frank hated that nickname and wouldn't let anyone but me get away with calling him that. He was sporting a *Zapata* mustache these days and really looked the part. "Or should I put a *Planned Parenthood* pamphlet in your Christmas stocking this year?"

"No, smartass. I got myself fixed," he added, smiling, his generous mustache twitching a little. Isabel glanced at him, loving approval evident on her face.

"You got a vasectomy?" I queried, astounded. Frank nodded with finality.

"Isabel tried every pill and patch you can think of. They all made her sick. So it was time to cut the ol' sperm tube."

After recovering from my shock, I congratulated them both, not mentioning that I thought it was high time for common sense to kick in. I knew that the tile-installation business was doing well enough, but feeding six mouths was straining Frank's budget. I'd hoped the family's on-the-edge-of-poverty cycle would end with Frank's and my generation. So far, it didn't look too promising. Especially with Roberto and Jesús in the mix, bringing down the income average.

Frank checked around to see if Roberto or the others were within earshot. I knew Connie and her doofus husband had moved to San Jose for some kind of job, but I hadn't seen them in town. Another call I had to make tomorrow. I'd invite them over for dinner at Aunt Flora's. The twins were a little over two months old. I could envision Connie changing their diapers on Flora's expensive brocade sofa. On second thought, maybe a trip to *McDonald's* would have to do.

After Jesús's and Roberto's six-month incarceration in a minimum-security federal prison in Arizona for their cyber-crime five years ago—selling used cars that weren't really for sale on *eBay*—it'd been difficult for them to find jobs. Frank had welcomed Roberto back into the family's tile business but not Jesús, figuring that keeping the two dumb-asses separate would be the prudent thing to do.

So far, Roberto had toed the straight and narrow, under Frank's constant scrutiny. Pop had threatened to disown him if he screwed up again. Frankie and Juan Pablo had threatened to break Jesús's legs.

Thank God for that, for I'd never seen Mama and Pop so distraught in my life. If Queen Elizabeth II called that one year of her children's scandals her *anno horribilis*, Mama and Pop called that year of Roberto's and Jesús' arrest and incarceration their *año de vergüenza*. Year of shame.

Jesús' sole accomplishment so far was proving to the

family that he had viable sperm. A chilling fact that was.

"How's that job working out for Jesús? What's he doing exactly?" I pictured him flipping burgers or washing dishes.

"He's driving a truck for Ramos Construction. I talked to Rick. He says Jesús's doing fine. He's got a guy keeping an eye on him all the time, so he's not tempted to mess up."

You could have knocked me down with a feather. I was so amazed. Boy, the shocks kept on coming this week!

"No shit? Even after denting the *Bel Air*, Rick gave Jesús a job?"

That horrible night of my college graduation party was forever etched in my mind, like with acid. Rick had shown up unexpectedly, and Jesús had run him off by taking a sledgehammer to that precious, restored *Bel Air*. I shook my head. Un-friggin'-believable.

"Hope Rick doesn't live to regret it," Frank grumbled, sliding a look over at Isabel.

"The Ramoses gave us a huge tile job, too," Isabel interjected, smiling broadly. "A big residential job. A development of new homes. Your father and Frank had to hire six more men. Now we can start saving up to buy our house."

"That's a long way to go for a tile job. Over an hour's drive, Frankie. How's Pop going to manage it? He's going in for surgery soon," I said.

"It's the biggest job we've ever gotten. Couldn't turn it down, especially now. And Pop's just going to do the desk work, ordering supplies, phoning the wholesalers. Y'know, that kind of thing. Until his surgery, anyway."

"What'd'ya mean, especially now?" My worry compass had halted on that one phrase.

My stomach clenched into a hard ball. What, another family crisis was brewing? Was there no end to these family problems? Frank leaned in closer, smoothing his mustache with a finger.

"Pop's got to retire . . .as soon as these new orders are in. You have to help me talk him into it, Dina. He wants to make it to his sixty-eighth birthday, but I say, no way. It's not worth the risk. The doctors want to schedule the surgery for next week. At the latest, the week after. After the surgery, he's got to retire for good."

"Shh—" I couldn't even finish my usual cuss-word.

"That's not all, Dina. The reason Pop hasn't retired, they don't have the money to pay all their bills. They had to mortgage the house to pay for Roberto's and Jesús' legal fees. You know, from five years ago. Pop's and Mama's Social Security checks won't cover everything, including the mortgage. They'll need an extra thousand a month."

"They have no savings?" I asked. A silly question. Of course, they had no savings.

"Are you kidding?" Frank gave me a look of what-planet-are-you-from? "Listen, if you can contribute two-hundred-and-fifty a month, Isabel and I put in the same, and Roberto and Pet and Juan Pablo, too, that'll be one-thousand. They won't have to sell the house."

Of course, Mama and Pop couldn't sell their house! This was home to all of us. As small and as poor as it was, a little stucco bungalow in a working-class Latino neighborhood, it was home. The front yard had just enough room for all of our cars, and the back yard was spacious enough for trees, a swing set on grass, and a patio fixed with a brick barbecue, table, and benches. For the most part, the neighborhood was safe, blue-collar, and near a city park. We'd all grown up there. It was home and always would be.

"What about Connie and Jesús? Seems to me they should put in, too." Hey, after all, fair's fair. It was Roberto's and Jesús's larceny that put Mama and Pop in this fix.

Frank frowned. "Not for at least a year, 'til they get back on their feet. Connie had to quit her retail job to take care of the twins. And Jesús . . .well, he's had odd jobs but nothing permanent. He's only been working steadily for a month." His steady gaze pinned me squarely as he sighed. "So, can you help out?"

"Sure, I'll be glad to," I said reluctantly. As I acknowledged Frank's and Isabel's grateful, relieved expressions, it dawned on me.

Shit! I might have to sacrifice my weekly golf game. Who was I kidding? I loved the game. I'd have to think of something else I could give up . . .my daily fix of *Starbucks*? Double shit! But hey, all those calories from that caramel in the macchiato wasn't doing me any good. I could feel my thighs beginning to bulge a little, just thinking about it.

No *Club Med*, for sure, this summer . . .or jetting to Cozumel with that scuba-diving group . . .or a party-ship cruise down the Mexican Riviera with my friend, Lisa. I might even have to teach summer school — Triple shit! Oh no, there had to be another way. Only a temporary lapse of sanity would inspire me to teach summer school. Maybe I could work at *Starbucks* next summer and get free lattes? Yeah?

I inwardly groaned but outwardly grinned encouragingly at Frank and Isabel. At least, I didn't have four kids to support. How were they going to manage?

By taking on big jobs, they couldn't refuse. Ramos Construction.

I was getting the feeling that Big Brother Rick Ramos was looking out for us in his own inimitable way. But why? He owed the Salazars nothing.

And funny it was that Rick never mentioned giving Jesús a job when we spoke at *Starbucks*. He could easily have reminded me that quid-pro-quo, I owed him a favor. But Rick Ramos, the gentleman, had said nothing. He hadn't wanted me to feel obligated to him in any way.

So like him. The old Ricky Ramos, anyway.

The new Rick Ramos, successful businessman and single father. Who was he, really? The other night, he'd sounded bitter. Angry. Even a bit anxious. He'd changed in some ways. That much I could tell. What was the new Rick Ramos really like?

Por favor, like I could care.

"Frank?" I temporized, pretending to study my fingernails for a moment.

"Yeah?"

"Why d'ya think Rick and his father hired Jesús? I mean, what would they stand to gain by doing that?"

"Rick hired him, not the old man. The old man's a real bear. If he knew it was Jesús who dented the *Bel Air* and served time, he'd never've hired him. He's a strict, old bastard — he'll hire Mexican illegals but not American ex-cons."

Frank paused and glanced at Isabel. "Hey, about the Mexican nationals working for ol' man Ramos, you didn't hear it from me, got it?"

I nodded and rolled my eyes. What, like I was going to run to *La Migra* and report the old guy. *Señor* Ramos was an icon. Everyone in Salinas admired what he'd accomplished.

"Why Rick hired Jesús, the family fuckup — I think he feels he owes it to our family. The *orgullo* thing, a matter of pride. Y'know, for what happened to you both . . ."

Frank looked uneasy at bringing up the shame of that broken engagement.

"Rick said he owes it to the Salazars. I told him he didn't, but he says he does. No matter what you think, Dina, he's a man of honor." I didn't know what to think. Another reason why I shouldn't hate the lying, cheating cad, perhaps? In any event, I was glad for Frank's and Pop's tile company, wary about Jesús's new job — beyond that, I refused to speculate.

"Frank, let's go talk to Pop. Let's put his mind to rest. He can't worry about money. That'll make his condition even worse."

Frank caught my hand. "Dina, Pop can't know about this. He'd, y'know, feel ashamed. We do this on the QT, give the money to *Mamá* every month. She pays the household bills."

I nodded, reached over, and hugged Frankie. Then I bent and hugged Isabel. We'd do what we had to do. And that was saving Mama and Pop from economic ruin!

It made me *orgulloso*, proud to be part of a family that rallied together when things got tough. The Ramoses didn't own a corner on pride.

Someone once said playing golf was as hard as doing calculus homework with a hangover. Why I persisted in attempting to play this sport was a total enigma to me. That it was a civilized, genteel sport played by my idols, Tiger Woods and Annika Sorenstam, was probably one of the factors. Another reason that kept me returning, I was the only one in my family to play the game. Not an earthshaking fact but one that I felt set me apart from my numerous, soccer-loving relatives.

Naturally, my Saturday golf date with Hugh the following weekend was, I have to admit, anticipated. But also dreaded.

We usually followed the 18-hole round with dinner and an evening at a ballet or concert. Not a Los Lobos concert but chamber music. I was usually half asleep by the time we got back to his condo in Palo Alto. The lovemaking was ho-hum as well, but hey, I was getting cultured. Wasn't that the price you paid for culture—boredom?

I loved the golf but not what followed. Maybe Hugh sensed my disenchantment, for he was pouring himself into his campaign to become the next DA and keeping me out of the loop. We were in a rut, and I sensed that both of us wanted out. Or at least, a change of some kind.

When he picked me up at Flora's, I was dressed in my best

golf togs — navy trousers with deep pockets for balls, a divet fork and a handful of wooden tees, a navy-green-tan-white argyle sweater vest over a white, long-sleeved, collared shirt, and tan-and-white, cleated golf shoes. I didn't bring my overnight bag for our usual Saturday sleep-together at his condo in Palo Alto because I had no intention of sleeping with him again. In my mind, this would possibly be our last outing together, but I wanted to end our relationship on a friendly, amiable note. So, like most people with a breakup on their minds, I wanted it to be in a very public place. I guess a public golf course qualified.

He greeted me with a feeble *hi* and a dry, puckered kiss. When I wrapped my arms around his neck, he drew his head back.

"I was hoping for a big hug and a big kiss," I said teasingly, trying to maintain friendliness.

What I needed was an open mouth, tongue-down-the-throat wet one, and a hard squeeze that promised fireworks later on.

You see, I was still trying to banish lingering thoughts of Rick's crotch in those suit pants, his flashing brown eyes, the way he grinned slyly at me. Even though he knew I hated him. I liked that kind of guts.

Hugh half-smiled and half-grimaced and took me into his arms. While he held me loosely and sighed, I inhaled his cologne . . .and the smoke that permeated his clothes. This was something I wouldn't miss, a smoker's acrid odor. My nostrils flared at the smell.

"Sorry, sweetheart," he murmured, then drew back. "We were out late last night. Y'know, another strategy meeting. I'm a bit hung-over."

At thirty-five, he'd reached a point in his life where he seemed to know exactly what he wanted. That was, I'd learned, a political office and a trophy wife. In other words, a woman who was educated, cultured, beautiful, and stylish. And if she had money on top of all that, that was okay, too.

How did I know this? It was sometimes shocking what a man's computer held—like a window into his soul.

One Sunday morning, while at his condo, I snooped around as he slept. Okay, okay, so I shouldn't have been prying into his email. But I'm convinced if more women did this, they'd see their men in a totally different light. I knew the password for his email retrieval because he'd said it to me once when he was boasting about taking over Ochoa's office. The password—politics. Did I mention that I wasn't the least bit shy? One email he'd sent to one of his former law school buddies, as a reply to the email he'd received and never deleted, told me what I'd needed to know. Hugh had revealed he'd be looking for this trophy wife. Just as soon as he won the DA's election in March.

In other words, he hadn't found her yet.

That alone had opened my eyes to the *real* Hugh Goss.

So why me? A blue-collar-raised Latina with a near-bankrupt but very proud family?

Heck if I knew. I was literate and had a respectable profession, but I was no trophy wife with connections. Except for Congressman Velásquez and the Latino Political Caucus. Was that what this relationship was all about? He needed the Hispanic vote in San Jose? I'd reached my own conclusions by now, of course.

The axiom I'd forgotten—never trust a politician—came rushing back like a slap in the face.

I knew it was only a matter of time before he moved on, as I already had emotionally. Although handsome in a blond, blue-eyed, nerdy, preppy way, he had a ruthless, ambitious streak. Overall, he could be charming when he wanted. But he was a Bill Clinton. Ambitious as hell and clever to boot. But dishonest to the very core of his soul.

"Strategizing again?" I commented sourly. "Hung-over, why?"

He slipped out of my arms—I felt more frustrated than hurt by the rejection—and cocked his head in that superior manner he had.

"We were celebrating. You've heard of that Trent Robertson case, the fertilizer salesman who's charged with the murder of his pregnant wife. Ochoa gave me the first chair on prosecuting the case. Do you know what that means, Dina?"

He waited like a professor who'd just asked the class dunce to answer a trick question, the smarmy look of conceit on his face almost unbearable.

"A high-profile case like that means lots of publicity for you, of course. What else?"

He looked disappointed, reminding me of my high school chemistry teacher who didn't expect any of us girls—especially the Latinas—to do well on the tests. That I aced every one of those tests really shook up his little world of stereotypes.

"It means if I win—ha, what's to lose—I'm a shoo-in for the DA's office. After the strategy meeting yesterday, I put my team together, and last night the four of us celebrated. Too much, I'm afraid. Too much booze, smoking—"

"Good for you, Hugh," I said, my voice flat, "but I think your celebration's premature. From what you've told me, it's a strictly circumstantial case. No physical evidence ties the man to the crime, and if you have a sympathetic jury . . ."

I shrugged. I read the newspaper coverage on the murder case, but what did I know about the jury system, never having served on one? I was just talking from common sense.

Hugh didn't look pleased that I'd offered a contradictory opinion.

"What do you know about *Voir Dire*? Don't you think my team will select a jury that'll fit our specifications? I've already hired a professional jury profiler and told her that we need at least eight women on that jury. It's a slam-dunk case."

"Nothing in life is a slam-dunk, Hugh. You have to find the aggravating factors that'll tie this case together. Just make sure to get that bastard and put him in prison for the rest of his life."

Aggravating factors, mitigating factors. Hey, no one could say I hadn't learned anything from dating a criminal attorney. Or reading crime fiction novels.

Hugh grinned smugly. In his mind, he'd already won.

I grabbed my golf bag, eager now to be on our way. I needed to be on that golf course, swinging at little white balls and clearing my mind, not arguing with Hugh over the nuances of jury selection. I was happy that he was getting this big break just before the March election but simultaneously a little sad about our dying relationship.

Another one was biting the dust. Oh well.

Also, I needed to stop thinking about this drug-lord uncle of mine who'd just died and all the rest of Grandma Gómez's shocking secrets.

I needed to stop worrying about Pop and his clogged-up arteries, impending surgery, and anemic bank account.

I needed to stop thinking about Rick Ramos.

I needed to hit a little ball and stop thinking, period.

Just for a few hours.

"Winning this high-profile case is just the added cachet I need," Hugh said, waiting on the front walkway while I locked the front door.

"Yeah, I suppose."

"The trial'll be broadcasted live on local channels. What better publicity could I get? We have to re-strategize my campaign, it looks like. And, Dina, I'll be working weekends, too. We may have to curtail our weekly golf game for a while until the trial's over."

"No problem," I said with false cheer. Hugh didn't look pleased by my cheery reply.

Three hours later, the tension between us had worsened.

For the first nine holes, I'd already been developing a slow burn, temper-wise. By now, halfway into what should have been a relaxing Saturday on the links, my irritation was a hard knot in the pit of my stomach. Then, all during lunch, Hugh discussed his campaign with Maury, his campaign manager, and Goree, the campaign's publicist and fund-raiser.

I'd been hoping for a stress-free day of golf, alone with Hugh, maybe discussing what had gone wrong with our relationship. Y'know, for future reference. Instead, I got three political fanatics.

Our little romance had already sputtered out. For months, I'd been gathering, like Hansel and Gretel, little crumbs of evidence that pointed to that conclusion.

Today was it.

"Quiet, please!" I repeated, poised to drive on the tenth tee-box.

I exhaled, focused hard on the *Day-Glo* yellow golf ball perched on its tee, and took a big, full swing. As I followed through and held my stance, I watched the ball soar into the blue sky, then plop down a disappointing hundred-and-twenty yards away.

"Shoot!" I muttered, having schooled myself not to swear on a civilized gentleman's golf course. Hugh disapproved of my cursing in English or Spanish, and I tried to curb my potty mouth and other temperamental impulses around him. It was like wearing an emotional straitjacket, but I had so wanted to fit in with his crowd.

"Not bad. At least it went straight," Hugh commented.

That was the highest compliment I'd receive that day, I knew. I bagged my club and hopped in the golf cart next to Hugh. Maury and Goree climbed into their own cart.

"I can't seem to hit it any farther, Hugh. What'm I doing wrong?" I asked as we raced down the freeway's cart path. I looked at my soon-to-be-ex boyfriend for advice. After all, he'd been playing golf for over fifteen years. I'd taken up the sport three years ago. To help me come out of my deep funk.

"You'll never improve if you don't play more than once a week."

"Can you be a little more specific? I mean, my swing." I held onto the armrest as Hugh whipped the cart around a tree and down a slope. "I mean, what is wrong, specifically, with my swing that keeps me from hitting the ball farther? I've seen Annika drive a ball three-hundred yards, and she doesn't weigh any more than I do."

In my heart of hearts, I suspected I meant a double-entendre, a secret one that I'd never admit. *What is wrong with me that you can't love me? That I can't love you?*

"Nothing," Hugh said, a hard edge to his voice.

He jammed on the brakes, and I had to cling to the back of our seat to keep from flying out. The cart fishtailed to the left and jerked to a violent stop.

"God-dammit!" I cried out.

"Do you have to swear? This is a golf course, not a salsa bar."

The sanctimonious prig, I thought. He practically ejects me through the windshield, and *he* makes snide remarks about my heritage. And it wasn't the first time, either. Could be that Mr. Goss, born to privilege and educated at *Stanford*, was tired of slumming. I wasn't expecting the Medal of Honor or even a Girl Scout badge, but I *was* proud of my achievements.

Or was Hugh already on the hunt for his trophy wife?

"You wouldn't be a gentleman in either place," I replied tartly. "You wouldn't be caught dead in a salsa bar. Too *cholo* for you, Hugh? Hell, you came to my parents' just that one time."

"Dina, we just don't—" He shrugged, not wanting to admit aloud the stark, naked truth.

I needed to confront him. "I may have issues with them, with some of them, anyway, but I need to go home for my birthday. It'd be nice to have you there. As a friend."

Maury and Goree had pulled up beside us in their cart but, hearing us argue, took off down the fairway.

"No, I'm not going back there."

"Y-you s-sonofabitch!" I was so angry. I was stuttering. I was thinking—this is it. The final test.

"I'll take you out instead. Great dinner, great gift."

"I-I don't want a great gift. I'd like you to come with me to my birthday party in Salinas at my family's home. If you were my honest-to-God friend, you'd make the sacrifice!"

"You know I have nothing in common with your family. Your brother's a felon—"

"Ex-felon."

"That brother-in-law of yours is a nutcase. That Jesús. He tried to hit me up for cash last time. Your mother hates me, and your grandmother doesn't even speak English, but I can tell she hates me, too. Your father isn't so bad, but he won't let me smoke in the house. I'm a fish out of water there, and I don't enjoy it. I'll take you anywhere you want to go but not there, Dina. You're different, special. Hell, you're not even like most Latinos I've met. That's probably why I was drawn to you—"

"You think that's a compliment? Puh-leeze! The truth is, Hugh, I'm no longer useful to you now that you've got the Latino Political Caucus endorsement. Am I? Which, by the way, was because of my friendship with Congressman Velásquez."

Hugh jumped out of the cart and grabbed a club. He looked furious.

By the time we arrived in cold silence at the fifteenth tee, I was so frustrated that I felt on the brink of irrational murder. A small, still lucid fragment of my homicidal mind wondered how many crimes of passion took place on golf courses. After bashing in someone's head with a golf club, what would be one's plea? Not guilty by reason of temporary insanity? Induced by what, total incompatibility?

At the fifteenth hole, to get on the green, we had to hit over a lake the size of Texas. Well, actually, it was a pond. But it looked big.

Hugh went first. The three guys, with their basketball-size driver heads, got on the green with their first drives. Having played this particular course before with Hugh, I knew this hole would be my most challenging. I took out my number-one driver, a Big Bertha, and noticed Hugh gloating, already enjoying my defeat. All the times before, after sinking two balls in the pond, I would cave in and cross the bridge, take the penalties, and drop the ball on the green.

Not today.

I had something to prove to Hugh Goss. What exactly it was, I wasn't sure, but I'd wipe that smirk off his face if it was the last thing I did to him. Or with him.

I sucked in my stomach and swung.

Splash!

After sending five balls into the drink, I was still determined to conquer that damned pond. I needed to drive the ball at least one-hundred-and-fifty feet. My longest drive was one-twenty.

"Give up already! You can't take that many mulligans!" Hugh yelled, gloating. The look on his face reminded me of a medieval Bosch painting of Lucifer, smugly reviewing the parade of sinners stumbling into Hell.

"Oh yeah, watch me."

Three more balls sailed into that damn pond.

"Dammit, give it up!"

"Mustn't swear, Hugh, this is a golf course, not a salsa bar," I said with mock sweetness.

"Aw, fuckit!" he shouted. He was the most enraged I'd ever seen him. All because I was trying to conquer Lake Texas?

Sure, I was holding up Hugh and the other men, but the more he hollered, the more stubborn I became. Mama didn't claim I had a *cabeza dura* for nothing. A hard head. But I'd need more than a hard head to get across that body of water.

I was insane with determination.

Four more balls disappeared. I'd just hit twenty dollars' worth of balls into that pond.

¡Mierda!

Hugh yelled another obscenity, then gave me a very un-gentlemanly finger. I began to sing the Spanish words to *La Bamba*. Maury and Goree had already sunk their balls on the green and moved on in their cart. Losing it finally, Hugh grabbed up his ball by the putting green flag and stomped back to our golf cart.

"You're one crazy broad!" he shouted, spearing me one last hateful look before jumping into the golf cart and gunning down the cart path. Fuming, I watched him disappear.

"Bite me, you jerk!" I hollered back. The asshole left me stranded with just my driving club and two remaining golf balls in my pocket.

I took a deep breath and swung again.

One made a small plop at the far edge of the pond. Not even a splash. Swallowed up by some monster of the deep.

My last ball, I carefully balanced on the little tee. I was a woman possessed, and it was do-or-die time. I took a deep, cleansing breath. Somehow, like a great liberating force that surged up from my belly, I found the strength within me, and I swung with all my might.

Holy Shit! It was a miracle. The tiny ball sailed low and

straight, landed and skidded on the fringe of the green, then bounced over. It rolled to a stop a mile from the hole, but it was *on the green.*

I did it! I did it! I did a little celebratory quarterback dance. Oh yeah, oh yeah! ¡*Buena chica, buena chica!*

I jumped up in the air. I pumped my fists and held both arms high above my head. Triumph and glory! It was Olympic gold-medal time! How sweet it was! No one saw it, but I knew what I'd done. I'd never be afraid of that pond again.

And I'd never be afraid of breaking off with a major prick again. Never.

Exuberant, I skipped across the bridge like a ten-year-old who'd just won a dodgeball game. If you think skipping on cleats is easy, you should try it. I plucked up my ball off the putting green and kissed it.

In awe of myself and my newfound strength, I hoisted the club over my shoulder like a soldier's rifle. Then, humming, I hiked back to the clubhouse.

It was a long hike. My game was over.

And so was my relationship with Hugh Goss.

CHAPTER SIX

Abuelita's motto—"*Con los hombres, cuando nada is la verdad, todo es posible.*"

Literally, with men, when nothing is the truth, everything is possible. Or, as Grandma Gómez explained once, anything that doesn't make sense is possible with men. In other words, where men are concerned, there can be only nonsense. One of the more intelligent things Grandma has said to us, although I was never quite sure why she wanted us to learn this. Now, in light of Grandma's revelations, I understood why.

"So you broke up with Hugh?" Lisa was prodding me to continue. I'd gotten sidetracked thinking about Grandma's warnings about men.

"Yeah," I replied, shrugging, "at the clubhouse. In front of his campaign manager and publicist. Then I made them call me a cab."

I was chuckling at the memory. Lisa looked at me, her spoon of green jello halfway to her mouth. She was on a jello diet, and I'd agreed to join her, just for support. Blessed with a curvaceous figure, in my opinion, Lisa was always trying to keep her voluptuousness under control. Svelte, she would never be.

"You don't look upset. You okay with it?"

I smiled to myself. Step one on the way to cleansing the heart of all unhealthy temptations was done.

"More than okay. It was long overdue. We had nothing in

common except golf, and that's not enough to build a relationship on. Besides, he was getting as fed up with me as I was with him."

"Fed up?"

"Yeah, we were using each other. I was using him for the cultural experiences that I felt I was lacking. And for the status, I'll have to admit. He was using me for political gains, for my connections to Congressman Velásquez. It was a mutual exploitation society, so how sick is that?"

Lisa squinted at me over her smart, tinted-pink eyeglasses, her head tucked down. "Didn't think you had it in you to use people. Hey, maybe you're more like me than I thought, Dina."

"Oh, I can be mean-spirited and selfish as much as the next person," I confessed ruefully, "though I try not to be. Maybe it's a family trait. Maybe I've got my uncle's genes, the one" — I broke off, wondering when I should reveal the family's secret about Grandma Gómez and her drug lord ex-husband and murdered drug lord son. Or if I ever should.

Lisa and her uncle, Leo, had access to intelligence agencies since Leo Luna used to be a Customs official before opening his business. Surely, they'd be able to answer some of my questions.

"Well," I went on, "it's difficult being good, especially to men. They're so deceitful. Hugh was not above deceiving me into believing he really cared about me. Which he didn't."

Lisa commiserated and helped herself to another bite of jello. How one bit into jello was beyond me, but we gave it the good ol' college try. We ended up slurping and sucking instead. Frankly, I was dying to sink my teeth into a turkey-breast sandwich at the very least. Or a cold salad of fresh romaine lettuce mixed with kidney beans and garnished with bacon, garlic, sweet onions, and crumbled Manchego cheese. Oh, yummy!

I also silently debated whether to tell her about Rick Ramos hiring my doofus brother-in-law and giving Pop's tile company more business than they could handle.

Lisa knew all about him, of course. One night when we'd had a few too many margaritas and were exchanging stories about lost loves, I'd told her about my college fiancé. And she knew that the guy parked in the red *Explorer* that day at school was him. I'd brought her up to date on my meeting with him in *Starbucks*, too.

We were in the teacher's lounge, having an off-duty lunch. Three other teachers were out on the playground, supervising. Somehow, it just didn't seem to be the place to talk about Rick Ramos. He was no longer The Hated One, but he was still in my eyes, The Scary One. An MTA — Man To Avoid.

Lisa was my closest friend, a woman I shared all my secret emotions with, all my dreams and foibles, all my failures. She, bless her heart, never judged me.

I made a decision.

"I have to tell you about my grandmother, what we learned about her last week. If you promise not to tell anyone, including your uncle." I gave her the stare as she crossed her heart.

Lisa had been out sick with the flu the week following *Abuelita's* *big* confession, and this was my first chance to sit down with my good friend and tell her in person the shocking revelations about my family in Mexico.

"Omigod, you're pregnant!" she whispered vehemently.

Making a face, I shook my head. That was the last thing on earth I needed, like catching leprosy just before your first TV appearance on the Miss America contest.

Hesitantly, my voice trembling a little, I told her everything, in between slurping down wobbly spoonfuls of jello. When I finished, she just stared, her red-lipsticked lips shaped like an O.

"Wow, no kidding!" Then she smiled. "I wish I had a story

like that to tell."

Actually, she did. She'd confided to me one day after we'd become close that she was an orphan and had been adopted by her mother's brother, her uncle, Leo Luna. When her mother died young from ovarian cancer, her father had fled to parts unknown, one step ahead of a truckload of creditors and *La Migra* officials, evidently. She occasionally received a postcard from him, each one from a different place in North America. She suspected that he'd return one day, but she wasn't really counting on it. She envied me the large family I had in Salinas, although I'd only complained about them at the time.

"My cousin, Teresa, is married to an accountant who works for the Juárez drug cartel. He works for Teresa's father, the drug lord. Or used to work for him. I don't know the current situation over there. Maybe things've changed. Maybe the accountant has taken over the cartel. Or maybe he's being hunted. Grandma Gómez hasn't heard any more news since her son, Roberto Martínez, was buried. The family in Chihuahua don't know any more than what they've already told my grandmother."

"The Juárez drug cartel? Hmm, I'll have to ask Uncle Leo about it. All I know is Mexico's got a bunch of cartels, and they all run things down there. They're more powerful than the federal government. Bet they tell the president what to do, when, and how. Probably why the Mexican government doesn't do anything about illegal immigration. In fact, they don't even discourage it. At the border, they give pamphlets away on where to cross, the paths through the desert to take, what to take to stay healthy. Things like that, but maybe all that comes from the coyotes down there who work for the cartels. For a price, they tell those poor migrants what to do. The places in Arizona, New Mexico, and Texas where crossing is easier, what to take with them, what to say to the American

Border Patrol when they get across. The more porous the borders, after all, the more drugs get through. It's all a lucrative, political game and the cartels seem to be behind it all."

Damn, I hadn't thought about it in that way. I thought I was cynical with worldliness. Lisa had me beat. But maybe what she said held some truth.

"Please don't say anything to your uncle about my family's involvement, my grandmother's son." With a quick nod, Lisa assured me she wouldn't. "You think it's really like that? The cartels are that powerful?" I grimaced at the next spoonful of jello. I was starting to hate the stuff and rethinking my promise to help Lisa keep to her lunch diet.

"Oh yeah, from what Uncle Leo says, it's like that. He used to work for Customs in San Diego after he did his army duty. He should know." She spooned up some cottage cheese from a store-bought carton. "Here, add some of this. It'll give it more taste and substance."

Into my bowl, she dropped a dollop of white, nonfat, small curds. I mixed it up with the green jello and winced a little before shoveling it into my mouth. Yuck! It was nearly as bad as tofu and cooked kale, which I'd tried on Lisa's last diet craze. Luckily, I was cooking that evening one of my favorite lamb dishes, Shepherd's Pie. Complete with mashed potatoes and melted cheddar on top. Just the thought of aromatic cooked lamb and its wonderful spices sustained me through the lunch ordeal.

"I wonder what life is like for my cousin, Teresa," I ventured, "She's close to our age, I think. *Mamá* read her letters to Grandma, said she was about thirty, had a son about seven years old. She went to the University of Guadalajara. Majored in Journalism. This is a cousin I never knew I had until a week ago. Imagine that!"

"You'd have a lot in common, you and your cousin," Lisa remarked, glancing at the clock in the teacher's lounge.

"Maybe she'll write to you."

"I'd like to know why my uncle, this drug lord, died. Why he was murdered. Maybe by a rival drug cartel, do you suppose? Undercover Mexican *federales*? If so, why kill his wife?"

Lisa shrugged. "Collateral damage? Let me know if you hear from her, from your cousin Teresa. Does she have your email address? There's AOL in Mexico, too, y'know."

It never occurred to me to tell *Abuelita* to write to Teresa through her sister, Carlota, and have Teresa write to me or email me directly. Lisa was giving me food for thought, although her information made me feel like a naïve child. I'd just assumed that anyone connected with the Juárez drug cartel wouldn't want to contact a law-abiding American, even if she was a relative. Then again, Teresa had been in touch with Grandma Gómez. Maybe Teresa had nothing to do with her father's business. So how could she marry someone who'd worked for her father, then? Maybe Teresa, herself, was a *traficante*. Shit!

Ignorance was bliss. Knowing more made you feel like crap.

"Dina, why don't you do a Google search? Get on the Net and do some searching. There's bound to be something about the Mexican drug cartels." Lisa was putting her diet lunch away.

"Huh," was all I could say. That was a new idea. I frowned. Was I afraid of what I might find?

The school bell rang. End of our thirty-minute lunch.

"Lisa, are you free this Saturday night?" I gathered up my brown bag, which held an apple and juice drink for later, and slung my hobo purse over my shoulder.

"Sure. Let's go off this diet — just for one day, okay — and have some pizza, watch a movie?"

"Yeah," I said. Lisa liked Lara Croft-type films, the kind where the kick-ass heroine did, well, kick ass. I preferred romantic comedy and sometimes mysteries and crime dramas. The kind that always ends happily. The boy gets the girl and vice versa. The cops get the criminals. Love conquers all. Justice reigns. Perfect solutions in a not-so-perfect world. Oh well, we'd compromise and see one of each.

Lisa and I agreed to get together that weekend. She didn't play golf, unfortunately, and didn't jog or go to the gym. In the future, I'd have to do all my exercising alone, it seemed. Lisa worked for her uncle's Security Systems and Private Investigations business on Saturdays but generally had her nights free. There was always Saturday night. Neither of us was dating anyone special at present.

She'd kissed her share of frogs, too.

We were both on hiatus from men. Date detox, she called it. At least, for the time being. I had a feeling it wouldn't last long. We weren't celibate nuns, after all.

On the way back to my classroom, I passed the girls' restroom. Standing outside was a little second-grader, one of Carol Johnson's students. I knew who the little girl was, for I'd been called into the principal's office to translate during a parents' and teacher's meeting.

"¿Evita, *niña, cómo estás?*" I asked her. The little girl and her parents were newly arrived from San Diego, I knew. Before that, Guatemala. Although the school was not obligated to check out the parents' documentation, I suspected they were illegal. The poor thing seemed totally out of her element. I noticed she'd been crying, so I squatted down beside her.

"What's the matter, Evita?" I asked her in Spanish.

At first, she said nothing but with a bit of coaxing, she opened up a little. The little girl swallowed back her tears.

"*Los muchachos allí,*" she said, sniffling, pointing with a thin, brown arm at two of my sixth-grade boys. Billy and Chip.

"What about them, *m'ija?*" I patted her shoulder, admiring

her long braids that fell to the middle of her back. Her long, black eyelashes were wet with her tears. Just the thing to tug my heartstrings.

"They called me stupid. And a retard. Am I a retard, Maestra Salazar?" She said the word retard in English.

The hairs on my back bristled. Billy and Chip were schoolyard bullies and were due some quality detention time. Like ten laps around the school, whether they liked it or not.

"No, you're not a retard, Evita. Soon you'll be speaking two languages, and they'll still be speaking one. Who'll know more then? Who'll be the retard, then?" I smiled at her, cajoling a wan smile from the little girl in return. "True, no?"

She nodded. "*Sí, verdad.*"

I stroked the top of her head, smoothing down a few stray, dark brown curly tendrils of hair. "Now, you go find Mrs. Johnson. Over there. Come to me if anyone bothers you, agreed?"

"*Gracias, Maestra,*" she said, then hugged me shyly.

She scampered off to join her classmates. I caught Carol Johnson's eye and nodded to her, reassuring her tacitly that everything was fine.

For a moment, I recalled Rick Ramos's kindergarten-aged daughter. I wondered if kids at school called her retard, what she felt, how it must've hurt. If that little girl didn't get help, she'd face similar problems as little Evita. Cruel kids tended to misunderstand immigrant children and exploit them, making them the butt of jokes and taunts. Even extorting them sometimes for lunch food or money. The average kid, free of prejudice, sometimes thought that not speaking perfect English meant you were retarded or mentally slow. Despite what their teachers told them.

Surely Rick would get his daughter tested and the help she needed. Maybe I had to find out if he, indeed, was doing this. He owed it to his daughter, of course, and maybe . . .just maybe I owed it to the Ramos family to make sure Rick did get her help.

I turned toward Billy and Chip, longing to shellac their little bottoms. Couldn't do that — against the law. But there were many ways to skin a cat.

Time to take care of two sixth-grade bullies.

Chapter Seven

"C'mon, fix yourself up for a change. Makeup, hair, dress. You're a knockout when you fix up."

To appease my aunt, Flora, who was taking me out for my birthday dinner, Friday night, I'd made the supreme effort. I'd fluffed up my pageboy, stuck a crystal-decorated comb along one side to hold my hair behind my ear, put on makeup and crimson lipstick to match the crimson, shawl-collared sweater I wore over my black wool slacks. My only jewelry was my gold cross, gold hoop earrings, and the opal birthstone ring I'd had reset with my long-ago engagement-ring diamond.

The diamond I'd kept after the Rick Ramos fiasco of an engagement—another battlefield of love reminder? Not really. It was so pretty, that diamond, and the only diamond I'd ever owned. I just couldn't return it—nor did I feel like I had to.

My family party in Salinas would be Sunday, although it was likely to be a subdued affair, even for us. My father would be undergoing surgery the next day, and we all were naturally worried. Grandma Gómez hadn't heard back from her Mexican granddaughter, and she was concerned. In truth, I didn't feel like celebrating anything, but Flora insisted. So did Lisa, who was going to meet us there.

She and studly Steve drove me to the *Asian Buffet Garden*, where you could pick from Japanese teriyaki, sashimi, and sushi on the left-hand side of this vast, long buffet table or stirfry Chinese dishes on the right side. Inexplicably, on mounds of ice in the middle of the table were dessert dishes—bowls of pudding, bananas in red jello, and platters of almond cookies, as many helpings as you wanted and all for $12.99. You wouldn't find any tiramisu, creme brulee, or New York cheesecake here, though. Flora had wanted to take me to *Le Tour d'Eiffel* in Menlo Park, but it would've cost her a week's salary, and I would've had to wear a formal and tiara to get in. I wanted casual and cheap.

The decor was funky Asian. In a resin sculpture, a giant, gold-painted dragon slithered across the room, separating the diners from the buffet table. Embedded into one wall was a huge aquarium filled with coral homes for all the colorful, tropical fish within. Red tassels hung from Chinese lantern lamps, the walls were painted scarlet, the tables were dark wood, and the chairs were upholstered, weirdly enough, in blue velvet. It was my kind of place. Lots of families seemed to agree with me. The place was packed with customers.

"Happy birthday to my dear, kooky friend, Dina!" Lisa toasted across from me, lifting her glass of wine.

"And many more lays, I mean days to come," Gil proposed merrily, sitting next to me on my left.

I elbowed him in the side and sipped my chardonnay. Lisa's short cousin and apartment-mate, Gil Luna, reminded me of a young Danny De Vito, but Gil had more facial hair than an ayatollah. He and Lisa were very close, had been raised together after Lisa's mother died, and she'd gone to live with her uncle Luna. Since Gil loved practical jokes, he and Lisa had a long history together of pranks. It was a miracle that they had survived childhood. I wondered if his and Lisa's gift was going to explode in my lap.

"Open your gifts," Steve encouraged. Tonight he was dressed up, he said, if a black *Adidas* warm-up suit with white racing stripes qualified as dress up. Flora was still in her business suit, a soft wool jacket, and skirt in Kelly green. With her auburn hair and gold jewelry, she looked a little like the first lady, only a Latina version.

"No, I'll wait till after dinner — is that okay?"

"I wanta see your face when you open what Gil and I got you," Lisa enthused, winking slyly at her cousin.

I warily looked at the oblong present, wrapped in *Barbie-doll* birthday paper. "Huh, maybe I'll wait till I'm alone."

Lisa and Gil looked disappointed but then broke into chortles over the table. Last year she gave me a *Frederick's of Hollywood*, crotchless teddy which I never wore. I could only guess what this year's gift joke would be. It was suspiciously the size of a vibrator. On second thought, this one might come in handy if my sex life stalled for very long.

I smiled at Flora, Steve, Lisa, and Gil as they passed over their gifts, then I thanked them for coming and honoring me with their presence. When they began to look at me like I was drunk already, not sure if I was being sarcastic or sincere, I stopped with the gushing gratitude. I supposed I was in a maudlin mood and chalked it up to Papa's surgery on Monday and finding out I was related to Mexican dope smugglers.

"Who else is coming, Flora?" I asked, indicating the two empty chairs next to Lisa.

She and Steve exchanged looks — Steve like the Cheshire cat and Flora widening her eyes like a dissembling Cruella de Ville — and I immediately knew something was up. This fairly pleasant day — my students had been extra-cooperative and had given me little, handmade presents — was going to take a decided twist, I realized.

"Who else did you invite, Flora?"

"An old friend who called last week. Mariana something-or-other and her boyfriend. She said she was an old college friend and lived nearby, so I told her about tonight. I invited her — I hope you don't mind. She said she'd lost your cell phone number but recalled my name. She's the one you ran into at *Starbucks* that day?"

111

I sighed with relief. "Yeah, oh, that's fine. I like her. You'll like her, too. I haven't met her—"

Just then, I glanced up at the restaurant's front window and saw Mariana and Rick walking to the door.

"Shit!" I muttered softly. My stomach lurched, and my appetite fled. I felt nauseous and froze in my seat.

Lisa wheeled around, following my gaze. "Who's *that*?" Her pert mouth made a perfect O, then clamped it shut, her wide eyes bespoke volumes. "That's *him*?" she whispered.

Flora reached over and placed her hand over mine. "Be nice, Dina. I had no idea Mariana would bring Rick Ramos. I did not invite him. It's too late now, so b-e-e-e nice. He's my client."

I straightened in my chair and pasted a smile on my face.

"No problem, I'm a nice person. I can do civilized and pleasant," I told her between clenched teeth. I picked up my fork and held it like a switchblade.

"Well, this's going to be fun," Lisa chirped, having overheard our exchange. She then explained rapidly to Gil who this man was walking through the door . . .this tall, handsome Chicano in the black turtleneck and tweed sports jacket.

He was holding the hand of a little girl. I stared.

Angelina Ramos. Her straight dark hair was braided in two long pigtails with blue ribbons at the ends. Her eyes were big and dark like her father's, but her face was all Anita's, round and pretty, her mouth a perfect heart shape. She was wearing a pink parka with white fake-fur trim and bright blue-and-pink ribbon trim at the hem and cuffs and down the front alongside the zipper. A stuffed white cat was clutched in her tiny hands. Rick's daughter. A pretty child.

Even though her mother was a skanky coke-junkie.

I pulled myself together, stood up, and hugged Mariana while Flora introduced Rick and his daughter around. He shook Steve's and Gil's hands, Gil adding, "*Hombre*," as a sort of machismo greeting. To that, Rick nodded, looking a little amused.

"*Mucho gusto*," he said to Gil. Lisa beamed and shook his hand, too, holding it longer than necessary. What was with *her*?

She was acting like he was some famous celebrity, like he was Benjamin Bratt or Jimmy Smits. Aye, Lisa can be sooo . . .She was making it so obvious that I had shared confidences about Rick.

"Joel couldn't come, Dina," Mariana explained. "He had a last-minute meeting with some clients and couldn't get out of it. I thought of Rick and how you two haven't seen each other in a while, so—"

"It's fine. So glad you could come," I said magnanimously, my frozen smile still in place as I introduced Mariana to everyone. I shot Rick a narrowed, wary glance and smiled at the little girl, and then we all took our seats. The Chinese waitress brought over a booster chair for Rick's daughter.

As we were giving our drink orders, Rick, seated across the table and down one, turned to me and held up a little silver-wrapped box tied with a gold satin bow. Our gazes met, his not wavering a bit. I wanted to run and hide behind the gold-painted dragon, but I held his stare for a second or two. Sheer will power.

"For you, Dina. Happy twenty-ninth birthday."

I glanced over at Flora, who was waiting with abated breath. I swear she was about to turn blue. For her sake—and because I'm not a total bitch—I smiled up at him and accepted the gift as graciously as my frozen smile allowed me. I unclenched my teeth so I could speak.

"Thank you. And this is . . ." Ha, like I didn't know!

"My daughter, Angelina. *M'ija*, say hello to Dina. It's her birthday today."

The little girl looked a little frightened, stared at my hair for a second like it was on fire, then tried to hide behind her father's shoulder. A broad one, it was at that, especially in that tweed sports jacket. His eyes were onyxes, as black as the turtleneck he was wearing.

"Hi, Angelina," I said, forcing a friendly tone into my voice. So this was the little girl I was going to help. I'd begun consulting the Special Ed resource teacher in our district that very week and had gathered some materials—mostly remediation books and games. Now I had a face to put with the name. Angelina. Pretty name.

The little girl peered at me from behind her father and said, "Hi."

"Is that your *gatito*?" I asked her. I was extra fluent in Spanglish.

The little girl's eyes widened, and then she answered in Spanish.

"My little cat's name is Guapito."

"I like that name, Guapito," I replied in Spanish. "And do you like school?"

The little girl shook her pigtails, the edges of her pretty, little mouth curving down.

"It's too hard. I like my teacher. She lets us play on the slide. And she lets us paint with our fingers." The stream of words was all in Spanish.

"She speaks only Spanish with my mother," Rick explained. "I use both languages with her, but at school, of course, it's strictly English."

"Does her teacher speak Spanish?" I asked him. The little girl seemed more comfortable with Spanish, but I couldn't really tell in such a short period of time.

He shook his head, helping her take off her jacket.

"I spoke to her teacher about getting her tested." There was a question in his eyes, but he hesitated to voice it. I knew he wanted to know about the remediation tools I was putting together. I'd called his cell phone and left a message about this. That was the day I'd spoken to little Evita and the two sixth-grade bullies.

"Good. Have the Special Ed teacher test her, not her regular teacher, if that's possible," I suggested, passing down the bottle of chardonnay. "I'll have all those things you need soon. Give me another week or two, Rick." Lord, but it was difficult to even say his name. Aloud and to his face. "Things've been kinda hectic—"

"Heard about your father. If there's anything I—my family—can do, let us know."

"Thanks. We'll know after the operation next Monday."

After that, people went up to the buffet tables and helped themselves to either Japanese or Chinese or both. Even though I managed to relax enough to eat a little, I had difficulty concentrating on the dinner conversations going on around me with Rick and his daughter sitting down the table from me.

I'd tune in a little to Flora and Steve discussing the latest movie DVDs on the market and what films and series were streaming online, then switch over to Gil, Lisa, and Mariana talking with Rick about the affordable housing shortage in Silicon Valley.

All the while, my gaze kept slipping back to the little girl, who seemed engrossed in feeding herself. Rick was solicitous with her and would occasionally murmur something to her, and she would nod or smile up at him. In general, though, he spoke with the adults at the table, throwing me furtive looks when he didn't think I was noticing. I confess I was doing the same.

Rick's relationship with his daughter seemed warm and loving. The daughter he and I could've had together, he had with Anita, the slut. It didn't seem fair. Yet, there it was.

His faithlessness, in the flesh. All three feet and thirty

pounds, more or less, of her.

At one point, I got up and took another helping of the broccoli-beef stir-fry. On my way back to our table, I spied Angelina standing in front of the wall aquarium, mesmerized by the illuminated undersea world. I went over to her, my plate in my hand. I like kids, what can I say. No matter who their parents are.

"Which fish is your favorite?" I asked her in Spanish.

She pointed to the yellow and black striped one that kept circling a spire of coral that looked like a castle tower.

"Ah yes, it looks like a tiger. It's beautiful, isn't it? Would you like your own aquarium, Angelina?"

The little girl looked up at me and nodded vigorously.

"You should tell your father that you'd like an aquarium for Christmas."

"A-uh-kwa . . ." She was having difficulty with the English word, which I had substituted for the Spanish one, which I couldn't remember. What can I say? The teacher in me came out.

"Acqua—agua, water—" I said each word slowly, starting with the Latin root, then moving to Spanish. Her eyes widened in sudden comprehension. " —a water tank or bowl for fish. A—qua—ri—um. Aquar-i-um."

She repeated the word in its English, three-syllable form several times, then smiled and dashed to her father's side. Rick's head bowed to hers as she made her new wish known. When I returned to my place at the table, he was smiling lopsidedly at me.

"Thanks," he said dryly. "She also wants a cat, dog, and pony. Now fish. I need a bigger home."

"When you get that home, you'll need a nanny, housekeeper, gardener—it goes on and on," Steve said, leaning forward to catch Rick's eye. "Small is good, believe me."

"What you need is a wife who can take care of all those

things for you," Gil interjected, then popped into his mouth a salmon-sushi. Lisa and I glanced at each other. My look said, can I kill your cousin now?

"Already tried that," Rick said flatly, "it was a disaster. Biggest mistake of my life." He looked at me pointedly.

"Oh well, get a housekeeper for the cleanup stuff and a mistress for the — ouch!" Steve bent over with pain. Someone had kicked him under the table, and it wasn't me. I smiled gratefully at Flora, whose face had reddened in anger.

For the remainder of the dinner, I refused to even glance Rick's way. Conversation turned to other topics, including golf, a sport that Steve and Gil also played.

I dilly-dallied with my food, hoping the evening would end soon. I could've been eating sea slug-sushi for all the attention I gave to my plate. However, my guests seemed to be enjoying themselves, so I guess I kept up my end of the pretense well enough to fool them into thinking I was having a great time.

By the end of the meal, my emotions were a roiling stew. I didn't know how I felt about anyone or anything by my last sip of oolong tea.

When our guests got up to leave, I thanked everyone for their gifts, which I said I would open on Sunday, my actual birth date. Lisa was disappointed, and when she said nice and loudly, "Darn, we were hoping to embarrass you in front of everyone — we got you a sex toy," I was glad I decided to wait.

Lisa and I hugged. "Grab him, Dina, or you're going to need that thing we bought you," she whispered into my ear.

"You like him so much. You go for it," I hissed back.

"Really, you mean that?" she said, her expression and tone of voice mocking me.

"Of course," I dashed off.

"You fool, you *tonta*. He's already taken." She let go, gave me a look of profound pity, and stepped back.

Mariana and I hugged, too. She gave me an apologetic smile—what was that about?—and I thanked her again for coming. Then she stepped back as Gil Luna came forward.

He said, "*Dame 'brazos, chica,*" and wanted a hug, too. I bent over double and squeezed him around the shoulders. They were all irrepressible. I thanked them for coming, for their gifts.

While Flora and Steve spoke to the little girl, the encounter that I was dreading—a face-to-face confrontation—happened.

"*¿Abrazos, también?*" Rick asked, holding out his arms and ignoring my extended hand. A hug, also? Before I could step back and hiss something like, "I don't think so, *cabron,*" I found myself engulfed in a big bear hug.

At first, I wanted to kick him in the balls, so I stiffened and arched back. But he felt so good. All hard chest and muscular arms and soft, clean-shaven face . . .and his smell—cologne, soap, and Rick's unique scent. I'd forgotten how comfortable, how safe I'd always felt in his arms. Within seconds, my body melted into his. My pulse was throbbing so hard in my throat, I couldn't speak. And I hate to say, my reaction was also . . .erotic. Something deep between my legs began to liquefy. I found myself caving into his long, firm body and wanting to stay there.

He mumbled something unintelligible into my hair, and then almost on cue, we both disengaged ourselves. When I looked into his face, surprise and—I think—fear registered there. Neither of us expected that kind of a jolt from a simple hug.

Frankly, I didn't want to make a fool of myself or offend anyone. I'd been on my best behavior all night, and my confusion and raw emotions were on the brink of spilling over, so it was with supreme effort that I smiled as though we were old friends enjoying a casual reunion hug.

Then I bent over and said goodnight to his little girl. I shook her hand, even said goodnight to the stuffed cat.

"*Buenas noches*, Guapito."

Angelina giggled, then clasped her father's hand as he turned to lead her to the door.

"*Buenas noches*," she said to me in a falsetto, pretend-cat voice, wiggling Guapito's paw, then covered her face with the stuffed cat and giggled some more. When Rick threw me a backward glance and grinned, I didn't know what to think. I think I managed a small wiggle of fingers.

In Flora's car, I tore open the silver-foil box. I flicked on the inside light and gaped at the jeweler's black-velvet case. Nestled on a bed of white satin was a pair of round, opal earrings mounted in gold filigree. You could see the iridescent colors of the rainbow, shooting like sparks out of the pale gold stone. My beautiful birthstone.

I was speechless.

"Holy smokes, Dina. Some gift," Steve crowed.

I looked at Flora, who was twisting around in the passenger seat and gawking, too.

"My God, those are Mexican fire opals. They're lovely."

I shook my head in wonder. "I don't understand. Just because I'm gathering that stuff for his daughter? Oh God, Flora, what does he want from me? A free tutor for his daughter? And why is he being so nice to the family? You heard about the big tile job he gave Frank. And he hired screw-up Jesús — why would he do all that?"

"Maybe he wants your friendship, Dina. Can you forgive him and accept his friendship? He's such a . . .a *caballero*."

"A what?" Steve asked, putting Flora's *Mercedes* in reverse gear.

"Oh" — Flora tried to explain — "literally a horseman. In Mexican culture, it also means a gentleman of substance. Of worth."

In spite of myself, my eyes were misting over. I was seeing his daughter's face, so like her mother's, in shape and coloring. His and Anita's daughter. Like a knife in the gut. We could've had a little girl as pretty, as endearing as Angelina. Or a little boy that was as sturdy and handsome as his father.

"So, Dina, can you forgive him and be his friend?"

"I don't know. I don't think so."

"You know, you shouldn't even consider being anything more than a friend, don't you? He's a heartbreaker, that one."

"I know, I know. I'm not a masochist," I ground out between my lips. Flora's cautionary reminders were beginning to annoy me.

"Good girl, let's not drink from the same well twice. Once fooled, shame on you. Twice fooled, shame on me. Isn't that how it goes?"

Shakespeare popped into mind, something like *methinks thou protest too much*. Was Flora trying to protect me, or was she lamenting the fact that she was too old for Rick?

"Hmm, guess so, sweetheart," Steve replied, apparently thinking Flora had asked him how the saying went. "So you going to wear those opals, Dina?" Steve asked me.

"I don't know." They were lovely. Even in the dimness of the back seat, I could see them shoot out sparks. "I really don't know."

That night, my reply was as certain as I could be about anything.

CHAPTER EIGHT

Cheez, all of a sudden, when my social calendar seemed as empty as Bridget Jones's, things got worse. After a nearly sleepless night, during which, I must confess, I obsessed over *the hug* from the night before, I awoke to my cell phone jangling its tune. I'd changed it to Ray Charles's *Hit the road, Jack.* I was hoping its message would remind me to stay single and unattached.

The first was my brother, Frank, calling to say that my birthday party had been postponed until the following weekend because the doctors wanted Pop to have a quiet, peaceful weekend before his surgery on Monday. He brought me up to speed on Pop's condition as well. Pop was so nervous that he wasn't eating, so convinced he was that the bypass surgery would be the death of him. So the doctors were building him up with megavitamins and special milkshakes and calming him down with mild sedatives. He was also taken off his blood-thinning drug.

Frankie agreed with Mama that everyone needed to stay away until after the surgery. I totally understood. When the Salazars got together, we were nothing if not loud, even raucous. Saliva was exchanged, and spit flew around the table like a dog shaking off water, no doubt landing a lot of pathogens into our food. A party at their place was the last thing Pop needed.

On Abuelita's behalf, my brother told me that Grandma's sister, Carlota, had passed on a letter from her granddaughter, Teresa. There had been no autopsy of her father's and mother's bodies, for it was apparent that numerous bullet wounds had done the job. Teresa's husband, Pedro Vargas, the husband and the Cartel's new finance manager, had taken over the reins of the business. Teresa wanted to know if one of us had an email address and could speak Spanish, someone other than *Abuelita*.

It sounded urgent that Teresa wanted to email one of us. Her visits into Ciudad de Juárez were being curtailed, and those visits had been her only means of communicating with Carlota. Evidently, from what she'd told Jaime, Carlota's son, the house phone calls were logged and recorded, and her computer was checked every night. The hacienda had become a prison. She'd warned Jaime to stay away, not to meet her in Ciudad anymore, too, for though they'd been extra cautious about their secret meetings, she was afraid one of the body-guards assigned by her husband would find out. And she couldn't risk that.

So Grandma Gómez had given her my email address, which I'd given Frankie, of course. Shit! Now I was being roped into some intrigue involving the Juárez drug cartel. Just what I needed.

I could just see some low riders pulling up to Flora's house and riddling it with *Uzis*. Riddling us, maybe. Or did these Mexican dope peddlers drive *Mercedes* and *Lexus* sedans? Maybe *Porsches* or *Ferraris*. Somehow, I didn't think I wanted to find out.

"The Juárez Cartel — that's one of the biggest drug rings in Mexico," Frankie informed me. "The Juárez, the Tijuana, and the Gulf Cartels are the three most powerful in Mexico. Holy shit, Dina, do you know what that means? Our cousin is mar-ried to one of the kingpins of the Juárez Cartel!"

"Great," I said dryly, "so you give her *my* email address. Why can't she just call *Abuelita* from time to time and be happy to jet-set around the world with her corrupt, filthy-rich husband? Why does she want to contact us? Why doesn't she leave us alone?"

"Because I think she's getting ready to leave her husband. She told Jaime that her husband was behind our uncle's death. So he could take over. She can't live with a man who had her parents killed."

"So if she has proof, she should go to the police. There are laws in Mexico, y'know."

"Dina"—Frankie sighed—"you don't understand. If her husband knew she had proof, she'd be dead already. We're talking ruthless motherfuckers here. They kidnap, kill, maim, push dope. Do you know that ten million bucks a day in drugs is trafficked by the Gulf Cartel alone? There's a two-thousand-mile border between the US and Mexico. It's like a sieve. Up to seventy percent of the cocaine coming into this country is through Mexico. Customs can search only one out of ten vehicles crossing the border. Only a fraction of the cargo containers on trucks, ships, and planes."

"How do you know so much about this?" I was astonished that Frankie could rattle off statistics on this topic.

"Hey, you're not the only one who reads in this family. There's a drug war between the Juárez and Gulf Cartels over who controls the border towns along the Texas border. Maybe that's what triggered this whole thing. Our uncle's murder, I mean."

"Frankie, I really don't want to get involved. Teresa needs to take it to the authorities down there."

Frank snorted loudly before ringing off abruptly. Yeah, well, happy birthday to you, too.

The second call came from Lisa, wanting to rehash the night before—how Rick Ramos looked, his cute little girl, how charming he was, how she felt he'd had eyes only for me, blah, blah, blah. None of which I really wanted to hear since he was the cause of my sleepless night.

"Yeah, yeah, *no me diga nada de éste*." I knew she didn't understand Spanish, but I felt in a surly, Spanish-speaking mood. Like I was Grandma Gómez incarnate.

Mirror, mirror on the wall, am I my grandmother after all? Yikes!!!

"Well, after all, who else do you have hanging around, giving you presents?" she asked, "And don't start on the Spanish, showoff. So, is it pizza and movies tonight?"

"Sure—" I looked at my clock radio. "Holy moly! It's almost noon!" I'd fallen back asleep after Frank's call. "Are you at work?"

On Saturdays, Lisa worked for her uncle at Leo Luna's Security Systems and Private Investigations company. Which reminded me . . .

"Yeah, working on a drop-dead funny case. A local fast-food restaurant, whose name I'm not allowed to divulge, wants us to prove that the chopped-off finger found in a patron's bowl of chili was actually planted there by the said patron. As we speak, I'm looking at their hidden security cameras installed by Uncle Leo's techies. This patron, now a soon-to-be plaintiff in a big lawsuit, is sitting down . . .Oh yeah, she's digging into her pocket and is taking out a tissue, is holding the bowl of chili in her lap—weird, isn't it? Who puts a bowl of chili in their lap before eating it?"

I listened patiently, suddenly curious myself, wondering if the hidden cameras would prove the woman guilty of fraud. Meanwhile, Lisa kept up a stream of descriptive narratives going.

"Ohhh, yeah . . .she's good . . .there she does it. It's barely noticeable, but these cameras are so good. Even though they've got a wide-angle lens, the focus is clear and crisp, and when you zoom in, you can see her taking something out of the tissue. Then she puts the bowl back on the table. I think we've got her. Aha! Let's see, how many years for a bogus lawsuit? Not to mention extortion."

"Years?"

"Betcha this woman's got priors, or at least prior lawsuits like slipping on water in grocery stores, spilling hot coffee on herself in restaurants. There are people like this who live from one settlement to another. They know all the tricks."

"No kidding. By the way, Lisa, tell your uncle not to bother about my uncle's death in Mexico. Sounds like his daughter, my cousin Teresa, already knows her husband was behind it. Or suspects it."

"No kidding!"

"Yeah, sad, huh. It's a real vicious jungle down there. My brother thinks she's going to leave her husband. Sounds like he had MOM, motive, opportunity, and method." I told you I read mysteries. "Lisa, he's now in charge of her father's cartel and my cousin's feeling trapped."

"That doesn't sound good, Dina. How's she going to get away?"

"I don't know. I guess she's going to email me when she figures it out. Do you think she's going to need our help?"

"Got me," Lisa muttered. "If she's the wife of the Juárez Cartel's head honcho, alerting them—the Mexican police— might not be a good idea. They will know, and the cartel will know, that she's trying to get help from her American family. They'll start watching the borders. Their proxies will start watching you and your family. Hold on."

I could hear her talking to someone in the background. Funny, I hadn't thought about the possibility that the Mexican police might be in the deep pockets of the cartel. What did I know of Mexico, other than *Club Med* in Guaymas one spring break? Or the cruise I took down to Cabo San Lucas one summer?

Or that the cartels had spies in this country.

Crap!

"Uncle Leo says you've gotta wait 'til she contacts you. From what you've said, most likely the honchos have bugged the phones at their house."

"From what I hear, they live in a hacienda near Ciudad de Juárez. She might have a cell phone, though."

"Yah, but her husband might've confiscated it by now or put a tracking device on it. GPS technology is everywhere these days. If he's expecting her to run, that is. That's what they do with their trucks, the ones that smuggle dope. Uncle Leo says these cartels have all the latest high-tech gear."

"Well, damn." Not good news, I realized. "She could be in real danger if her husband finds out she's going to leave him. *If* she's going to do that. She married a man who worked for her father. Surely, she knew what kind of a man he was."

That *gabacho*! Already I hated him. Still, maybe Teresa wasn't the real victim here. After all, we didn't really know her.

"You've gotta sit tight and wait for her to contact your grandmother again. Or you. That's my advice, Dina, and Uncle Leo's. If you hear from her, let me know, and we'll go from there."

I rang off after wishing her a fun date with Mark McDuff. He was the new vice principal at our school and had asked her out for lunch today. Still, as I lay back in bed, trying to stir myself into action—shoot, I had so many exciting things to do that day, like catching up on dirty laundry and shaving my legs—I was beset with uneasy feelings and worries.

Uneasy about Lisa's date with Mark, in essence, one of our two bosses at the school—was it ever a good idea to date one's boss? And even more than a little worried now that Lisa had mentioned the technical sophistication of the Mexican drug cartels.

What if they traced one of her emails to me? Would they come barreling through my door in the middle of the night and shoot me full of holes? Or would I simply disappear, maybe cut up into little pieces and fed to the fish in San Francisco Bay?

My overactive imagination went on churning mercilessly. Did my cousin really have a chance of getting away from her husband and his murderous cronies? Would he kill Teresa as he probably did her father and mother? Whatever possessed her to risk herself and her child when she'd grown up in the cartel, her father had been one of the kingpins, and she'd married one of them? Didn't she know what she was getting herself into when she married the man? A part of me was sympathetic, and a part was just plain dumbfounded. And a tiny bit afraid.

Like a song suddenly cut off, I banned those thoughts and turned to what I was about to do in the kitchen.

"You're going to love this, Lisa. And it's about as low-fat as a pizza can get," I gushed happily. Determined to put my worries over my Mexican cousin's situation out of my mind, I focused on one of my favorite hobbies, cooking.

"You shouldn't have gone to all this trouble," Lisa said. "I'd've been happy with a frozen one."

"Yuck, no. You want *sabores naturales*," I explained, tossing in a little Spanish for effect. Natural flavor. My pizza was going to be a masterpiece of culinary prudence and pleasure. Low-fat and very tasty.

I sliced thin medallions of smoked turkey over the marinara sauce, added chopped scallions, sweet onions, chopped mushrooms, and artichoke hearts. Over it all, a generous sprinkling of low-fat mozzarella cheese and freshly grated parmesan.

"You see how thin the crust is," I pointed out, placing it in Flora's oven. "Now for some wine—a mild Chianti, I think. Flora's got the best collection, tells me to help myself whenever she's not home." My aunt was in San Francisco for the weekend.

I poured us two goblets, and we clicked glasses.

"*Salud!*" I said. Lisa eyed me over her raised glass.

"Have you noticed you're speaking more Spanish these days? Ever since you heard about your Mexican cousin? What's with that? Hey, not that I mind. I need the practice, myself."

I shrugged. Hmm, the Chianti was excellent. I'd have to remember the label. Great with pizza.

"I'm not aware I lapse into Spanish that often," I explained. "Sorry, don't mean to be rude."

"No, you're not. I should learn. I really should." Lisa and I sat at Flora's pub table, both dressed in our grubbies. Tonight was casual girls' night. No need to impress anybody.

We wore sweats and tees, no makeup or jewelry — well, except for our earrings. Lisa tended towards hoops. I was wearing the fire opal studs.

"Maybe you could teach me a little. Uncle Leo says if I learn Spanish, he'll send me on field assignments for his Mexican clients. I'd really like to do more field work. Investigative stuff, y'know. He's got me working in the office on Saturdays, helping him catch up on filing, paperwork, accounts, boring stuff. Today was the most exciting thing I've done — reviewing the videotape from that hidden surveillance camera."

I was surprised. "You mean you'd leave teaching if you had the chance to work for your uncle full-time?"

She demurred, taking a moment to sip her wine.

"I might. Mark was shocked to hear me say so. He doesn't understand how . . .how dull it can get, working with kids all the time. I like the adult world, Dina."

I nodded, understanding completely. There were times when I longed for more adult interaction and companionship in the workplace. Kids were fun and endearing, but they could also be trying and frustrating.

We talked, sharing ideas and feelings, until the pizza was done. Then we mostly ate in silence, enjoying the wonderful aromas and flavors of my homemade pizza.

Until my cell phone rang.

"Rick?" I widened my eyes at Lisa, whose mouth was at the moment stuffed. "Am I busy? Not exactly. Lisa and I are having pizza and talking."

He was on his way home from a dinner meeting with clients and wanted to come by to pick up those materials I'd collected. If it wasn't an imposition. If I wasn't busy.

My heart was racing a mile a minute. Lisa made a gesture to leave, but I grabbed her arm and held on tightly.

"Sure, drop by," I told him before snapping my phone shut. I wasn't letting Lisa's arm go. "Oh no, you're not leaving me alone with him. You're staying. He'll be here in just a few minutes."

She sat back down, and I let go of her arm, relaxing a trifle.

"Just say the word, Dina. I saw how you two looked at each other last night. I could almost see the electricity crackling between you both. I can disappear."

Panic surged up from my belly. "Don't you dare." I looked down at my dirty, holey sweat pants. Shit! Gulping down a large swallow of wine, I jumped down from my chair. "Be right back."

I dashed to my room, threw off my sweat pants and t-shirt. In my undies—not so virginal black ones—I washed my face and hands, brushed my hair into a neat ponytail, applied scarlet-red lipstick. Then, as I hopped around in my *huaraches* which I wore around the house, I shimmied on a clean pair of jeans. Rummaging through a couple of drawers, I found a V-neck sweater in green, red, and tan stripes. The red would highlight the copper in my hair, the green would bring out the greenish tint in my hazel eyes—my pale olive complexion wouldn't look so, well, pale and indoorish.

It'd been weeks since I'd been outside for any length of time, and except for the Lincoln All-Stars' twice-weekly jog around the school, I'd been sedentary. A state that I was never happy with for very long.

Too bad Rick Ramos didn't play golf. I could forgive anybody anything if they'd play golf with me.

But he used to run . . .

Before returning to the kitchen, I double-checked the fire opal earrings in my earlobes. There! Not so bad for a hasty, thrown-together look.

By the time Rick showed up, Lisa and I were lounging in Flora's luxurious living room, perusing the stack of DVDs she'd brought for us to choose from. I was asking about the folder she'd also carried in with her when the doorbell rang.

"Remember, if you want me to leave," Lisa whispered to me, "just—I know, cough three times. Right in a row. That'll be the signal."

I inhaled deeply and shook my head. "He's staying just a few minutes. I'll get him out of our hair as fast as I can."

Somehow, my assurances fell flat, for Lisa sat back, smirked, and rolled her eyes.

I'll have to admit, my mouth did gape when he walked in. He'd never looked so debonair! Wearing a navy, three-piece suit and white dress shirt, he appeared quite the elegant businessman. Already, he was stuffing a navy and red-striped tie into his jacket pocket. Rick Ramos looked a little embarrassed over his attire.

"Sorry to interrupt your . . ."

"Girls' night in," Lisa piped up, grinning from ear to ear. Her whole demeanor changed. She looked like Flora, preening for her man. "Would you like to watch a movie with us? I brought over *Crouching Tiger*, that Chinese martial-arts film. It's about a woman warrior . . ."

Inwardly I groaned, not only because of Lisa's movie

choice but because she was inviting Rick to stay. I didn't want to share the same room with him for two or three hours. Last night's ordeal at the restaurant was harrowing enough.

In truth, with each encounter, I was finding my resolve to avoid him slipping a bit.

"There's also the second Bridget Jones movie," I found myself offering. Maybe he'd flee at the sight of a chick flick.

Rick looked from me to Lisa, appearing indecisive. Perhaps he'd hoped to catch me alone so he could talk about his daughter and the materials I'd gathered for him. Or maybe he'd wanted a heart to heart—no, that I couldn't handle. Not now. Not ever.

"Well, I just dropped by . . ." He shrugged and smiled. "Why not? I've got my neighbor's daughter babysitting Angelina for the evening. Guess it won't hurt to stay."

With a lingering, questioning look at me, I finally smiled. After all, I had to be courteous, I rationalized. Look at all he'd done for my family, for Pop's and Frankie's tile business, for Jesús and Connie—

"I don't have any beer, but there's wine."

"Wine's good." He unbuttoned his suit jacket, took it off, and folded it over a wing chair. Then he eased himself down, rested his long arms on the chair's arms, and crossed his legs. As though a little uneasy, he rubbed his dimpled chin. A familiar gesture I knew very well.

Lisa and I were watching him like we'd never before seen a member of the male species. He looked again at the two of us, first me, then Lisa, back to me. His gaze lingered on my ears. Then traveled southward. I shook myself mentally.

"Right. Wine. Be right back."

Already it was starting. My skull was tingling, and my belly was quivering. Not a good sign.

Oh, Dina, you fool. You're making *a big mistake.*

Three hours and too many glasses of wine later—I thought

that movie would never end — I jumped up from my place on the brocade sofa.

"Better make coffee. Rick, there's some pizza left. Home-made pizza, if you want some. I can warm it up."

"Sure, I'd like that. Let me help," he said.

In the kitchen, I kept silent while I cut off two large pie-shaped slices, placed them on a dish, and microwaved them. Then I put the coffee on after first grinding the coffee beans.

"You're going to make someone a good wife," he said finally, as the grinder whirred to action. I wasn't sure I'd heard him correctly.

"What?" I handed him the plate of pizza and watched him take it over to the pub table. The grinder stopped. The grinding of my teeth didn't.

He looked over at me, pausing as if contemplating his next choice of words carefully.

"Never mind," he said, taking a bite.

I fiddled with the coffee machine, burning inside. Right, fella, don't you dare mention *wife* to me. After ditching me to marry that tramp! Bet Anita couldn't make anything but tacos. Wouldn't know a coffee mill from a blender.

He made small, masculine noises of pleasure.

"Ummm, great pizza. How do you come up with these concoctions? I remember that pork roast you made one time with peach and mango salsa —"

"Yeah, well, being a good cook doesn't seem to be a major requirement for marriage these days. I don't know what young men want from a woman, but a good cook isn't one of 'em."

"It is for me," he quipped around a mouth full.

"Could've fooled me." I shot Rick a look to kill, then poured him a cup of black coffee. The wine had loosened his tongue, and I was having none of it.

"Dina, you know I didn't want to marry her," he said

quickly after a hard swallow. "You know how it was that summer. I had to drop out of school. My father needed me to get my contractor's license so we could buy that roofing business. I was an American citizen, and there would be no questions about a loan and documents. I was in a foul mood, and you were in DC. I thought you had a crush on Velásquez. Chrissake, if she hadn't gotten pregnant, do you think I ever would've married her?"

I waved him to shut up. We'd dredged it all up before, six years ago, when I'd learned he'd cheated on me and gotten Anita Hernández pregnant on that terrible summer before my senior year in college. I'd barely made it through my last semester once I'd discovered the truth. How I kept my sanity and made it to graduation, I'll never know.

"Don't even go there—"

"So the prickly porcupine hasn't put away her spines?" Rick huffed a big sigh. "Dina, why won't you forgive me?" He'd almost whispered this plea as I snatched his plate and carried it into the living room. He followed with a cup of coffee.

Practically dropping the plate on the coffee table, I went over to the dining table in the adjoining room. The books and manipulative games that Rick was supposed to use with his daughter were in a brown grocery bag. He was leaving— now!

"Here, I think these'll help," I said archly, reining in my emotions. Lisa was sifting through the papers in that folder she'd brought, trying to avoid looking at both of us.

"Holy cow!" she exclaimed, ignoring Rick and me. Lisa held up some sheets of computer printouts.

Rick and I both halted and stared.

Lisa looked up, appearing startled. Taking in Rick's presence, she dropped her eyes and was silent. Well, now I was curious.

"What's that?"

"Nothing," she mumbled, "just stuff I printed out from that Internet search I did this afternoon. About the Juárez Cartel. You know . . ." She glanced meaningfully over at Rick, suddenly mindful that he probably didn't know about my grandmother's connections to Mexican dope smugglers.

"Your brother, Frank, told me all about it," Rick offered, realizing my sudden discomfort. "He wanted my opinion—"

"Damn that Frank," I exclaimed. "Don't tell anybody, Rick, please. Even Flora doesn't know. Grandma didn't want anyone outside the immediate family to know."

The materials on the dining table were forgotten, and I returned to Lisa's side, anxious to hear what she'd uncovered. Rick came back and sat down, too, helping himself to that second piece of pizza.

"I was just reading this article from the *El Paso Times*. Your uncle, Roberto Martínez, had a price on his head. A five-million-dollar reward. He was one of the top ten international fugitives wanted by ICE, the US Immigration and Customs Enforcement agency. He and his cartel were generating about one-billion American dollars monthly—give or take a few million. The Juárez Cartel was responsible for nearly twenty percent of the narcotics that reached American streets from Mexico." Lisa paused to look at us. "Man, your uncle was one successful drug lord. He even had a fleet of *Boeing* jets, all privately owned, to carry cocaine from Columbia to his warehouses all over the state of Juárez."

To say I was stunned would be an understatement. Rick stopped chewing and stared at me, then Lisa.

"How successful is dead?" I wondered aloud.

"There's a whole lot more. Fifteen people with suspected drug ties disappeared near Juárez. Witnesses said the kidnappers had *INCD* on their black uniforms. That's a Spanish acronym for a Mexican federal anti-drug agency. So that means he'd bribed corrupt federal officials into doing his dirty work. The bodies of these fifteen people were found in the desert. They were suspected drug peddlers who wanted to break away and form their own network."

I was beginning to feel physically sick, and I had a headache from too much wine. Shrinking back into the cushions, I closed my eyes. Lisa was silent. So was Rick.

"Go on," I mumbled. What difference did it make if Rick or anyone else knew the horrible facts about an uncle I never knew? What did it matter if our family history was now tainted — no, bloodied by the life of a man whose existence had been a total mystery to us until two weeks ago.

"Want to know how he died, Dina? It's all here. In this article in the *Frontera del Norte* newspaper. It's been translated to English." Lisa hesitated. I nodded, sighing deeply.

Might as well hear the ugly truth.

Lisa read on, as intrigued as I was, "Roberto Martínez Carrillo — your grandmother's maiden name is Carrillo? Anyway, he was indicted on twenty-six counts of drug trafficking and money laundering, accused of transporting more than ten thousand pounds of cocaine and fifteen thousand pounds of marijuana from nineteen-eighty-five to two-thousand-five. The indictment was a result of an American investigation conducted by several federal agencies, including the DEA and ICE. Let's see, if caught by Mexican or American authorities, he would have faced multiple life sentences, forfeiture of more than fifty-million dollars' worth of property, and profits from street sales in US cities of cocaine, marijuana, and methamphetamines as well as millions in fines. Believed to have resided somewhere in the state of Juárez. The American agencies issued Mexican authorities an extradition request last year along with a warrant for his arrest. US agents were working closely with Mexican authorities . . ." Lisa seized my arm. "Are you okay? Do you really want me to go on?"

I opened my eyes, saw the concern in her expression, glanced at Rick, and saw the sorrow in his face.

"I want to hear it all."

Lisa glanced at Rick before continuing.

They were just as riveted as I was.

"Roberto Martínez Carrillo was a pioneer in the use of large aircraft . . .huh, sounds like an epitaph . . .here it is. While undergoing plastic surgery in Ciudad de Juárez, liposuction and facial reconstruction to alter his appearance, it is believed that at the end of the eight-hour surgery, an injection of a lethal combination of sedatives and anesthesia was attempted but foiled by — listen to this — his daughter Teresa. Later attempts by rival drug cartels were made over the years, but they were always uncovered and stopped. Mexican officials believe he was ultimately killed last month by rivals within his own organization."

Lisa gasped. "So your cousin might be right."

I blew out cheeks full of air.

Rick remained silent.

"Well, now we know." I wondered if Grandma Gómez knew. Unless Frankie had gotten hold of the same article and told the family, I doubted it.

"Wow," Lisa exclaimed. "Maybe your cousin's husband was behind it all. Maybe her husband did it for all that money."

We were all silent for a few minutes. My gaze fell on Rick, so quiet and still in that wingback chair. His father was an illegal though he had enough fake documents by now to run for mayor of San Jose. Rick understood that family back in Mexico lived in a different world than their gringo relatives up north.

We were the blessed ones — most of us, anyway. There were still barrios in the States filled with desperation and hopelessness. Immigrants, legal or otherwise, who couldn't or wouldn't assimilate and take advantage of what opportunities American society offered them. Rick's father certainly had and had thrived. His entire family had prospered because his father had the brains, guts, and determination to do what he had to do to make it work for him. Ramos Roofing and Construction was a testament to that determination.

I couldn't help but wonder what Rick thought of me now.

His big, brown eyes raised to meet mine. In them, I saw only compassion . . .maybe a little pity. I bet he had stories to tell, or his father did, about Mexico — such an alien world.

"I hate to sound mean," Lisa broke in, "but people who live by the sword die by it. I know he's your uncle, Dina, but look at the life he led. How many people became addicts, suffered, and died because of him and his cartel? You have to think of the damage that man did. And now somebody just as bad is going to take his place. The whole cycle of greed and violence continues."

Lisa shuffled her papers and stuffed them into the folder. "You read the rest when you feel like it. There were ten articles in all. I read part of just one. I'll leave it for you."

I nodded my thanks. My thoughts were dwelling on Teresa's son. A seven-year-old boy. If his father was taking over the Juárez Cartel, the boy would eventually be groomed to take his place.

Oh God, the whole cycle, from father to son. Suddenly, Teresa's wanting out began to make sense. If that was true, that she was preparing to leave her husband. None of us really knew if it was true or not. Could we even trust her word?

How did one leave the cartel, anyway? Grandma Gómez had fled but had to leave a baby son behind. That was sixty years ago. Assuming Teresa even wanted to, how could she just leave and take her son? It seemed to me there was only one way a person left the cartel . . .in a pine box.

"Would you like us to stay with you for a while?" Lisa

asked me, including Rick in the offer.

All of a sudden, I didn't want to be alone. "Yeah, thanks."

Rick pushed to his feet. "I'll pour the coffee." He went to the kitchen and my gaze, like a magnet, trailed after him.

Lisa tapped me on my shoulder. "Want me to leave?"

I looked down at the folder of printouts, feeling both depressed and anxious. A lost romance was the last thing on my mind just then.

"Don't you dare."

CHAPTER NINE

Abuelita's motto — "Beware the power of the one-eyed snake."

This was Grandma Gómez's metaphor for sex. The word, sex, was never mentioned by her, but in her advice to Connie, Perpetua, and me over the years, this was the metaphor I recall her using the most. The one-eyed snake.

It was powerful, evil, tantalizing, seductive. It could make you forget all the Catholic rules and teachings you took to heart as a young schoolgirl. It could make you lose your mind and soul and do things that would send you straight to hell when you died. It could make you commit the blackest of mortal sins.

Connie, Pet, and I were naturally intrigued. Our little Catholic hearts quaked with trepidation while, at the same time, we couldn't wait to see the one-eyed snake. Sort of like a Mexican version of the boogeyman.

Well, Connie saw her one-eyed snake by her junior year in high school. That was how she ended up with the family screw-up, Jesús Morales. As a result, Pet was a little more cautious and didn't meet up with her one-eyed snake until Beauty College. By then, she'd had a little more time to scope out the boys at Salinas High, a little more time to mature and realize just what kind of man she wanted to commit her body and soul to for the rest of her life. Juan Pablo was good-looking, had prospects — translated to be, he had intelligence, fundamental job skills, and was devoted to her.

My native pessimism told me I wouldn't be so lucky, and so while the other girls began sharing their most intimate body parts with pimply-faced, high school doofuses, I buried myself in books, schoolwork, and school sports. I played girls' soccer and joined the cross-country team. While jogging five miles one day after school along with the rest of the coed team, I met Enrique Ramos.

He was a ladies' man — at least, the girls all thought he was — had a wild reputation and a tattoo on his right forearm. I'd thought he was a member of the *norteños* and consequently steered a wide berth around him. It was not until we met again in a freshman literature class at San Jose State U that I realized he had a good head on his shoulders, actually read books — albeit mystery and science fiction novels — and was the only son of a very traditional, strictly Catholic immigrant family.

I began to trust him, and we became good friends, although I refused to date him. Even then, I'd sensed his one-eyed snake was more potent than all the rest. I was determined not to fall under the control of any man, at least not until I was thirty. Ha, ha!

How I got on this tangent of the one-eyed snake, I don't know. But this topic preoccupied my mind during the entire two hours of my drive down to Salinas the weekend following Pop's surgery.

I was remembering the last time Rick and I had made love. Rick had caught me writing a paper for one of my Ed classes. My roommate was out, and so, as if storm-driven, he'd flung himself at me. It'd taken a moment for me to get swept away by his lust, but I let him carry me to my bed, strip me in his urgency, watched him fling his clothes off. All the while, he'd said little, just had this dark and stricken look, like he'd just lost a part of his soul.

There'd been no foreplay, just an incredible, desperate

clinging to each other. Our climax was explosive, and while I went limp with panting, he'd continued rocking and pumping, like he couldn't believe it was over. Like he'd wanted our coupling to go on . . .maybe forever. Then he'd started to weep. Big, tall Enrique Ramos, all two-hundred pounds of almost pure muscle, was crying over me. His face was buried in my neck and hair, and as his weeping went on, I grew scared.

Had I just allowed a psycho to make love to me?

That's when he finally told me. He'd had a fling with Anita Hernández while I was in DC. He'd gotten her pregnant, had found out a month ago. His father insisted that he marry her, legitimizing the child. Do the right thing. Be a man and accept responsibility.

Funny thing, I couldn't recall what happened after that.

I must've lost it somehow . . .but my memory was truly a blank. All I knew was that was the end of our engagement, our romance, our friendship. The true end of my innocence.

After that passionate sexual encounter with Rick, my heart was broken, and romance for me was a poison plant, like bella donna.

What Grandma said was true. The one-eyed snake was a curse.

When I arrived home in Salinas, everyone was already there. They'd practically set up camp in the house and yard. Everyone wanted to see Pop after his heart surgery. The atmosphere inside was like a wake. A Mexican/Spanish wake. Which meant, of course, there was plenty of food, music, kids, and noise.

"*Mamá*, don't you think all the kids should be outside?" I greeted her with a brief, stiff hug. "Pop should be resting."

"He is, *m'ija*. He's lying down with his earplugs."

Frank told me that whenever Pop wanted or needed to tune out the family hubbub, he'd escape to his bedroom and listen to the small, portable TV on his bureau with the ear-phones Frank had bought Pop. No one—especially the chil-dren—was allowed in at those times. Evidently, he hadn't emerged from his room since he got out of the hospital. There was an enormous painted-clay bowl of *migas* left, and the nine adults around the table—Connie and Jesús, Pet and Juan Pablo, Frank and Isabel, Roberto, Mama, and Grandma Gómez—were helping themselves to this high-cholesterol, ar-terial-bursting Spanish breakfast dish.

The main ones absent were my Salazar grandparents, who had left three weeks before for a two-month vacation in Spain, visiting distant cousins whose parents had remained in the old country. Flora and Pop's other siblings and their families would be visiting next weekend after Pop had a chance to re-cuperate more fully.

My brothers and sisters and their spouses greeted me in their usual ways.

"Dolores—uh, Dina!"

"Aye, *bonita*." This was my favorite brother-in-law, Juan Pablo. Pet always just smiled and gestured a V with her fin-gers.

"Hey, *dolor de culo*, happy belated birthday," Frankie teased. "Sorry, we had to postpone it."

Grandma Gómez, long since convinced by Mama that Dina was only my nickname, narrowed her eyes and gave me a critical, once-over look, apparently disapproving of my loose tunic and snug tights. Did she think I was trying to hide a pregnancy? Or joining a Robin Hood band of merry twits?

When I told her what Lisa and her uncle had said about waiting to hear from Teresa Vargas first before we could do anything, Grandma Gómez just snorted loudly and left the room. Mama frowned at me like I had kidnapped Teresa and was holding her for ransom.

Well, piss on a brick, don't shoot the messenger, I thought.

It wasn't my fault that my Mexican cousin had married a man in the cartel business. This accountant turned drug lord, Pedro Vargas. Of course, I'd said nothing to either Grandma or Mama that Pedro Vargas had now taken control of his father-in-law's cartel. A meaningful look from Frankie conveyed to me that it was best to keep them both in the dark.

Most likely, he'd heard from Rick Ramos, I thought. Before Rick had left Flora's house a week ago, I'd told him it was okay to pass on the information to Frankie if they happened to meet on the job. Since then, too, I'd spoken to Frankie on the phone and shared the rest of that computer search Lisa'd done.

"Those *migas*," I said, pointing in horror at the bowl in the center of the table, "are ninety percent fat, the bad fat, not the good fat. The same crap that clogged up Pop's arteries. We shouldn't be eating that stuff." Why I bothered to say this, I haven't a clue, for it was a waste of breath.

"Our arteries are young," Roberto offered. "We don't hafta worry for another forty years at least. Shit, by then, we'll be dead from terrorists or global warming."

"Or the big earthquake that'll make California crack off and disappear into the ocean," Jesús said, chuckling.

"But it's what we eat now and the next forty years that'll — oh, never mind," I retorted weakly. By now, I could smell the heavy garlic scent wafting up from the bowl of fried dough, garlic chunks, and pieces of aromatic chorizo. Pet inserted a tall, white candle into the middle of the bowl of *migas* and lit it.

"Happy twenty-ninth!"

I smiled as they sang *Feliz cumpleaños a ti*, the Spanish version which we'd learned as children.

Mama was quiet and just stared into the candle's flame. Maybe this was going to be a very long weekend, after all. She and *Abuelita* were somehow going to blame me for not doing something to help cousin Teresa. If she wanted to leave her murdering, cartel-boss husband, what could I do? What was I supposed to be now? An ATF agent?

"Dina, come and eat," Connie invited warmly. "Jesús, take your plate to the counter. Make room for Dina at the table."

Jesús shrugged and stood up. I stared.

My miscreant brother-in-law, now duly employed thanks to Ramos Construction, was sporting a black beard with four dangling, beaded braids, an oversized *San Diego Clippers* jersey over baggy Bermuda shorts, and ropes of cheap but colorful plastic beads. He looked like a cross between Blackbeard the pirate and a reject from a drunken Mardi Gras party.

"Is that your Halloween costume?" I asked, gawking.

"Yah, dude, how did you guess? Can't wear it Halloween night. Don't wanta scare the little kids. Like my punked-out braids?" He leaned over and let them dangle in front of him.

Well, I always knew his elevator didn't go to the top floor.

"Yeah, guess you fit the look," I tossed off.

Jesús was never one to quit while he was ahead.

"Hey," Jesús prattled on, "I hear Rick Ramos ditched his 'hood ho cuz he never got over you. Man, he's gotta hard-on a yard long for you, *chica.*"

Mama gasped. My sisters naturally reacted angrily, and the guys broke out laughing. Connie reached out to slap Jesús's arm but the idiot, throwing his head back and chuckling, made a quick evasive move out of her reach. The braids on his beard swung back and forth as he, like a small gorilla, swayed back and forth tauntingly. Connie threw a piece of fried dough at his face but, wouldn't you know it, the ape caught it in his mouth. Everyone laughed.

Except me. It was time to take evasive action on my part as well.

"As usual, Jesús, I have no idea what you're talking about." I sniffed. "Rick Ramos wanted my professional opinion on his daughter's learning problems. Nothing more."

Several at the table exchanged amused glances. Others looked sheepishly down and continued eating their platefuls of Pop's favorite cholesterol-laden, artery-busting dish.

I'd already begun to picture Rick's hard-on in my mind. My memory was very vivid on what *that* looked like. The traitorous one-eyed snake. I'd seen it only once. Still, *the hug* outside the restaurant lingered in my mind. As well as how he'd looked in that navy, three-piece suit the other night.

"Just don't make Rick sorry," I warned Jesús, "that he hired you. If you screw up, Jesús, so help me, I'll tell *Señor* Ramos that it was you who dented the *Bel Air*. Then he'll call Customs and have you deported."

Jesús laughed defiantly, did a bump-and-grind with his hips just to watch the colored beads on his beard-braids spin around. I glanced over at my sister, Connie, who looked amused. She actually thought her whacky husband was funny!

What did I tell you about the power of the one-eyed snake! Even though Jesús's was probably a worm compared to Rick's cobra.

I hadn't seen or spoken to Rick in a week — but hey, who's counting? I'd called Mariana to let her know I couldn't come to her housewarming party, which was tonight. She'd told me that Rick was coming, as far as she knew.

That reminded me — shit! — that I'd forgotten to call that cute cop and get him off Rick's case. It had been almost a month, I think.

"I'll be right back," I told everyone. "Save a plate of *migas* for me. I have to make a phone call."

They resumed their conversation at the table — as usual, nearly everyone speaking simultaneously — while I looked into the living room. Five rug rats, having already eaten, were gathered around the TV set, watching Disney's *Beauty and the*

Beast movie, all more or less contented. I did notice that Connie's and Jesús' twins were sleeping in their portable bed with Frankie's and Isabel's baby, Tomas, while Pet's and Juan Pablo's daughter was protecting her *Barbie doll* by biting her brother's fingers. Frank's eldest two, Frankie junior and Linda, were apparently told to supervise their siblings and cousins. Surprisingly, they were doing a halfway competent job of it, occasionally barking out a warning to settle down or be outcasted to the backyard.

Fleeing the nursery scene, I went out to the front porch. I fished the officer's card out of my wallet and punched the numbers on my cell phone. Incredibly, he picked up immediately.

"Officer"—I read from his card—"Dalton, this is Dina Salazar. I'm the teacher at Lincoln Elementary who called that day—three or four weeks ago, I think—to report a...a mysterious man in a red *Explorer* outside my school. He was waiting in his SUV."

"Oh, yeah, I remember. I input his name and driver's license into our database. Nothing so far, just a few traffic violations. The sex offenders' database showed nothing, too."

"Well..." I hated to be put on the spot like this, but it was my own fault. Lying was sometimes helpful, even necessary, but I had to admit I'd blown it this time. "I want to report officially that I made a, uh, a mistake...when I told you I didn't know him."

Uh-oh. How was I going to avoid getting in trouble, myself?

"You made a mistake?"

"Yes, sir." It wouldn't hurt to lay on the politeness. "You see, I went home—" Creative sparks ignited in my imagination. "And just happened to be looking through my high school yearbooks. That man, Enrique Ramos, was one of my classmates. And then I recalled that he's on the reunion committee—you know, to plan and organize our high school reunion. I recently joined this committee, and it turned out Mr. Ramos was just trying to contact me since he'd lost my cell number and didn't have my home-phone number. We've been in touch since then, and he explained everything. He's a nice man . . .an upstanding citizen."

Wow, was I impressed with my own bullshit! I was hoping Officer Dalton was buying it.

"Oh, I see," he said. "You're that redheaded teacher at Lincoln Elementary, aren't you?"

"Y-yes," I replied cautiously. Uh-oh, he remembered me. My hair was auburn, not red, but I wasn't about to correct him.

"I'll have to come by and have you sign a statement. Miss . . ."

"Miss Dina Salazar. Oh sure."

I was so relieved that my racing heart rate immediately plummeted back to normal. After I gave him my available time after school on Monday, we hung up. I blew air out of my cheeks and tossed the cell phone in my purse.

Now, you see, sometimes telling white lies was a good thing. I'd see that cute cop again and get Rick Ramos off the hook. And off my mind. All I had left to do regarding Mr. Ramos was to give him that bag of stuff I'd gathered for his daughter, which he'd forgotten to take when he left Saturday night. After that, we were square, as far as I was concerned, and I hoped to never see him again. What lame Jesús had said was his usual idiocy.

Rick hadn't gotten over me and divorced his *'hood ho* because he was still hung up on me. What a crock that was! I had nothing to do with his pitiful marriage and its outcome. It was a forced marriage doomed from the start. Anyone could see that. Little Angelina was just lucky that one of her parents turned out to be a decent sort of person. Decent, honorable . . .and loving.

Why that vision of Rick's one-eyed snake lingered in my mind, I'll never understand.

I'd no sooner finished my guilt-laden portion of *migas* than Grandma Gómez reappeared, holding a piece of paper.

"Here, read this, Dolores," she ordered. Mama and the others remained at the table, staring at me. I began to wonder if this was my official excommunication from the Gómez/Salazar family.

Instead, it was a Mexican telegram. I read the message in Spanish. It was from Teresa Martínez Vargas. She'd signed it simply TMV. I digested it slowly, considering its implications.

"We already know what it says," Roberto provided. No doubt Mama had translated for everyone.

"Okay, so Teresa's left the hacienda and is on her way to the city of Chihuahua. Her destination is Monterrey. She doesn't know where she'll be staying — possibly with friends. She took her son with her. She'll be in touch."

I looked up at the anxious eyes of my grandmother. "*Abuelita*, that's all she says. But this is good news, right? At least she's okay."

"What do you think, Dolores?" Grandma asked me in Spanish. "How can we find her? How can we help her leave Mexico before her *bastardo* of a husband finds her and kills her?"

I gazed around the table, then back at Grandma. Her lined, seventy-nine-year-old face appeared especially haggard. Even her usually neat bun was disheveled. It was clear she'd been worrying herself into a tizzy over Pop and Teresa as well as grieving over her son, Roberto Martínez. It was also clear she and the others were expecting me to say something intelligent — like, you're the college graduate, so show us how smart you are. I was on the hot seat — again.

"Monterrey. It's a fairly large city. There's a beautiful

cathedral there. *Abuelita,* if you don't hear from her in the next week or so, let me know, and I'll call the office of the bishop down there and maybe enlist the help of the church."

Well, I thought it was a brilliant idea. The looks of everybody around me registered bewilderment. Grandma Gómez stared at me as if I'd suddenly been infected with the Jesús Morales-dumbass virus.

"*¡Qué mensa! ¿Qué pueden hacer los clérigos?*" How dumb! What can the clergy do? Grandma pulled a handkerchief from her apron pocket and patted her forehead. "Dolores, *nina,* Mexican priests don't do anything that will disturb their comfortable, little lives. Especially a bishop! Who do you think donates money to buy the gold in the altar of those cathedrals? The rich of Mexico, of course, and the richest of the rich are the drug traffickers. How can you think such a thing?"

Grandma was speaking Spanish so fast, it took me a moment to catch up. Before I could object, she grabbed my wrist, yanked me out of the chair, and led me down the small hallway. Pop and Mama's bedroom door was closed, and Pop was napping. I was not to see him until later.

"I want you to see something," my little, feisty grandmother said, letting go of my wrist when she realized I was following her, although reluctantly.

I hadn't been in my old bedroom for years, not since Grandma Gómez had taken it over. I remembered it as being small but light and airy. Now it was like a cave. She'd had my father paint it a dark, antique gold color. All the drapes were drawn, and the only light in the room was emanating from the candles on her double dresser. There must have been twenty candles at least, all arranged around three shrines. It was a miracle that she hadn't burned down the house by now.

When I approached, still following her lead, I saw the pictures at each of the three shrines.

A large, black-and-white, framed photo of her parents was

on the left, surrounded by candles of various heights and widths. On the far right of the dresser stood the gold-framed photo of her and Grandpa Gómez on their wedding day in Texas. I inched closer to the middle. The central shrine was dedicated to a handsome, dark-skinned man with black hair, dressed in a fine suit and standing next to what appeared to be a black *Mercedes*. The photo was colored and framed in gold-painted wood, draped with a black scarf. The same image she'd shown us before.

"Your uncle, Roberto Martínez Carrillo. My son."

I stared at his face for a while out of respect. In a way, I could see the resemblance between the man and Mama. My brother, Roberto, had the same smile and complexion. The same shock of straight, dark hair as my long-lost uncle.

"He was too young to die, Dolores, only sixty-two. Your mother's twin brother."

I wanted to remind her that we'd already heard her story. I wanted to remind her that he'd been a violent man who had people killed. That he'd run a dangerous organization that fed the addictive habits of hundreds of thousands of Americans. That he'd been on ICE's Ten Most Wanted List for drug trafficking and money laundering. That I couldn't feel anything but contempt for a man like that. But out of respect for her, I kept quiet.

"It's a sad story, Dolores. I was married to a man with no heart. He made me leave little Roberto—"

And this was Grandma's lifelong scar that'd never healed.

"To assure I would return," she continued. "I almost did. Perhaps I should have. But Roberto's destiny was made the moment I married that man. He had to follow in his father's footsteps whether I was there or not."

"That's true, *Abuelita*. If you had stayed, the outcome would've been the same. You didn't fail him. His father did."

My grandmother absorbed that message in silence. Then

her dark brown-eyed gaze flicked up at me, holding me in a steady, level gaze. "You know that I have learned through Jaime and Carlota that Teresa regarded her father kindly and with love. Though he was stern and strict—"

Huh, I didn't have to wonder where he got *those* traits.

"Too bad he died before you got a chance to see him . . .in person, *Abuelita*." Grandma Gómez gave me a strange look, a mixture of guilt and ferocity.

"That would never have happened, Dolores. I would never have been allowed near the hacienda. It was like a fortress with guards with bandoliers and guns and thick, stucco walls that made a tall fence. On the top were pieces of broken glass. He—Senor Martinez—would never have allowed me to come back to that fortress. That prison."

That was how Grandma remembered the hacienda. Now, I'd bet, there were security cameras all over and huge Doberman Pinschers prowling the estate. Guards with automatic rifles. Maybe helicopters that patrolled regularly.

"Jaime told Carlota that Teresa believes her parents were killed by her husband, this Vargas *serpiente*," Grandma continued. "She must be correct. Dolores, she is like you. My granddaughter, Teresa."

I looked at her, feeling all of a sudden weirded out.

"She is educated, smart, brave. She has set her mind to leaving this ruthless murderer of her parents, this Pedro Vargas, for the sake of her son. I know this. I know how she feels, that she must somehow protect her child from this . . .this way of life. She must protect the boy from becoming like her husband—"

And like his grandfather and great grandfather, I wanted to add.

"If what Frankie says is true, that this cartel employs a gang of former Mexican soldiers, like ex-army commandos with bazookas and machine guns. If this is true, these men are mercenaries and will do whatever this Vargas *diablo* tells them to do. That is why I am so afraid for Teresa and her son."

I nodded solemnly, wondering how Grandma knew about army commandos. Maybe she knew more about American life than I'd given her credit for. Then I noticed the dish of *calaveras*, Mexican cookies in the shape of skulls-and-cross-bones. They'd been whitened with powdered sugar and lined with brown frosting, rather artistically done, no doubt by Grandma, herself.

"*Calaveras*," I muttered, "*el Día de los Muertos*." Day of the Dead, or All Saints' Day, the day after Halloween, which was this coming Wednesday. Tuesday night was Halloween.

"*Sí*." Grandma Gómez sighed, a corner of her mouth turning down sadly. "We have to honor the dead in our family. We have to show our respect, our love, our appreciation for their lives. Without our ancestors, where would we be? I made more. They're in the freezer for you to take back to your school. You teach your students about *el Día de los Muertos*, Dolores?"

"Yes, I do," I said. I'd take those skull-and-crossbones cookies and give a short lecture on the Day of the Dead, also telling my kids about my grandmother's shrines. Many of my Latino, Asian, and New Delhi-Indian students had similar shrines in their homes, and I knew it might provoke an interesting discussion about honoring one's ancestors. My Asian kids could relate to that idea, also.

"Do you see why we must find my granddaughter and great-grandson? We must help them escape that horrible world of the cartel and come to the United States. They must have a better life, a good life — one full of hope and goodness."

Grandma Gómez looked at me fully, and there was no pleading in her face, just intense scrutiny and ferocious logic.

"Yes, *Abuelita*, but why can't Frankie or Roberto do this?"

She shook her head vigorously, one of her side combs

pulling loose from her sleeked-back black hair.

"No, you're the smartest one, Dolores. You're the one who must figure out a way to do this."

What could I say? I couldn't speak anyway. Something was causing the back of my throat to ache all of a sudden. Like I was coming down with a sore throat. Even the picture of *Tío* Roberto, which I began to study again, blurred in front of my watery vision.

So Grandma thought I was the smartest one in the family? All these years, I'd thought she held me in scorn. In reality, she admired me?

I couldn't speak, my throat was so clogged, so I nodded instead. Grandma had given me the challenge, and, some-how, out of a combination of respect, fear, and surprise, I had just agreed to take it on.

Omigod, what was I getting myself into?

CHAPTER TEN

Grandma Gomez—"*A buen hambre, no hay pan duro.*"
When you're starving, there's no such thing as hard bread.

Or beggars can't be choosers. One day, I retorted with the American version of her *buen dicho,* and she just shook her head, her brows furrowed like angry caterpillars. Maybe that was just one of the many wise sayings I had misunderstood. Perhaps because I'd never been close to starving in my life. Who knows?

"Dina, I can tone up the red in your hair and make it more red, y'know, flashier if you like. Come to my salon after five today. JP can take the kids out to *McDonald's* while we do our thing."

Pet was always trying to glam me up, much to my chagrin. I always did my own hair, figuring a drugstore shampoo and conditioner, plus my round hairbrush and hairdryer were all I needed for my simple pageboy-coif. I'd never been to a beauty spa, and the only couturiers I knew were the salesgirl and alterations lady at *Nordstrom*—and I only saw them during their big annual sale. What did I know—much less care?

Nevertheless, I had to admire the short cap of chic, dark curls on Pet's head. Even Mama had the same permed 'do.

"No, but what about a manicure?" I asked.

"Yep, at the very least. Your nails look like you've been scraping them on bricks."

"I've been helping my students make their pyramids and

ziggurats for their Egyptian project. We've been making tiny bricks out of *Quik-Set* cement. And I've been working in Flora's garden, planting bulbs," I explained defensively.

I felt that women wearing painted flowers and rhinestones on two-inch-long acrylic nails were one of the modern mysteries of our American culture. Didn't these women ever cook or clean? Besides, how many books could be read in the time it took to have that done?

"Okay," I finally relented.

When was my last manicure? Last Christmas? I could see a few tiny patches of coral polish on three of my fingernails. Now I remembered—little Tomas's baptism. I was his godmother and had dolled up for the event. I'd actually worn pantyhose and a skirt for that occasion.

No wonder I could never be a trophy wife for Hugh Goss. Hmm, from out of the blue, I wondered if Rick was looking for a trophy wife. Didn't he say he liked a woman who could cook?

I quashed that thought, like a fly on the kitchen counter that you swat with a dishtowel.

"Good. I have to get back to work, Dina, but you come in at closing time. Maybe we'll try passion-flower scarlet or ruby-red this time. Deeper, jewel colors do well in the wintertime."

"Whatever," I muttered. "You're my fashion consultant."

"By the way, what you're wearing today—the tunic and leggings—is so over. I mean, totally."

Pet was starting to talk like a Valley Girl, and I don't mean San Joaquin Valley. San Fernando Valley, like LA. Maybe the lingo came with the beauty business world.

"What'd'ya mean?" I asked crossly. "Women were wearing this last year."

She glanced over at Mama and Grandma Gómez, who'd just checked in on Pop. He was still napping and couldn't be awakened.

"Overweight women over fifty—yeah, trying to hide all their bulges. With your figure, you should be in hip-huggers and cute, colorful cami tops, or heeled boots and short skirts. How're you going to get a man if you dress like a sixty-year-old prudish school teacher?"

As much as I loved my sister to death, that remark pricked my ire.

"Hey," I began cooly, "I wear high-heeled boots with my jeans. If I wore short skirts to work and bent over, I'd be written up, probably fired for indecent public exposure or contributing to the delinquency of minors."

Pet laughed. "Well, at least wear tighter clothes and show off your shape a little more."

I grumbled and groused a bit while Pet started putting things back into a tote the size of Vermont. It seemed like she always carried around a portable beauty shop in her bag.

"What was this nonsense Jesús said about Rick Ramos?" I finally asked. I couldn't leave it alone. Damn! If curiosity killed the cat, it was sure going to do me in. And I was more intelligent than your average domestic feline. At least, Grandma Gómez thought so.

Connie, Pet, and Isabel looked at each other, then glanced over at Mama and Grandma Gómez. We were the typical female sewing circle, except no one was sewing.

"What?" I asked, throwing up my hands, palms outward. Now what, I wondered, and why was I the last to find out.

"Jesús thinks—" Connie began. From the expression on my face, she could tell my opinion of her ex-con, lamebrain husband's credibility was zero. Zilch. "I know what you think of Jesús, Dina. Go ahead. You think he's a little crazy. Everyone does."

Ha! Crazy for him would be two levels higher than he deserved.

Her shoulders rose and fell as she shuddered back tears. The other women, all except Grandma Gómez and me, quickly assured her that Jesús was a reformed man, a good husband and father, and a responsible, able provider.

Now I knew where all my bullshitting talent derived. The bullshitting gene ran in our family. *Abuelita* and I were silent, wryly observing Connie's restored spirits. Of course, if I were in her shoes, I'd need to delude myself, too.

"As I was saying, Jesús thinks Ricky Ramos wants to win you back."

I sighed loudly. Okay, I'll bite.

"Why, pray tell, does Jesús think that?"

Connie frowned. "You don't have to sound so nasty, Dina. So haughty," Connie protested.

Of course, Mama clicked her tongue at me disapprovingly.

Forcing contriteness in my voice and demeanor, I said, "Okay, I'll try."

I swear, ever since *the hug*, I'd been a class-A bitch.

Connie continued, "He—Ricky Ramos has been doing all these nice things for the family." Did Connie think we'd mistakenly believe it was Jesús doing all these nice things? I had to keep myself from shaking my head in exasperation. "And now he's paid down fifty-thousand dollars on *Mamá* and Papa's mortgage loan, so their monthly payment is lower."

"What!" I half-rose from my chair.

Mama waved me back down.

"Don't tell your father about this," she ordered. "He isn't supposed to know. You know how very proud he is. He wouldn't accept it."

"*Sí, muy orgulloso,*" Grandma Gómez chimed in.

"Rick found out from Frank that we were all chipping in because their house was mortgaged to pay Roberto's and Jesús's legal bills—" This was Isabel who, like me, deeply resented the financial problems the two family bozos had caused our parents. Even Connie's gaze slid downward in an expression of her shame. "And because Papa's had to retire because of his health problems."

"I'm going to get a job," Mama interjected, her chin thrust upward, "as soon as your papa recovers from the operation and is back on his feet. I don't want my children paying our mortgage bill."

My head was swiveling back and forth from one woman to the next so fast, I felt like I was at a tennis match.

"So, anyway," Isabel continued, "Rick gave Jesús a check for fifty-thousand dollars made out to Frank because he knows Frank does all of Papa's banking."

Rick gave a fifty-thousand-dollar check to Jesús? And the nitwit didn't endorse Frank's name and caught the first plane to Vegas? Oh my God, were miracles really possible in the 21st century?

Or had Rick Ramos lost his mind? Why did he give a check for that kind of money to Jesús, a convicted con-man who'd once tried to bash Rick's brains out with a sledgehammer? More importantly, why did he give that sum of money to my parents? What was he hoping to gain by that? I was going to give him advice about his daughter for free!

"Now," Pet added, "the mortgage debt is only forty-thousand, and we only have to put in one-hundred each month."

"No, you won't have to do that at all," Mama piped in, "just as soon as I get a job. I can work part-time at the high school. They need a Spanish-speaking clerk to call home to report daily attendance. I can earn enough to pay off what's left of the mortgage in two or three years."

I gawked at my mother. As long as I'd known her, she'd never worked outside the home. As a young woman, she'd worked in the fruit canneries and later for a food service company, but that was eons ago. I couldn't help but look at her with a new measure of respect. Way to go, Mama!

"Jesús asked Ricky why he was doing this," Connie went on, "and Rick said, *to make it up to the Salazar family.* You know, for breaking off his engagement to Dina, hurting her, and embarrassing the whole family. And then Jesús—well, y'know how he blabs things out—he asked Ricky if he still loved Dina."

Shit! I knew this was coming. All their gazes pivoted on me. They wanted front-row seats to my reaction. They knew Rick had given me fire opal earrings for my birthday. I think Flora must've said something to Pop. Like an electrical current, it must've run through the entire family like the county power grid.

My emotions—my pain, my anger—would be on display for the world to see if I showed how I really felt. Well, maybe not the world, but to bare my soul in front of the women closest to me was still an impossibility. I still didn't know why.

Consequently, I schooled myself into showing an impassive face to them all. Remember, I was a skilled liar.

"Ricky said, quote, I never stopped." Connie nodded her head for emphasis. "He never stopped loving Dina."

Like a supreme fool, I felt the tears well up behind my eyes. I pushed myself up from the table.

"That's ridiculous." I laughed derisively and fled the kitchen.

A moment later, I knocked on Pop's door. After I heard a gruff, "What now, Concha?" I entered. When Pop saw me, he relaxed and beckoned me over to the bed.

"Sorry, *m'ija.* Your mother's been fussing over me, and it's driving me crazy. Hey, come over. Look at this postcard your grandparents sent from Spain. It's from Granada, where my father's family is from. Look, this is the Alhambra."

I sat next to Pop on my parents' queen-size bed. Pop was wearing an undershirt beneath his pajama top, so I couldn't sneak a look at his scar. Then I recalled he had no chest scar, for the surgeons had gone up to his heart through his femoral artery. He hadn't needed a double bypass, after all, such miracles of modern medicine, those arterial stents. Those angioplasty balloons squashed down the plaque that had been collecting for sixty-odd years, and now the stents were holding the arterial walls up and keeping them clear. The blood-thinning drug was doing the rest. Twenty years ago, my sixty-seven-year-old father would've had a two-foot-long scar down his chest.

His earphones were lying next to him, and a long, thin cable connected him to the TV set on the bureau opposite the bed. With the remote, he turned the set off.

I gazed at the Moorish palace known for its beautiful, intricately carved-plaster fretwork. This was the area of southern Spain I'd visited last summer, where the Salazars hailed from a century ago. My paternal grandmother's family—the Rodríguezes—were from the north of Spain, where fair-skinned, blue-eyed blondes were commonplace. The ancient realm of the Iberian Celts. Pop, Frank, and I looked like the Rodríguezes. More *rubio* than *moreno*. So did Flora. The other aunts and uncles looked like the Salazers, more darker-skinned from the Moorish influence. How strange and complex human genetics was.

"They called, and I told them not to rush home. What's the point? If I died on the operating table, being here wasn't going to change anything. And now there's no need."

I looked at Pop. And noticed with a pang the pallor of his skin, the dark smudges under his eyes. He was clearly in some discomfort, still. Yet, he'd always had a philosophical, upbeat attitude about life and death. Like, if it's going to happen, it'll happen. So make the most of the present.

It seemed that Mama and *Abuelita* had the same pessimistic outlook I sometimes had? Was that a gene that got passed down from the Mexican side, I wondered? Souring experiences with distrust and fatalism and causing people to sabotage their own happiness? Or the Celtic side, and that's why they needed those mournful bagpipes?

I hugged him. "Pop, you haven't shaved. Your gray whiskers are showing," I teased.

He rubbed his cheeks and frowned.

"I know, I'm getting lazy . . .and starting to mope and feel sorry for myself. Now I have to quit work, Frank says. How can a man be a man if he doesn't work? What will I do with myself, *m'ija*?"

I lay down beside him and flopped an arm over his slightly bulging belly, covered by a sheet and blanket. He gave off a warm scent of coffee, eucalyptus lozenges, and masculine muskiness.

"Pop, maybe take up golf and come out on the links with me."

He laughed shortly, which turned into a brief coughing spell. After a moment, he calmed down.

"Damn, wouldn't you know, I caught a cold at the hospital. They saved my life, but I got a cold. Did you say golf? Begin playing the hardest sport in the world at my age? No, Dina, I'll enjoy my grandchildren, do some fixing up around the house. Maybe take your mother on a trip to Spain or Mexico. Better yet, I'll keep working at the desk at the business and pay down that damned mortgage."

He tossed the postcard on the bed with a shrug, then put an arm around me, inviting me to lay my head on his shoulder, which I did, happily. I wanted to tell him about Rick Ramos's largesse, his fifty-thousand-dollar gift but couldn't. I'd promised the rest of the family I'd keep mum. Pop was not to know that Rick, our galloping knight, had just ridden in and dropped a check off for fifty-thousand big ones.

"You know, *m'ija*, I want to see you married and settled before I die. I want to see a good man taking care of you, looking after you. I don't like to see you alone."

"Right, so you can't die for at least the next twenty years, Pop," I teased him, "'cause it'll take that long to find somebody. Besides, I live with Flora. I'm not alone."

"I know that, but my baby sister is not the kind of woman I want you to be. I mean, she's intelligent and educated, but she doesn't live the way I want to see you live. No, I want to walk you down the aisle and hand you to a good, decent man. A man I would be proud to call my son. 'Course, knowing you, you'll have your wedding on a golf course somewhere, and you and me'll come riding in on one of those damned golf carts." He chuckled, and I joined him. Pop's swearing meant he was in a bit of discomfort.

"Hmmm, not a bad idea, Pop. Not a bad idea. I'll keep that in mind."

After a minute or two, I summoned my courage.

"Pop, this hasn't happened, naturally, but what would you do if you found out that *Mamá* had cheated on you? Y'know, had an affair with another man?"

"My God, Dina, are you trying to give me a heart attack right after the doctors worked so hard to save me?"

"No, Pop," I hurriedly replied. "It's a hypothetical question of forgiving and forgetting. Would you—knowing yourself and how you think and feel about people and life—would you be able to forgive and forget? Really forgive and forget?"

Silence. Pop wasn't one of those men who ruminated out loud. He frowned deeply.

"Well," he finally said, "I know I couldn't forget such a thing. Forgive? I don't know. I may seem like an easygoing guy on the surface, but some things in life are hard to forgive—maybe impossible. I would have to consider all the circumstances, y'know. But I don't know if I'd be able to forgive such a . . .a terrible betrayal. But you know, us men and our macho pride."

I kissed Pop's stubbled cheek. I was so happy, so grateful my father had survived the operation. My eyes misted over for the second time that day.

"You're *muy macho*, Pop."

But I was thinking, women have pride, too, Pop. Sometimes strong egos, sometimes fragile ones, just like men.

And there was the paradox, I felt. My ego and pride were strong, even robust, in most cases. After all, it took a fairly strong ego to kiss off Hugh Goss, considering I'd only recently discovered what I wanted in a man.

I wanted a *caballero*. In the best sense of the word, a man of worth, a stallion—not a mule.

But where one man was concerned—Rick Ramos—my ego and pride were as fragile as a paper-lace doily. I'd almost gone crazy the last time he shredded both my ego and my pride.

I couldn't let that happen again.

No, never again.

CHAPTER ELEVEN

I was just finishing up my grading of that day's student papers — avoiding the *Starbucks* by Villa Florentine — when Officer Dalton dropped by my classroom.

"Miss Salazar?"

I looked up. My memory served me well. He was a cutie. No, not cute, *gorgeous*. Tall — at least six-foot-four — built like an Adonis, with long, muscular legs and broad shoulders. He could've been a male model for *Esquire* or modeled briefs for *Calvin Klein*. Although his hairline was receding — heck, whose hairline after thirty wasn't? — his light brown curls were thick and cropped a little short like a fluffy skullcap. He had an incandescent smile, accented by dimples an inch deep on both cheeks. His face was so boyishly cute, you wanted to step up and pinch his cheeks. Of course, if you did, you'd end up catapulting over his head from some martial-arts flip.

His forty-five automatic sidearm was intimidating, I'll have to admit, but not as intimidating as the rest of him. He exuded 50,000-watt sex appeal in his light gray uniform.

"Officer Dalton, come in. I'm done here."

"So am I, just clocked off-duty. Wanta grab some coffee . . .while you write out that statement?"

"Sure," I said, a little taken aback. Was this going to be my first date with a real, live cop? Well, well, there was a first for everything — and I knew just the place. "Do you like *Starbucks*?"

"Who doesn't?"

I smiled with malicious intent.

Walking into my favorite after-school hangout—which I was determined not to lose—with a handsome, uniformed cop was so sweet, you have no idea. Behind the espresso machine, Manny didn't dare blurt out his usual taunting banter.

"Call me Tyler." My new best buddy-cop smiled. His cheeks were dimpled.

I was so grateful that he'd bought my lame story about not recognizing Rick Ramos in his SUV that day, I could've kissed him on the spot. Instead, I signed his revised police report and agreed to have dinner with him the following Friday evening.

As we left *Starbucks*, I shot my teasing barista a smug, little grin. There was something sublimely satisfying about having your own gorgeous, well-armed, kick-ass escort.

By Wednesday, *el Día de Los Muertos*, I'd made two other tough phone calls. One was to Mariana, apologizing for missing her previous Saturday-night Oktoberfest party and hoping everyone had fun. I'd called her before to explain about Pop's surgery and how I had to get home. Mariana sounded pleased that the party had gone so well as she threw in a mention of Rick Ramos. He'd shown up with an attractive blonde woman, ate some bratwurst and sauerkraut, and then she lost track of him.

Well, of course, he did. Show up with an attractive blonde. What was I thinking? That he was spending his Saturday nights pining and moping over me? Had I actually believed what Jesús told me, told the family—that Rick said he still loved me? Either my ding-a-ling brother-in-law misunderstood him, or Jesús was playing a practical joke on me by rattling my chains.

Some joke! I felt like I'd been hit with the flat end of a shovel. It was all I could do to keep my voice normal before ringing off with Mariana. Then I'd spent the next hour jogging around the Rose Garden neighborhood near my aunt's house.

In the dark, I ran so none of the neighbors around her house would see this crazy girl jogging past, crying and wiping her face with a tissue.

Still, I knew I had to square any debt I may've owed Rick Ramos for his generosity with my family. He'd forgotten to take, that Saturday night of Lisa's and my pizza-and-movie night, the bag of remedial books and games I'd collected for his daughter. So I called him and reminded him to once again come by and pick it up.

By then, I'd convinced myself that Rick and I could not be friends but cordial acquaintances. Now that I had Tyler Dalton, my gorgeous cop to swoon over, one man at a time was all I could keep track of, anyway.

Tyler was my Rick antidote. No more obsessing over Rick's hard-on or *the hug* or what Rick told or didn't tell Jesús. Ha, like I could believe Jesús, the bozo, the black sheep of the family! Connie had to keep him off her computer, for Jesús was so dumb, he'd fall for every Nigerian life-insurance scam that cropped up.

I'd decided to beef up my romantic life — who better to do this with than beefcake Officer Dalton? So I'd stop thinking and behaving like the sixty-year-old prude Pet thought I dressed like. How jacked was that! I think her observation scared me more than I wanted to admit. I'd even begun dressing a little more age-appropriate. However, wearing miniskirts to school and showing my fanny to my sixth-graders was still out of the question.

Back to Rick Ramos. How could I continue to hate him with a passion? How could I hate someone who'd given Frank and his tile business such a lucrative contract? Who'd given wacko Jesús steady, law-abiding work, so my sister and her twin daughters wouldn't starve? Who, on top of everything else, had saved the Salazar siblings from financial hardship and kept my parents' home from being sold?

Simple. I couldn't.

Still, I wasn't about to nominate Rick Ramos for sainthood. I had moved his name from the MTA list to the FO — Friends Only.

I didn't know how I felt about him, except that hate had morphed somehow into grudging respect and gratitude. If there was more to it than that, my stubborn mind had closed itself to any other possibility. I was willing to advise him about his daughter's learning problems and what I could do and still maintain my emotional distance. I was sure of it. No one was going to make a fool out of me a second time!

Meanwhile, all week I was fretting about my cousin, Teresa, and her son. What had happened to them? Were they safe somewhere or dead in some desert ditch?

When I hadn't heard from her — no email or phone call — I decided to do a People Search one day after school. Sitting at my laptop PC, I Googled several People Search sites — SA, the UK, Japan. Strangely enough, there were three for Mexico! I logged in and typed in her full name — Teresa Dolores Martínez Vargas. A half-minute later, a university directory showed up. She was listed as an alumnus of the University of Guadalajara. A local campus address was given. That was all. There was no email address or home address. No phone number.

It was as if she'd disappeared after graduating from the university. As far as I knew, she probably married then and moved back to the hacienda south of Ciudad Juárez.

I called Lisa and told her what I'd done. "Most likely, her father made sure she couldn't be traced back to the hacienda, the cartel's headquarters. If Teresa had old school chums or roommates from college, she'd have to contact them. Dina, you don't know who her university friends were, where they live, if she's in touch with them."

"Where else can I go?" I asked, stumped by the Internet

dead-end I'd arrived at.

"Let me think," she murmured. Silence ensued for a few seconds as Lisa's mental wheels sped up. "You said she'd go into Ciudad Juárez to meet secretly with her cousin, Jaime. Your cousin, Jaime. She probably shopped in some upscale stores, being the daughter of a very wealthy man. If you could get a directory of Ciudad Juárez"—Lisa pronounced it see-you-dad—"You could call some of the best shops and ask them if they've seen Teresa Vargas. I'd think the local people around there would know she was the big drug lord's daughter and would treat her like royalty."

"But they wouldn't tell me—some stranger with an American accent who calls out of nowhere. Why would they trust me, even if I happen to get a hold of a friend of hers? Maybe the Cartel is bugging *their* phones, expecting Teresa to call one of her friends in the city."

"Hmm, hadn't thought of that. If the cartel is that sophisticated, and Uncle Leo says they are, it probably wouldn't be a good idea to call down there. They could trace the call back to *you*."

That comment gave me pause.

"Do you think the cartel—or Pedro Vargas, the new honcho—even knows about us? Teresa's American family?"

"Don't know. Probably not, or why else would she sneak and meet Jaime on the sly? Most likely, Teresa didn't want her father or husband to know that she was in touch with your grandmother's sister in Chihuahua or her family. She sure wouldn't want them to know she'd been in touch with her grandmother in the States. Not if she's been planning to leave for a while."

What Lisa said made sense to me, and I said so.

"Yeah. My gut feeling tells me she's smart, so she wouldn't have wanted her father and her husband to find out about us. Or Carlota and Jaime. I think she's been extra careful. Maybe she's been planning her escape for quite some time. Or maybe she began after her parents were killed."

"Dina, hate to tell you this, but you're going to have to wait 'til she contacts you."

I had to agree. Trying to find her was like looking for a needle in a haystack, with machine-gun toting thugs watching you. Besides, how many millions of people were there in Mexico? Close to 102 million? One database carried 37 million names in Mexico. Vargas and Martínez were like Smith and Jones. There could be tens of thousands of Teresa Vargases or Teresa Martínezes.

Then I remembered what Grandma Gómez had told me the previous weekend. And the map of Mexico we'd looked at on Sunday.

"Grandma got a telegram from Teresa. She was on her way to Chihuahua, the city. Then on to Monterrey. She's going south. Know what I think, Lisa? I think she's got friends in Monterrey and Teresa wants to get out of Juárez Cartel territory as fast as she can. Monterrey's in the state of Nuevo León, one of the biggest cities in that state. That's south of the state of Chihuahua. Maybe she plans to get to Mexico City and fly out. Or get to one of the coastal towns along the Sea of Cortez. Then she could get to San Diego more easily. Pay a coyote to get her and her son across the border."

"Yep." Lisa nodded and clacked one long, black-polished nail on one of her front incisors. "She might be that desperate."

I just couldn't see Teresa, a woman accustomed to great wealth, joining a parade of poor illegals dashing through holes in chain-link fences. "No, she's gotten in touch with us for a reason. She's not stupid and wouldn't take such a risk of getting caught at the border."

I sighed heavily. Damn, I wished she would email me. Although Grandma didn't know an email from an emu, she had somehow passed on my email address to Carlota and Jaime in one of her correspondences to Chihuahua. Or so she told me last Sunday. Still, I was completely stymied as to what to do next. "Guess I just have to wait and see."

"Sorry, Dina. Wish I had more ideas. Keep me abreast of Teresa's flight to freedom, okay?"

Flight to freedom. Yes, that's exactly what it was for her and her son. If they weren't already found. If she wasn't already dead.

When Rick showed up on Wednesday, I was in the middle of preparing *osso buco,* a veal shank casserole that Flora and I would consume over the next few days. I thought Steve, her . . .ahem, personal trainer, would be joining us that night for dinner before their session. Instead, Porter Hilborn, her dancing partner and usual Tuesday/Thursday date, had appeared unexpectedly.

Flora had given me no advance warning, and so I was more than a little surprised by the change in her social calendar. She admonished me silently to keep quiet by her special, wide-eyed look, so I prudently said nothing. I pretended that nothing was out of the ordinary.

What an understatement! The evening turned out to be anything but ordinary.

"Smells good, Dina," Porter commented," but sorry, we won't be joining you. We have reservations at *Chez Louie's.*" His deep bass voice seemed incongruous for such a slim man.

Frankly, I didn't know what to think about Porter. He was closer in age to Flora, silver-haired and trim of physique though I never saw him in anything other than an expensive suit. He had a pleasant enough face though I wouldn't call him handsome or even good-looking. I knew he owned lots of property in Silicon Valley — which, of course, meant he was a multimillionaire — and used to be an engineer at HP. We'd had little verbal contact over the months that Flora had been seeing him because Porter always seemed to whisk her away.

They'd met, actually, at the *Starlight Ballroom Dance Studio* and had been regular dance partners from the very beginning. According to Flora, on one of those rare occasions when she spoke of him, they had clicked from the very first dance together. In my usual skeptical way, I wondered if they would've clicked so well together had he been a poor carpenter or sales clerk.

Lately, I'd become aware that Flora was regularly packing her cosmetics and wardrobe bags with her on Thursdays. The last two Thursday evenings, she'd slept over at Porter's house in Los Altos, a posh town in the valley's western foothills. From what she described, his grand, eight-thousand-square-foot stucco and stone manor made her place look like an abject gardener's cottage. Something was up, I suspected, since Steve's night this week had been pre-empted all of a sudden. I wondered how Steve was taking his sudden demotion.

"We're going to a *milonga* tonight," Flora excitedly gushed. She was dressed to kill in a flouncy, crimson-red cocktail dress with matching spike heels and clutch-purse. I estimated the cost of her outfit was the equivalent of one month's paycheck. *My* paycheck, not hers.

The men had whistled appreciatively, their goblets of wine momentarily forgotten. I glanced at Rick, who'd arrived about the same time as Porter. His casual attire, a dark green crewneck sweater and light-gray cargo pants, made me feel a little more comfortable, at least. I was in black sweatpants, a black V-necked tee, and white cross-training sneakers. Devoid of makeup and my unruly side locks pulled back and fastened with large, plastic barrettes, I felt like the dowdy stepsister to Flora's glam belle-of-the-ball.

Hell, I didn't have to go to Mass with Grandma Gómez. I already was a sixty-year-old prude! Having my pushing-fifty aunt in the room, all dolled up and the focus of male attention, made me want to run to the nearest spa for a complete make-over, followed by a shopping binge at Nordstrom. Damn, wish I'd at least dabbed on a smidgen of *Glow* by JLo.

"A *milonga*? What's that?" Rick asked, gazing steadily at Flora and Porter. At least he wasn't ogling my aunt, but he'd barely looked my way since Flora had welcomed him in through the front door.

"It's a special dance for tango enthusiasts," Flora explained, fingering her fake crystal-and-pearl chandelier earrings. Or maybe they were real diamonds and pearls—in any case, I hadn't seen them before. Hmm, I wondered if they were a gift from Porter.

Porter's gaze was glued to her every move. Clearly, he was besotted with my beautiful, brilliant aunt—maybe he'd fallen in love with her. But did she reciprocate his feelings? Or were gifts of bling enough to entice Flora away from her hunky trainer?

If Steve was permanently out of the picture, she probably saw in Porter somewhat of a future. Was my nudging senior-status aunt finally ready for a mature relationship? Had she let down her guard finally and fallen in love? I wanted to believe it.

"There's a live tango band from Argentina," Porter broke in, "called Bocha Lopez, playing at the ballroom tonight. They feature a bandoneon and guitarist from Buenos Aires. Everyone dances strictly Argentine tango. All night. It's a blast."

Oh well, that explained everything. Rick and I exchanged puzzled looks. What the heck was a bandoneon?

"The Argentine tango," Porter continued, "is very sensual and seductive"—he and Flora swapped heated looks—"but the dance is also interpretive and improvisational. The man talks with his body and gets feedback from the woman's body. The moves may change because of that feedback. He might move in closer or move faster or slower. He might take his time for certain steps, building up to a dip. Much like sex."

Gulp. I took another swig of pinot noir. Rick did, too, his gaze averted, appearing to study Porter's necktie.

I may sometimes dress like a dowdy spinster, but at least no one can say I can't pick the right wine for the dishes I make. However, tonight in Flora's kitchen, I could see no one was giving a rat's ass what kind of wine they were drinking. All four of us grew silent as we digested Porter's description of the tango and sex, each with our own different mental images, to be sure.

"Well, we must be off," Porter downed his wine and set his stemmed glass on the bar table, where Rick was sitting on one of the stools. "Flora, do you have all your things?"

"Yes, they're in the living room." She smiled at Porter and caressed his well-padded shoulder. There was no hint of the sexy, schoolgirl silliness she'd often demonstrated with Steve. Again, I wondered if this relationship had depth and meaning. Here I thought she'd sworn off love forever. Maybe not. Then I began to wonder how long it'd be before I had to start looking for new quarters. Damn!

Wait a minute. Didn't Porter have a mansion? Why couldn't Flora move in with him?

They were off in a flurry of goodnights and a swish of silk and chiffon. Leaving me to face Rick Ramos alone. Shit!

"You seem to have everything under control, so I won't offer to help and muck things up." He grinned, stared at me for a long moment, then looked away hastily as he sipped more wine.

Maybe it was the wine and the kitchen heat — the oven was on at 375 degrees and waiting for the casserole — but I felt hot and flushed. I kept fanning my face with a potholder. Hurriedly, I added broth and some wine to the marinara sauce and poured the entire fragrant sauce over the browned veal shank, new potatoes, and broccoli flowerets.

"Are you hungry?" I asked, noticing his deep whiff of the dish's pungent aromas as I passed by to put it into the oven.

"Yeah. Haven't eaten since lunch." His gaze had trailed the casserole to the oven like a ravenous wolf. "It's been that kind of a day. I've been running around all day from job site to job site. Grabbed lunch on the run — can't even remember what I ate. Maybe I didn't. It's been that kind of a day. Picked up Angelina at six. She'd already eaten at my mother's, and you said to come over by seven."

"Where is she now?"

"The high school girl upstairs comes down to babysit. Don't know what I'd do without her."

"Well, unfortunately, the *osso buco* takes two hours to cook." He looked disappointed. "I know, have some spinach dip and veggies. I live on this stuff when I'm not in the mood to cook."

I put out a tray loaded with baby carrots, cucumber rounds, uncooked zucchini sticks, and cherry tomatoes. The dip was fresh, and I urged him to dig in. Then I poured him and myself more wine, trying not to stare at him. What did he think tonight was all about? Dinner and sex? Hell no!

If I was going to get through this nerve-racking evening, I figured it wouldn't hurt to be half-zonked. Jesús's mindless remark about Rick's hard-on kept resurfacing in my mind, distracting me. I tried to think of Tyler and our upcoming date on Friday night.

"I remember all the great home-cooked meals I had at your apartment at State. You were a good cook even then," Rick said in his husky baritone.

"Yeah, well, cooking skills aren't everything," I remarked dryly. "Look at Flora. She's got men lined up, and the only thing she cooks are accounting books — uh, I don't mean it that way. Not illegal stuff, I mean."

Flustered, I stopped talking and sipped more wine. On top

of being dressed like a slob, I was now blathering like an idiot.

"I know what you mean, Dina." He chuckled. "You need a special night out—a romantic dinner and dancing. You could dress up in a killer dress, the kind that looks like a slip, and load up on the mascara and lipstick. Fix your hair. The kind of things you chicks like to do. You interested? Or are you still in thick with that pompous ass, Hugh Goss?"

Caught off-guard, I just stood there, speechless. How did Rick know that romance was exactly what I needed? Even before I'd realized that fact, myself? Damn, not only was he a successful contractor, he was psychic!

"Did I tell you, I met him?" he asked, not waiting for my reply to his date offer. He *was* asking me out, wasn't he? Or I might've misunderstood. Maybe he was asking if I was interested in a romantic night out—but not with him.

Certainly not with him! *Dios*! What was I thinking?

"Met who?" Boy, was I flummoxed and flustered!

"That Goss guy. He spoke at the Small Businessmen's Action Committee. I'm the Committee's vice-chair. I invited him to speak to us—wanted to check him out."

Hmmph. I reminded myself, never underestimate a Ramos.

"And you thought him a pompous ass?"

"Yeah, keep wondering what you see in him. The badass in me wouldn't mind stealing you away from that *gabacho*."

Now that got a smile out of me. I loved the Spanish word *gabacho*.

"Well, I don't see much in him . . .anymore. We split up."

"Why?" I could see Rick was trying to suppress a smile.

"Mutual disenchantment."

Rick erupted into deep, sonorous laughter. The dimple in his chin smoothed out, and he showed a row of white, straight teeth. Oh my, was he handsome! His dark brown hair glistened in the kitchen light. His broad shoulders were thrown back, his long legs spread apart. He looked so healthy. So sexy.

"Dina, you make me laugh," he gasped between gulps of air. "Only you would say something like that. I really miss that about you . . .besides other things. I miss the fun we used to have."

"Yeah, like running out of gas in Tahoe in the middle of a snowstorm."

"But do you remember what we did in the car waiting for the storm to pass?"

He laughed again and I, embarrassed as I was by the memory, joined him. Rick had always had an infectious laugh. Not to mention a fine set of teeth. I caught myself staring at the slight cleft in his chin, his smooth-shaven face, and thick shock of dark brown waves. He appeared to have just gotten a haircut. My gaze wandered to his neck. No hickeys there. I wondered what that meant. Didn't the beautiful blonde know what she'd missed?

"Or the time we got locked out of my car at the gas station, and it was raining," he contributed, "and we had to wait for the roadside assistance to show up. I think we found a staffer's cleaning closet that time."

"Yeah, you and me and cars always got into trouble."

"Oh, I don't know," he said, his black eyes sparkling mischievously, "we had some pretty good times in my father's *Bel Air*."

I knew exactly what he was talking about, all the times we steamed up the windows making out, the first time I lost my virginity, all the subsequent lovemaking. We'd mastered the fine art of contortionism in that *Bel Air*'s back seat. Straddling Rick's naked lap had been my favorite kind of cheap date. We were like horny little rabbits.

I fanned my face. Those were *not* the kind of memories to have with him standing in front of me.

"We were young, stupid, and horny." I looked away, grabbed a cracker and dug into the spinach dip, sipped some wine. Rick was silent as he did the same. I latched onto a more neutral topic. "Does your father still own that *Fifty-seven Chevy*?"

"Oh yeah, he'd get rid of me before he'd get rid of that car. For *Papá*, it symbolizes the American Dream."

I noticed his face was a little flushed. He stood and took a couple of steps closer to me, a certain look in his eyes. Maybe the memories were spiking his internal temperature as well.

I straightened in sudden alarm. "Eat up, Rick. I'll get you those workbooks for your daughter."

Observing that he'd consumed half of the crackers, all of the cherry tomatoes, and half the spinach dip, I offered to make him a ham and swiss-cheese sandwich, to which he gladly nodded. While I did this, I kept the conversation going. Heck, as long as we kept talking and eating, there was scant chance for us getting naked together and ruining what little, tenuous friendship we were trying to resurrect.

Swallowing a whole lotta pride, I took a deep breath.

"I wanted to thank you for everything you've done for my family. Giving Frank's and Pop's company that job—you could've hired any number of tile companies in San Jose. It was a big boost for them. And helping Jesús, of course, went far beyond the call of duty. That should earn you the Humanitarian Award of the Year. But the fifty-thousand dollars, Rick—how can my parents ever repay you? Or any of us ever repay you?"

He shrugged and smiled slyly. "I'll think of a way," he quipped. I was standing next to him, handing him a plate with the sandwich cut in half. He'd settled down again on the pub chair and glanced down at the plate, then up at me. With one smooth turn of the chair, he opened wide his legs and caught my hips in a vise.

Ohhh, this wasn't good.

Chapter Twelve

"We used to have a lot of fun, you and me," Rick said huskily, his dark eyes smoldering under a half-lidded stare. His suggestive grin evoked another hot, little memory that sprang to my mind, unbidden. "It's not too late to have some more."

Wow! This was exactly what I was longing for to escape my prudish tendencies — a handsome man who turned me on. We could have fun, I knew that. With Rick Ramos, I'd be swept up in a tornado of lusty pleasures and fulfilled desires.

His big hands, smooth now, not callused as they used to be when he was a roofing laborer, caressed my shoulders, then slid down my arms to my wrists. He easily encircled my wrists but did not squeeze them. The inside of his legs, clothed in chinos, continued to apply steady pressure. Involuntarily, my gaze flicked down to his crotch. Oh yes, I recalled like it was yesterday the power of Rick Ramos's one-eyed snake.

I made the mistake of hesitating. He was ducking his head, leaning forward to kiss me. My pulse was racing, and I found myself leaning into him. Then — drat it — alarms like my school's fire drill bells began shrieking in my head. I shook myself out of my sensual fog.

"I'm serious," I protested weakly. I reluctantly squeezed myself out of that Ramos leg-sandwich. Too close to the family jewels there, I figured. Too close to toxic temptation.

"I am, too," he said, his dark-eyed gaze wavering over my breasts. "We'd do it better this time. I wouldn't make any dumbass mistakes and lose your trust, Dina. It could be just as good as it used to be. Even better. I won't hurt you again. I promise."

I backed up into the kitchen, put a couple of yards distance between us, and started talking a mile a minute.

"Uh, would you like a glass of milk to go with your sandwich? Better than wine. I don't have any beer. Flora and I don't drink it."

"Yes, sure." His facial expression told me everything, like he'd been slapped in the face. Shock, dismay, hurt, then a cover of indifference.

I got the gallon of cold milk from the fridge and poured him a glass. By now, the wine had given me a mild buzz. I should have switched to milk, myself, but I didn't, for some perverse reason. However, my hostess formality and courtesy were enough to cool the air and give us both time to compose ourselves.

Rick took a swallow of milk, then cleared his throat.

"Jesús said your father's angioplasty went well. On behalf of Ramos Roofing and Construction, I sent a bouquet of flowers to the hospital. When did he go home?"

"A week ago. And thanks for the flowers. My father appreciated them." It was my turn to clear throats. "*Mamá* wants us all to stay away for a couple of weeks, give him total peace and quiet so he can recover from a cold he caught right after the surgery. The Salazar uncles and aunts are visiting this weekend and will probably wear him out, so he doesn't need us on top of it."

Boy, was my chest warm! I felt hot and buzzy and fuzzy, which was why I was giving my mouth full throttle while my mind cowered in fear. I then launched into a summary of the most enjoyable units I'd taught since school started—the ancient Greeks and Egyptians, their history, culture, and architecture. By the end of that curriculum summary, my mind had relaxed in neutral.

He laughed when I told him my students were mummifying chicken legs with a process I invented that replicated the ancient Egyptian priests' method.

"Salt and baking soda?" He was shaking his head in wonder.

"Then the kids wrap up their chicken legs in cloth, check the drying process once a week, and measure the loss of tissue mass. They record their data in their science notebooks."

"Your class sounds like fun, Dina." He was smiling that crooked grin of his that always spelled trouble.

Trouble for me, that is.

"Did you ever go back and get your degree?" I asked finally.

"No, never did. I was too busy building the business and then moving to San Jose. I got my general contractor's license and started expanding into new residential construction."

"And your sister, María Theresa?"

"She's a sophomore in high school. Helps with Angelina after school. She's doing well. Like you, she loves to read, thanks to the tutoring you gave her that summer. She's good at sports. Right now, she's on the tennis team, so she just helps out at night if I have a meeting and my mother's too tired."

"Wonder if she'd like golf. That's my favorite sport at the moment. It's consumed me for two years." I went on to tell him about my conquering the pond I'd dubbed Lake Texas. He laughed when I told him about the twenty balls I'd sunk into that pond, trying to prove myself.

"I believe it. You haven't changed, Dina. You're still the stubbornest woman I've ever known." I must admit his eyes twinkled as he said it.

He'd finished the sandwich, and so we were moving to the dining room. Impulsively, he tugged gently on a length of side hair that had come loose from the barrette. "Maybe I'll take up golf. I need a relaxing kind of exercise on the weekends, if you can call it a weekend. Sunday's my only full day off."

My heart and stomach were doing so many flips, I took a long draw from my glass of wine. The buzz in my head grew louder, like a hundred crazed bumblebees.

"You'd like golf. Rick, maybe we could go to a driving range some Sunday and practice hitting balls. I haven't played in several weeks. Ever since . . ." I trailed off, not wanting to reveal the circumstances of my breakup with Hugh Goss.

"Sure, I'd like that. You can help me pick out some clubs, all the gear I need. If that's okay with you."

I nodded, smiling, leading him over to the dining table.

Wait a freakin' minute! My mind was yelling at me. Which I was ignoring successfully. Hey, everyone needs a golfing buddy — what was the harm in that? No way could Rick Ramos seduce me on a golf course. And if he tried, I'd have my Big Bertha driver to hit him with.

"So, are you interested?" he asked.

"In-in what?" Somehow, I'd lost a thread that he'd managed to pick up. I wanted to add, *wait a minute. What about your attractive blonde girlfriend?* How had I forgotten *her*?

"In a date, y'know, dinner and dancing? The whole enchilada? You can do a Flora, and I'll put on a suit. We can go to *Habanero's* and salsa all night — well, half the night, anyway. The other half, maybe we can find something else to do . . ."

Did Rick the slick Ramos think I'd fall into his lap, clothed or unclothed, just because he gave my parents fifty-thousand smackers? Just because he was showing an interest in playing golf with me. Well . . .

"Uh, here it is." I pointed to the stack of remedial workbooks on the dining table. "I have everything set up. Phew, it's hot in here." I pulled on the collar of my tee and puffed a little.

Once in the cooler air of the dining room, my head began to clear. And sanity returned. Just in time, too, for I was sorely tempted to accept his invitation and all that it implied.

He downed the rest of his milk and set the glass on the table. I could feel him close behind me, then he rubbed the front of his chinos against my rump.

"What're you afraid of, Dina?" My heart raced, and I felt dizzy. For a second, I wanted to just surrender to the heat that threatened to overcome me. Surrender to desire, just like you read about in books. But I jumped away like he'd scorched me.

"You," I quipped. And truthfully. "You're a heartbreaker, Ricky Ramos. You've got a blonde girlfriend you took to Mariana's party, and now you're asking me out? Sorry, I'm not going there again, ever again. So forget it."

"Blonde girlfriend? Mariana's party? Y'mean, Jody? She's my neighbor. Her teenage daughter babysits for me. I took her to Mariana's party but not as a date. Just so she could meet some of the neighbors. She's new to the condo complex, so I was hoping you'd be there, but then I remembered your father's surgery, and you were due for a visit to Salinas."

"Oh." My heart leaped for joy despite myself and my cynical attempts to dampen all things joyful. "Well, I-I didn't know. Mariana said—never mind. Look, Rick, so long as we just stay friends, we can play golf together." I had to look away. "I've started dating someone—the cop—the one who was hassling you that day at my school."

"Great," he murmured in a surly tone, "*that* cop."

I glanced at his now peevish expression. He looked like he'd developed a sudden toothache. Oops, must've hit a sore spot there.

"I squared things with him. He's not going to bother you."

"Thanks." He scowled. "So now you've dumped the

gabacho and you're going out with the cop. Why?"

"He happens to be—" Drop-dead gorgeous, I thought. No other reason than that, except to keep you at arm's length, Rick Ramos. "Single, never been married, no children," I said instead. "You and I have too much history, I'm afraid. Bad history."

I wondered how he was going to take that charge. He had his hands in his pockets and was standing still, rocking a little on the balls of his feet. Six years ago, Ricky Ramos would've pounded or kicked something. The thirty-year-old Rick just stood there, looking unhappy but staying cool, calm, and collected. I was impressed.

But because he was no longer teasing and joking, it was time to switch modes here. Turn on the professional and get down to business. I clasped my trembling hands together and took a deep breath. Looking away from his somber face helped.

"Take a seat, Rick. I'll walk you through all this stuff."

Under the crystal chandelier, our end of Flora's dining table was covered with workbooks, manipulative games of assorted sizes, and children's books appropriate for Angelina's age group. I'd taken them out of the grocery bag and spread them about. Overwhelmed, Rick dropped into a chair and blanched.

"Don't panic. I'll explain what all this is for. This textbook, *Exceptional Children*, was required reading for elementary credential candidates. I've tagged the chapters and pages you should read. You don't have to read the entire book. There's a whole section on prenatal exposure to cocaine and other drugs—"

"And alcohol," he added ruefully. He deeply inhaled as if staving off deep emotion. "Anita tried everything when she was pregnant. Still is, from what I hear. She's an addict, though what her current drug of choice is, I couldn't say.

She's serving time in *Coachilla Women's Correctional Facility,* but I hear the inmates still get the dope smuggled in."

"My God, what for?" I could guess, however.

"Drug possession, peddling, prostitution. Dina, I tried to get her into rehab for over two years, but she wouldn't do it. Not even for Angelina's sake. After I left, she went off the deep end, hooked up with some dudes, some pimps."

Our gazes locked, and I could see the pain in his. The man had suffered, maybe more than I had. Something inside me was wrenched with compassion.

"There's a section on fetal alcohol syndrome," I said, returning my attention to the book I was holding. "The good news, Rick, is that the latest research indicates if the symptoms are mild enough and IEI — intensive early intervention — occurs, the effects can be reversible. A child can catch up to their peers. The learning disability need not be permanent or debilitating."

I wanted to stay focused on Angelina's problems, not hear about his doomed marriage to Anita Hernández. I honestly didn't think I could handle it.

The look on his face showed me that I had his rapt attention. He even began to tear up, which made me tear up. Oh, damn! So much for the professional in me. I wasn't expecting to feel his pain nor the hope he felt concerning his daughter. I put aside my wine and struggled to focus.

"Has Angelina been tested by her kindergarten teacher or the Special Ed teacher at her school?"

"Yeah, they gave her a test" — he mentioned the name — "and she failed it."

"Hmm, that particular test is not a very good screening device. Most kids fail it, especially the nonverbal ones. Is she still not talking much in English?"

Obviously upset, he could only shake his head.

"If Angelina's especially fearful and reticent, it's no

wonder she failed. There are many other tests, better ones, in Spanish, too."

"You know how we are, Dina, my sisters and brother and I are all functional in Spanish, if not bilingual. Maybe the Spanish we speak at home with my mother, maybe that's kept her back a little."

I nodded.

"If the screener was a stranger who spoke only English, perhaps Angelina felt shy and was afraid to speak."

"I think she was. The teacher said she clammed up." Rick looked away and took another deep breath. "I want a second opinion. The teacher said they might put her in a special day class for the retarded. Dina, I know she's not retarded. And her hearing has been tested. It's perfect."

His elbows braced on the table, he let his forehead sink to his raised, folded hands. Slowly, he moved his head from side to side. "*Chingado*, Dina, help me."

"I will," I assured him. Rick looked stricken.

"I should've taken Angelina when I left Anita. She was almost two years old! God knows what she must've gone through in the six months she was alone with Anita and her string of addict-boyfriends. When I was still living in that house, my family and I offered some protection for her. After I left—I couldn't take it anymore, Dina—things went from bad to worse. I blame myself for Angelina's condition, whatever it may be."

I sat quietly, wishing I could comfort and console him but not knowing how. All I could do was touch his arm and clasp his hand. Our fingers intertwined, and he looked up. A weary, unhappy father returned my gaze. Gone was the brash, cocky teenaged Rick that I'd first fallen in love with during my freshman year in college. I was now looking at a grown man with a weighty problem.

"I can have her tested by a school psychologist if you'd like.

The woman in my district freelances on the side. I'll arrange it. The least I can do for all that you've done for my family."

That seemed to offend him. "You don't owe me a thing, Dina."

"I know. As a return favor for a friend, then."

I gazed into his deep brown eyes, into the very soul of Rick Ramos. A distraught father, a kind, decent man whose very being I'd adored for nearly ten years. Even when I was hating him for hurting me, I was loving who he was, the essence of him.

If that made any sense. It certainly did to me.

And it scared me to death.

"Rick, there's another way to do this. A better way to get her tested again. I want you to give this list of tests to Angelina's teacher. They are three of the best assessment devices for kindergarteners. They measure a child's readiness for academic learning, including pre-reading and pre-math skills in addition to socio-emotional development, gross- and fine-motor skills, and general cognitive development. Insist on two of these three tests, at the minimum. That is your right as a parent. Angelina should not be placed in special day classes until at least two more assessment tests are given. Got that? You insist on it. Don't take no for an answer. If you need me to back you up, just let me know."

Thirty minutes later, I'd reviewed and summarized all the other materials on the table, including explaining how to use the manipulatives to develop pre-math and motor skills. When he read the children's books to his daughter, Rick or his mother or sister was to follow up each page of graphics and narrative with a progression of questions, beginning with *who, what, where, when, how, and why.*

This would stimulate her innate cognitive abilities in a non-threatening context. The little girl could answer in Spanish or English and was not to be criticized or prompted to use only one language. Whatever made her comfortable and secure.

The workbooks consisted of games to help develop reasoning and verbal skills. He didn't have to use all of the materials, just the ones he felt comfortable with. Maybe thirty minutes a day for the rest of the school year would catch her up to her peers. It was a start, anyway.

Satisfied that he understood what had to be done on a near-daily basis, I packed up all the supplies in that large, sturdy shopping bag and stood up.

"I'll make an appointment to see her teacher tomorrow," Rick said stoutly, looking much more buoyant and hopeful. He stood, also, and picked up the bag of materials.

"Have you heard from your cousin in Mexico?"

I shook my head. "Not a word. She sent a telegram to my grandmother. Teresa's on the run with her young son. She's going south to Monterrey. That's the last we heard from her."

Rick stood a moment, scooting in the dining chair with his hip. He chewed on his bottom lip, a nervous habit that drew my attention again to his sensuous mouth.

"A couple of my framers are from the town of El Porvenir. It's not too far from Ciudad Juárez. They're brothers who left home when they were young, looking for work. They got roped into working as *picaderos* — peddlers of dope in the cartel's shooting galleries. They saw and heard a lot, finally risked their necks and got away and sneaked across the border. They learned firsthand about the Juárez Cartel."

He had my attention. "Like what?"

"This Pedro Vargas, your cousin's husband. He used to work as a foreign-exchange manager for the Bank of Mexico. He quit to go work for the cartel. Roberto Martínez recruited him, then married him off to his daughter. This Vargas was groomed to take Martínez's place."

He paused and stuffed the bag under his arm. The look on his face was troubled as though there was more he knew but was reluctant to share.

"Anything else these brothers found out about this Vargas?" I asked, a sinking feeling filling my chest.

"Yeah, but it's not good, Dina."

I sighed. "Just tell me."

Rick took a deep breath. "The syndicate was beginning to expand their operations into child pornography and human trafficking."

"Human traffic—" I broke off, the realization of what he was telling me hitting me full force finally. "Shit. Maybe that's why Teresa finally had enough. Drugs are one thing but the exploitation of children and—" I didn't even want to verbalize it. I'd seen enough television documentaries about the slave trade and child porn to have an idea what kinds of larcenous monsters would do such things.

"These brothers were sickened by what they saw, got out of there as fast as they could. Risked their lives. Dina, this Vargas is one evil creep."

I nodded, patting his arm.

In kind of a daze, I went back to the kitchen to pack a plastic container filled with the now fully cooked osso buco, potatoes, and broccoli. He watched me in solemn silence. Then we started moving toward the front door.

The mood of the evening had sufficiently changed so that I wasn't nervous about walking him out the front door and to his *Explorer* at the curb. The cool night air slapped me in the face, all at once waking me up. The previous hour and a half had already sobered me enough. Reality did that to people, I guess.

I felt good about the evening. I'd helped Rick understand the kind of intervention that was necessary to help his daughter begin the first step of catching up to her five-year-old peers. As well as the importance of getting her tested again and this time, correctly. I hadn't made a *tonta* of myself by melting in his arms. And we'd made plans to meet at one of the local, short-nine golf courses on Sunday. All in all, a successful visit.

Then Rick went and ruined it. Or rather, I did. I ruined it. He turned around after stowing the shopping bag and the plastic food container on the front passenger seat. I may have been standing too close, granted, when out of the blue, he seized me.

The next thing that registered — his enveloping arms crushing me against the full length of him, all hard masculine body of him — powerful chest, rigid abdomen, sinewy thighs. His warm mouth at first sipped gently at my mouth. Then prying open my lips, his hot tongue tangoed with mine. How my hands found their way around his muscular back and then slither down to cup his nicely rounded rump — I swear I have no idea! The kiss was divine and profoundly stirring, our mutual touching even more so. There was a lot more neediness in that kiss than I'd expected from us both.

Shameless hussy that I was, the kiss ended much too soon.

"We could say good-night . . .or you could invite me back in."

His voice was deep and raspy. I knew exactly what would happen if I did. For several long moments, while his hands explored the front and back of me, and his lips trailed warm kisses along my neck and throat, my mind wrestled with my body.

And curse my very nature — my mind filled with fear and won out.

"You should go," I managed to croak, pulling back a little. I was still in his arms, though, firmly held.

"No, I shouldn't, Dina. You don't want me to go." He trailed hot kisses down my temple and around my ear. I shuddered with desire. A few more minutes, and I'd be lost.

Somehow, I found the strength to step back. Slowly, he shook his head, dazed. He and I were panting like a couple of horny teenagers. It was déjà vu time. If there'd been a *'57 Bel Air* nearby, I would've been jumping in the back seat.

"I saw your neck, Dina. No love-bites. Remember all the hickeys I used to give you. You loved it, but you had to wear turtlenecks and scarves when you went home."

Damn him! Rick was pulling out all the stops. Man, did I remember those love bites.

"You better go," I repeated weakly. There was little conviction in my voice. My steel had melted and puddled somewhere in my lower female regions.

"You're a tough one." Then he smiled like a fox. The old Rick, the slick seducer, was back. "If you're not letting me in, I bet you're not letting the other guy in, either."

"What do you mean?" Letting them in—my house, my heart, my . . .uh, vagina, for Pete's sake?

A raised forefinger pointed at me.

Mockingly.

"You keep the gates up, Dina girl. 'Cause I'm the only one who's gonna knock down that wall around your heart."

Damn good line, I thought as I watched him drive away.

Wall around my heart.

Hmmm . . .

Visions emerged. The Great Wall of China? Hadrian's Roman wall? The impregnable wall of Troy?

The cognitive dissonance was making me tremble inside. So much that I'd have to admit the wall around my heart was already beginning to crumble.

CHAPTER THIRTEEN

"How was the *milonga*?" I asked Aunt Flora when she returned home from her overnight visit in Los Altos.

Since Wednesday evening, I hadn't seen her even though she'd left me a note on Thursday explaining that she would take Friday off to drive down to Salinas to see Pop. I was appreciative that she had done this, and she'd reported that Pop was sleeping well and recuperating nicely from his cold.

"Won-der-ful," she cooed, drawing it out as if it were a foreign word. "Porter's a heavenly dancer. The tango brings out a side of him that people rarely see."

"Have you met any of his family or friends?"

Flora looked uneasy. "No, not yet . . .well, I have met his housekeeper and a few others on his household staff."

"Wow, how many servants does he have?"

"I counted at least five, including two gardeners."

I had to ask. "Flora, is he married?"

Her pretty blue eyes flicked away, giving me the answer I dreaded. "They're separated. His wife is in London with their youngest son, who's attending Cambridge."

"How long have they been separated?"

"Five months."

I did some quick mental calculations. Flora had been seeing Porter since August. Three months.

"Have they filed for divorce?"

Flora sighed as she poured herself a cup of coffee from the pot, which I'd just brewed. I was tired from the week's strain of standardized testing—not to mention Wednesday's sleepless night after Rick's visit—and felt I needed a caffeine infusion before my date with Tyler Dalton.

"Porter says it's complicated, what with all their property and other assets held in joint tenancy."

I restrained myself from rolling my eyes. "So, if he divorces his wife, he's just half as rich as he is now? That certainly won't put him in any soup kitchen lines."

Guess she didn't appreciate my sarcasm. Flora blew over her cup and returned her attention to the daily newspaper, shutting me out, clearly not wanting to pursue that line of inquiry.

"Just be careful," I counseled, not wanting to see her hurt, "he could be just using you."

I'd never dated a filthy rich man like Porter Hilborn, but I knew enough about men and their assets to suspect that Flora's tango partner was protecting his own . . .ass. A wife in London—how convenient!

"You should check him out. Maybe hire a private investigator or something. My friend, Lisa Luna, at school, is a part-time PI. She can do an online check, then dive deeper."

She continued to ignore me. All of a sudden, I felt again like the sixty-year-old prude giving advice to an ingenue. Then it hit me!

Caramba! I was already Grandma Gómez. Well, that bites, as my brother, Roberto, would say.

"How did it go with Rick the other night?" Flora asked suddenly, glancing up over the rim of her paper.

"Fine."

She gave me that CIA stare.

"Okay, it got a little emotional when he was telling me about his daughter and what she may've been exposed to, living with her cokehead mother. I felt so sorry for the little girl . . .and for Rick. Anyway, I gave him all those materials and showed him how to use them. Y'know, to help his daughter catch up with her peers."

"And that's all? He didn't come on to you?" Flora was resting the newspaper on her lap.

"A little," I said uneasily. Didn't I return a bit of his passion at the end of the evening? Wasn't I the one who copped a feel on his butt? Didn't I return his hot, wet kisses?

"Dina, watch out for him," Flora said archly, "I dropped his quarterly report off to him one evening last week. Guess who was coming out of his condo about the same time I arrived? A pretty, voluptuous blonde, that's who—a little old for him, I thought. He's taking you for a ride, Dina girl, if he's trying to take up where you two left off years ago. He knows you're a homebody, you're a good cook, you like kids. Have you ever thought he may be hunting for a readymade wife and mother so he can continue his prowling, womanizing ways? That's the attitude of a lot of Hispanic men, you know."

A pretty, voluptuous blonde. Well, it could've been innocent—that neighbor, perhaps, the mother of his babysitter. Then again, perhaps not. Was Flora right? Was Rick seeing me as just someone who could solve his daughter's problems? A homebody, someone's wife and mother? Well, what was wrong with that—if the right man came along?

Still, I had to retort Flora's assertion about Hispanic men.

"My father's Hispanic, and he's not like that. Neither is Frankie or Juan Pablo. Jesús, I don't know—he's such a nitwit. A lot of men are faithful to their wives," I reasoned.

"Probably true, but a statistic I recently read said up to eighty percent of husbands in that survey confessed to cheating on their wives. It makes it so a woman can't trust any of them. Or they can until the honeymoon's over. I've always believed that the man a woman marries is the most important choice she ever makes in her life. A lot of women spend more time choosing their hair color." Flora snapped her newspaper shut and went back to her coffee.

While my aunt held her ground, I mulled that piece of wisdom. "Well, Flora, I told Rick to forget it. We have too much bad history."

"Good girl, now that's smart thinking, Dina." She blew on her cup. "After one business meeting with Rick and his father, Rick said that he often went dancing at *Habanero's* on Saturday nights. Has he ever told you that?" I shook my head. "I thought not. He's not moping around like a lovesick hound dog, Dina. He's out there making his moves, just like most single men."

For a moment or two, I felt truly crushed. Rick had invited me on Wednesday night to go dancing at *Habanero's*, what used to be our favorite salsa bar. Now, to hear that he was a regular there, like all the men who went by themselves to pick up women, was another puncture in my romantic balloon. My schoolgirl notions of true love conquering all were dashed again. I sat there, feeling too stupid and lethargic to move. Tyler was coming to pick me up in thirty minutes, and I felt like a zombie.

Maybe I needed a hormonal transfusion as well, for I wasn't feeling at all sexy. I wasn't anticipating my date with the gorgeous cop. What was wrong with me, I wondered. I should've been hopping around with excitement. Tyler was handsome, built like an Adonis, and he apparently — though God knows why — was attracted to me. Maybe even had the hots for me.

I left Flora at the kitchen bar table and trudged to my room. Rummaging through my closet, I pulled out the shortest denim skirt I owned — it barely skimmed my thighs — how decadent was that! Then, my high boots with the three-inch heels. Next, I found just the thing in the plastic container where I kept my sweaters — a bloody-red, lambs-wool clinger with a low, scooped neckline.

The hell if I was going to be *Abuelita* before I even turned thirty! The hell if I was going to fall for Rick's lines again! Both scary thoughts motivated me to pin up my hair in a shabby-chic twist with hanging tendrils of side curls. Pet had brightened my hair color — made the red stand out — just like she'd promised. The effect complimented my complexion, a very light olive. After tossing aside my curling iron, I applied *nude* foundation, blush on my cheekbones, black eyeliner, and mascara, then the creamy, deep scarlet lipstick — which, by the way, matched my nails. Compliments of Pet, my own personal stylist.

When I stepped back to view the results, I was stunned by the trampy vamp staring back at me in the mirror. My flighty imagination sprang alive, and I began to consider possible changes in my lifestyle. I could work as a scantily clad cocktail waitress in Vegas for probably twice my teacher's salary, including tips. I could slither and shimmy as a pole stripper or lap dancer — naw, I would have to lose about ten or fifteen pounds and get silicone implants. And let sweaty, hairy strangers touch me. No, no, chica! Otherwise, Dina, the dangerous vixen, might've been tempted.

Nevertheless, my new persona, the *femme fatale*, was ready to give the gorgeous hunk, Tyler Dalton, a new version of the schoolteacher he'd somehow found appealing.

Screw homebody! Most of all, screw Rick Ramos!

Even Flora, when I appeared beside her to gauge her reaction, in the middle of sipping coffee, slurped a little on herself. Don't ask me why I was doing this — putting on this mild masquerade.

Well, I knew, of course. Who was I kidding?

Ever since Wednesday night, when Rick left me shaking in my shoes like a cowering virgin, followed by a sleepless night, I'd decided to fight off the power of his one-eyed snake.

Yeah, I was convinced I'd be putty in his hands once that happened — us getting naked together. I knew I wasn't ready for that kind of total surrender to a man, especially a man like Rick Ramos. The man I thought I knew but probably didn't.

Hearing the doorbell, I ran to open the door.

My anti-Rick drug was here!

"Hi, there," Tyler greeted me, smiling, his eyes opening wide. Pleased that he was delighted by what he saw, I glanced back at Aunt Flora. She was standing behind me, waiting to meet the new man in my life.

Struck dumb, Flora could barely unstick her tongue enough to mumble a few words. I hustled Tyler out of there before she could start exercising her considerable charms on my date.

In his SUV, a hulking, black *Lincoln Navigator* the size of an Army tank, he leaned over and kissed me.

"You look so pretty," he said, dimples cratering, "I had to do that. Hmm, taste good, too."

I almost said you look so pretty, too. He was wearing a western-style, red and blue plaid shirt, snug blue jeans, and red-leather boots. I was wearing denim and boots, too. How psyched was that? We were in sync in fashion, anyway. That we were members of the same mutual-admiration society was a definite plus.

"Do I have a surprise for you, pretty girl!"

"Really? Where're you taking me to dinner?" I was thinking, the *Outback* or *Texas B-B-Q*. We were certainly dressed for the place. But maybe he had a special, ultra-chic and expensive restaurant in mind. One where there were two tuxedo-clad waiters for every table and candlelight and real flowers graced a white-linen tablecloth.

"I want my mother to meet you. She's cooking for us."

My face fell. "Huh?" I had to think fast. I didn't want to meet anyone remotely related to this cutie-pie. All I wanted that night were fantasy and romance. "Tyler, I don't want your mother to go to any trouble for me. Let's just go to a steak place. The *Outback* has delicious ribs."

"Too late, sweetie, she's already started cooking. She's making a dish I love—liver and onions. But the first place I'm taking you is really special. It's close to where we live, so it's on the way."

"Where *we* live? You live with your mother?"

"Oh, sure. I'm her only child. Gotta take care of Mom, especially since Dad died."

"I'm sorry—"

The cell phone attached to his belt played a short tune, the first few bars of the William Tell Overture. *The Lone Ranger* theme. Cute, I thought, not yet willing to give up yet on my gorgeous hunk. A cop and *The Lone Ranger* theme.

"Hi, Mom . . .yeah, she's here with me. She's a sweet, pretty girl. You'll love her. We're going to the range first. Be there in two hours. I'll check back later . . .yeah, I'll call just before we leave the range."

"Range? There's a range in Silicon Valley?" I was thinking, cattle range, like in Texas. Of course, he meant driving range, as in golf.

He smiled. Damn those dimples! He had the straightest teeth that I'd ever seen on a man. Then again, he was an only child. His parents could've afforded the braces.

"Sweetie, the firing range. Thought you might have some fun out there. And I've got a present for you."

I was still trying to compute—firing range. What was that? A present, however, I understood.

"You don't have to get me presents, Tyler. We barely know each other—uh, where is it?"

"Under your seat. It's not loaded, so don't worry. It's Mom's old thirty-eight *Lady Smith and Wesson*. She's moved on to a forty-caliber automatic. Revolvers are good to start with. You'll like it."

"A gun? You brought me a gun?" All this talk about

calibers, automatics, and revolvers was making me nervous. "Are you serious?"

"Go on, take a look."

He was obviously pleased about his choice of gift. Well, this was a first. A gun for a gift . . .on our first date, no less. Hmmm.

Gingerly, I felt under my seat. My pulse was beginning to skitter. If the damned thing went off in my hand and shot off my fingers, I'd sue this lunatic and his crazy, gun-toting mother. Oh right, it wasn't loaded.

I opened the rectangular-shaped, blue plastic box. Inside was a greasy paper-wrapped package nestled in gray foam. I fished inside the paper wrapping and put my thumb and forefinger around the stock, or handle, of what turned out to be a black-metal, snub-nosed revolver. Holding my gun like it was a tarantula, I looked over at Tyler.

"I've never held a gun before. I wouldn't know how to shoot it, much less load it."

"That's okay, Dina. I'll show you, that's my job. Look, we'll stop at the range. You can practice with it for a while. If you like the feel of it, the way it performs—it's yours. It's worth over three-hundred bucks."

"The range? A shooting range, a gun range?" I was still trying to wrap my head around the idea. On our first date?

An expensive gift, I mused, crinkling my forehead. What did he expect in return for this gift that I didn't ask for and didn't want? And why the hell was he taking me to meet his mother?

"My mother and I," he went on, "felt you needed some protection. You and your aunt are single women living alone. You two need a gun."

"Thank you, Tyler."

I kept thinking, Shit! Shit! I don't want to shoot a gun. I want to kill my inhibitions, not some poor, innocent bystander.

I decided to go along with his date plan out of gratitude for his innovativeness and concern for my personal safety. I would draw the line at shooting live critters, though. What did I know about firing ranges? Maybe they had live bunnies scampering across a field, and you were supposed to practice shooting them.

No, I'd definitely draw the line at live critters.

He patted my bare knee, then left his right hand lightly strumming the bare skin of my lower thigh. Ten minutes ago, I would've liked his advances, but now I wasn't so sure. Under the circumstances, I chose not to protest. Wasn't it prudent to be extra nice to people who carried guns in their cars?

Twenty minutes later, in the Saratoga hills, I was standing in one of the twenty stalls of this vast, brightly lit firing range. Tyler had loaded the revolver with five bullets—it was a five-shooter, not a six-shooter like the Old West cowboys used to twirl around. He'd bought me a box of fifty *Winchester* pistol-revolver cartridges. While he loaded, I watched intently but couldn't hear a thing he said. The rubber-padded earmuffs I was wearing blocked out all speech and muffled most of the explosive bangs going off around me on both sides. It was an intriguing though nerve-racking place. Not a great place to chill out in, especially if you're wired on caffeine.

In the distance, in front of each stall, were individual alleys with designated targets, white paper mounts with black bulls-eyes. My fellow shooters were taking the whole affair very seriously. Concentration levels were high, and I noticed a couple of other women present doing target practice. Their guns were bigger than mine.

Okay, I thought, I can do this.

"Now take it. Hold it like this. Place your forefinger loosely on the trigger. If you want less of a kick when you fire, cock the hammer slowly with your thumb. Like this. Then gently squeeze the trigger."

I'd taken off one of the rubber earmuffs to hear his instructions. If I was going to survive this night's ordeal, I figured I had to learn how to shoot the damned thing without killing someone, including myself.

Tyler flipped the earmuff back over my ear, kissed me on the lips, then put the revolver in my right hand and stepped back.

For a moment, I regarded his lusty look and tasted his kiss. It was minty and warm, indicative of his behavior. On the surface, he was considerate and sweet to a fault, but my antenna was out and wobbling. I was beginning to sense that Tyler, the competent cop and possible Mama's boy, got his rocks off being the macho-guy helping the damsel-in-distress. Or got a hard-on scaring the daylights out of damsels under the guise of helping them.

Hmmm. I wasn't sure which.

Like I'd seen in movies and on television, I held out my right arm as straight as possible, steadied it with my left hand grasping my right wrist. If Sandra Bullock could do it, so could I! Then I fired. The recoil was so strong, I yelped, stumbled back, and nearly dropped the revolver.

That made Tyler move quickly to stand behind me.

I fired four more times, progressively getting accustomed to the kick of the gun after each explosive discharge. Tyler reloaded the revolving chamber and stood back. After a few minutes of observing me, he moved to the stall next to mine. I glanced over at him when he began firing his .45 automatic. There was a sharp gleam in his eye, and the smile on his face was almost orgasmic.

What was it about men and their guns? I wondered if Rick had fired a weapon or had gone hunting since our breakup. Not that I knew, anyway, probably he was too busy firing nail guns into roofs.

Then I knew. I preferred men who got their charges hitting little balls across expanses of green grass and over tree tops. To me, that was sexy.

Or men who took care of their families and put their loved ones' welfare before their own. *That* was sexy.

With a puff of exhaled air, I blew some bangs out of my eyes. I aimed again and fired. Forty-two bullets to go.

It was going to be a long night.

When I returned around midnight, Flora was still up. Porter, who refereed college basketball games as a hobby, was away on a trip somewhere in Utah, Flora'd said earlier.

I plopped beside her on the living room sofa. In a mauve, velvet bathrobe, she was watching a cable movie and looking forlorn and lonely. A bowl of half-eaten vanilla and cherry ice cream sat on her lap. My beautiful aunt, brooding and breaking her diet! She must be crazy in love . . .or worried sick about something.

I probably looked as forlorn and lonely. "Uh-oh, your face is telling me it didn't go well. Now, how could you not have a great date," she reprimanded gently, "with that Greek god? I'd enjoy just staring at him all night."

In a nutshell, I told her what we'd done. I put my blue plastic box with the *Lady Smith and Wesson* inside on top of Flora's glass and brass cocktail table.

"At least, I got a gun out of it. And I got over my fear of handling them, too. Well, somewhat."

Wasn't there always a silver lining to every black cloud?

"If Steve tries to break in," Flora suggested, "you can use it on him. He's been plaguing me with incessant phone calls — at least ten today."

"Oh, didn't you let him down easy?"

"I thought so. I had no clue he'd become so . . .so dependent on me."

Yeah, he's got monthly car payments to make. You'd be dependent on your paycheck if you were in his shoes. My face must have reflected what I was thinking.

"I know what you think, Dina, that I paid him for his...um, services. The truth is, I didn't. Steve has family money. He's a trust-fund baby. He owns that gym where he works. Fitness is his passion. But I felt the relationship wasn't going anywhere—he's such a little boy in many respects. And, I have to admit, I'm weary of trying to keep up with him. He's twelve years younger than I."

I tried to look shocked. I really did.

"Yes, that's the God's truth. I'm twelve years older than Steve! Perhaps with Porter, there's a chance for real happiness and stability. As soon as he divorces his wife, that is."

Well, blow me over. I didn't know this about Steve—that he was rich. Nor that Flora actually nursed feelings for him.

"He really loves you, then," I said. "Steve, I mean."

Flora shrugged. "I suppose. Did you have a nice dinner, anyway?" she asked me. Then she winked lasciviously. "And a nice make-out session afterward?"

"No to both. We had the ghastliest meal I've ever tried not to gag on—liver and onions, both overcooked, with hard-as-rocks rice. His mother can't cook a stick though she was nice enough, in a creepy kind of way. Like that Stephen King book, *Misery*, where the nurse pretends to help the writer. Normal on the surface, but a sadistic lunatic underneath. I got all these strange vibes from his mother. I couldn't relax with all those loaded guns around, anyway."

Flora laughed. "And afterward? Why didn't that work out?"

"Tyler wanted to, naturally, but after four hours of doing what *he* wanted to do, trying to please both him and his mother, I wasn't in a mood to do the GF thing." Flora looked baffled. "The girlfriend thing. I told him I had a sore throat and a killer headache. All I gave the gorgeous hunk was a peck on the cheek and a hug. He was lucky to get *that*."

I pointed to the box. "Well, he did give me that, after all. Now I can protect us. Wanta see it? It's not loaded. I don't think so, anyway."

Flora cast me a strange look and shook her head severely.

"Don't ever load that thing. Not unless obsessive, off-his-rocker Steve shows up in the middle of the night."

She chuckled mirthlessly, looking demoralized. I wondered if she had more feelings for Steve than what she let on. A second later, both expertly-waxed eyebrows raised.

"Rick called tonight, asking for you. Your cell phone was off, and he thought you might be here. I told him you were out — didn't say who with or anything. He said he's been trying some of those workbooks and games you gave him."

"Good. I'm glad he's helping Angelina."

Flora shrugged noncommittally. Then I recalled that I hadn't told her about Grandma Gómez's secret life in Mexico once upon a time, nor about my Mexican cousin, Teresa, now on the run from her murderous husband. It had been building inside me like lava in a volcano. She was wise, wasn't she? Maybe she'd have some advice. Pop hadn't told me not to tell anyone except to be discreet. I got up to get some ice cream, too, then came back and spilled the beans. The whole pot full.

Halfway into my story, she'd put down the bowl of ice cream and wrapped her arms around her knees, looking first astonished, then pensive.

I finished with, "So what do you think?"

Flora looked away, her expression pensive, thoughtful.

"Your *abuelita* is a tough woman to figure out. She's closed off emotionally, y'know. You're a little like her, Dina, though I know you hate to hear that. I think she felt it cast shame upon her to admit that she abandoned her baby boy and left him to be raised by her criminal husband and his second wife. I think she didn't want all of you to hold her up to scorn. Sounds like she's never forgiven herself, especially how things turned out. And now the sins of the father are visited upon the children, so to speak. Your cousin's trying to prevent her son from following the kind of life her father led. You can imagine what the boy's father is like, this Pedro Vargas."

I concurred heartily. "He's worse than *The Godfather*. He has people murdered, and he's untouchable. According to Carlota, Grandma's sister in Chihuahua, Teresa is convinced her husband had her father and mother killed. Maybe had tried once before while her father was undergoing plastic surgery. Who could live with a man like that? I bet he's sent his men out looking for Teresa and his son."

I sighed deeply, staring at the blue plastic gun case on the cocktail table. "Grandma Gómez wants me to find her before it's too late. Before Pedro Vargas and his men find her. She wants me to bring her to the US."

Flora stared at me in alarm. "What?"

Shrugging, I went on, "But I haven't gotten an email from her, or a phone call or telegram. I only know she's on her way to Monterrey or was planning to go there. I don't know where she is now or what's happened to her and her son. What can I do?"

"Maybe you need to talk to an agent in the DEA or Border Patrol, someone in Texas, someone who's dealt with the drug trade across the border. Didn't you say Pedro Vargas's Juárez Cartel has a monopoly in the state of Chihuahua? Ciudad Juárez is near the Texas border, across from El Paso, isn't it? Talk to someone in El Paso."

I frowned. In the past week, I'd consulted maps of Texas and Mexico to get my bearings, but Flora's logic didn't make sense.

"Teresa, according to that last telegram, is headed toward Monterrey. That's in a different state. Nuevo León. That's south. She should be going north to Tijuana, shouldn't she? Then I could go down to Tijuana and maybe smuggle her and her son across."

She stared at me like I'd lost my marbles.

"Just because you've fired a gun a few times doesn't mean you can turn into an armed coyote," Flora said flatly. "Besides, Dina, you'd be breaking the law, committing a felony. You'd lose your teaching credential. Do you want that?"

"Of course not!" Man, this was not going to be easy.

"Knowing that she's on her way to Monterrey—or so she said—helps you narrow down her location," Flora pointed out, "but it doesn't get you the help you really need to get her and her son out of Mexico safe and sound. You need to go to the American authorities, Dina."

"Not the Mexican authorities, the federales?"

"No, definitely not the Mexican authorities."

She was firm in her conviction, I could see. This was the general consensus of everyone I'd spoken to about this. Of course, I couldn't do this—help rescue Teresa—without support from government officials—the proper government officials.

Flora should know. She was brilliant, except about men.

"I'd start with a DEA agent, Dina, if I were you," she added. "One in Los Angeles or San Diego. Then get Teresa to come up to Tijuana."

I jumped up from the sofa, energized. Yes, that was where I had to begin, not with Mexican authorities but American ones.

"Do you think the DEA would really be interested in helping Teresa and her son?" I asked, feeling optimistic about my mission for the first time.

"The wife of Pedro Vargas, the new *jefe* of the Juárez Cartel, and all the information she could give them—you bet they'd be interested!"

Now her logic was making sense!

I hugged her and said goodnight. There was a lot to think about and to do. Tomorrow, first thing, I was going to drop by to see Lisa at her uncle's business. She could help me get up the courage to call the DEA in Texas. Maybe they wouldn't laugh at me and hang up.

Well, tonight wasn't a total failure, after all, I consoled myself. I'd picked up a new skill—handling and firing a gun—and had managed to earn a *Girl Scout* badge—and many brownie points in Heaven—for politeness and patience with creepy Mrs. Dalton and her doting son. And, thanks to Flora, I now had a handle on how to approach the Saving Teresa mission *Abuelita* had assigned me.

And maybe, just maybe, I'd get the consolation prize—an erotic dream or two. If Rick was in it, I wouldn't half mind.

Hey, after all, it'd only be a dream. Dreams were safe.

Real men were not.

CHAPTER FOURTEEN

"She's in the back office," Leo Luna greeted me, waving me towards the rear of his establishment.

Lisa's fifty-ish uncle always reminded me of a Mariachi musician with his barrel chest, bola ties, and big belt buckles. He had a wide, gap-toothed smile, handlebar mustache, and a double degree in electrical and mechanical engineering. In his youth, he'd worked for Customs while putting himself through college. He was one of the wisest men I knew.

At the moment, he was sitting at his vast metal desk, speaking with a well-dressed client, a man in a pinstriped suit.

His establishment, Luna Security Systems and Private Investigations, was quartered in a converted automotive-garage strip mall. There were four bay-doors, permanently closed as far as I could tell, and four connecting garages in which high- and low-tech apparatus were displayed on shelves and tables. From run-of-the-mill surveillance cameras with motion sensors to the tiny, hidden kind in the eye of a teddy bear or flower pin. From listening devices to sophisticated satellite GPS transmitters and receivers. You could see into the displays through a large glass window, which Lisa said was bulletproof.

Walking down the main hallway of the front office, I glanced again as I had before. One day, Lisa and her uncle would have to take me on a tour of all that techie stuff. Not that I had any use for that stuff, but one never knew. I would've liked to have a hidden camera in Rick's condo, come to think of it—maybe in a fake fly on the wall. Bet I'd learn a lot about the new Rick. I'd know whether I could trust him or not. However, right now, I was focused on contacting Teresa.

I found Lisa at her desk in the back office. She had her hand cupped over a cordless telephone handset, a cup of coffee in the other.

"Good, thank you. I'll have my client mail you those things you requested." She rang off, catching my eye, and smiled broadly.

"Lisa, I don't know how much I can pay you," I ventured, figuring their clients weren't likely to be poorly paid teachers.

"Don't be silly," she gushed. "You can buy me lunch today. There's a new salad at *Wendy's*. I've gotta stop there, anyway, and tell the manager he's off the hook. The woman dropped her charges once we told her what the hidden cameras picked up. Ha! I just love larceners—huh, is that a word, Dina?"

I waited for her to wind down. She was clearly excited about her latest successful investigation. Also, when I'd called her earlier to tell her I was dropping by for help in contacting a DEA official, she said she'd do it for me pro bono—on *behalf of her client*.

"Dina, this was a first, my very first call to the DEA—the office in Los Angeles. I told them the whole story. My client—whose name must remain anonymous for the time being—doesn't want her cousin to be put in any more danger than she already is, yadda, yadda, yadda. He said he needed proof that the cousin was really who she, you, I claimed she was—Pedro Vargas's wife and Roberto Martínez's daughter. The DEA knows all about these guys. They just can't touch'em, of course, unless Mexico extradites them. Which doesn't happen too often. So, anyway, if your grandmother has any photos of her and her father or her and her husband—oh, and Teresa's birth certificate or passport. Have her make copies, and we'll mail them to the DEA guy. He'll get it all to the appropriate agent." Lisa took a breath and raced on. "The guy I spoke to said when Teresa's identity has been verified, he'll put one of his agents in touch with you. I specifically requested a Mexican-American agent who spoke Spanish—in case he has to speak to your grandmother or your cousin. I offered to give him your cell phone number and Flora's home number, but he said for you to send the photos and ID copies. I think he was treating my call as a crank call, not taking me that seriously. Anyway, here's his name, address, and number."

I sat down opposite her, impressed beyond words.

"Wow!" I smiled my gratitude. "Thanks, Lisa. I was dreading having to make that phone call, afraid they wouldn't believe me."

"Well, they don't, not yet. Give them what they need for verification, and they'll start believing you. At least we started the ball rolling. Does your grandmother have those photos?"

"I've seen a picture of Roberto Martínez. I don't know if she has any others. I'll call her today and find out. If she does, I'll get them next weekend when I make another trip down to Salinas."

"Good, let's hope Teresa sent her some photos over the years. She probably had to sneak them out if her father didn't want her contacting your grandmother. Or if she contacts you, you have her *FedEx* those photos and ID stuff. Or email all that stuff, take a photo of her passport."

I frowned. "I've been thinking, Lisa. At first, when my uncle was younger, he was told his mother and sister had died in Texas during their visit—Grandma and Mama. Later, he might've found out they were still alive and living in the US. You would've thought he'd have contacted his own mother despite what she did, despite his blaming her for abandoning him."

While sipping from her cup, Lisa listened, indicating if I should want a cup, but I shook my head, my thoughts in a swirl. It seemed I had only speculations instead of concrete proof.

"He must've been a very hard man, no doubt thanks to his father's influence. I feel so sorry for Grandma Gómez. Imagine that—feeling sorry for a woman I've disliked most of my life! What a predicament she found herself in—forced to make a choice to stay with her abusive, violent husband or leave and abandon her small son."

Lisa nodded solemnly in commiseration. I pondered something that had been nagging me in the back of my mind for days.

"The last Grandma heard, Teresa was on her way to Monterrey, running from Pedro Vargas and his thugs. Do you know how big a city that is? Over three million, the third-largest city in Mexico. Don't you think they'd have *Starbucks* cyber cafes there?" Lisa was nodding vigorously. "I stopped at Fuentes Market on the way here. Y'know, that place that sells empanadas and pan dulce and those huge burritos, all custom made. They send money orders and telegrams to Mexico, too."

I took a deep breath, unsure whether what I did was the right thing. Hey, what do I know about private investigations! That course didn't come with Ancient Civilizations and The Literature of the Spanish-speaking Peoples.

"I sent a telegram to the *Western Union* in Monterrey. Teresa's telegram to *Abuelita* came from a *Western Union* office in the town of Chihuahua. Remember, I told you she signed it, TMV—that was her way of using her initials but letting us know that it was really her. So I addressed my telegram to TMV and included my email address. I wasn't sure she'd gotten it from Grandma, who, I think, had given it to Carlota and Jaime. This was kind of a backup to make sure she could email me from one of those cyber cafes in Monterrey. We can finally establish contact, one-to-one. Then she can let me know where exactly she is in Monterrey or where she might go to next."

I waited for Lisa to groan, but she didn't. "That's brilliant, Dina! Way to go."

"Do you really think—" I began hopefully.

"Yes, if she has any brains at all, she'll go back to that same telegram office to see if she got a reply. And if she's our age or close to it, she's bound to be a little computer savvy. She can get an email account under a false name or use someone else's account, someone she might be staying with." Lisa leaned back in her executive's chair. "My theory is she's hiding out with friends or people she trusts, maybe friends from her university days. People that her asshole-husband wouldn't know about."

I considered that a moment. I'd assumed she had money and was staying in hotels, but no, Lisa's theory made better sense. Hotels check identification, and Teresa wouldn't risk that. The Juárez Cartel's arm was long, and they had plenty of money to throw around. They'd be watching all the border towns, maybe the airports, too.

How the hell was she going to get out of Mexico alive?

"Lisa, I think you may be right. So this DEA agent . . ." I looked down at Lisa's neatly printed letters on the back of her card. "This Joe Torres is waiting until I give him the proof that Teresa is who we say she is. Oh God, my heart's pounding. How can I repay you?"

I smiled sheepishly. "I know you're dating Mark now, but if you're free tonight, come out with me on an adventure."

Lisa perked up. "Can't tonight. We're going out." She made a face as if giving the idea a second thought. "What kind of adventure?"

"Uh, have you ever done . . .what do you call it, when you sit in a car and watch and wait for someone—"

"A stakeout. You want me to do a stakeout on someone?"

I didn't like the sound of that—stakeout—especially when

she widened her eyes enticingly and smiled wickedly. Adventure sounded less sinister and underhanded. Less sneaky.

"Yeah, the spying kind," I explained. "I want to spy on this salsa bar. *Habanero's*. Do you know it?"

"Sure, my cousin, Gil, goes there all the time to pick up girls. He says it's easier than asking for dates. Some of the girls put out like they're wives for the night. Such slutty dumbasses. Why do you—oh, don't tell me. I may not want to know."

I confess, I lowered my gaze guiltily, like some housewife trying to catch her cheating husband. I shouldn't, though—feel guilty, I mean. After all, I was doing research into a man's character. Such research was legitimate and prudent.

Lisa's dark brown eyes narrowed to slits. "You want to catch a rat."

"Dina! So glad you came!" Mariana cried, ushering me inside her and her fiancé's condo.

As I met her fiancé, Joel, in turn, I glimpsed her guests milling about inside. Two men and four women in their twenties, thirties, and forties, all dressed in California business-casual, were apparently socializing with drinks in hand. Apparently, a business meeting of Joel's had spilled over. I'd chosen a bad time to drop by to give Mariana and Joel their housewarming present since I wasn't able to come to their Oktoberfest party. I'd brought a bottle of *Sonoma Valley Pinot Noir*, one of my favorite wines, and had attached to the neck of the bottle my recipe for *osso buco* on the inside of a congratulatory card. They were gracious in their appreciation and invited me to join them. I declined, of course, thanking them anyway and left, promising Mariana I'd call soon.

Their condo was on the third floor of a four-storied building. It was quite a trek up those stairs, but at a glance, the fairly new condo was well-appointed with tall ceilings and crown moldings. Compared to our previous student quarters, it was luxurious. I was so happy for her!

It was the Wednesday night following my first golf date with Rick, which had turned out to be an enjoyable two hours of hitting balls at a nearby driving range followed by a casual dinner at a family restaurant. He'd asked me again to go out dancing, but I told him I needed more time to think about it. We'd parted on friendly terms with an agreement to meet the following Sunday for an actual round of golf.

He'd told me to drop by his condo any time and watch him tutor his daughter to see if he was doing it correctly. I knew this was just a ruse, but as I left Mariana's place, I thought, why not? So I turned right at the pool by Mariana's condo building, followed the walkway by the clubhouse, and the second building on the right was his. His condo was on the ground floor, number 108.

Just outside his condo, I saw him. I was about to walk around a large shrub outside the clubhouse but halted in my tracks and cowered beside it. Rick was as casually dressed as I'd seen him in a long time. A black t-shirt stretched across his muscular back and was tucked into a pair of snug-fitting faded jeans. The only problem was he was embracing a slim, pretty blonde. His back was to me, and the woman's face was turned away.

Neither of them saw me. For a second, I froze, and then I backtracked in my steps until I was entirely out of sight.

My head was screaming, I told you so! I told you so! He's a lying, cheating bastard, and he'll always be one. You're such a fool, Dina, to fall for his pity-me act.

I was so choking with anger, I couldn't think straight. My hands and feet were on automatic control, obeying orders that came from somewhere within me. I felt myself running to my car but didn't know where the strength came from.

I was such a fool! Such a dolt! Such a *tonta*!

Like an idiot, I'd fallen for his lines—he'd never stopped loving me, he told Jesús. Interested in a romantic night out, he'd asked. Are you going to invite me back in? I'm going to knock down that wall around your heart.

That last line was especially good. And now so hurtful.

He lied to me. He's still lying. *Still lying.*

When I got home, I dashed to my room. Flora was out with Porter, either dancing or doing whatever women did with wealthy men they wanted to rope into marriage. I could well imagine!

Dispiritedly, I flung off my clothes and desultorily put on jammies and a bathrobe. Maybe I'd end up a frumpy, old spinster with my nose in a book every night like Jane Fairmont at school. She was still teaching at sixty-eight, had never married, talked about her ten cats as if they were her children, and dribbled food on her chest at lunch. Why retire when there was no one to stay home and do things with?

Automatically, like I'd done every evening for the past two weeks, I turned on my laptop and logged on to my email. There was something from Frankie.

Rick said you two had fun driving balls last Sunday. After this job in San Jose, he's got a residential development in Milpitas he wants us to do. Eighty upscale homes near the old mission. It is great to have friends in high places.

Yah, yah! What was that about, anyway? Why was he still being nice to my family? I couldn't figure it out.

There were two pieces of spam, one email from a college friend who wanted to travel with me next summer. She was teaching in New Mexico and thought we could take a trip down to the Caribbean.

Then—one from an unknown email address—sja94@aol.com.

Who the heck was that? Fearing a deadly virus would destroy my hard drive if I opened it, I was about to delete it. Then I noticed it was in Spanish. It had to be from Teresa!

It was!

Translated—

Dear cousin, I am in Monterrey, and we are safe. It has been a terrible three weeks, but we are with friends who cannot be traced. I know now how your American slaves felt before the War Between the States when they ran away and had to rely on the kindness of strangers to keep them safe. The Underground Railroad, I think they called it. As you can see, I am using my dear friend's email address so that my husband cannot track us and find us. I am confident that I do not dare to use the airport or go near the borders, for la organización has been alerted. My son was distraught and frightened, but he now understands why we must leave Mexico. Can you help us? I will check back tomorrow. I pray that you will receive this message and reply to this address. God bless you, TMV.

I sat there trembling a little, feeling her fear seeping through the electronic distance to me. Teresa wrote in simple Spanish, not knowing, of course, how fluent I was. When I replied in Spanish, typing on my keyboard with shaking hands, I told her that I was in contact with the DEA, the Drug Enforcement Agency. Was that okay with her, I wanted to know. I, and several others whose advice I trusted, felt certain that DEA agents could help her and her son escape Mexico. But they needed proof that she could help them in return. Could she send me, by *FedEx* or *UPS* or the Mexican equivalent, evidence of her identification? Even a photo of her ID? Copies of her passport or Mexican driver's license? Also, they wanted at least one picture of her and her father and perhaps one of her and her husband. A family portrait? Could she send those as soon as possible?

I concluded with.

I pray that God will keep you and your son safe. On behalf of your American family, I wish you both well. We look forward to meeting you soon. Love, Dina.

I sent it with a silent prayer. Then I called Grandma Gómez to tell her that her Mexican granddaughter and great-grand-son had gotten in touch with me and that they were safe.

I didn't add, for the time being.

CHAPTER FIFTEEN

We were in Lisa's car in a lower-middle-class Hispanic neighborhood southwest of downtown San Jose. It was a dreary night, and the car's ignition was off, as was her heater. We were bundled in jackets, waiting. *Habanero's* had changed a lot since I'd gone there last with Rick. They'd gone uptown a little, adding on a restaurant at the side of the bar lounge. The place had been upgraded from the outside with a cosmetic makeover, new stucco and tile trim, and a new Spanish-style fountain in front. It was Saturday night, and the place was packed. That much hadn't changed.

We were on a stakeout. Waiting to catch a rat in the act.

"Well, this is boring," I commented flatly.

"That's what a stakeout is, Dina. You sit and wait for something to happen. Just hang on — I know this is kinda tedious. Eat your hamburger and fries. God, I love this stuff!"

Lisa Luna, her long, dark-brown hair in a moussed-curly 'do, was excited. Her dark eyes were flashing both mischief and merriment. That's one reason I liked her enormously. She was intelligent and fun to be around. And we both had a penchant for seeking adventure. And if trouble found us, we always felt ready for it.

We felt like the female versions of James Bond, but without the shooting car and other cool gadgets.

She was munching on one of the *Big Macs* she'd stopped and bought for us on the way here. Off her diet of jello and cottage cheese, now that she'd lost five pounds, I guess I was resenting her enjoyment of what I tended to regard as prettily packaged lard. I'd brought hot, nonfat macchiatos from *Starbucks* to help keep us toasty, but I'd forgotten how icy a car could be on a cold, drizzly night in November.

I was worrying aloud about Lisa not getting a superior evaluation if she didn't sleep with Mark, our vice principal. She'd been out on three dates with him and so far hadn't put out. I told her she was playing with fire by going out with one of our administrative bosses. Especially if she had no intention of having sex — or having sex but breaking it off later. Men didn't like that, no matter what job they had or how gentlemanly they behaved at work. I told her that revenge from Mark McDuff would be a poor or unsatisfactory evaluation and a stain on her otherwise sterling teaching career. In fact, it could cost her a good job, maybe even a career as an educator.

Never underestimate the fragile male ego and its need for revenge.

Naturally, she probably didn't appreciate my grandmotherly admonitions, especially coming from me, a girl who'd screwed up royally in the boyfriend department. But she took my words of caution equally, taking another bite of her *Big Mac* and mulling them over between hardy chews.

My incurably curious and pessimistic nature overrode my fatigue and secret desire to take a hot bath and return to a romance novel I'd started. I was suddenly plagued by a hefty dose of guilt, too, for spying on Rick Ramos. But it was Saturday night, and I just knew he was coming to *Habanero's*. For what — besides dancing — I was longing to find out.

I'd played a round of golf with him that very day despite my catching him embracing that blonde outside his condo a few nights before. He'd had a rare free Saturday and was eager to try out his new skills on the greens. He'd struggled to drive the golf ball straight down the fairway, struggled even more at putting, but ended the four-hour, eighteen-hole golf experience feeling satisfied and wanting to do it again—with me.

Again, he'd asked me to join him for a night of drinks and dancing, and I'd declined again—even though we'd had a lot of fun on the links that day. Rick had driven that golf cart like a ten-year-old kid with a homemade go-cart. Despite myself, I'd laughed 'til my sides were splitting. Golfing with Rick was fun, and I didn't have to suppress my potty mouth around him. We both swore every time we hit badly, which was often. When other golfers came near, we'd switch to swearing in Spanish. And when we arrived at Lake Texas, he patiently waited for me to hit the ball across. It took me only five mulligans this time.

I updated him, too, on the initial email contact I'd had from Teresa. He agreed with Flora that going to the DEA for help was a sensible next step. Since Wednesday night, I'd been waiting to receive a *FedEx* mailer from Mexico or another email, but nothing had arrived. Rick was impressed that Lisa and I had already gotten in touch with a DEA agent in Los Angeles, the very one who'd requested the verification of Teresa's identity.

We were parked across the street and down one house from the salsa bar. *Habanero's* was an anomaly, a commercial building in the midst of a residential area, but it had been there forever. We were waiting for Rick to leave, having already spied his red *Explorer* in the parking lot.

Lisa took a hefty bite and sighed. Having finished my non-fat macchiato, I scowled and sucked on the straw inside my cup of *Diet Coke*. I was going liquid tonight.

"You have the metabolism of a hummingbird, Lisa, and you've got curves in all the right places. But for me, every bite of this *Big Mac* turns into five-hundred extra fat cells that I don't need."

Lisa snorted. "And I have a plot of land in the Mojave

Desert to sell you. Sorry, not buying your envy of my metabolism."

Someone was coming out of *Habanero's* entranceway, and since it and the parking lot were well lit, we had no trouble seeing who it was. I stashed my drink and grabbed Lisa's binoculars, nestled at the ready on her center console.

"It's Rick! Who's the woman — d'ya know her, Dina?"

It took a few seconds to focus on the tall man and shorter woman walking to a dark blue car.

"I know her," I murmured, thinking aloud, "yes, I know her. That's Esther, Rick's sister."

"How many does he have?" Lisa was peering through her *Nikon's* telephoto lens, the camera in one hand and the half-eaten *Big Mac* in the other.

"Three, he's the oldest and only male. Funny, I thought Esther was married and living in Los Angeles." I put the binoculars down, watching through the front windshield as Rick bussed her cheek, then held her car door open for her while she got settled in the driver's seat.

By the time Esther drove off, I was feeling weighed down with guilt. Frowning, I scooted down in my seat while he returned to the bar. Then, when Lisa called the coast was clear, I sat back up. Awash with shame and guilt, I unwrapped my *Big Mac* and drenched it in ketchup from four of those little baggies.

"So, when do you think he'll leave?" Lisa queried. The amateur sleuth.

I mumbled something unintelligible from my stuffed mouth.

"How many dates have you and that cute cop been on?"

My thoughts harked back to Tyler Dalton, my strange but hunky cop-friend who lived with his wacky mother in a lovely, multimillion-dollar Saratoga home. I hoped we were still friends, but I wasn't so sure after that fiasco of a date two weeks ago. He hadn't called back, anyway. Which was fine. I wasn't in the mood for any more target practice.

"None after the first one. Just call me One-Date Dina. It's really okay with me, Lisa. There's more to a man than looks."

"So true. That's why we're here. To dispel or confirm your suspicions and get down to the gritty truth." I could tell Lisa was relishing this stakeout. I think she really missed the sleuthing during the school year.

"Yeah, Jesús said that Rick said he never stopped loving me. If he's out here picking up women, I'll know that he was lying."

"Are you sure you want to find out," she mumbled as she chewed, "if he's dating other women?" Not waiting for me to swallow and answer, she hurried on. "I mean, we already knew Rick Ramos hasn't been a monk all these years since you two broke up. Right? If he's dating someone else, why should you care? You don't date him. In fact, you've refused to go out with him, and golfing doesn't really constitute a date in your book. So you have fun with him on the golf course, and you've made it clear that you just want to be his friend. Right?"

I sighed and nodded, saying nothing, impatient for this stakeout to be over and done with. Unlike Lisa, it was anything but exciting and romantic for me. It was cold, and I was tired. And now, I felt consumed with guilt for invading Rick's privacy. Then I thought of the boyfriends whose computers I'd sneaked into. Strange, I hadn't felt guilty about invading *their* privacy.

We waited some more, ate, and washed our humungous calories down with our *Diet Cokes*, naturally. Somehow, gorging on calories and cholesterol did nothing to dispel my mood.

"Or you're in love with him but don't want to be and catching him leave with another woman will make you miserable but will give you another excuse not to trust him. Not to love him again." Lisa paused long enough to take a long suck from her straw. "This, of course, makes some sense to me because I've done the same thing myself once or twice."

She looked over at me, for I'd gone very still and had stopped eating. "I just hate seeing you miserable, that's all. If he goes home alone, what does that accomplish? You'll tell yourself, good, he couldn't find some — how did you put it — wife, for the night, but he'll find one next week. And you'll still feel miserable because what you really want to do is feel free to love him again. But you're afraid. Hey, not that I blame you. In your place, I'd be scared silly. And I don't scare easily."

When she noticed my mouth hanging open, like some village idiot, Lisa quipped, "Dina, did you think I minored in psychology for nothing? Really!" She was smiling self-deprecatingly.

I felt foolish. Lisa was so right on target. "I never said I was falling in love with him," I protested feebly, "and if I am, I shouldn't be. Not after what I've been through with him."

"Well, don't worry," Lisa quipped, "he's the father of a little girl. It's a package deal with him. Any woman he marries has to love his child. You'd have to win over his daughter for it to work, anyway. She might not like you, so that'd be that."

I rewrapped the remainder of my *Big Mac,* having lost all desire to gorge myself. Lisa's insightful comments hit so close to home and heart that I was no longer in the mood to indulge. These were weighty matters, indeed, and suddenly hoping to catch Rick the Rat in the act of going off with some woman he'd picked up at *Habanero's* didn't seem like something I could handle. I wasn't dating him and so had no claims on him, and, anyway, I had just decided I was better off not knowing.

"Lisa, I've changed my mind. Let's get out of here."

"You sure?" she asked. "Yep. Sorry for all this."

Lisa started up the car. "No problem. It's good to practice my PI skills. I never know when Uncle Leo'll ask me to go undercover for him." Lisa put her camera under her seat and the binoculars in the glove compartment. She shot me a look of wry resignation.

"Don't worry about Mark McDuff and me, Dina. I'm a big girl and can take care of myself. If I sleep with him, it'll be because I'm horny and he'll scratch my itch. If we stop seeing each other and he tries to make a big deal about it, I'll charge him with sexual harassment. Don't look so shocked, either. I'm not a bleeding heart like you. I don't take men seriously like you do. Nothing against that, I'm telling you. Just that, we're different when it comes to men and sex and love."

We began to giggle over the absurdity of it all—this stupid stakeout and all it implied. The heater purred into life, and my anger and fears seemed to melt away. I began to feel at peace with myself. No matter what, I was doing the right thing.

"Y'know, Dina, when you love somebody a great deal, you make yourself a hostage to his actions, his decisions. Heck, his fortunes in life. It's a huge commitment and leap of faith. I think you'll know when you're ready to do that again."

I nodded, grateful for my good friend's confidence in me and in my judgment. I'd deal with Rick Ramos and his daughter when I was ready. And if he had to pick up a hundred girls in the meantime to satisfy some urges of his, so be it. I wasn't going to rush into something for fear of losing my second chance with him. And if I needed more time to work through my fear of being hurt again by such a man—well, such was life.

My heart. My terms.

I didn't want it any other way.

The following Thursday, after a half-hour of jogging with the Lincoln All-Stars and two hours of grading student papers while nursing one venti, nonfat caramel macchiato, I went home to Flora's.

There, on the front porch, was a *UPS* mailer from Mexico.

I dashed inside and opened it, my heart beating like a hummingbird's. Spilling out on the dining table were several photos clipped together and two pages of a handwritten letter attached to three *Xerox* copies.

I examined each colored photo. One showed Roberto Martínez, a woman who might have been Teresa's mother, a young, dark-haired man, and Teresa in a maroon suit and matching heels. The men were in dark suits, the older woman in a cream-colored suit, all looking elegant and prosperous. On the back, she'd written in Spanish — *May 15, 1994, my graduation day from the University of Guadalajara. Mamá, Papá, Brother Roberto, Teresa.*

Brother? He looked older than Teresa. Where was he now? Did he work for the cartel? Grandma Gomez hadn't mentioned him.

It was a medium shot, so I couldn't really see her or her brother's face that well.

The second photo was clearly a formal wedding portrait of Teresa and Pedro Vargas. Her mother was still alive at that point, standing beside her husband on one side and the married couple on the other. I looked closely. Teresa was a pretty woman, had small features, and was petite like Grandma Gómez and Mama. Pedro Vargas had pale skin and light brown hair, wore spectacles, was handsome in a geeky way. He looked more like an accountant than the murdering usurper of the Juárez drug cartel. Roberto Martínez, Teresa's father, appeared much huskier and stouter than the other photo I'd seen of him.

The third photo was a close-up of Teresa and her son. In the picture, the boy looked about six, maybe taken a year ago.

On the back, she'd written — *Alex, age seven. June 2004.* The boy resembled Teresa a little but had an almost ivory complexion, blue eyes, and dark blond hair, nothing strange about that. There were many blue-eyed, blonde Mexicans. Perhaps Pedro Vargas had a mixed, Northern European heritage. Teresa's features were more apparent, her makeup flawless. She wore her dark hair in fluffy curls about her face, no longer than her jawline, and diamond studs in her ears. The mother and son seemed close.

I was saving the letter for last, so I next looked at the photocopied sheets. Two were of Teresa's and Alex's passport-picture page, with their passport numbers and signatures. The third was a copy of her birth certificate and one of her father's. On the fourth sheet was a photocopy of her declaration of matrimony to Pedro Antonio Vargas Aguilar.

Putting these aside, I snatched up her letter. She sent salutations to my family and me, said she was happy to hear from me and felt that there might be hope for the first time. She mentioned that her brother, Roberto, had finished his medical degree in Salamanca, Spain, and was a resident physician specializing in cancer treatment in Madrid. Their maternal grandmother had died of ovarian cancer, and that had influenced Roberto to be an oncologist. She added meaningfully that her brother was nothing like her father and had refused to join the family *negocios*.

As before in her email, Teresa wrote in simple enough Spanish for me to translate immediately as I was reading it. The next part, however, caused me to slow down and read the paragraphs several times.

It has been challenging for us, and I lament my son's unhappiness. We have been living at both the mercy and generosity of very kind and trustworthy friends. These are friends with whom I have served in the Cruz Rojo *and the* Sociedad de Tratamiento del Cáncer. *They know my situation and are willing to risk their lives* to protect my son and me. However, Alex and I cannot leave the apartment where we are currently living for fear that my husband will have the building watched. He does not have the names of these friends, for I have been meticulous in keeping them secret, but I know well enough the power of the Organización. They have ways of finding out the deepest of secrets. Through their sobornos, they can learn anything from anyone. In any event, I do not wish to jeopardize the well-being of these friends any more than I already have.

I have known for a long time that my son and I would have to leave someday. To that end, I have prepared extensively. My ultimate goal is to join my brother in Spain. However, such preparations are futile if I cannot leave my country safely with my son. To do this, I give you permission to communicate with any federal agency of the United States government that can help us. Show this agency all that I have sent you and if you need more validations, let me know. My friend risked a great deal to mail this to you. Every communication and correspondence has been through her kindness and courage. You may continue to email me at the same address as before. sja94@aol.com. 1994 was the year that we graduated from university. I cannot tell you anything more about her than what I have already divulged for her sake and for the safety of her family.

Also, cousin, I speak, read and write a little English. If you cannot translate this in safety, I can try to write in English. Our grandmother assures me that you will have no difficulty understanding my correspondence. I look forward to meeting you, dear cousin Dina. Abuela said your name was Dolores. Dina must be an apodo, a nickname? I have one, also. My father used to call me Teacup, for I was so tiny as a baby.

Despite what you may have read about him, my dear father was kind to Roberto and me, although not very kind to my mother. He had an inferior role model as a father, himself, from what our abuela has written to me. I mourn his death as I daily grieve my mother's.

While the only proof I have of Pedro's involvement in my father's death was overhearing a brief conversation that he had with another man, it was proof enough for me. I have written a transcript of that *conversation between Pedro and this man, an enforcer in the Cartel, so that the government agency you communicate with will know this is true. This transcript is safely hidden with the other documents of the* Organización's *affairs that I was able to copy. I am hoping these documents, which I keep close to me, will provide us our safe journey out of Mexico, the land of my birth, and give us a haven in my grandmother's adopted country.*

Teresa signed off in the usual formal Mexican way.

Today was Thursday. I'd call that DEA agent, Joe Torres, tomorrow during my lunch break and set up an appointment to see him on Monday. I'd take the day off and fly down to LA and show him Teresa's photos, proof of her and her son's IDs, and all her correspondence. We'd see where we could go from there.

If there had been any past reluctance on my part to get involved in rescuing my Mexican cousin and her son, it had vanished by now.

I was committed.

CHAPTER SIXTEEN

For the past four Sundays, I'd been shamelessly feasting my gaze on Rick's masculine body, all six-foot-two of him, sinewy muscles and all. In somewhat conventional golf togs, he looked every bit a Michelangelo's David in my eyes. When he drove a ball, I'd watch as if my very life depended on my memorizing every motion of his arms, twist of his torso, and stretch of his legs. His nice, taut rump was well defined in his khakis as he followed through, his arms upwardly swept and cocked in the air.

I dragged my attention off him and gazed after the ball.

"Sorry, couldn't track it. It just soared, lost it in the sky." I turned to him ruefully. He just shrugged good-naturedly.

"I think I hooked it—again!" he grumbled, then issued forth an expletive in Spanish.

"Well, you're still doing better than I am. I don't understand it. You've barely been playing a month, and you can drive farther than I can. It's just not fair." I took my place at the white tee-box and balanced my ball precariously on the tee I'd just pushed into the grass.

"You tense up, Dina, just before you swing," Rick informed me flatly. "You've got to loosen up, relax your whole body. Here, like this."

He came up behind me, snuggled in close, nearly spooning me but bracketing my arms with his and clasping a hold of my club.

"Okay, so how do I relax with you rubbing against my—" I broke off, not wanting to mention the body part he was so

229

expertly touching. He chuckled.

"Just go with me on this," he urged, "feel the full swing potential. The golf pro said it's all in the technique, and you can't have good technique if you don't relax."

I leaned my head back, stretching my neck and rolling my shoulders a bit. Feeling his chest and belly and groin behind me like a blanket—if we were horizontal, he'd be lying on top of me—was not at all conducive to releasing tension. Nevertheless, I tried to follow his example of loosening up my swing. We went through the motions a few times, then I asked him to step back. A few seconds later, he puffed out a short laugh and released me.

I knew he was watching me from behind, so I wiggled my rump and took a few practice swings, trying to relax. It was true. I *was* tensing up, and I could feel the difference when I practiced.

I swung my driver and—lo and behold! My ball sailed up and over the fairway at least a hundred and fifty yards—my all-time best drive ever!

"Yes, yesss!" I screamed in a very unsophisticated golfer's fashion. He exulted with me, and we bumped fists in delight.

A half-hour later, we were tossing our bags in our respective car trunks. It was one PM, and my stomach was growling.

"Let me treat you to lunch, Rick," I offered, closing the trunk and calling out across two-car widths. "Least I can do for your helpful lesson. Besides, I want to show you something."

"Oh yeah? Did you buy something at *Victoria's Secret*? If so, you can show it to me later tonight."

I gave a short laugh, for a second wishing to retort about a certain slim blonde I'd seen him with. That I restrained myself was a sign of my growing maturity, I felt. Or a sign of something—I wasn't sure what.

In the clubhouse grill room, over my salad and Rick's club

sandwich, I watched him pore over the contents of that *UPS* mailer Teresa had sent. He studied the photos, the photocopies of Teresa's and her son's passports, then read the letter.

"Wow, sounds like she's going through hell." Rick stuffed the contents back into the mailer, then paused to sip his beer. "To be on the run like that with a child, having a cartel after you . . ." He shook his head in disbelief. "She's very brave or very foolish."

"If her husband—this Pedro Vargas—is aware that she's carrying cartel secrets with her, I doubt she'll have a chance to get out of Mexico. What do you think, Rick? Does she have a chance?"

The look of genuine compassion he turned my way was like a balm to my fears. At least, he could sympathize with my cousin's situation. And my dilemma.

"Honestly, Dina, I don't know."

"I'm flying down to LA to see this DEA agent, this Joe Torres that I've spoken to. He said to come and see him or mail all this stuff down to him. I want to see him in person. Maybe it'll make for a stronger case if he sees me, a representative of the family, the people related to Teresa and her son. Anyway, I've got a ten AM appointment on Monday to see him."

He looked surprised. "You going alone?"

I nodded. "Sure, I've got ten paid sick days a year. My brothers don't, and my sisters are busy with little kids. My father's still recuperating and needs my mother. I won't ask Flora. It's not her family that's in trouble. And Grandma Gómez—well, let's say, now that I know she came here illegally, I don't think her seeing a federal agent is wise."

He smiled wryly, his big brown eyes glinting. "You're absolutely right not to take your grandmother. This Torres guy speaks Spanish? She'd say the wrong thing and find herself under interrogation at *La Migra*."

He took his mobile phone out of his pocket and flipped it open. Punching in a series of numbers, he smiled at me in complicit silence.

"Hello, Sue? Rick Ramos here. I need you to make a phone call for me. *Southwest Airlines*. Book two tickets—" He paused and looked inquiringly at me, and when I shook my head, he went on hurriedly. "Yeah, two tickets down to LAX and back. Seven or eight AM flight. Back on the three, four PM one. Cancel my Monday appointments—all of them except Templeton. Reschedule for Tuesday, if possible. He's the architect on the Milpitas project, and . . .yes, that's it. You're one amazing *mujer*, dollface. I owe you. Okay, dinner for two at *Il Fornaio's*. Got it."

He rang off before I could raise an objection or insist that I could handle it independently. Besides, who was this Sue? Was she his secretary, mistress, or both?

"Done," he said, all businesslike. I opened my mouth to issue a specious protest—frankly, I was relieved someone was coming with me. "Federal authorities can be intimidating, Dina. I don't want you saying something that might jeopardize your grandmother's or mother's status here. Believe me, I've had a close call or two regarding my father and his false papers and a few of the men working for me. Sometimes you have to walk a razor's edge to protect the people you care about. If nothing else, I'll be there to give you emotional support." He waited for me then to protest.

I sat back, overwhelmed by his show of friendship. As long as I'd known Rick Ramos, he'd been bold, decisive, a doer as well as a thinker, an efficient man who, once he knew what had to be done, spared no effort to do it. Hesitation or fear was not in his vocabulary. It was a trait I'd always admired.

I smiled and thanked him. "Who's Sue?" I had to ask finally.

His gaze flickered over my face and hair for a second

before lowering. He was trying to conceal a slightly smirking smile.

"My secretary. Don't know what I'd do without her."

"Is she a slim, attractive blonde?"

Rick snorted. "Good thing she isn't. I wouldn't get anything done if she was. No, Sue's a fifty-something grandmother who keeps threatening to retire any day now. But I pay her well and buy her gift cards when she has to work on Saturdays. For five phone calls today, she's getting a great dinner for her and her husband. I say, not a bad deal."

I disliked his allusion that pretty blondes would offer a distracting influence, but I was still happy he was accompanying me. It was a meeting I was both dreading and anticipating. My scalp tingled at the very thought of meeting an agent of the Drug Enforcement Agency and begging him to help us.

"Thanks, Rick," I said, displaying affection to him in my voice for perhaps the first time since we'd become golfing buddies. "You're a good friend."

I meant it.

Perhaps it was my imagination, but he looked down at his sandwich like it'd suddenly turned into stale, week-old bread.

We flew down on the eight o'clock flight to LAX and took a taxi to the Federal Building in downtown Los Angeles. Rick had monopolized the conversation in the plane, laying out the plans for the Milpitas project amid the time frame given to him — happily taking my mind off the meeting that awaited us. One of the upscale homes he was under contract to build, in the developer's concept of a combined residential and commercial village, was going to be his and Angelina's new home — a 3000 square-foot, Spanish-style villa. Did I know anyone who wanted a 1500 square-foot, two-bedroom condo in a luxurious condo complex off the Alameda? Yeah, me! I wanted to say, meanwhile yearning to see what that Spanish villa would look like. The woman who married Rick Ramos might have a nice life — wouldn't be forced to work, most likely. She could stay home and play housewife, cook to her heart's content . . .

Oh, and stepmother to a cute, little five-year-old.

Another woman's child. Rather, a cokehead's possibly learning-disabled child.

It was an uncharitable thought, I had to admit to myself, but the possibility of a stepchild was enough to give a gal pause. That is, if she was frank about making this man and his daughter happy.

Por favor, like this gal was me?

All the while he was talking, I kept noticing little things. Like the way his short, cropped curls clung to his temples and neck, his strong jaw line and well-formed neck. The line of his shoulders under the suede sports jacket, the cut of his V-neck sweater, which showed the white-tee neckline underneath. The glint of his gold chain holding the crucifix he'd received at his Confirmation. So much was different about this older Rick Ramos, and yet so much was the same as the man I'd been madly in love with six years ago. Half-listening to him, I was mentally trying to blend the two, I suppose.

Too soon, we were in the lobby of the Federal Building, walking through the metal detector, getting wanded by a uniformed officer, then riding up in the elevator to the seventh floor.

Ushered into the waiting room of the DEA's warren of offices, we sat down. I nervously clutched that *UPS* mailer to my chest, straightening my caramel-colored leather blazer and matching straight skirt. The pumpkin and gold-tinted tweed sweater underneath went nicely with Rick's birthday gift to me — the fire-opal stud earrings. We looked respectable and highly credible. That I might have to tell a few white lies to a federal agent made me quiver inside. Overall, he had to believe me and, through me, Teresa Vargas.

If he didn't, God only knew what might happen to her.

A heavyset, middle-aged Hispanic man approached us, and we stood in unison. His hair was salt-and-pepper and cropped even shorter than Rick's. He was swarthy-complexioned and clean-shaven, and if he wasn't smiling, at least his dark eyes twinkled in a friendly manner.

"Miss Salazar? Special agent Joe Torres," he said, shaking my hand. He looked up at the taller man by my side. "Your brother?"

"No, this is Rick Ramos, my friend. He came to give me moral support," I offered, smiling in a way that, I hope, inspired confidence. They shook hands and sized each other up in the way that Mexican-American men do. I think it's a cultural thing. A few seconds of suspicion, an unspoken challenge to define yourself.

Whatever. By the time we were seated again in Joe Torres's office, a walled-in one with a glass wall and door—unlike the other cubicles of lesser agents, I supposed—Rick had inspired a sense of trustworthiness and sincerity. Good traits to evoke if you're meeting with the feds.

Without much preamble, I turned over to Agent Torres the contents of that *UPS* cardboard mailer. For several minutes, he scrutinized the photos using a handheld magnifying lens, then the photocopies of the two passport ID pages, verifying their numbers on a separate paper on his desk. When he read the letter, it was apparent that he was fluent or at least quite functional in Spanish.

I noticed he wrote a few things on a yellow pad as he read, including Cruz Roja's name and the Cancer Treatment Foundation that Teresa and her friend had worked with. Rick and I were sitting side by side in armchairs, and once during the ten-minute silence as the agent perused the documents, we exchanged a meaningful look. Yes, I knew what I had to say in case he asked about Grandma Gómez and Mama. Sure enough, it wasn't long after that when the moment came.

Agent Torres sat back in his swivel, padded chair and steepled his hands. "Tell me again, Miss Salazar, your connection to this Teresa Vargas, Pedro Vargas, and Roberto Martínez."

I took a deep breath, then launched into the whole story, only changing one part. A small detail, perhaps, but Rick thought it was an important one.

"Grandma Gómez — well, then her maiden name was Carrillo and her married name, Martínez — went to Texas to visit her brother and his wife who was expecting a baby. She helped her sister-in-law with the newborn, and before she returned to Mexico, she learned that Martínez had divorced her. Her son, little Roberto Martínez, was just two years old at this time, and my grandmother was not allowed to come back and claim him. So, brokenhearted, she stayed in Amarillo with her brother, eventually met and married my grandfather — well, my step-grandfather — Pablo Gómez. They had my mother, Consuelo, and ten years later moved to California, to Salinas."

By telling this little white lie, that my mother was born in the States, I hoped, my mother was assured of her legal status. What was a two- or three-years difference in age between Mama and her dead brother?

"Roberto Martínez was sixty-two when he was murdered. How old is your mother?" Agent Torres was taking notes on his yellow pad.

I felt Rick's foot nudge mine. "Fifty-nine, I think. Her birthday is in September." I glanced over at Rick. Good, his look was saying. I was hoping Agent Torres wouldn't check her Social Security number and other facts in those Big-Brother government computers.

"When did this Teresa Vargas begin to contact your mother?" Agent Torres asked.

I frowned. Was he trying to trick me, catch me lying, or did he genuinely forget what I'd told him on the phone two weeks ago?

"My grandmother. Teresa discovered she had relatives on her father's side of the family while at the University of Guadalajara, from an ancestry register. She phoned Carlota, Grandma Gómez's sister in Chihuahua, and they corresponded through Jaime, Carlota's son. When Teresa went to Chihuahua or Ciudad Juárez to shop, she'd sometimes arrange to meet Jaime secretly. She had to do this because her father had forbidden her to have anything to do with the Carrillos, my grandmother's family. So three years ago—" I sighed, tired of having to repeat all of this again. "Teresa began sending letters to Grandma through Jaime. That way, she could keep the correspondence secret. As far as she knows, her father never found out and her husband, Pedro Vargas, never knew, either."

Agent Torres was nodding his head. So far, I'd kept my story straight, and the detail about my mother's birth was a new one that I'd never spoken about before. Unless he looked more closely into it and discovered that Mama was the same age as this Roberto Martinez drug lord, I could simply say that Mama's age was what she'd told us it was. Looking at the man, the way his gaze leveled on me as I repeated my story, gave me the impression that he wasn't interested in pursuing anyone's immigration status.

He had bigger fish to fry.

"Do you know anything about these documents Teresa Vargas mentioned in her letter? It appears she's given much thought to her flight from under the Cartel's iron fist, and she has something to bargain with. Normally, we wouldn't be interested in helping a kingpin's daughter or wife escape from a lifestyle beyond our control or jurisdiction."

"I understand," I said. "And no, I've never seen those cartel documents or copies of them. According to her letter, she's not letting them out of her sight. They're with her at all times. Whatever that means."

Agent Torres retrieved a thick folder from the big briefcase on the floor by his feet and placed it on top of the yellow pad.

"I haven't been ignoring this case, Miss Salazar. We sent one of our undercover agents down to Monterrey to do some scouting. He's looking into the Red Cross affiliation your cousin has, possible friends from her association with them. Everyone's clammed up. One possible reason is this." He handed me folded newspapers. Glancing at the headers, I realized these were a sampling of Mexico's leading newspapers. A *Mexico City daily*, a *Tijuana weekly*, a *Guadalajara daily*, a *Monterrey daily*, even a *Yucatán tourist weekly*.

I gasped. In each one, circled in red felt-ink was an article declaring in various headlines—Teresa Vargas and Alejandro Vargas, wife and son of business mogul Pedro Vargas of Chihuahua, were missing. Feared kidnapped. A five-million-peso reward was offered for information and their safe return. Their photos, the passport close-ups of Teresa and her son, were featured.

Stricken with fear, I passed the news articles to Rick, who looked as visibly shaken as I felt. Agent Torres was watching us closely.

"It appears Pedro Vargas is determined to find them. What do you think would happen if they're discovered, and these documents that your cousin has managed to smuggle out are found? Perhaps he already knows about them."

To Torres's rhetorical question, I could only frown and bite my lower lip. I didn't want to visualize how my cousin might suffer for running away from this man and his evil empire.

"Can you help her?" I pleaded, feeling my eyes smart with suppressed tears.

He slowly nodded. "Possibly. I need to get authorization from my bosses here at DEA. Also, ICE will be involved,

Justice and the Border Patrol. You contend she's in Monterrey at present, hiding in a friend's home—"

"Friend's flat, I think," I interjected, feeling a little encouraged. "In her emails, she hasn't given me the address."

"Just as well, if she feels her emails might be tracked electronically. When you write to her, do it in code—"

"Code? Like Morse Code?"

Agent Torres smiled for the first time since meeting him.

"No. Your own code. Don't mention DEA or my name. Just friends or Sammy, as in Uncle Sam. You're a clever girl. Think of ways to avoid mentioning details and specifics." He held his steepled fingers against his full lips, evidently pondering the next move. "It wouldn't help to know her exact location. We wouldn't be able to get her across the border, especially in light of those news alerts. Our undercover man says there are news flashes on television and total media coverage on the missing wife and son. Vargas is pulling out all the stops to recover them and no doubt not strictly out of kindly sentiment."

I looked mournfully at Rick, and he replied in his own way by taking my hand, clasping it over our chair arms. His hand felt warm and strong and helped diminish the trembling inside me.

"Vargas might find them soon if the entire country of Mexico is out looking for them, hoping to claim that prize—about half a million dollars' worth. Somebody's bound to give them up sooner or later." Joe Torres dropped his gaze to his desk and rapped his yellow pad with the point of his pen. What he'd just said made my stomach plummet to my knees.

I hadn't considered that her husband would put out what was basically a country-wide, All Points Bulletin on his wife and son. He was trying his damnedest to find them. And like Teresa had said, the Cartel had a very long reach.

"There *is* a chance at one of the border towns. Nuevo

Laredo. That's probably the most porous spot along the border. It's given us lots of headaches, I can assure you. She's already in the state of Tamaulipas, and the Gulf Cartel owns the border towns in Tamaulipas."

At Rick's and my puzzled looks, Agent Torres paused and unfolded a large, laminated map of Mexico. He pointed to Monterrey, then traced his forefinger northeast to Nuevo Laredo, a town across the Rio Grande from Laredo, Texas.

"The Gulf Cartel is run by a pack of thugs that's in competition with the Juárez syndicate, which is northwest to Tamaulipas. We know for a fact that the kingpin, a man by the name of Aguilar, has clashed with Roberto Martínez on numerous occasions. Probably why Martínez was killed. The Gulf might've approached Vargas with a kind of promissory truce or cut in the action if Martínez was eliminated. Might've been a ploy, however, to upset the leadership of the Juárez. Killing two birds with one stone, you might say. Eliminate Martínez and upset the higher-level management at the same time. That'd buy the Gulf Cartel a little time to make their moves into Juárez territory, take over warehouses and shipment routes.

"You see, these two crime syndicates are like rival Mafia families. They'll do any underhanded thing it takes to upset the business and profits of the other cartels, especially if the Juárez is trying to infringe on the Gulf's territory. And vice versa. Which we think may be happening now. Kind of a drug war going on, a war for supremacy. We've seen that already with the Tijuana Cartel when one of the two Solario brothers died suddenly. The eldest used to be one of Roberto Martínez's friendlier associates, so to speak. Your uncle's generation is dying out. Now the younger *jefes* are all jockeying for position, territory, power, and profits."

I'm sure I still looked puzzled. What did all this have to do with getting Teresa and her son out of Mexico?

"So you're saying . . ." I prompted.

"I'm saying, Miss Salazar, that if you can persuade your cousin to leave the relative and very probably temporary security of Monterrey, go up to Nuevo Laredo, which is about two hundred miles to the northeast. If she could stay there until I can get authorization to go down and get her and her son out of the country, you'd be doing your cousin and us an enormous service. She apparently trusts you. And we have undercover people down there in Nuevo Laredo who'll give her sanctuary and watch her back. People we pay well, who won't be persuaded by that reward money. Besides, anybody claiming that reward money would earn a big target on his back from the Gulf Cartel."

I glanced over at Rick, who shrugged in response. What could he do? What could I do that I hadn't already done? There was nothing more I could do except to follow Agent Torres's advice.

"I'll try. And you'll arrange to give her political asylum or something like that?" My hopes began to rise.

Agent Torres grinned. "Not political asylum, but I'll certainly try to arrange a special immigration entry for her and her son." He jotted down a note on his yellow pad. "One more thing, Miss Salazar. Your cousin mentioned Cartel documents in her letter, documents she's bargaining with. If you could get her to send a sample either through the regular mail or in her email to you, that would be helpful in persuading my superiors."

"Okay," I agreed. It seemed that Teresa was guarding these documents with her life and would be reluctant to give them up. But perhaps one page or half a page. Of course, I had no idea what these documents might contain, having no insider's knowledge about Mexican crime syndicates. Perhaps names of people involved in the *Organization*, as Teresa called it. "Could she send it to you directly?" I asked the federal officer.

Agent Torres exchanged an amused look with Rick. "Not a good idea. If she could slip the sample to my undercover man down there, it'd take longer for me to get it, and the risk would be greater. I assume she's having her friend post her mail for her, and she's using her friend's email address, I see. Warn her against using cell phones unless her friend has a GSM phone with an international prepaid SIM card. Before she moves to Nuevo Laredo, she should have her friend purchase in her own name or someone else's name a mobile phone with an international SIM card."

I whipped a piece of paper and pen out of my purse and made a note of that. I knew what he was talking about but had never used one myself. Lisa had told me once her uncle, Leo, used those international prepaid cards whenever he went to Mexico.

"What if she refuses to go to Nuevo Laredo? As hard as it is for her and her son in Monterrey, hiding inside all the time, she feels safe there."

The gaze he directed my way underwent a subtle change from amused detachment to profound pity.

"If she refuses to go to Nuevo Laredo, then I can't help her. I'm sorry, but that's the best possible border for her to cross. Her picture and her son have been plastered all over the country. Vargas's men have most likely alerted all the major airports and bus terminals. I can give her a fairly safe haven in Nuevo Laredo. For a while, anyway."

Fairly safe. For a while. There were so many qualifications to his statement that my hopes sank like a ton of bricks.

"Okay, I'll email her and tell her all this." I mulled over his conditions. "You're sure I can't just go down there and bring them back—like in a tourist RV or something? I could go down to the Baja coast and pretend I'm there to camp for a few days. Or the mainland coast of Mexico. I know of a campground north of Puerta Vallarta. Lots of gringos go there."

Agent Torres heaved a sigh. "Miss Salazar, you'd have no problem getting there, but you'd never make it back across the border. It's too risky. You'd become another statistic, I'm afraid." He stood up and extended his hand. Apparently, the meeting was over. "Do your part, and I'll do mine. Leave it to the professionals, Miss Salazar. Please."

I shook his hand, and so did Rick.

"Good luck," was Agent Torres's parting.

Rick and I looked at each other.

We were going to need more than luck.

Teresa and her young son, too.

CHAPTER SEVENTEEN

"**W**hat kind of pizza do you want, Dina? I've got pepperoni or mushroom and sausage. Or both?"

"Mushroom and sausage," I called out to Rick, "but only two small pieces. Pizzas are hip and thigh-spreaders." I was making a giant salad to balance the cholesterol in the pizza.

"There's nothing wrong with your hips or thighs," Rick said, peeking around the corner of his open-counter kitchen. He winked at me. "In fact, I've been thinking a lot about those hips and thighs lately. And what's in between . . ."

I gasped in mock horror, then hushed him as Angelina appeared in the living room. She'd vanished the moment I'd stepped foot inside their condo, and despite Rick's coaxing, she wouldn't emerge. I had a feeling the aroma of newly baked pizza had lured her out of her bedroom.

She went straight to the kitchen, ignoring me and the present I'd brought for her.

"*Papá*, make her go home. She's still here." The little girl looked back at me and glared. Boy, if looks could kill . . .

What had happened to that sweet little girl the night of my birthday dinner?

Quién sabe! Rick kept reassuring me she'd come around, but I was beginning to have my doubts. However, I'd promised Rick I'd be very patient with the child, and I was keeping to my word.

It was Saturday night following our meeting with DEA agent Joe Torres, and I'd been invited over to watch Exhibition Football. Our favorite team, the *Forty-Niners*, was playing against the *Dallas Cowboys* and Rick wanted to make our little, informal get-together cozy and relaxing.

It was turning out to be anything but.

Last night he'd gotten a babysitter, the teenage daughter of the pretty blonde woman upstairs — the one I'd seen him hugging that night in a very innocent embrace, so he'd explained — and we'd had our first date. Over an Italian dinner, we'd talked about our jobs and our families, trying to catch up on each other's lives over the intervening years. One topic we'd tacitly agreed on was off-limits — our romantic relationships during that time. I didn't feel I could handle knowing about his, and I suppose he'd felt the same way. Definitely *verboten*.

Our trip down to LA to meet the DEA agent had changed things for me. Call me a fool, but at that point, I realized I was ready to take a risk on our resumed friendship. Simply put, I wanted Rick Ramos, and he wanted me. If the whole thing blew up in our faces, well, so be it. If my Mexican cousin, Teresa, could risk her neck to save her son from a life with a crime syndicate, I supposed I could take a few risks with mine.

Anyway, later last night, after meeting Rick for coffee, we'd returned to Flora's, sat in his car, and talked some more. Flora had left with Porter to spend a weekend in Reno right after work, so I wasn't forced to tell her I was seeing Rick again. Frankly, I was in no mood to hear her lectures about drinking from the same well twice or her admonitions about Rick's unfaithful history.

I knew — God, did I know — the considerable risk I was taking, but it didn't seem to matter for the moment. Call me *estupida,* but I was hoping and praying that it would be different. This time.

Still, despite my willingness to gamble with my whole heart and soul, I wanted to take it slowly.

Our Friday night casual coffee date ended at Flora's door even though it took every ounce of willpower to send him away. We hadn't slept together yet, though, *Dios sabe*, my nether regions—all the erogenous zones in my body—were throbbing with desire and need. Tonight was no exception.

"Angie, if you're not going to be a nice girl, go back to your room," Rick told the little girl in Spanish. "Dina's my guest, and you're to treat her with respect, or you can eat by yourself."

"Fine!" The five-year-old stamped her foot and held out a plate. "I don't want to eat with her! She has ugly hair and a butt face—"

Cara de culo. I had to suppress a smile, for I used to call my brother that when we were small.

"That's enough!" Rick hissed at her. "Go to your room. I'll bring some pizza to you when I'm damn good and ready. Now go!"

Angelina turned her big, brown eyes up at her father, her lips quivered, and tears began to roll. Dissolving into tears, she ran to her room. We could hear her sobbing loudly from the living room.

I felt guilty and saddened all at once. Without wanting to, of course, I was coming between Rick and his daughter, and we weren't even officially together as a couple.

Rick brought in a tray with two plates and two glasses of cold lite beer. He placed the tray on the sturdy, oak coffee table and sat down. Every feature on his face showed tension.

"I think I've lost my appetite," I said. "Maybe I should go. Maybe we're moving too fast. I mean, Sunday golf, then Monday down in LA, then last night and now tonight."

"We're not moving fast enough for my taste," he replied, handing me one of the glasses of beer. He smiled and clinked his glass with mine. "Dina, it's been too long. All I can think about is you." He leaned over and kissed me. "*Querida*, don't let her get to you. She's jealous, probably feels threatened because she senses how much I care about you. You females are all like that, y'know, just get two together with one man, and there's sudden competition for his attention and affection."

"Oh, are you accustomed to this? Has Angelina behaved this way in front of your other girlfriends?"

I could've bitten my tongue, but the words and all they implied just tumbled out.

"No, not lately anyway. And no again. You're the first woman I've brought home. This is new to her, and she feels threatened."

I wasn't sure I believed this, but I appreciated his attempt to make me feel better. I took a sip of beer, then another.

"She wouldn't even look at the toy keyboard I bought her."

"I know." Rick smiled in commiseration. "I apologize for her. She's acting like a real *mimada*. And maybe she is, a little. She's been my whole world—well, her and my work. My mother dotes on her—my sisters, too. Maybe we've tried too hard to make up for what Angie's been through. We've spoiled her."

"I'm hoping one day to see the charming little girl I met that night at the restaurant." By now, I needed to relax, and so I took a few gulps. The pizza, though smelling heavenly, I knew I wouldn't be able to force it down my throat.

"You will, I promise," Rick assured me, about to take his first bite of pepperoni, his attention already on the television. The kick-off had just happened, and the stadium crowd was roaring its excitement.

Over the television noise, we could hear loud wailing from behind the wall. Rick rolled his eyes.

"Now she's being melodramatic."

"She's probably hungry," I suggested.

Two minutes later, he jumped up and took a plate and a glass of milk to the little girl's room. I sat there, wondering what I'd gotten myself into. If Rick's daughter persisted in her *Hate Dina* kick, I doubted whether Rick and I stood a chance as a twosome, let alone a family.

Maybe, just maybe, Rick and I weren't meant to be. Y'know, like the star-crossed lovers of Shakespeare and medieval lore. Maybe it wasn't in the stars.

At halftime, I made excuses about a Roman mythology test that I had to create and word process for Monday's history class. Rick saw through that lame excuse but nevertheless accompanied me to my car.

"Something else bothering you?" he asked sympathetically, his big hand clamped firmly on my shoulder.

"You know I emailed Teresa in care of her friend in Monterrey as soon as we got home on Monday. I told her all about the meeting with Agent Torres. Only I put it all in code like he said to do. I said that *Tío* Jose would be consulting with *Tío* Sam about coming down to Mexico to visit family." Rick was nodding his approval. After all, he knew how good I was at concocting tales. "I also told her that *Tío* José wanted to see some of the real estate papers that her family had. She was to send them to me so I could show them to *Tío* Sam. I made it sound as if their visit to Mexico depended on those papers." Rick was holding me close and kissing my hair, trying his best to distract me, I think.

"Have you heard from her since then?" he murmured against my temple. His body was radiating heat, making me struggle to focus on my cousin Teresa's problems. His groin was pressed against my left thigh, and the hard bulge I could feel was unmistakable.

"Yes, this morning." Today was a work day for both of us, so we hadn't had the opportunity to talk much. "She said her friend didn't have the real estate papers but would send the men's suit that I'd requested. She hoped the size would fit. Which I thought was strange, but it must be *her* code that she was sending what Agent Torres wanted. She also said that leaving where she stayed was out of the question. Not possible, she said. That was it. She's afraid, Rick. She and her son are safe now, and she's afraid to leave."

"You'll have to persuade her, Dina. Otherwise, the DEA can't help her."

I mumbled something like, yeah, before turning my body and reaching up around his neck. I pulled the scruff of his hair at the nape and playfully tugged. Then we kissed. Long and deep.

My nether regions throbbed some more. Our kisses made every vein inside me pulsate with yearning. Our touches were fervent and frantic, born of desperation and sexual frustration. I sensed that fear played a part, too. Fear that no matter how we longed to make it work as a couple this time, there were now three of us.

Funny, what a five-year-old child can do to two adults.

The hours between six and eight seemed to be the Salazar clan's communication time. I started calling home regularly to check on Pop and to give Grandma Gómez updates on Teresa and her son in hiding in Mexico. She hadn't received any messages from Teresa since that telegram. Grandma was more than a little annoyed about my contacts with the DEA, ever fearful of any communication with American authorities. Still, I'd made a good case about the need to involve them, making sure she understood that Agent Torres was Mexican-American and sympathetic to Teresa's situation.

I also reassured her that the feds would not show up on her doorstep with a deportation warrant. If she were ever asked, Grandma was to tell people that Mama was born in Amarillo, Texas, two years after she left Mexico. She'd even clucked her tongue disapprovingly over my admission that I'd lied to a federal agent.

Hel-lo! I gave up trying to make her understand why I had to do that. Grandma seemed to believe that since Mama came to the States as a baby, she became an American citizen. Trying to make Grandma understand the maze of immigration laws when I didn't understand half of them — well, that was a task better left alone.

With the need to communicate again with my family in Salinas in mind, I took my cell phone out to the spa in Flora's back garden. Soaking in the nude in 100-degree heated water and sipping from a glass of *Napa Valley* syrah were the equivalent, to me, of an hour with a high-priced shrink. And a whole lot cheaper.

I'd had a rough day at school. Juan, one of my favorite Special Ed kids, got bloodied up in a fight with a future linebacker from Mrs. Collins's sixth-grade class. A new kid, recently transferred from East San Jose and upset over his parents' impending divorce, the linebacker tried to set the hallway's garbage cans on fire, and Juan tried to stop him. Both boys, blubbering and apologetic, were suspended for three days, and their parents were called.

Then, after lunch, one of the girls whose recent essay I'd given a C blurted out that she hated me, then ran crying out of the room.

And there wasn't even a full moon. I didn't know if it was raging prepubescent hormones, lousy karma from all those bratty incidents in my childhood, or if I was a failure as a teacher. By two-thirty that afternoon, I was revisiting the possibility that one of Grandma Gómez's wicked, Chihuahuan ancestors had put a curse on me.

Then we had a practice fire drill, which ramped up the kids' adrenaline levels for the remaining half-hour, followed by a dull, protracted staff meeting. The Lincoln All-Stars had to forego their fitness jog around school, and I missed the opportunity to exercise off my frustrations.

By the time VP Mark McDuff informed me in an icy voice, at the conclusion of our staff-snooze, that he'd be doing a formal classroom observation of me the following week, I felt a melt-down coming on. Lisa had broken it off with Mark, and now he was associating his pain at rejection—caused by her, not me!—with her closest friend. *Yours Truly.* I was already planning a defense in case I got an *unsatisfactory* evaluation. Sexual harassment by association.

My cell phone played its new tune, a few bars from *La Bamba*. This was one of Rick's favorite rock 'n roll numbers.

"Hey, *dolor de culo*, how're things?"

Frankie was calling me, probably on his way home from work.

"Hmm, so-so, *cara de culo*. Tell me again why I chose teaching as a career."

He chuckled. "'Cause you love kids and kids love you."

"You got that wrong," I groused, pausing to sip some wine. "A couple of my kids are making me wig out . . .or get me fired. And Rick's daughter hates me."

"Aha, I thought so. I mean, I thought you two'd get back together. Don't get me wrong, Dina, I like Rick, but I hope you're not doing this because of the fifty-thousand he gave the folks. You know what Grandma says about selling yourself to the highest bidder—"

"No, Frankie, it's not that at all. I've been . . .*enamorada* with him all these years." I couldn't say the words, in love. The Spanish sounded less . . . I don't know . . . serious?

"Huh? You drunk?"

I laughed. "Not yet. I'm on my first glass of wine—haven't even gotten a buzz yet. I'm sitting in Aunt Flora's spa, relaxing, trying to mellow out. It's been that kind of day."

"Yeah, I know what you mean. Isabel wants me to put in a hot tub—you said Rick's daughter hates you. So you've met her?"

"Uh-huh. She's a cute little girl—listen, Frankie, you've got four kids. What do you do to get them to love you?"

"You shower 'em with expensive gifts and let 'em watch all the TV they want. You let 'em stay up as late as they want—"

"Really?" Was he pulling my leg?

"No, *tonta*, none of the above. All that does is earn their contempt. 'Course, you might get that, anyway. No, what you do, you earn their respect. Simple as that. Don't show your fear or anxiety. It's a dog-eat-dog world, and kids can smell fear like dogs can. So, if you want to impress Rick's daughter, you earn her respect."

I considered that. Frankie was smart.

"'Course, you know, hooking up with a man with kids, it means you're always second-place. You have to be able to live with that. So can you live with that, Dina?"

"Truthfully, Frankie, I don't know." I didn't like the sound of that—second place—but then, didn't all parents have to put their kids first before the comfort of their spouses?

"Believe me, sis, it's not all fun 'n games, this raising kids business. So what's new with our cousin in Mexico? *Mamá* said you've been getting emails from her. And you saw a DEA agent that might help her get out."

I filled him in on the meeting with Joe Torres in LA.

"The last one, three days ago. It was a concise message—I think she's scared and paranoid, and I can't blame her. She's afraid her husband'll find her and kill her. She's staying with a friend right now in Monterrey, but she's hoping we'll be able to help her cross the border. She doesn't want to use a coyote. It's too dangerous. You know what some of those coyotes do. They leave 'em in the desert to fend for themselves or even lock 'em in trucks and suffocate them. No, we definitely don't want her to go that route. But the longer she stays in one place, the greater the danger. That's what Agent Torres believes, anyway. He wants her to go to a border town called Nuevo Laredo." I sighed audibly. "That's basically it. And I'm expecting to get some papers from her, some cartel documents she took. The DEA seems very anxious to see those."

"Okay, so what's next?"

"Then I send Agent Torres those papers. Then we wait for him to get approval to go into Mexico and get her out."

"Well, keep us informed, okay? And good luck with Rick's little girl. Funny, I can't picture you a mother."

"I can't, either," I said, frowning. I wasn't being flippant.

We rang off a few minutes later. Well, Frankie's advice helped a lot!

How was I supposed to earn the respect of a five-year-old girl? Do I impress her with my culinary skills? Do I take her to a driving range and show her how far I can hit a golf ball? I was stymied.

I sat there, on the spa's submerged seat, totally hidden from prying neighbors. Flora's spa was enclosed on three sides by trellised screens, covered by *Morning Glory* vines and climbing *Star Jasmine*. The rain had stopped, and the evening air was pungent and fragrant with wet earth and sweet blossoms. Four solar-powered garden lights dimly illuminated the little, curved flagstone walkway extending from the French door of the sun room to the spa. I'd kept the overhead patio lights off so that I could mellow out in the darkened silence of Flora's lush garden.

Since the internal spa light was on, I raised one foot and glanced down at what remained of my pedicure polish. Not much left. I wondered if Rick would notice and consider me a frumpy slob. I'd barely had the time to shave my legs and underarms before coming out here, the primary purpose of which was to relax and get in a sexy mood for Rick's visit. He was due in an hour after getting dinner for Angelina and reading to her from that *Berenstain Bears* book I'd taken over on Saturday night.

In the five weeks we'd been seeing each other, I still hadn't slept with him. I know that by today's moral standards, that made me a first-class prude. Not that I didn't want to, believe me. I just wanted to give us some time to get used to each other. And I wanted to feel out Angelina, to see if there was a chance we could be friends. That night of my birthday dinner, I certainly thought so. Lately, though, every time I saw her, she ran to her room and flatly refused to even speak to me. Rick reassured me that she'd eventually thaw out, but I wasn't so sure.

Perhaps Frankie was right. I had to earn the little girl's respect and get used to being number two. Romance, adventure, and sex would always take a back seat to a child's needs and concerns, as they should be.

I frowned. Is that what I wanted? Or needed?

Still, I'd made the decision to crank up our relationship a notch. Rick and I were both tired of saying good-night at the door. Tonight was *it*.

My cell phone played *La Bamba* again. Maybe it was Rick, having to cancel out because Angelina was throwing a hissy-fit about his coming to see me. Or she stuffed a marble up her nose and had to be taken to emergency. Whoa, Dina! Was my resentment against the little minx starting to seep up to the surface?

"Hi, Dina! It's Hugh."

I almost dropped my phone in the spa. It danced in my hand threateningly until I got it firmly in my grip. Well, knock me over with a feather!

"Hugh . . .uh, how's life?"

Like I wanted to know. Like I cared.

"Okay, I guess. Actually, not so good. My campaign's stalled, and that murderer Trent Robertson got off—"

"The guy who murdered his pregnant wife?"

The newspapers were all over this notorious case. A young husband was facing two counts of first-degree murder and death-by-injection. The case, on which Hugh was the lead prosecutor, had hinged on a multitude of solid but circumstantial evidence. The team of expensive defense attorneys, smelling a high-profile case, were clever, relentless sharks — as Lisa called them. Lisa Luna and I were convinced the man, a chronic liar and serial philanderer, was guilty as sin. We were also confident that Hugh's career either soared or stank based on the jury's verdict.

Oh shit, better get out the deodorizer. "I'm so sorry. I wanted justice for that poor woman and her family." Perhaps Hugh, the trial attorney, had been too distracted by his political campaign. Too much gladhanding and schmoozing with the local big wigs? Or too cocksure about his own talents? Had he let the guilty verdict slip through his hands?

"Huh! Justice is blind, and the jury's a bunch of mindless morons. My career is toast. I couldn't get elected dogcatcher in this town."

So true, I thought, I wouldn't vote for you. But what about the electric power-grid supervisor for the state of California? Now, there was a job. What, with all those brownouts we had last summer. I could see the people lining up. I almost suggested it out of spite.

"I'm sorry, Hugh. How can I help you — as a friend?"

I almost gagged on that last little phrase, but, hey, you don't earn brownie points in heaven by kicking a man when he's down.

"I-I miss you, Dina," he whined. "Can you come over?"

Yeah, come over to stroke his bruised ego. I coughed down a nasty retort.

"Well, Hugh, I'm sorry. There's a new man in my life."

I broke off as another call was coming through.

"I have to go. Sorry, Hugh, I hope things improve for you.

Good luck."

Boy, was this Grand Central night! It was the DEA agent, Joe Torres.

"Dina Salazar? Teresa Vargas's cousin? Joe Torres, Drug Enforcement Administration. Sorry to call so late—it's eight-thirty here in San Antonio. I'm talking to some people about the Nuevo Laredo connection—the possibility of getting Teresa across the border here. It *is* possible, but ICE wants to have a peek at those cartel papers she has. Have you gotten them yet?"

I told him no but didn't add that Teresa said she wouldn't leave her safe haven in Monterrey. I figured there was still a chance I could talk her into it once Agent Torres gave us firm assurance that she and her son would be taken care of in Nuevo Laredo.

He went on to say that he'd need a couple of weeks to confer with the INS, the FBI, ICE, the USBP, and the DOJ. Talk about a blockade of government bureaucracies!

If all went well, Torres said, he'd make it possible for Teresa and her son to immigrate to the US legally in exchange for information about her father's and husband's organization. It took me a few seconds to decipher some of those government acronyms. The rest, I took his word for it.

"Okay."

"I just need a little time to make arrangements—get approval, documents, set things up. Oh, and I need to speak with your grandmother to find out what other information Teresa Vargas has passed onto her. I'm fluent in Spanish, so that's not an issue—"

I told him I didn't think my grandmother would speak to him, explaining how I was the family's designated liaison, and Grandma Gómez refused to talk with American officials.

"I see," Joe Torres said after a pause. I think he understood the situation without my having to spell it out—the reason for

Grandma's reluctance. As an illegal, she was fearful of having American authorities check her identification papers too closely.

I was fearful, too. The last thing I wanted was for Grandma Gómez to get deported to Mexico. My family would never forgive me if that happened. Omigod, the family brat turned family rescuer, would then become the family pariah!

"I'll get back to you, then, as soon as I get the okay. My partner and I are calling it, Mission—Saving la familia. As the family representative, Miss Salazar, I'll need you to be there when the time comes."

"Huh? When the time comes? What do you mean?"

"I mean, when we cross her at the border, you've got to be there. We'll need her trust and complete cooperation. Also, we need you to make initial contact with our undercover man."

"What border?" My mind wasn't making the leap.

"The Texas-Nuevo Laredo border. She's in Monterrey. Laredo's the closest border town in Texas. It's too risky for her to travel across Mexico to the California border sites. That's where they expect her to cross. She'd be going into territory that's controlled by the Juárez and Tijuana Cartels."

His voice carried a nuance of irritation as though he'd explained all of these problems before. Maybe he had, but suddenly the idea that I was supposed to help her physically cross the border kept interfering with his message.

"Tell her in your next email that she must prepare to go to Nuevo Laredo. Not right away but in the next couple of weeks. Better yet, tell her to stay put until further notice."

A lot of what he said made no sense to me but what registered was the first sentence. "You want me to go to Laredo, Texas?"

Well, this was a new wrinkle. I'd never been to Texas in my life, nor had I ever met Grandma Gómez's brother and his family, who were still in Amarillo.

Heck, I didn't even know where Laredo was. Then I remembered that map in Joe Torres's office. Shoot, Laredo was somewhere in the desert country by the Rio Grande. It wasn't even close to Playa Blanca or Cancún. There wouldn't be any *Club Meds* down there. Just cactus and sagebrush. And probably cartel bandidos with machine guns.

"You speak Spanish, true?" Agent Torres asked me in Spanish.

When I said yes, then followed with a bit of demonstration, he went on, "Good. You'll need it. Nuevo Laredo and Matamoros are Gulf Cartel headquarters. But first, let me do my job and grease some wheels around here. Send me those documents as soon as you get them."

When we clicked off, I found my heart racing.

Shit! What had I gotten myself into? Did Grandma Gómez realize the danger she was going to put me into? And how was I going to help a federal officer rescue my cousin from dangerous drug-cartel desperados? Would Agent Torres allow me to take that .38 *Lady Smith and Wesson* revolver with me? Would I have the nerve to use it if I had to save Teresa, her son, and me? My skin started to creep and crawl. This was a world I wanted no part of.

Was that why *Abuelita* needed one of the intelligent Salazars to do the job? Smart or not, what the hell was I supposed to do in that border town in the midst of this Gulf Cartel? And how was Spanish going to help? Didn't the Mexicans in those border towns speak English, like they did in Tijuana?

Suddenly, I heard the wrought iron gate latch jiggle and the gate creak open. Rick must be early, and I was still soaking in the spa, naked. Oh well, why not?

My thoughts quickly skipped to a much more pleasant topic. I'll invite him to join me, I thought, suddenly excited. My heart tripped to racing mode. My nipples perked up. All my e-zones became liquid fire.

A dark male figure stumbled into the dim light of the garden. He mumbled something.

Shit!

"Steve!"

CHAPTER EIGHTEEN

"*Mas te a gachas, mas te miran.*" The more you bend over, the more they look. Grandma Gomez liked to remind us girls that if you tempt men by behaving in a lewd way, the more you will pay for it. One of Grandma's favorite cautionary tales. Not that we took it to heart, I hate to admit. Oh well, some lessons I guess women never learn.

His eyes half-closed, one hand holding the neck of an open beer bottle, Steve weaved to the left, then to the right.

"Thought y-you were Flora . . .w-where's Flora?"

I tried to cover my bare breasts and pubis with my arms and hands. In a dark sweat suit and sandals, Steve was slurring his speech as if he'd been injected with a massive dose of *Lidocaine.*

"Sh-she's out, Steve. Come back . . .uh, tomorrow night."

He smiled sardonically and lurched forward, his eyes bulging like a clown's.

"Sh-she doesn't want me . . .did you know that, Dina? Sh-she dumped me for some old dude with lots o' bucks. Hey, I got lots of bucks — h-hey! Y-you're butt naked."

"Steve, you're drunk. Go home and sleep it off . . .or go inside and sleep it off on Flora's bed. C'mon, you'll feel better. Now go inside, and I'll come and make you some coffee."

I was speaking fast, trying to cajole him into leaving so I could get out of the spa and grab my bathrobe, which was lying across one of the chairs on the patio.

It wasn't working. Steve was pulling his sweatshirt over his head. Next, he began untying the cord around his waist. I started to panic. When he shimmied out of his sweatpants and kicked off his *Birkenstocks*, I was past panicking.

"No, you-you can't come in. My boyfriend's coming over. He'll get angry —"

Steve barked a pathetic laugh and stripped off his black bikini briefs. Fortunately, his penis was as flaccid as a wet flag. This was studly Steve? With a weenie the size of a goldfish?

I was more ticked off than scared. If Rick showed up now and saw a naked man in the spa with me, what would he think? Lots of terrible things about me, I knew. I'd lose him for good!

"I'm mad, too. Flora said I was her man . . .and . . .and then she dumped me f-for some . . .loaded, old guy."

He let himself into the spa, submerging completely. When he came up, he was sputtering water.

"Ha, I see your bush, Dina. F-funny, I always thought y-your hair was fake. H-hey, did you know . . .Flora dyes h-hers to match her hair? And-and she's not . . .not thirty-nine. Sh-she's goddamned f-fifty years old. F-fifty years old! I've been fucking a f-fifty — hey, y'know, I don't even care. I l-love her —"

"Steve," I pleaded, moving to the far side of the circular spa, "get out. You can't be in here. I don't want you in here —"

"Hey, I always liked you . . .though you're kinda prissy. You always have a rod up your b-butt. D-Dina, don't you like me? If Flora doesn't want me, why don't you . . .y-you and me get together?"

I glanced at his crotch. Even through the bubbling, swirling water, it was apparent he was getting aroused. Either that or the water was magnifying parts of his anatomy. His goldfish had grown into a herring.

"Hey, let's show Flora . . . lets you and me do it. Bet you knew we didn't just do abs and glutes in her bedroom—huh? W-whaddya say?"

Then he did the unthinkable. He lurched toward me and grabbed my breasts. I lost it. I started screaming—I can't remember what I cried out or if I even put words to my panic. I think, mostly, I just shrieked and cursed like a longshoreman.

Flailing my arms, I tried to slap away his hands. Then I began to kick, but he was standing too close. I tried kneeing him in the groin, but he moved to the side of me. For a drunk, he was pretty agile. As I pushed against his chest, I could feel one of his hands grope between my thighs.

I screamed some more. A fragment of my mind hoped a neighbor would come and rescue me. I screamed louder and fought more vigorously.

With no help in sight, I managed to twist aside and turn my back to him. But Steve was relentless. He bent over me, grabbing my buttocks this time and encircling my waist with one arm, pinning me to him.

I was getting tired, as much from screaming as from fighting him. But the thought of submitting to him was not an option. The very idea of being assaulted by such a spoiled, stupid oaf made me furious.

For a couple of seconds, I relaxed to recoup my energy. I let him paw me while I clenched my teeth. I drew deep breaths of air. Steve relaxed, too, thinking most likely that I was ready to play ball. Or else, in his drunken stupor, his strength was sapped. He loosened his grip around my waist, just long enough for me to renew my struggle.

Screaming as loudly as I could, I sprang up to a step and kicked back with all my might. My heel connected with something hard, probably Steve's face, and I heard something crack. Steve cried out in pain. With another leap upward, I hit the wooden spa deck, bounced off, and landed on my knees on the damp grass next to the spa.

Then I cried out in pain. My heel hurt like hell!

And Steve had disappeared under the water's surface.

Only then did I hear a noise by the same gate Steve had pushed open.

Rick's tall shape quickly came into view. "What the hell's going—"

"Rick, Steve—he-he was trying . . ." I looked back. Steve still hadn't surfaced. "Oh my God, he's drowning!"

The next blur of events happened in intense silence.

Rick threw down the bouquet of red roses he held, kicked off his shoes and jacket, and jumped into the spa. I stood there, naked and shivering, while Rick lifted a dead-weighted Steve and propped him over the edge of the jacuzzi. Submerged to his waist, he glanced up at me, scowled, and said nothing. After climbing back out, his shirt and pants sagging and clinging to him, drenched to the skin, Rick dragged a limp Steve to the grass. He laid him on his stomach and straddled him.

"For Christ's sake, Dina, put on something and call nine-one-one. His nose is bleeding. I might not be able to revive him." Rick began to massage Steve's back, pushing upwards from his waist.

"Yes, nine-one-one." I grabbed my bathrobe from the patio chair, wrapped it around me, then searched for my cell phone on the spa deck.

"Rick, I kicked him. Really hard. D'ya think his nose is broken?"

I seized the phone and punched in the numbers.

"What were you doing in the spa with him? Naked?" Rick eyed me accusingly.

"I was by myself, having wine, talking on my cell. Then he showed up, and he was drunk—"

I broke off to report the emergency. Embarrassed, my

explanation to the dispatcher was another white lie. I told her that the man—my aunt's friend—was drunk and slipped, hit his head, and knocked himself out while climbing out of the spa. Another friend was attempting to revive him, and then I gave my name and address.

By the time I rang off, Steve was moaning and spewing water. Rick had rolled him onto his back and was crouching beside him. That's when I explained to Rick who Steve was and the entire situation—silently praying that he would believe me. Good grief, I didn't want him thinking I'd invited Steve to join me in the spa just before he was due to arrive. I didn't want Rick to think I'd ask Steve to anything, anywhere.

A minute passed while Rick, heaving from the exertion and adrenaline rush, sat on the grass next to a slowly stirring Steve. Soaked all over, he took a scan around him, absorbed the whole scene, the haphazard pile of Steve's clothes, his bottle of beer tossed absently on the grass, my single glass of wine by the spa.

Dear God, make him believe me, I prayed, and I promise you I'll never go skinny-dipping again. Ever!

"I can't decide if I should punch him or strangle you. You should have a lock on that gate. What're you and Flora thinking? I heard you screaming before I got out of the car. You didn't exactly sound like you were having fun. Man, where did you learn to swear like that?" He sounded very annoyed.

I felt a smidgen of contrition. Where did he think I learned—with two older brothers and growing up in a Salinas barrio? I wasn't much of a lady, but at least I knew how to fight back.

"I had to kick him to get him off me," I pouted.

He swung his head in my direction and gave me head-to-toe scrutiny. "Are you okay?"

I nodded, still a little shaken. I felt so relieved that Rick believed me that tears welled up and began to slowly trickle down my cheeks.

"You want to call the police? Charge him with attempted rape?"

I looked over at a naked Steve, eyes still closed, gingerly touching his face with one trembling hand. He was so bombed that I doubted he knew what he was doing.

"Look at him, Rick. He's wasted. He never would've done this, sober. He's basically a nice guy — well, used to be. Flora dumped him, and he's not taking it very well."

Steve moaned softly. "Flora . . .help me."

My gaze steadied on Rick. I was confused and torn. The old Steve was goofy and weird in a sweet way. With a significant Mommy complex. The new, angry and drunk Steve was capable of God-knows-what. Yet, another word from Rick, and I probably would've called the cops.

Rick's fulminating frown answered me. "It's your call."

I let Steve off the hook. This time.

Twenty minutes later, after the medics administered first aid, applied a neck collar, and carried Steve and his clothes away in their ambulance, Rick and I went to the laundry room. I'd already put Rick's bouquet of red roses in a vase, and now we were ready to get his clothes dry.

"I'll make some hot tea. Or coffee?" I offered between shudders.

"Never a dull moment with you," he griped, stripping off his blue and white striped, button-down shirt, tan khakis, and navy socks. He stood there in his white, *Fruit-of-the-Loom* briefs, looking exhausted. His head-cold had worsened since I'd seen him for dinner Sunday night. His eyes were watery, the rims of his nostrils reddened. Wet and cold, he probably felt like shit.

Nevertheless, he had an enormous erection that was poking out the front of his briefs. As I threw the shirt, pants, and socks in Flora's dryer and set it for air, I couldn't wrest my gaze away from it — or him.

"I'm so sorry, Rick. I could make you some chicken soup. That'll make you feel . . ."

I'd kinda lost my train of thought as my gaze roamed all over him. Despite his head-cold and ill humor — who could blame him — Rick Ramos was beautiful. His body had always enthralled me. Tall, muscular, and flat-stomached, he had broad shoulders you could rest a board on. His waist and hips were narrow, and he was nearly hairless. His skin was a *mélange* of bronze and light olive. His nipples were chestnut brown, and his pecs well-padded.

Oh sure, Tyler Dalton had a more classically attractive face, but Rick was the epitome of the handsome Hispanic male in my view of things.

When he peeled off his wet briefs, my gaze naturally strayed downward. The narrow line of straight, black hair, which arrowed down from his pecs to his belly, widened to a nest of nearly black curls. His penis, lighter in shade than the rest of him, was thick and long, big enough to satisfy me, I recalled with pleasure. I would've continued my perusal of the finer aspects of his male pulchritude, but something hit me. A surge of desire and hunger shot through me so strong that I almost gasped.

I stopped shivering immediately.

I untied my bathrobe sash and drew apart the front, hoping he wouldn't be too repulsed by what he saw. I was no Jennifer Lopez or Salma Hayek. I knew my body had flaws. Hell, I'd studied them to death in my lowest moments. But I also knew that Rick found me attractive, so that knowledge emboldened me.

I glanced down at the beige, shag area rug that lay on the tile floor of the laundry room. He caught my smile a second later. His sensuous lips twitched into a smile.

We didn't need to speak a word. We flung ourselves at

each other and collapsed in a mingled heap on the rug. There was no need for preliminaries. No foreplay — hell, we wanted to get it on! Anyway, the past five weeks had been foreplay enough.

In one fluid motion, he thrust himself into me — no need to fumble or guide him in. He was like a mariner who knew precisely where to find his favorite port. I wrapped my legs around his hips, and we rocked a few times. Rick sank more deeply into me, and then we rode the waves together until we crashed onto the shore. Wave after wave of spasms shook me until my toes tingled. Rick uttered one long groan.

All the metaphors in the world couldn't describe how I felt in those moments. We lay together quietly for a minute or two after the tension in our bodies slackened.

Finally, I had to break the silence.

"Who was it who said — it was in a movie — the guy said, sex was the most fun he had without laughing."

"Woody Allen in *Annie Hall*," he said.

Like me, he was a movie buff, and he remembered how we'd laughed over that line. We continued to hold each other.

"Are we going to screw it up this time?"

Omigod, where did that come from? In horror, I clamped my mouth shut so hard that my teeth were practically biting through my lips.

"I'll try not to." He nuzzled softly against my cheek. "What about you, baby?"

"I'll try not to."

After a moment of sipping my lips, he braced himself up on his forearms and gazed intensely into my eyes. "You sure? Dina, you know Angelina and me. She's my daughter."

"No need to argue your case. You're a package deal. I accept that."

I couldn't believe these words were coming out of my mouth. Had the filter in my brain suddenly gone to sleep?

What was I getting myself into? But if I was saying this—and my screwball, distrustful mind wasn't editing it out—these words, this decision must've come from somewhere deep within me. I had to trust my instincts on this one.

And hope and pray I wouldn't live to regret it.

"*Me alegras, corazón.*" You make me happy, sweetheart.

Spanish was such a romantic language that it was a good choice for such a moment. English, on the other hand, was for hardcore, practical matters.

"Will you be able to come to family parties and tolerate my mother and grandmother? You know how they can be."

"I've always liked them. Didn't you know that? They're hard and stern like my parents. I understand people like that."

"Huh, I didn't know that."

"Enough with questions. Let's find a bed."

What followed defined my idea of heaven on earth. Lying in bed with Rick in a dark, quiet house, I felt cocooned in love. A real love fest, without the fest.

We'd made love again, this time in my bedroom sanctuary, then talked—both done languidly, luxuriantly as if time were standing still, just for us. Like a special effects freeze-frame in a video, but we were the only ones moving and talking. Ah, absolute heaven.

He was nibbling my rump as I lay in that relaxed half-state between consciousness and sleep, sated somnolence.

"I like that," I said drowsily.

"What's not to like? I love tasting you."

I moaned. "Celebrity mags call what you're doing a Bennifer. You ever read them?"

"Nope. I read blueprints by day and children's books by night. I'm getting a hands-on, practical American education, kindergarten style."

"What're you doing?" Of course, I knew what he was doing, and it was divine.

"I'm marking my territory. In case some other dude catches you in the nude."

"I'm going to look like I've had liposuction."

"You planning to show your bare bottom around? Do you have another date lined up with that cop?"

"Oh no," I purred. Who needed him when I had the Latino lion right in my bed? I flexed my knee and swung my foot up, hitting him in the shoulder accidentally. "Oh, sorry."

"Oww, that hurt so bad," Rick mocked.

"While you're down there, look at my heel. I think I broke it when I kicked Steve."

"Can you ask nicely?"

"*Cielo . . .*" We were back to our customary teasing and bantering like six years had never come between us. I felt Rick move my foot, flex it at the ankle.

"It's bruised, not broken. If it swells to double the size, then you'll know it's broken."

"Boy, wait'll I tell Flora. Hmm, is she going to be pissed that I broke down and slept with you?" For a second, I wondered if she'd be so angry that she would throw me out of her abode.

Oh well, it might be time to start looking for another place to live.

I rolled over to my back, and we joined again. Smoothly and slowly. The side of my neck became his subsequent territorial claim.

"What does she know about love?" he whispered against my flesh. "She's never stayed with any man for very long. Follow your own heart, Dina." He groaned softly. "I wish I could spend the night."

"It's okay. I'm sure I'd be dead by morning if you did."

We both chuckled. Then we sobered up and got down to

business.

Afterward, while cuddling in the letdown of another fire-works-shooting, earthquake-shaking climax, our talking continued.

"Dina, we need to make time for ourselves. It's going to be tougher this time."

"Making love again?" I was still on one train of thought.

"No, I mean . . .being together. We both have demanding jobs, a child to think of, busy lives."

"I know. Whenever is fine with me. Come over when you can."

"Not fine with me," he chided. "It's nice having a cheap date, but—" I pinched his nipple, the one closest to my right hand. He yelped and grinned. "I'd like us to be a family."

I said nothing in reply. What was Rick asking of me? Was he asking me to marry him? Move-in and live with him and his daughter? Without a wedding ring on my finger? What would our families think? He said nothing more, and neither did I.

An hour later, he got up to leave. After retrieving his dry clothes, he dressed in my bedroom, gazing at me while he did so.

"Tomorrow's Thanksgiving. Do you have plans?"

My head was braced upon my raised palm, my gaze following his every move. I was not going to miss a second of his body, naked or otherwise. I nodded.

"Yes. Going home to Salinas. But I'll be back on Friday or Saturday."

"Want to take a drive down to Carmel? Just you and me?"

My face must've registered rapture all of a sudden, for he looked pleased that I was excited.

"This time, no cheap motel. We'll stay at the *Pine Inn* on Ocean. We'll feast like kings, and we'll play the links at—"

"Pebble Beach?" Eighteen holes at Pebble cost five

hundred dollars per person!

He nodded. I was so charged up, I practically bounced on the bed.

"I told you I'd check out the green fees—*chinga madre!*—nearly a thousand bucks for the two of us, but it'll be fun."

I threw my arms around his neck. I was Rick's for life.

"You sure know how to show a girl a good time."

My hero, Rick Ramos!

CHAPTER NINETEEN

A common toast of Mexican men—"*Salud, dinero y amor sin suegra*." Health, money, and love without a mother-in-law! This was Grandpa Gomez's favorite *buen dicho*. Most men prefer love and sex without being forced to get married. When my sisters and I heard that one, we looked at each other and frowned. So, where did that leave us? The message I got was, get a career! Don't depend on marriage! Don't depend on a man!

It was Sunday night, and we'd just returned from a heavenly weekend in Carmel. As Rick pulled up alongside the curb, I noticed the absence of Flora's *Mercedes*. She was still in Lake Tahoe, visiting Uncle Ralph, or was on her way back. It was a five-hour drive through the mountains, and since the Sierras had been blanketed with the first snowfall of the winter season, the pass was probably clogged with slow-going traffic.

As we strolled up the flagstone walkway, I saw it. A *UPS* package, the size of a dress box. In minutes I'd flung it on my bed, not even bothering to take off my jacket. Rick was beside me as I opened the cardboard outer mailer. Inside was a white, light cardboard box, the kind stores give you for gift wrapping. On the lid were the words, printed in black felt ink. *Solamente para los ojos de Dina y José.*

Only for Dina's and Joe's eyes. Meaning Joe Torres, of course. Teresa didn't want anyone else to see the documents apparently, out of concern for their welfare, perhaps.

What about my welfare, I thought uneasily. That worry, I quickly squashed as I took off the lid. Inside, under cover of tissue paper, lay . . .a brown suit! A lady's suit jacket and skirt. From the looks of it, a size 4 or 6 and made of costly material — a blend of cashmere and merino wool, I thought. The brown color was lovely, a shade darker than caramel with minute threads of dark chocolate interwoven into the fabric. Costly fabric, I was certain.

Rick and I exchanged dumbfounded looks. "Look at the note," he said, pointing to the folded piece of paper pinned to the lapel.

With anxious fingers, I unpinned and opened the paper. In Spanish, it read —

Take out the lining very carefully, please. I'd like to wear this someday, Dina, perhaps one time when we go out and celebrate my freedom in California. Inside the lining is the interfacing, which I have written on with permanent fabric ink. Send the interfacing to Joe. There are five pieces. Be careful not to damage them. God bless you, Dina. I hope this will be enough. Tell him there are four more suits and a lot more information about the Organización.

I opened the jacket and stared at the shimmery, dark gold satin lining.

"Teresa made this suit," I told Rick. I knew enough about sewing to recognize a handmade suit, and I knew what interfacing was. My mother encouraged me to take sewing classes in high school, even though I was mostly taking college prep classes. It's an excellent practical skill, she'd said. I think it was the only thing we'd ever agreed on.

"What's *inter-forro*?" Rick asked, running one finger over the smooth satin. I was rummaging through my closet, looking for my sewing basket.

"It's the stiffening fabric that goes inside the lining. Couturiers still use it on high-end, tailored clothing." Finding it, I dragged it out and looked for the seam ripper. "Yes!" I exclaimed happily, clutching the handy little tool and returning to the bed.

Slowly and carefully I worked, ripping out the tiny seams that connected the lining to the wool fabric. Meanwhile, bored Rick took off his jacket, placed my overnight bag on my desk chair, then went into Flora's kitchen to make coffee. By the time he returned with two steaming mugs, I had the lining of the jacket apart. Teresa had sewed the interfacing as one piece with the satin lining, and so I had to rip more seams to separate the two different fabrics.

"Holy shit!" Rick yelped, bending over to take a closer look.

I perused the black print on the inside of the interfacing, the side that had lain against the satin, protected by its smooth texture. Teresa hadn't taken any chances that the ink would rub off by friction with the wool. Very clever girl, my cousin was!

We looked more closely, peering at the small print in Spanish. One piece of interfacing, Rick took and held it up to my bedside lamp. I drew up the second piece and left the third jacket piece on the bed.

"This has three columns, Dina. Names in one column, phone numbers and addresses, I think, in the other two."

"Is one of those names Eduardo Cárdenas?"

"Yep. Number four. Torres said he was the top enforcer of the Juárez Cartel. What does yours have?" Rick looked over my shoulder as I held it up.

"There's a list of numbers and names of places, I think. Dates, weekdays, times. What do you think?" I handed the piece of marked interfacing to him.

"Shit, I think these are VINs and shipment schedules."

"What're VINs?" I asked, still in an amazed, mental fog.

"You know, Dina, Vehicle Identification Numbers. All cars

and trucks have them. These are drug shipment schedules and the trucks, I suppose, that carry them."

"Shit," I echoed, staring at Rick's face. His skin had lost its color as if the blood had drained all of a sudden from his cheeks.

"These places," he went on, scrutinizing the piece once more, "some of these are factories—*fábricas, maquiladoras.* Y'know, since NAFTA, those Mexican factories near the border towns are making all kinds of American goods for companies that want to save on labor costs. I bet the Cartel's storing the drugs in these trucks that bring over the merchandise from those *maquiladoras,* in secret panels or in the cabs." He dropped the piece of interfacing and went to my open bedroom door. "Stay here."

My stomach did a somersault as I realized what we were holding. If the Cartel only knew what we had, we'd be toast. No, burnt toast! I could hear Rick moving around Flora's house, probably making sure doors and windows were closed and locked. Probably checking outside in the street, making sure no Cartel thugs were driving by with *Uzis* pointed out of their windows. He'd already put a lock on the backyard gate, but there were a dozen places thugs could break in through—

"What the hell—"

Rick had caught me pulling the blue plastic gun box out from under my bed, and now I was gingerly inserting bullets from my ammunition box into the revolving chamber of that .38 snub-nosed revolver. He was standing behind me while I pointed the gun at my double-dresser mirror.

"Do you know what you're doing?" he demanded, alarm deepening his voice. "Where did you get that gun?"

I snapped shut the chamber after loading the fifth and final bullet. "My cop friend. He gave it to me and showed me how to use it." I said this with a tinge of pride, I had to admit. "He took me to a firing range on one of our dates."

"You're not still seeing him, are you?" he growled, backing up as I swung around and deposited the loaded gun inside the second drawer of my bedside table. The blue plastic container and ammunition box I replaced under my bed.

"Of course not," I said blandly.

Rick's mouth curled into a lopsided grin. "Remind me not to cheat on you again," he said dryly. I punched his arm. Hard.

"Don't even joke about that," I warned him hotly, narrowing eyes at his mock-fear expression. He clutched his arm in exaggerated pain and groaned loudly.

"*Cabrón!*" I called him. We both broke out laughing, forgetting the Cartel secrets lying on my bed. Our embrace and kiss were sincere and heartfelt. Too bad he had to go home tonight. Angelina was waiting for him at his mother's. A moment later, another thought occurred to me, pushing aside the Cartel secrets on my bed.

"Rick, do you see yourself marrying again?" There, I'd asked it bluntly, like a reporter digging for an expose from a celebrity. "Do you see another marriage in your future?"

He looked away, glanced at the second drawer of my bedside table where I'd stored my loaded revolver, and then shrugged.

"In all truth, I don't know. The last one was such a fucked-up mess."

His dark-eyed gaze met mine, locked together briefly, before we turned back to the bed. We stared again at the three pieces of interfacing strewn on the bed. The skirt probably hid a few more. In all, the kind of secrets — stolen documents — that people were killed for taking. In the eyes of the Juárez Cartel's leadership, kingpins such as Pedro Vargas and his ilk, this was theft punishable by death.

"You're sending it down to Joe Torres, right?" Rick asked.

"Yeah, I'll go to a *UPS* store first thing in the morning."

Rick started gathering up the three pieces, then unfolded the skirt. "No, send it off tonight. I know a store that's open twenty-four-seven. I don't want you to have this shit under your roof all night. It's too dangerous."

He was right.

"Okay." I sat down to rip the seams open on Teresa's beautiful skirt. The sooner I rid myself of these documents, the safer I'd feel, for sure.

I didn't tell Rick that Agent Torres wanted me to go to Mexico, into that border town, and help rescue my cousins. He'd flip out, I knew.

But hey, I wasn't married to Rick. Maybe never would be if he was so gun-shy.

Gun-shy, I mused. Hmmm, wonder if Joe Torres would let me take my .38.

The following night, after a long day at school, wondering when Agent Torres would receive the *UPS* overnighter and what he'd think of it, I was in Flora's kitchen cooking. On tonight's menu was lasagna Florentine with fresh garden salad, accompanied by a bottle of cabernet sauvignon. I was on pins and needles, expecting a call from the DEA agent any moment. My cell phone was on the counter just in case.

Flora breezed in just as I was putting the garnish on the salad. Two goblets of cabernet were already on the pub table.

"What's this about you breaking Steve's nose? He called me from the hospital, but I didn't believe him. Did you know he followed me up to Tahoe? He barged in on my brother and me in the Sage Room at *Harvey's*."

I explained that Steve slipped as he climbed into the hot tub, joining Rick and me in the spa—okay, so I was frosting another wedding cake. I couldn't very well tell her the truth, anyway.

"You and Rick—" She stopped to shake her head—

melodramatically, I thought. "Don't tell me you went back to him—that lying, cheating cad!"

I ignored that. "Steve was drunker than a skunk, so maybe he doesn't remember it exactly the way it happened. Anyway, we called nine-one-one, and an ambulance took him to *El Camino Hospital*, I think—"

"Well, of course, his father's on the Board of Directors there. Are you sure you didn't kick him in the face, Dina? That's what he said—"

I hesitated but only for a second. Even if I told Flora the truth, she'd never believe me, I sensed. That Steve was assaulting me, and I had only defended myself. Flora only saw in her men what she wanted to see. But then, maybe we all did.

"I may've kicked him accidentally as I was helping Rick lift him out of the spa. He was a dead weight, you see. He was knocked out cold for a few minutes. So drunk he couldn't see straight. Mooning over you, griping about how you dumped him."

Might as well turn the tables, I thought. There was no way I was going to take the blame for what happened.

My cell phone played the first few measures of *La Bamba*.

My perverse memory kicked in at that very moment, and I recalled the way Rick had made swirls around both my nipples with his tongue. The pleasure was so aching, the memory so vivid that I almost couldn't speak. I must've croaked a hello.

"What's the matter with you, Dolores?"

Mama. Oh, shit. Why do mothers always call when you're in the middle of an erotic memory with a man who's not your husband?

"Nothing, *Mamá*. What's up?"

Mama made a small grunt. She always seemed to know when I was lying or covering up. Flora left the kitchen, peeling off her suit jacket as she went.

"Dolores, this is important. A man called from Mexico. Your father answered it at first but didn't understand him, so he gave the phone to me. He said he's a lawyer in Ciudad Juárez, my brother's lawyer, and he's handling his estate. He said my brother, Roberto, left me a lot of money. Me and my mother. He wanted to know where Dolores Martínez lived."

Red flags flew up. "So the man didn't know she's now a Gómez?"

"Yes, I thought that was odd. Everyone knows she's Dolores Gómez, even your cousin, Teresa in Mexico, and her sister and nephews in Chihuahua."

My blood ran cold. "What did you tell him, *Mamá*?"

I held my breath, the hair on my spine bristling with fear. If indeed he was a lawyer, the lawyer was most likely one of the Cartel's men. One of Pedro Vargas's hirelings. Mama's brother, the cartel's late kingpin, had known Mama and Grandma were alive but had refused to correspond with them. He had received letters from Grandma Gómez over the years—his own mother—but had never written back. Over the years, he'd made no move to contact them and, according to Teresa, forbade her to have anything to do with them. Her grandmother and aunt.

So why would he leave his mother and sister a lot of money?

Something didn't sound right.

"The lawyer said he found our phone number among Roberto Martínez's personal things in his journal. His will had mentioned our names and phone number."

Now it was making sense. Teresa might've inadvertently left Grandma's—my mother's and father's—phone number on a scrap of paper or something. Or maybe it was found in my uncle, Roberto Martínez's personal things that Teresa left behind and hadn't known about. If Pedro Vargas was scouring the country, looking for his runaway wife and son, he'd try all the phone numbers he found among Teresa's things. Especially a North American phone number. He'd maybe put two and two together. Teresa might've even mentioned to him at one time that her father's mother and sister — grandmother and Mama — were alive and well in California.

Oh. My. God. The last thing we needed was Mexican cartel assassins showing up at Mama and Pop's doorstep!

"So, *Mamá*, what did you tell him?" I held my breath and mentally crossed my fingers.

"Well, it seemed strange that he didn't know my mother was a Gómez. If he really knew what he was talking about, wouldn't he also know that her Martínez husband divorced her and that she remarried? I also think it's strange that my brother would've left us money when all those years, he never wrote back to my mother or me. He wouldn't even let Teresa write to us."

"I think this lawyer guy was just fishing around," I told her.

"Yes, that's what I'm telling you, Dolores. You don't listen. I think if he was really a lawyer and telling the truth, he'd know Grandma's real last name was Gómez. Her legal name."

"I'm listening, I'm listening. Go on."

"You see, after Roberto — my brother — found out his mother was alive, he was told she'd abandoned him. He was so full of hate all those years. My mother sent him Christmas cards, tried calling him, but he would have nothing to do with her. Or me. And my mother signed those cards with her Gómez name. Roberto knew her legal, American name. Roberto would've put Gómez, her legal name, in his will. So, anyway, I told him — this probably fake lawyer — that no Dolores Martínez lived here, that we bought the house two years ago when an old woman died."

"Good thinking, *Mamá*." I breathed again. Those lying

genes were strong in our family, no doubt about it.

"I don't want any drug money, anyway, even if what the man said is true. Then he asked me if I knew a Teresa Martínez Vargas, if she had called our house, and I said no, the only Vargas I knew was a butcher in Salinas."

"Way to go, Mom!" I was so impressed. What a damned good liar my mother was!

"So if anyone calls you from Mexico, even someone saying she's Grandma's sister in Chihuahua or one of the Carrillo cousins, asking about Teresa Vargas, say you don't know anything."

"'Course. I know absolutely nothing."

"Your poor father's all worked up and told Roberto and Frankie to bring him their guns. He says if those Mexican drug-gang, *hijos de puta*, show up, he's going to blast 'em."

Jeez, I didn't know Mama could be so *cholo*! Of course, I didn't tell her about my loaded gun tucked away in my bedside table. And I didn't tell her that my brother, Roberto, an ex-felon, was not allowed to own a firearm.

"Don't worry, *Mamá*. I'll call Joe Torres, the DEA guy I've been talking to, and see if he can help."

"We don't need help, Dolores. Roberto moved back in and is sleeping on the sofa in the den. He's got a shotgun, and your father's got one, too. He and your father are guarding us." I heard her sigh aloud over the phone. "Hey, you tell Ricky Ramos to behave himself. You, too, Dolores. I hear you're seeing each other again. Keep in mind, you're not married to him, and you know men. They all want the milk but don't want to buy the cow."

"Yep, *Mamá*. We'll behave." Aye, the wedding cake was growing taller.

Hmmm. Grandma's one-eyed snake and Mama's dairy cow.

The one-eyed snake was not so scary.

But no one asked, what if the cow wants the bull in her pasture but just not all the time? What then?

We hung up. I looked at Flora, who'd returned to the kitchen. She glanced at me peculiarly while she set the table. I supposed it was time to update her on Joe Torres's Mission—Saving La Familia. Especially now that the deadly Cartel secrets were no longer in her house.

I carried the serving dish of lasagna and the salad bowl to the table, poured the wine, and sat down.

"Flora, you're not going to believe this."

CHAPTER TWENTY

Flora Salazar — "In the journey through life, everyone travels with baggage."

It was the week after Thanksgiving, and I was still in a dreamy state after Rick's and my romantic weekend in Carmel and Monterey, deluding myself into thinking that maybe my life wasn't cursed after all.

Flora and I hadn't been graced, thank Heaven, with a return visit from Steve, although I did overhear her talking to him on the phone once — consoling him with soothing words in a motherly tone of voice.

Because Steve kept insisting to her that I'd kicked him, I finally broke down and told Flora the truth. How Steve had scared the living daylights out of me, how I'd broken his nose trying to get away from him, how Rick'd rescued Steve from drowning. I was sure she felt sorry for Steve the most, with his broken nose and broken heart, instead of me, who was now afraid of going in her hot tub alone. Even though Rick had put a lock on the backyard gate.

I was keeping that *Lady Smith and Wesson* by my bed, safely concealed but loaded. Lisa said an unloaded gun was like a baseball bat made of balsa wood. It might look scary, but it was essentially useless. It gave me comfort to know it was close by, however. Common sense told me, one little, ol' snub-nosed revolver by my bed was no guarantee of safety. Like everything else, it was the illusion of safety that kept it there.

Or maybe my old pessimism was kicking in, and I was expecting something truly horrible to happen—like having the Sword of Damocles hanging over your head. But in general, life was swell, as they used to say in those old thirties movies that Flora and I started watching on that cable channel. Although it was a sore point with Flora, Rick and I continued seeing each other several times a week, enjoying golf and savoring everything else we shared together, if you know what I mean, *chica*.

There were only two glitches in my now-perfect life—concern over my cousins in Mexico and Rick's daughter, Angelina.

The little girl's stubborn refusal to accept me didn't bode well for the three of us, I had to admit. She was a child who'd been traumatized and was ten times more distrustful than I'd ever been at her age. And that's saying a lot. Each time I left her, I resolved to be more patient and give her time to adjust to me. But let me tell you, trying to win her over was the most challenging thing I'd ever had to do . . .other than forgive her father.

No matter what treat I brought over, from a jar of blue *M&M*'s, her favorites—know how time consuming it is picking out the blue ones from five large bags of mixed-colored ones?—to a homemade strawberry-custard pie. She didn't like it and would have nothing to do with it.

One day, I brought her a cute little sweater that I'd bought at *Baby Gap*. It had bright pink and pumpkin stripes and a matching knit cap and mittens. Heck, I wanted one just like it. Nope, she didn't want it. Refused to try it on. Not one word of thanks or even a smile. That stubborn little girl wouldn't talk to me, wouldn't let me touch her. As far as she was concerned, I was the village leper who came to infect her father.

Her recalcitrant behavior was annoying Rick, for he could see I was trying to woo her. He remarked one day—out of earshot of his daughter, of course—that Angelina was more like her mother than he'd realized. But I know he didn't mean it or want to mean it. Actually, I had to confess, she reminded me of *me*. Most likely, it was that same *cabeza dura* gene that made us stubborn and willful. I wondered if it was just a general human defect, like a flawed DNA-thingie somewhere on the double helix-doojiggie.

Mostly, I fretted over Teresa and her son. I hadn't received an email from her since the package arrived. Agent Torres called Tuesday as I was walking yard duty at lunch. After his call, I sought out my friend, Lisa, who was far wiser than I in the ways of this wicked world.

"Hey, Lisa," I called to her. She waved me over to her.

Her curly, dark hair was drawn back into a long, high ponytail, making her look eighteen instead of closer to my age. She was standing at the edge of the play yard, eating a ham sandwich and drinking from a bottle of cold tea. I'd taken out with me my ubiquitous plastic bottle of water—my lunch since I'd been too upset to eat anything. At least, there was one benefit in this whole mess with Teresa Vargas. It was better than the *Atkins diet*.

"Dina, you look like your puppy dog just ate a poisonous piece of meat—"

"God, do you have to be so graphic, Lisa?"

"Sorry, it comes with my overly fertile imagination. So what's the latest? You said Mark made a formal observation of your classroom last week. Has he written up the evaluation yet?"

I nodded. "Fortunately, he gave me a *good* rating."

I was pacing back and forth in front of her, so nervous was I. My feet couldn't stop moving.

"I was hoping he'd do that. Y'know, not let our breaking up interfere with his professional duties. You look upset. Did you hear from Teresa or Agent Torres?"

"Torres just called. A bunch of DEA agents pored over those pieces of interfacing I told you about. They were, to quote Joe Torres, blown away. When he heard that she had four more suits filled with Cartel secrets, he said he had all the proof he needed to convince his superiors that Teresa and her son were worth saving. That's exactly what he said — worth saving. Of course, my cousins are worth saving! What is he thinking?"

I was pacing behind her but stopped mid-stride.

"It finally dawned on me, Lisa. They had no intention of helping her until they saw with their own eyes all the information she'd taken — actually, stolen — from the Juárez Cartel. If she hadn't done that, she and her son would be lost. They wouldn't have a prayer of being rescued."

Lisa threw her head back and took a long swig of tea. "Look at it from their perspective, Dina. They're American authorities with no legal jurisdiction in Mexican affairs. Only when the drugs and violence hit our streets does it become their job to intercede in some way. Too bad they don't get enough cooperation from the Mexican feds, but basically, their hands are tied."

"So why do they need this information?"

"Probably to stop the shipments once they cross the border into the States. If they know when and where, from what direction and road, they'll be able to stop a lot more than they've been able to. They'll be able to clean up El Paso if nothing else."

I pondered her assessment. Then I told her that Agent Torres wanted me to talk Teresa into going up to Nuevo Laredo and that he wanted me to go there, too, when the time came to rescue her.

"What do you know about that town?" I asked her.

"Nothing, really. I'll ask Uncle Leo and get back to you. So when're you and Agent Torres going into Mexico, that border town?"

"I don't know. After Teresa and her son show up there. After he gets the okay to go down there. I guess I'm on call. I'll have to drop everything and fly there when the time comes. If the time comes," I added with uncertainty.

I stopped pacing and stopped an errant ball that one of the older kids had kicked. Absently, I threw it back to him.

"You don't want to go alone, Dina. Let me go with you — it'd be fun! An adventure, like our stakeout, only much more exciting. I don't speak Spanish, but I'll watch your back. Ask this DEA agent if it's okay if you bring along a friend."

She looked so expectant, her ponytail bobbing up and down in her excitement. It wouldn't hurt, I supposed, although I was kind of planning to ask Rick to come along. But he'd already taken off work one day to fly down to LA. I hated interfering with his crowded work schedule, especially since his Milpitas development project was about to get underway. Besides, I didn't think Lisa was really serious.

"Okay, I'll ask him," I said to placate her. "The most he can say is no."

Lisa looked so pleased, her ponytail practically went airborne. "Good. I'll do all the research on this place, this Nuevo Laredo. We'll be prepared. Besides, I haven't taken a day off yet this year. I'm due for some *mental health* days."

Two and a half weeks remained before Christmas break. I wondered whether Teresa would be out of Mexico by *La Noche Buena* or if Pedro Vargas and his thugs would find her first. Just the idea alone put a damper on my holiday cheer. Already, the stores were filled with Christmas decorations and tons of merchandise meant to separate the American consumers from their money. Our classrooms at school had gold and silver garlands hanging across the ceiling. Big red and green paper bells, like Christmas tree ornaments, were suspended from the middle and swayed every time the door opened. The kids had written narrative essays on their most memorable Christmas. Of course, this was the time of year when our students were on their best behavior. None of them wanted a call home from their teachers.

Lisa was silent a moment, her eyes crinkling as if seeing a plan on the horizon. "We'll go undercover, pretend to be gringo tourists in Nuevo Laredo—"

"I think we'll have to go with Joe Torres's strategy, whatever that may be. He's calling the shots, Lisa."

"Oh sure," she said, her voice rising gaily. I looked at her with awe, my feet no longer restless. No doubt about it, I really liked gutsy people. She was serious.

"You'd do that, Lisa? You'd risk your neck and come with us?"

"Ha! My life is so dull, I'd risk my very life for a little excitement. Of course, I'll come with you."

I was so grateful. I could've kissed her. In a spillover of emotion, I hugged her tightly, my chest feeling lighter than it'd felt in weeks. My wonderful, loyal Latina sister. *Mi hermanita.* Together, we'd save Teresa and her son from those damned Juárez Cartel thugs.

The little devil on my shoulder—my *diablito*—was curiously quiet. I took that as a good sign.

"Y'know, Lisa, forget Mark McDuff. It's never a good idea to date your boss. Keep the faith. One'll come along eventually."

Her wide smile was inscrutable.

Funny how life turns on the whim of something you have no control over. Like a fickle weathervane. Or the death of a tiny, unknown thing inside your body. As a somewhat-practicing, on-and-off-again Catholic, I'm supposed to believe in guardian angels. Sometimes I do, sometimes I don't. If I had one, he/she/it was doing a reasonably decent job of protecting me so far. Whenever, as a child, I used to ask Mama or Grandma Gómez if I had one, their mysterious reply was always, "Light a candle, Dolores. Keep your *diablito* in fear."

I took that to mean that I probably had a little guardian angel on one shoulder and a little devil on the other. One liked the light, and the other wanted the darkness. I figured my angel might be the stronger of the two. After the following Friday night, I no longer had any doubts.

"Rick, come and taste this," I beckoned to him, lifting a stirring spoon. Contrary to the old stereotype about Latino men, some can cook and even set the table. Well, maybe a few.

Since Rick had cooked spaghetti the night before—albeit the sauce was bottled and the pasta as hard as *Pick-Up Stix*—I was doing the honors that night. I was cooking at his condo one of my favorite winter recipes, leg of lamb with red wine and dried cherries. The aromas emanating from the kitchen were intoxicating, the wafting of which into the living room kept drawing Rick to my side by the stove.

Between his moves to the dining table with plates, glasses, and utensils, he'd return to me. We sipped cabernet sauvignon—a nicely turned *Russian River Valley* vintage if I do say so—as he snuggled up behind me and watched me dabble. His hands kept traveling up the front of my turtleneck sweater—yep, thanks to all my new hickeys, I was wearing turtlenecks again.

"All right, Martha Stewart, tell me what you're concocting."

"Stop it." I giggled, trying to wriggle out of his caresses. I then whispered, "Remember, *la niña.*"

"Aw, she's got to get used to the fact that I'm loco about you."

"Or just plain loco. Keep your hands still, and I'll tell you. Here, have a taste. Maybe that'll take your mind off . . .other things. This is the marinade. When the lamb is cooked, I'll pour this mixture over it. It's a very simple marinade — garlic cloves, some of this cabernet, some dried cherries, salt, and pepper. I'll reduce the liquid a bit, make it a reductionist sauce. Hold on, let me check the potatoes and broccoli in the microwave."

I stuck out my denim-clad rump, making him scoot back a step. But not for long. I probed the contents in the casserole dish with a fork, but as soon as I returned to the stove, Rick was back to his canoodling.

Not that I minded. If a five-year-old child hadn't been in the condo, no doubt we'd be doing the nasties on the dining table. It was difficult suppressing the tendency to act like newlyweds when we were now together every other evening. Although I'd never done an overnighter at the condo for Angelina's benefit. Call me old-fashioned, but I didn't think it was a noble example to set any child. If we'd been engaged, it might've been different.

We hadn't talked about marriage again, not seriously, anyway. I think we were both waiting to see whether Angelina would come around or not. Or maybe I was enjoying having the bull in my pasture but just not all the time.

Suddenly, tonight, she appeared at the kitchen's threshold. Reacting to Rick's display of affection — he was snuggling behind me, circling my waist with both arms — she looked us up and down, propped her hands on her tiny hips, and frowned.

It was eerie, that scowl, like Grandma Gómez in the body of a five-year-old. Yikes!

"*Papá*, I'm hungry. She's taking too long."

According to Angelina, I did not have a name or one that she was willing to utter. It was always, "She's here, again," or "When is *she* going to leave?"

I was the proverbial unwanted corner of a domestic triangle. I think the only reason Angelina tolerated me was her little girl's fantasy that I'd suddenly disappear in a puff of smoke.

"*Papá*, I said I'm hungry!" With that, the little girl turned on her heels and stormed out of the kitchen.

"Take Angelina these carrot sticks. That'll hold her 'til dinner's ready."

Rick smiled warmly, kissed my cheek, then went to the living room.

"No! I don't want them!" Angelina screamed, "And I don't want what *she*'s cooking! It smells stupid, and I hate what she cooks!"

To her credit, Angelina was extending the length of her sentences. Guess she figured one-word protests were getting her nowhere. The little girl had passed the Spanish version of those Special Ed tests and stayed with her mainstream first-grade class, only being pulled out for additional English remediation. The exposure to her English-speaking peers was paying off, evidently. Also, the nightly remediation exercises with her father. Those gave Angelina her father's exclusive attention, and she seemed to thrive on them. Rick would come over only after Angelina had fallen asleep, and the upstairs teenager was more than happy to earn five bucks an hour, babysitting a sleeping child.

"Fine, then starve," Rick snapped back. "I swear, *m'ija*, you're becoming a real class-A brat."

"Well, *Papá*, I don't want *her* here. I *hate* her hair, and I *hate* her clothes, and I *hate* her cooking."

"Too bad, Angie. I like her hair, her clothes, and her cooking. Most of all, I *love* Dina, so get over it."

After which, the slamming of a door could be heard as, once again, Angelina ran to her room in tears. A moment later, Rick appeared at my side. He lifted his glass of wine and emptied the contents in one gulp. I actually felt sorry for him. He was caught in the middle of this little domestic war. I was beginning to wonder who would be the first to wave the white flag, her or me.

"I'm thinking of sending her to Flora's and keeping you. Is that okay?" he quipped.

He leaned over and brushed my lips with his. He tasted of wine and marinade. His dash of *Old Spice* from that morning's grooming lingered in my nostrils. I returned the kiss.

I smiled weakly. "If only it were that easy—besides, Flora would kill me for disrupting her quiet home."

"Yeah, well, my little brat of a daughter is disrupting mine," he grumbled, "and I don't know what to do. I'm sorry about this, about her bad behavior. I've never seen her like this. She's usually sweet-tempered. She's turned into a little witch—I don't know why it's taking so long for her to warm up to you."

"What happened to that sweet little girl who came to my birthday dinner?"

"Ha! She was displaying her party-manners. You weren't a threat to her then. Y'know, I think she dreads having a mother-substitute. I think she remembers her own mother more than I realize."

"Go talk to her, Rick. Reassure her that I'm not like the mother she used to have. I'm different."

"No, I'm done talking to her," he announced with finality. "I've been talking to her for over a month, and it hasn't done any good."

"She's tenacious, all right. I can hear *Mamá* and Grandma Gómez saying, you're getting your just desserts, Dolores. I was just like Angelina when I wanted my way. I'm sure I taxed my parents' patience to the limit. Even now, my father calls raising me, Extreme Parenting. Like Extreme Sports, bungee jumping off the Golden Gate Bridge. My mother used to tell us, if I'd been born first, they wouldn't have had any more kids."

Rick laughed and squeezed my waist. I smiled ironically.

"I don't believe it," he said, then gave me a wink. "Or maybe I do."

I flicked some bangs out of my eyes with a hardy puff. "So you see, she can change. I can't believe I'm saying this, but I see a little of myself in Angelina. She's a fighter. She's got spirit."

Rick chortled in his throat. "I'd like to see less spirit and more cooperation."

Paradoxically, the more Rick groused and complained about his daughter, the more patient I became with her. Call it perverse or pigheaded. Me, the cynic, the pessimist, the wiseass, the stubborn smart-aleck — I was all of these at various times but never a quitter.

Then and there, standing over the stove, I made a decision. I'd never give up. Angelina might hate me the rest of her life, but I'd never give up on her. And damn if I could explain why. If Grandma Gómez was born to fear, Mama born to sneer, and I seemed born to jeer, then maybe I could get Angelina to — cheer? Spend the rest of her life cheering and feeling good about herself, especially after such a rotten start.

Most of all, she was Rick's child. His flesh and blood.

Halfway through dinner, while Rick kept up a forced-pleasant stream of conversation, Angelina, though glowering at me, began to eat the slices of lamb on her plate. I think she liked the cherry flavor in the marinade or the port wine in it was having a mild sedating effect on her. A half-minute later, she even forked half of a new potato and started munching on it.

Well, I guess if trainers can get wild elephants to dance on little boxes by using food rewards, I could eventually get a resentful five-year-old to behave civilly toward me. Maybe food was the key to Angelina's heart.

"*Dios*, this is good, Dina. I've never had lamb that tasted this good. This sauce is out-of-this-world incredible."

I cut a piece of tender, succulent lamb, but my appetite had suddenly vanished. All day menstrual cramps had plagued me, worsening just before we sat down to dinner. I'd been popping *Motrin* all day like jelly beans. The pain had abated for a while, and now it was returning like gangbusters. A wave of nausea engulfed me. I tried to ignore it.

"Did I tell you, I got another email from Teresa in Monterrey. I wrote to her that Uncle Joe was working on a plan to move her to Nuevo Laredo. My message was in our usual code, so her return message was in code, too. She said her friend in Monterrey was having a problem. Two strangers were watching her friend's house. I told Joe Torres, and he said they weren't his men. He said it was time to move her and the boy to Nuevo Laredo. Right away."

Rick stared at the way I was leaning back and grimacing.

"Are you okay?" he asked, putting down his fork.

"Yeah, I—" I broke off on a hard gasp.

"Dina," Rick said, frowning, "you're in real pain."

"Teresa's going to Nuevo Laredo soon, and I suppose—" I sat back and moaned. "Oh, Rick, I need to lie down—I feel sick."

Rick stood up and threw down his napkin, worry lines creasing his handsome face. "Let me help you—"

I waved him off. "No, finish your dinner. It's just cramps."

"Did you take another *Motrin*? Do you want some water . . .or something else? Dina, talk to me."

"Uh-uh." I was too nauseated to speak. Holding my belly like a pregnant lady, I made my way, none too gracefully, to his sofa. On the way, I overheard Angelina ask her father a question.

"Is Dina sick, *Papá*?"

The little minx actually knew my name but wasn't about to use it in front of me. After that, my mind was distracted by the pain I felt. I lay down, closed my eyes, and tried to will away the cramps.

I didn't understand it. The pain was no longer dull and achy but was now sharp and stabbing. Never a wussy, I nevertheless began to cry. I was frightened, too. Something was definitely wrong. The pain was so bad, it took my breath away. Combined with the nausea and rolling surges of heat, then chills, I knew this was no ordinary menstrual cramping.

Rick cleared the table and came back to the sofa.

"Dina, how do you feel?" When he noticed I was crying, he grew even more concerned.

"That bad? What can I do, baby?"

I opened my eyes. Time to face the music.

"What you can do—y-you can take me to the hospital."

He looked scared. Not half as frightened as I felt, though.

"My God, Dina—"

I sat up, my face contorted with the pain. "*Now!* These are *not* cramps. Rick!"

He helped me into my jacket, all the while muttering a string of encouraging nonsense in English and Spanish.

I sat on the sofa and alternately shivered and moaned. In a flurry of activity, he got Angelina's jacket and his own, turned off the oven, grabbed his wallet and keys, then came over and gathered me up. Without a word, Angelina picked up my purse and gave it to me, solemn-eyed.

Her little, round face was pinched with anxiety, her brown eyes huge with fear. All this didn't really sink in at the time, for I was lost in a fog of mindless, excruciating pain. All I could think was, get me to a doctor . . .help me . . .save me . . .I don't want to die.

Later, though, I recalled that look on Angelina's little face.

The next hour was a blur of half-remembered images and sounds, like a dream-montage. Riding in Rick's SUV. The hospital's bright lights. A nurse was drawing blood. The anxious voices of strangers. Someone was saying something about my white count. Rick's murmuring something into my ear. A doctor pressed on my abdomen. The horrible pain! My screaming. Folding in half from the hot, searing stabs in my right side.

A prick on my arm. Then blissful nothing.

CHAPTER TWENTY-ONE

"*Si no lo quiere, come leche frita.*" If you don't want it, eat fried milk. Said with a heap of exasperation and directed at spoiled children. One of Grandma Gomez's *buen dichos* that I never understood and probably never will. But it came to me as my foggy mind began to clear.

Leche frita.

Weird how you rise to consciousness, up through layers of dreamy images. You see in fast-forward images of childhood, adolescence, adulthood — people you love, tatters of scenes, fragments of conversation. I kind of saw my life passing before me — but thank God, not in the moment of my death. I like to think my guardian angel intervened on my behalf and snatched me out of the jaws of . . .whatever. Death?

When I came to, I looked around and tried to focus. In my hospital room, Rick was sitting in one of those uncomfortable metal chairs. He was slumped over, dozing. Angelina was lying across his lap asleep, her head supported in the crook of his arm. My gaze was then drawn to the window. The blinds, angled partially open, showed horizontal slivers of a light grayish sky. Good God, it was morning! What had happened?

I was swathed like a newborn baby and hooked up with cables and tubing like an old-fashioned computer terminal. My abdomen felt raw and taut. I tried to sit up but couldn't, but I did succeed in making the IV bag jiggle on its hook.

Rick woke up. He yawned and smiled simultaneously. It

struck me as funny, almost hilarious.

"What happened, Rick?" I was curious but strangely unconcerned by my new surroundings, my wrapped-up body. At least, the excruciating pain was gone. Thank heavens!

"Oh, baby, you scared the shit out of me."

He lumbered to his feet, still holding the sleeping little girl. He carried her, still in her jacket and jeans from the night before, to my bed and gently set her down by my feet. Instinctively, she curled up, deep in slumber.

"Dina, the surgeon removed your appendix. He said it melted right in his hands, so he got to it just in time. There was leakage, he said, so he put in a drainage tube. He said two hours more and you wouldn't have made it. Peritonitis would've set in."

Nothing he said made sense.

"I have to go to school. What time is it, Rick?"

It was early morning, and from the shadow of whiskers on his face, Rick hadn't yet shaved. He smiled peculiarly.

"Dina, you're in the hospital. I called Flora and your parents after they took you to surgery. I called them back again when you came out. They said they'll be here around noon."

"Surgery? I had surg—" I looked down at my body. Ever so slowly, the memories of last night began trickling back. Most vividly, I recalled the pain . . . and nausea. And my uneaten lamb with wine-cherry reductionist sauce.

"My lamb? I never got to eat my lamb. Or maybe it was *leche frita*?" I could faintly hear Grandma Gomez's scolding tone of voice.

"You had an acute appendicitis attack last night," Rick slowly said as if he were talking to a child.

"There was nothing cute about it," I said, starting to laugh. Not a good idea, I suddenly realized, as I caught my breath. A stabbing pain lanced through my abdomen. I expelled my breath with difficulty. "You've been here all night? You and

Angelina?"

He played with the fingers of my right hand and smiled.

"Don't laugh, Dina. You've got stitches and staples and a drainage tube. Yeah, we slept here. Angie wouldn't leave. I wanted to take her home and leave her with Susie and Sharon, my neighbors, but Angie didn't want to leave."

I was hopscotching in Lalaland, thanks to the cocktail of drugs in my IV drip.

"Is today Saturday?" I raised my head a little. The child looked peaceful at the foot of the bed.

"No, baby, Friday." He lowered his head to hover over mine. "You had a close call, sweetheart. We're both lucky—all three of us are lucky."

He kissed me lightly on the mouth, and I beamed as much as it was humanly possible while doped on modern medicine's miracle drugs. I was flushed with pride and gratitude that he had stayed with me all night. But he looked like he'd been hit by a truck.

"I have to get up, get dressed. My class starts at seven-forty-five. You two should go home and get some rest," I told him, then squeezed his hand.

He was looking at me oddly. "Dina, you'll be here for a while. In the hospital."

"Ha, ha, you're funny. I love you, Rick. Thanks for coming. Maybe we can go dancing tonight or tomorrow night?"

My gaze danced around the white-walled room, from Rick to little Angelina, to the IV tubes and bed railing. Like seeing the world through a gauzy veil.

"*Te quiero, corazón.*" His voice was quivering with emotion. His dark, luminous eyes blinked, releasing two streams of tears. When I saw that, I got a lump in my throat, and my eyes welled up, too. Then I noticed Angelina. She was sitting up and gazing at her father and me.

And *no me diga*. She was actually smiling at us.

Rick's emotion and her emotion were the only reality that penetrated my drug-infused mind.

"Dina. *Papá.*" That was all she said. Then I noticed her tears, too, like tiny pearls.

My cheeks got wet, too.

"Dina." Someone touched my arm. I opened my eyes.

"Flora," I said, smiling lazily. She was leaning over my bed. Behind her, a still opalescent sky peeked through the half-open blinds.

"How're you doing, Dina?"

"Fine, I think." I squinted to focus because I wasn't sure whether my eyes were deceiving me. My usually perfectly groomed, made up, and coiffed aunt looked — well, like a human wreck. She looked like a homeless woman who'd just been turned away at a soup kitchen. Her hair was disheveled, as were her clothes — a wrinkled, slightly soiled sweatsuit. Her pretty face looked pale and fragile without makeup. And distraught. She actually looked her age!

"My intestines are temporarily paralyzed," I went on, "according to the nurse. It's called Paracelsus. Sounds like a Greek philosopher to me. I can't have anything in my stomach until my guts start working again."

Maybe I told her more than she wanted to know, but I thought this little medical development was interesting. I had no idea that the intestines could stop working. Weren't they the ones that always made noises when you didn't want them to, just to prove they were functioning?

"Are you in pain?" she asked, clasping my left hand in hers. It appeared that the nurse had removed the hookup on my left arm while I slept. My right arm was still tethered to an IV drip.

"No, but if I move, my abdomen hurts. The stitches are right down the middle — no bikini cut for me, darn it. The surgeon stopped by and told me he had to do an exploratory because he thought my ovaries were infected. When he looked to my right side, he saw my swollen appendix. He said he got it in the nick of time. It split apart right in his hand."

Compared to Aunt Flora, I probably felt much better than she looked, but I hesitated to ask what was wrong. In my, ahem, delicate state, did I want to deal with an emotional crisis of hers? I don't think so! Not that I'd ever seen Flora in an emotional meltdown. She'd always been private, circumspect, and above all, super-sophisticated about such feelings as love. Add cynical to super-sophisticated, also.

"Your father had his appendix out when he was about your age, long before you were born. And Frankie, too, come to think of it. When he was about twenty-five —"

"Oh yes, I remember that. Do you suppose appendicitis, or atrophied appendixes — that's what the doctor called it — run in the family? Maybe it's a genetic thing like weak bladders or early dementia."

I could tell Flora was barely listening to me, nor was my topic exceptionally cheerful or enlivening. But, heck, weren't hospital visitors supposed to be the ones to do the entertaining and take the patients' minds off their ailments? Flora's face held a dark storm cloud.

Without warning, the cloud burst and down flooded the tears. Flora covered her face with her hands and turned away toward the window. Her shoulders hunched together, her head bobbed a little as she succumbed to sobs.

"I'm s-sorry, Dina," she said, calming after a minute. "This is the worst time and place to break down."

"Hey, I'm not going anywhere." I sighed, striving to be sympathetic. "I'm already bored with this place. So tell me what happened."

When Flora brought herself under control, she plucked half a dozen tissues from the box on my hospital tray and wiped her face. I patted the side of the bed with my unhampered hand. She came over and perched her hip, her eyes downcast, the balled-up tissues at the ready.

"Porter left me — he says he's going back to his wife. He's leaving for London tomorrow. H-he's going to spend the holidays with his family."

Uh-oh. Not that this news deserved a headline or banner. In fact, I wasn't terribly surprised. I'd had a hunch from the way Porter acted one night that something had changed. Perhaps his outlook on the whole affair — the romance not quite jiving with reality or some such thing. Or maybe he started thinking about all the money he'd lose in divorce property settlements and alimony.

Flora's attempts to revive the old magic — she'd hosted several candlelit dinners at her house, catered by one of the finest chefs in San Jose — were, to me, patently pathetic. Men don't need candlelight and music — most men, I thought. That's a female thing to put *them* in the mood. Rick told me once that most men come pre-armed, ready for action. They just need a receptive female, a woman who turns them on.

I think what Flora couldn't accept was that she no longer turned Porter on. Or maybe the millions he'd kiss goodbye in a divorce were Porter's real love.

But hey, who am I to judge? Didn't I once dress up in Reno-hooker's garb just to entice my hunky cop-friend? The memory of which, I have to tell you, now made me wince.

"I'm so sorry, Flora." What else could I say?

"I think I'm still in love with Steve," she said softly. My eyes popped open in alarm.

"Oh no, that can't be true, Flora. After all that jerk-off's done, no intelligent woman in her right mind" — in panic, I was laying it on thick — "who's certifiably sane and rational would ever entertain the idea of taking Steve back. And, Flora, you are rational . . .aren't you?"

She shrugged and dabbed at her eyes. "I-I don't know. I'm confused."

In my fear and fervent desire to set her straight, I tried to sit up, but the tightness in my abdomen and sudden, sharp pain changed my mind.

"Flora, what he did was no boyish prank. When Steve's drunk, he's gets a little crazy."

Flora gazed at my flimsy hospital blanket, looking pensive. She smiled nervously.

"Dina, he came over last night, sober and apologetic. He cried and begged me to forgive him. He said he didn't know what he was doing, he was so drunk. He's not deranged. He says he loves me so much . . .he wants to marry me." She paused and met my eyes. "Dina, I'm lonely. I should have married years ago."

Shit! I couldn't believe that she, brilliant, beautiful, independent Flora Salazar, was actually forgiving the louse. She was excusing him for assaulting me!

"Flora," I pleaded, "he's whacked! If he comes around, I won't feel safe. I'll have to keep that damned thirty-eight revolver loaded just in case . . .Or at the very least, carry around a can of *Raid* for pest control."

She glanced up and glared at me. So it was a feeble joke. How could she even consider taking him back without breaking down in hysterical laughter? Steve, the man who assaulted her niece!

"You've forgiven Ricky Ramos, and look what he did to you. You two were engaged, and he got another girl pregnant and married her. Then six years later, he waltzes back into your life, and you rush back to him—"

"I didn't rush back," I retorted defensively, hurt by her comparison, "and Rick never assaulted anybody. He hurt me emotionally, that's true, but he hurt himself even more. And he never once hurt me physically."

"Oh, please! You were so brokenhearted, you wouldn't date for years! You lost weight! You turned into a frightened, little, frumpy prude! You don't call that being hurt physically?"

Her words were hurtful even though they were true. "Rick's different now, more mature. He wants us to become a family."

Chrissakes, why was I trying to point out the differences between the two men? Wasn't it obvious? Or was I offering as many excuses for Rick as Flora was for Steve?

"Men don't change, Dina. They just get older and more difficult, more set in their ways. That's why I need a younger man in my life." She softened her voice but still looked hard at me. "Rick is a catch, but you watch out. A man that good-looking is going to be tempted by women throwing themselves at him. And he's no saint. He's proven that."

I was in no mood to debate the differences between Rick's and Steve's characters. One thing was clear. We were both in love. Perhaps blindly so.

"Look, you've been working so hard," I suggested, "why don't you take time off, travel, go to Spain. Maybe look up that old flame of yours? Just don't do anything rash."

"Oh, Dina, not everyone is as lucky as you—to find love again in an old relationship. It's been almost twenty-five years since I was in Spain." Her voice became soft and dreamy. "Antonio was a medical student at the University of Madrid. He was three years older—God, we were mad about each other!" Her blue eyes darkened into black coals. "I left him to return to the States, to go back to school."

Flora sighed profoundly and dreamily gazed at the window.

"Did I tell you, he begged me to stay and finish my education in Spain? My parents wanted me to come back, and I didn't have the money to stay over there. Antonio couldn't afford to pay for both our educations, so I returned to California. I threw our love away. Oh, we wrote for a while. But then, the letters tapered off, and we moved on." Her voice had grown frantic. "Don't you see, Dina, I can't throw away what I have with Steve. I'm too old to keep throwing away relationships. I've done that for twenty-five years!"

So Antonio, a physician in Spain, was Flora's secret love! And all these years, she'd hidden her feelings. What she had with Steve was a fantasy, a delusion of youth, not a substantial love. At least, that's how I saw it. All right, it was time to get down and dirty. I took a deep breath and said a silent prayer.

"Flora, Steve knows you'll be turning fifty soon. He told me while groping me in your spa . . .that he couldn't believe he'd . . .uh, um, screwed a fifty-year-old woman. Honest to God, that's what he said."

Flora looked like she was going to go ballistic.

"Why should I believe you, Dina? Even your own grandmother says you tell enough white lies to frost a wedding cake."

Yeah, yeah.

"He also said it didn't matter, you're being fifty. He was in love with you," I said frankly. "Maybe his groping me was his way of striking back at you—he was crushed when you broke it off."

Was I crazy? Was I actually speaking in Steve's defense? I clammed up then for fear my charity would go too far. Next thing, I'd be scattering rose petals at their wedding.

I sank back in bed and closed my eyes. "Flora, maybe you should go." I made my voice sound drowsy. "I'm feeling tired," I lied . . .a little. I felt Flora rise from the bed and pat my arm.

Suddenly I remembered something. My last phone conversation with Joe Torres. The two strangers who were watching

Teresa's friend's building in Monterrey. Joe telling me that Teresa and her son had to leave right away for Nuevo Laredo, that Mexican border town under the thumb of the Gulf Cartel. A hundred yards away to the north, the Texas flag whipped in the desert breezes just across the Rio Grande in Laredo.

"Flora, hand me my purse. I need to make some phone calls before I drift off."

"Yes, of course. Dina, get some rest. Don't worry about any of this. Everything'll be fine, you'll see."

I made small noises, somewhere between agreement and farewell, then dug my cell phone and Agent Torres's card out of my hobo-styled purse. I signaled goodbye when she walked out of the room.

Then my attention turned to more serious matters. Rick had called my school to let them know I was in the hospital, but I informed the principal's secretary I'd be out at least a week. Have the District call a long-term sub. That's what the surgeon had said, anyway. A week of bed rest, followed by a week of walking around and taking it easy.

Which, of course, did not mean I couldn't fly down to Texas and help Agent Torres rescue my cousins. Compared to teaching sixth-graders, I figured evading Cartel thugs would be taking it easy.

My next call was Joe Torres. When I told him where I was and what had happened, he sounded worried.

"I'm sorry to hear this, Dina. The fact is, we need to get her and her son out of Monterrey ASAP. Her husband must've gotten the word that she's in hiding with old Red Cross friends from her university days. He's drawing in the net. My undercover guy has the apartment building and the two men under surveillance. There seems to be a one-hour window mid-day when neither man is there. That's when my guy'll be showing up in a furniture truck as if he's delivering something. You email Teresa to be ready tomorrow at one o'clock—she told you she checks her friend's email every morning, every noon, and every evening, right? So tomorrow at one, my guy—Santiago's his name—he'll say *Tío* José sent him. He'll unload a specially constructed chest of drawers. Inside under a special lid on the chest is a small trunk, which the boy is to hide inside. Santiago'll have old clothes for Teresa to wear, and he'll load up the trunk in addition to their suitcases. All this is to be done very quickly, in a matter of fifteen minutes at the most. Tell Teresa she is to ask no questions and offer no resistance. Time's of the essence, and this man's risking his life for her and her kid."

"Just a sec, Joe," I said, frantically taking notes on a paper towel resting on my hospital bed's tray-arm. "Okay."

"Another thing. Teresa should change her looks, cut her hair, color it—anything. Also, the boy's hair. Change the dark blonde to brown or black. Remember what I said about having her friend buy a mobile phone with a prepaid international SIM card?"

I murmured I did.

"Well, forget that. Mobile phones have electronic serial numbers which allow service providers to track. If they're on to Teresa's university friend, they'll already have their electronic tracking devices in place. So forget the mobile phone. When she gets to Nuevo Laredo, to the safe house there, she can use their email address to contact you."

"Are you sure it's safe, Agent Torres? This safe house in Nuevo Laredo?"

"As safe as we can possibly make it, Miss Salazar. One of our undercover guys—actually a woman—lives there. Teresa will be passing as her cousin from Guadalajara, there on a visit. That's all you need to know for now. Can you contact her right away? Do you have a wireless setup in your hospital room?"

"I don't know, my laptop's wireless. But the room here—"

I looked at the phone hookup provided by the hospital. A phone was attached, but I didn't know if the hospital provided computer service as well. I pressed the nurse's emergency button. "I don't know. It may take a while to find out. Joe—" I skipped formalities in my nervousness. "Maybe you should email her. Tell her what happened to me but assure her that I'll be there in Nuevo Laredo with you. When it comes time to pick her and her son up and bring them across the border. Okay? Oh, and I'm bringing my friend, Lisa Luna, with me."

That agreed to, I gave him Teresa's friend's email address. Then I asked him to call me when Teresa and her son arrived safely in Nuevo Laredo. We rang off, and I flipped my phone shut.

I blew out a long breath of air and closed my eyes. Stuck here in a hospital bed, with tubes snaking out of my body, unable to move my body very much, I felt totally helpless. There was nothing I could do except pray.

Which I did. Sincerely and heartily.

What was it about hospital rooms that made people want to unburden themselves? Catharsis venues were supposed to be psychiatrists' couches or the priest's Confessional, not the bedside of a recovering patient. Maybe the specter of our mortality, our somewhat vulnerable bodies, inspired people to bare their souls and their fears. I don't know, but hours later—after a lunch of IV cocktail and a family visit—Lisa Luna joined my parade of visitors that day.

Pop, Mama, Grandma Gómez, Frankie, and Isabel had paid their visits around lunchtime until the nurse came to change my dressing. They said they'd return later that evening with Rick and Angelina. My social life was getting busy enough to hire a personal secretary. Or at least enough to get a PDA. Maybe my cell phone's social calendar would have to do.

Hoisting a huge, cellophane-wrapped basket filled with eatable goodies that went great with good coffee, bless her heart, Lisa presented it with fanfare.

"On behalf of the entire staff of Lincoln Elementary, I wish to bestow upon my dear friend all our wishes for a rapid recovery."

"I'm so honored. Thank you all," I said in my best British accent.

We laughed. Rather, Lisa laughed, and I tried to, limiting my mirth to a mere chuckle—damn those stitches!

"There's frosted and chocolate-dipped biscotti in here, so when you break it open, call me, and I'll help you eat them."

I smiled at Lisa. She was already off her latest diet. "I'll take it to school, and we'll have them with our morning coffee. I'll share the basket with everyone."

"Oh, good," Lisa said, pleased. "'Cause I really like that chocolate biscotti. Boy, what you go through to get an extra-long Christmas break. Two weeks off, plus two for Christmas. Not bad."

I groaned inwardly. Writing lesson plans for two weeks—shoot, maybe I could go back to work in a week. Then again, my wrap-up unit tests were already made. I just had to email the attachments to my sub. The kids would finish up with a few Christmas crafts, which any sub could oversee. Besides, what could I do? I again tried to sit up—well, maybe not.

I'd already told her about Flora's affair with Steve, their breakup, the incident in the spa, and my breaking his nose. Now I added the latest about Flora maybe marrying the looney-tunes twit.

"Sounds like he should be in jail if he assaulted you. But if he's going to come around your aunt's again, maybe you could move in with Rick or get your own place. You're welcome to stay with me, but my place is small."

I'd been there. Lisa lived over her uncle's garage in a two-bedroom apartment she shared with her cousin, Gil. I shook my head but thanked her anyway.

"I can't move in with Rick," I said.

What was stopping me, I wondered. Oh yes, Angelina. She was beginning to thaw, or so I thought. Was I imagining things or early — very early — that morning, didn't she smile at me? Still, moving in with them might throw her into a rebellious tizzy. The very thought sent chills up my spine.

Another reason, of course, was my family and Rick's family. I couldn't live with a man I wasn't married to without being branded a slut, a tramp, a *puta*. Of course, I could do it, anyway, and defy my family's code. The code implied that women were to remain virtuous, whereas men could do whatever they could get away with. But I was a rebel, not an anarchist. I could not destroy the love and respect of my family. It was as simple as that.

Moreover, I wasn't ready to give up my independence, and I certainly needed more time to test Rick's loyalty. Maybe Flora was right, that he was the kind of man who couldn't resist temptation. A devilishly handsome man whose libido would always cause him problems.

"Hey, Dina, Mark's requested a transfer for next semester. He claims the staff at Lincoln isn't friendly. Heck, we — rather I was too friendly. Turns out he's the one who confuses business and pleasure. When it didn't work out between us, he couldn't take it. I had no trouble keeping things separate, compartmentalized. He's the one who kept saying, no problem, our little romance won't interfere with our professional relationship. Oh well, the male ego, what can you do?" She laughed while I did a grimace-chuckle. "Just find me that prince you keep talking about. I'm tired of insecure, little pricks."

I lifted one shoulder. There wasn't much else I could move

on my body except that and one arm.

"Do you still want to come with me to Mexico — to help rescue my cousins?"

She nodded vigorously. "Gil thinks I need to restore my *buenas vibras* by taking a trip with you. So, yep, I'm your girl."

Lisa was so excited that I imagined her smacking her lips and rubbing her hands together in anticipation. I smiled in gratitude. She was a great friend.

"Thanks, Lisa. I'll feel better having you with me, especially now. We might have to leave fairly soon — take off work. Agent Torres has to postpone the rescue 'til I'm outa here, though. That's a wrinkle in his plan. Another week, for sure. Two at the most. So maybe it'll coincide with Christmas break."

"I'll be ready. Just let me know. I'll make up lesson plans just in case we have to take off before Christmas break." Lisa paused to shoot me a contrite look. "Y'know, Dina, you're right about not dating your boss. That whole thing with Mark McDuff didn't work out well at all. I should never've gone out with him. Should never've had sex with him. Damn, why do smart women do dumb things?"

I snickered softly. "I'm walking testimony to that — or rather, lying down testimony. I spent two years avoiding all men. Then nearly four going from one loser to the next."

"And now?" she inquired.

I pondered that a moment. "Now . . .I don't know. Maybe I'm chasing a dream that I can never have." I shrugged that one shoulder again.

We smiled warmly at each other. Reflectively, our gazes slid to the window. Through the blinds, early twilight shone its pinks and oranges and violets.

What a night and day this had been! But as long as there was another day, I thought, there was hope. As long as you learned from a bad experience and moved on.

And if you didn't learn?

Then, as Grandma Gomez would say, *"Canta, tonta, no llore."* Sing, silly, don't cry.

On Saturday, the nurse attending the other patient in my room and me announced that I was not to have anything to eat or drink. I could suck on ice cubes, but that was it! My intestines hadn't begun to work yet, and I had to continue to fast, even from drinking liquids. Well, that truly sucked!

A forced diet just before Christmas!

The nurse issued that stern warning when she saw my siblings enter my room with an extra-large box of pizza, a tub of *KFC* chicken, and two liters of *Classic Coke*. They hadn't been informed of my condition, and no one really explained to me medically what would happen if I ignored her warning. I concluded something dire from the way the nurse looked and spoke, like exploding guts. Yet, I could smell the heavenly aromas, which caused me to salivate like one of Pavlov's dogs.

Much to my torment, my siblings and their spouses — even Pop — had a fiesta in my room after pulling the curtain behind them for privacy. I felt sorry for my roommate, who was well enough to glower at each of them. Most of my family had come up from Salinas for the day, but some would stay overnight at Flora's or with Jesús and Connie at their two-bedroom apartment. We'd never grown up with lavish hotel stays, so we were accustomed to bunking it. As long as there was a toilet and running water somewhere, we could manage. Tonight, Mama and Grandma Gómez had stayed behind at Flora's to take care of all the children.

Everyone came over to my bed and kissed me on the forehead or cheek. I even think I saw Pop's lips quiver with emotion. My family seemed truly happy that I'd survived my little, cute appendix ordeal. I was now trading places with Pop.

Last month he was in the hospital, and now it was my turn. When he and I exchanged looks, I think we conveyed our relief silently that we'd both lived through it.

Jesús had shorn his pirate-beard and now sported a handlebar, Joaquin Murrieta-style mustache. And believe it or not, a black-and-silver Mariachi sombrero. He'd even brought his guitar, but the nurse had warned him against playing it. I swear the man was a frustrated performer or celebrity impersonator. His arm draped around Connie's shoulder, Jesús was joking with Roberto, pretending to shoot, with his fingers as a syringe, something into my IV tubing. Liquid cyanide, maybe?

Frankie and Juan Pablo began stuffing their faces with pizza while Pop, ignoring his new diet but appearing in good color, began munching on a drumstick. All this food was stacked tantalizingly on my bed, like a picnic spread on a blanket. All that was lacking were ants!

My stomach growled, but my intestines remained frozen.

Damn my uncooperative, gutless guts! Didn't they know I was starving?

Isabel, Connie, and Pet elbowed the guys out of the way and approached me. They looked pointedly at my left hand, ring finger. Nope. No ring. They were as disappointed as *Oscar* losers, smiling bravely but looking crushed nonetheless. Pet whipped a brush out of her purse and soon was hard at work, restoring some style to my flat, straggly bed-hair.

"I'm not ready, and he hasn't asked," I said evenly, trying to ignore their disappointment.

"Here, fix up some," Pet urged me, handing me a damp washcloth and my lipstick tube, "so you'll look nice when Rick shows up. We saw him and his little girl in the parking lot."

Pop, looking thinner but healthier, nodded approval between bites of chicken. "You make him wait, little girl. If he's serious, he'll stick around."

"Rick wants Frankie and Roberto's company," Connie piped in, "to do all the tile work for this Milpitas development. They'll have to hire at least six or eight more guys. They might have to move up here."

Jesús overheard this and winked. "Think I'll ask for a raise. Rick's going to be rolling in dough — "

Just then, Rick and Angelina appeared at the break in the curtain. Wearing a different outfit from the one she'd worn all night, Angelina was riding his hip. Poor Rick looked worn out and frazzled. He'd probably spent the day running around, tending to business, tending to Angelina, trying to catch up on lost sleep. My family greeted him in various ways, but mainly Rick shook hands with the men and kissed the cheeks of my sisters and Isabel.

Then our gazes met, and he beamed. Even Angelina smiled sheepishly. I don't mind saying, my heart soared to the ceiling. I couldn't help it — I was in love and desperately needed the little girl to like me. Rick held up a *Starbucks* cup.

"When I told Angie I knew you'd be dying for your favorite coffee drink, she talked me into buying this. It's no longer hot, though."

"Thank you, Rick. Angelina." I put it on the tray with repressed longing. "My intestines are still paralyzed. Can't eat or drink anything 'til they start working again. I'll save it. Maybe tomorrow, I'll have them heat it up."

He made a moue of pity, bent over, and kissed me on the mouth. As he straightened, he whispered in Spanish to the little girl. From her hand behind her back, she thrust forth a stuffed green and yellow dinosaur the size of my fist — a cute, little brontosaurus. She shyly gave it to me.

"A dinosaur for Dina. A Deena-saurus," she said, giggling at her father. Rick smiled broadly.

Everyone laughed in appreciation at the child's cleverness,

although I knew Rick was behind the pun. The women fawned over Angelina, frightening her a little, making her cower against her father's side. In a brilliant move, Rick placed her on the bed, where she sat and gazed at me and all my hookups with open curiosity.

"Thanks, Angelina, I love it," I said, playing with the little stuffed toy on the bed. I was genuinely touched by the gift but especially by her willingness to speak to me and sit so close. No doubt, I looked fearful and strange, but Angelina just stared at everything frankly and with acceptance. My God, it took almost dying to finally get the little girl to warm up to me a little, but it was worth it. I'd do it again in a New York minute.

I could be a wife—especially Rick's wife. But instant step-mommy hood? Was that what I wanted? What did it mean to me? I wasn't sure, frankly. Right now, in my weak physical state, it was enough to make me want to turn up the painkiller drip and drift off into fantasyland. Later, I knew once I'd returned to my robust, healthy, and sassy nature, it'd be just another life challenge that I'd be willing to take on.

Maybe.

Maybe not.

Tentatively, I took Angelina's hand. Our fingers clasped together for a long moment before the child slowly shifted her shy gaze and withdrew her little hand. I held up the stuffed dinosaur and made it bow to the child.

"I'm Dina-saurus," I told her in a cartoonish, falsetto voice. "What's your name?"

She covered her mouth and giggled. I looked about me, noticing that Rick was radiating pleasure and Pop was leveling a steady, speculative look on me. Frankie was frowning all of a sudden.

Twenty minutes later, Frank lingered behind and whispered something in Rick's ear. Then Rick looked worried. By the time he returned to my bed, I was beginning to feel scared. Something was wrong, and I had a feeling it had to do with my cousins in Mexico.

"Rick, what happened?"

"No, nothing bad. Frank wanted me to tell you that your cousin, Teresa, is now in Nuevo Laredo—that border town across from Laredo, Texas. Teresa called from a pay phone and spoke to your grandmother. She knows you've had emergency surgery, but she still got panicky. She's fine but scared. The woman she's staying with is keeping her and her son in hiding, but the woman's a stranger. Also, Teresa learned that the woman's husband knows some of the Gulf cartel militia, so Teresa's afraid someone in that gang'll find out about her and her son. Your cousin's got a price on her head. The word's gotten out that Pedro Vargas's wife took off with his son, and he's got half his thugs looking for her. Vargas wants his son back but doesn't care about the condition that Teresa's brought back under. That's gang code for dead or alive."

Dammit! I had to call Joe Torres right away! We had to get her out of Mexico as soon as humanly possible. I had to warn him that she might not be as safe as he thought she was. And here I was, tethered to an IV cable, incapacitated.

"My cell phone, Rick," I urged breathlessly, pointing to the purse on the window sill ledge.

Rick glanced meaningfully over at Angelina, who was standing at the doorway, watching the nurses come and go. Then reluctantly, frowning all the while, he rummaged in my purse.

"Dina, maybe you should let Frank and Roberto go to Texas and get your cousin out. You're in no state to go anywhere."

He pulled out my phone and held it raised in his hand.

"Dina, think about it. That border town is one of the most lawless. You read those news articles. Just this year, the mayor of Nuevo Laredo, the police chief, and a reporter were gunned down by Gulf Cartel commandos in broad daylight. All because they tried to do something to stop all the violence. Nearly eighty American tourists have disappeared from that town so far this year. God knows what happened to them. Gulf thugs either murdered them or sold them into white slavery—you know that happens. And it's getting worse. It's like a Wild West town—whoever's got the biggest gun or the most guns wins." He drew a deep breath and ran his fingers through his hair. "Dammit, Dina, think of Angelina and me. You may not believe it, but we *need* you."

I was—honestly, I was—thinking of them. Seen from his perspective, maybe I was being foolhardy, stubborn, and selfish. Nevertheless, I'd committed to Grandma Gómez, Teresa, and the DEA agent, Joe Torres. The only thing Frank and Roberto could say in Spanish was *cerveza*, Jesús was a loose cannon, and my sisters all had children to care for.

But I wasn't a mother, and neither was Lisa.

And I had sworn to Grandma Gomez that I would fulfill this mission.

That old saying about the road to hell was paved with good intentions. I didn't believe that.

To me, the road to hell was not trying.

CHAPTER TWENTY-TWO

A cute or ugly appendix wasn't going to keep me out of operation for longer than one week. There was too much joy in my life to keep me down, so I put on a panty-girdle to cinch in my lower torso. The girdle was so tiny, unstretched it looked like a size 0. Although a little shaky, I went back to work the week before Christmas break.

My guts — about time — were back doing the job they were meant to do. Which meant, of course, I could eat and drink and restore my strength. I was still on painkillers but mending nicely, according to my surgeon, and my head was clear enough to survive a full day of sixth graders. My kids showed sympathy by restraining themselves and marking time until Christmas vacation. I showed my appreciation by giving the class a hot chocolate, marshmallow, and peppermint candy-cane party.

Well, almost. By the middle of the week, I was feeling a little quivery by the end of the day. Fortunately, Lisa Luna helped out by combining our classes one day for a field trip to San Francisco to see the ACT production of *A Christmas Carol*. She'd organized the entire trip, made the reservations, sent out and collected the permission slips, and rented the motor coach for our trip into the city. What a friend!

Then, bless their hearts, four of my kids' mothers chipped in and helped with the class Christmas party on Friday. So, after hugging the kids and wishing them *Merry Christmas* and *See you next year*. I stowed away all my gifts from the sixth-grade mothers, the PTA, and the kids themselves in my trunk.

The decorations in my classroom could wait until St. Valentine's Day to take down, as far as I was concerned. Then I snagged Lisa before she could take off for our holiday break.

"Come with me for a *Starbucks*," I told her as she was doing the same with her Christmas stuff, filling her trunk. "I have kind of a surprise for you. I swear, on my grandmother's rosary, you'll like it."

Knowing all I had to do was arouse Lisa's curiosity, I pressed her, and she agreed.

"I don't have much time," she pointed out. "I haven't even started Christmas shopping, and it's in—"

"Six days," I supplied.

"I promised everyone no more tree ornaments, hand-made or store-bought. I gotta be a little original this year, or my family's going to fry my butt. And we're leaving tonight?"

I'd been ready to leave for Mexico as soon as I was released from the hospital, but Joe Torres wanted to postpone things. He claimed he had last-minute arrangements to make, but I thought it was because he didn't want to cart around an invalid. He said he needed me strong and healthy to carry out his plan. *The plan*—he was keeping secret until Lisa and I could meet him in San Antonio.

"Thirty minutes, tops," I assented eagerly, while inwardly grinning up a storm, adding mysteriously, "you said you wanted some excitement in your life."

A short while later, we were sipping our customized coffee drinks, and, I have to admit, my gaze kept wandering to the store's entrance.

Even though I was aware that *the best-laid plans of mice and men often go awry*, to quote Bobbie Burns, the risk was worth it in this case. Of course, I was going with my gut feeling on this, but I sensed that Lisa would thank me later. Besides, this was my way of thanking her for being a good friend and arranging that superlative field trip for my students and me.

Lisa looked especially attractive that day. In fact, most men would call her *hot*. Her curly dark hair was gathered up in a high ponytail, which always looked great on her. Her makeup was flawless, and she wore a snug crimson sweater with a red Stuart-plaid skirt. Red pantyhose and red stacked heels completed the pert, Christmassy ensemble, but the little bit of jewelry that drew one's attention was pinned at the tip of her deep V-neck collar.

Well, if one could call it jewelry. Anything flashy and sparkly counted as jewelry in Lisa's book. An enamel, cherubic-faced Santa Claus with a white mustache and beard smiled impishly on a pin, its red nose lighting up and its blue eyes flashing every time Lisa flicked a switch on the side of its face. It was typically Lisa—perky, tongue-in-cheek, with a touch of gaudy.

I saw him at the door and waved him over, at the same time telling Lisa not to turn around. Tyler and I had talked for a long time on the phone a week before. He knew all about Rick and our relationship, although my little, white lie stood—that Rick and I had become reacquainted through our high school reunion committee work. The ostensible excuse for this meeting was to return to him that .38 caliber revolver he'd given me. Joe Torres told me in no uncertain terms that Lisa and I couldn't bring any weapons with us to Mexico.

"Why are you so mysterious, Dina?"

I looked up, and then Lisa glanced up at the gorgeous hunk standing next to our table. Tyler was still in uniform, and, yep, it fit him like a form-fitting ski suit. He could've sold tickets to women to let them come and gaze at him all day.

"Tyler, this is Lisa Luna. Lisa, Tyler Dalton."

While I pondered whether I could become a model's agent and enlist Tyler as my first client, Lisa and Tyler locked eyes and clasped hands. For a very long moment. When he took a seat at our table, Lisa sat up straighter, jutting out her breasts a little.

"Hey, is that one of those pins—" Tyler pointed at her bosom.

Lisa flicked on the switch. Santa's eyes flashed on and off like a carnival clown's. Tyler smiled appreciatively—his inner little boy tickled, no doubt—his sweet dimples cratering, his pretty mouth curving upward. He nervously ran a big hand through his thick, curly brown hair, unable to take his attention off the blinking Santa. When he finally raised his gaze to Lisa's dark, now smoldering eyes, Tyler had set his square, oh-so masculine jaw in the same decisive way that I'd observed at the firing range when he was shooting at the target with his .45. The steady, intent gaze of a male predator on the prowl. This time, Mama's boy found a new target.

"I've got just fifteen minutes, Dina," Tyler said to me, though still looking at Lisa. "Doing an overtime shift tonight."

"Lisa's a part-time private investigator, Tyler," I informed him, "so I thought she could use that *Lady Smith and Wesson* you and your mother so kindly gave to me. After much thought, I think I'll stick to *Mace* or some kind of pepper spray."

Lisa reacted with alarm. "But, Dina, what if we need it in Mexico?"

I shook my head dismissively. "Torres said absolutely not. If it's a matter of life or death, we'll have to rely on the DEA."

Tyler looked at me as if I were the looniest human on the planet. Then, like an electric switch flicked on, he turned to Lisa.

"What's this about Mexico and the DEA?"

What followed was Lisa's two-minute update on how she and I were working with a DEA agent to bring out my cousin and her son and Teresa's history and involvement with the Juárez drug cartel. She skipped the part about how my grandmother and her son, my drug-lord uncle, played a role in all of this.

This FYI segued into a serious, ten-minute discussion about CIs, perps, criminal profiles, CSI techniques, bunko schemes, insurance-fraud cases Lisa had investigated, felons Tyler had brought in and brought down in the line of duty, their choice of weapons for various occasions—there were different crime occasions?—locked breeches, 7-shot magazines, and grip and thumb safeties.

I couldn't understand half of their conversation, so I spent the time sipping my heavenly macchiato and planning my sexy look for the evening. Rick was finally taking me out on our romantic dinner-and-dancing date, and I planned to look like a sultry siren.

After one week in the hospital, thanks to my frozen guts, and one week back at work, Rick and I would be celebrating much tonight. My survival, my tentative, new friendship with Angelina, his new contract to build that complex in Milpitas, and, of course, Rick wanted to see me before I took off for Texas.

I was just waiting for the phone call from Joe Torres, telling me what time to meet him tomorrow in San Antonio. Lisa and I were already booked for the midnight flight out of San Jose to Dallas. Then from Dallas to San Antonio on a hopper.

All other problems and potential risks would be shoved to the back burner tonight. I was so engrossed in my thoughts that I'd barely noticed Lisa slipping Tyler her PI card with her personal cell phone number on the back.

"That twenty-two of yours won't stop any of the perps I've encountered," Tyler was telling Lisa. "Maybe you'd like that thirty-eight snub-nose Dina's giving back to me. It's perfect for undercover work. Easily concealed. 'Course, you'll have to register it and get a license to carry."

"I already have one for the twenty-two, not that I've ever

used it. My uncle has me confined to mainly office research. But just in case I get out in the field someday, it might come in handy. I'll just have to get used to the extra recoil."

Lisa smiled brightly—ha! Like she had any doubts about her ability to handle such a trifle as the recoil of a gun.

"When you get back from Texas, I'll take you to a range by my house," Tyler offered. "In an hour, you'll get accustomed to the kick."

By now, Lisa and Tyler had shifted their chairs so that their forearms were touching.

"Okay," Lisa replied, "got all my shopping done early, so I'm free." She glanced at me and grinned slyly. "What about yours?" she asked a captivated Tyler.

"My . . .what?" Apparently, Tyler's mind was on a slightly different topic.

"Your Christmas shopping? Have you finished?"

Tyler's matinee-idol face flushed a bit. "No . . .uh, I still have to buy something for my mother. So when do you leave for Texas? I'd like to take you out for lunch and maybe some Christmas shopping after your trip."

"Don't know when we'll be back. Probably by Monday. This is just a weekend trip," Lisa said, flicking her long, dark eyelashes at him.

While Tyler reluctantly checked his watch, Lisa threw a meaningful, wide-eyed look my way. I tried hard not to smirk or snicker but failed, I'm sure, to conceal the smug delight I felt in bringing these two like-minds together. Now, if Lisa could get past Tyler's controlling, clinging mother, the two might enjoy each other. Knowing Lisa, she'd find a way to avoid creepy Mother Dalton.

I turned over to Lisa the blue plastic gun case, hugged them both, and wished them a Merry Christmas in the parking lot. Rick had told me about a hardware store that sold over-the-counter pepper spray in canisters that could easily fit into a purse. He'd bought a couple for me in case Steve came around and gave me trouble. Instead of a gunslinger, I'd be a pepper slinger. Somehow, it seemed a more natural fit for me.

I was about to turn on the ignition when my cell phone jangled.

"We're good to go, Dina," Joe Torres said without preamble. "Get here by tomorrow. I'll meet you at the Federal Building in San Antonio at five PM."

We spoke briefly, and then I hopped out of my car. I waved my cell phone in the air and caught Lisa's attention. She ran up to me, and we both started jumping up and down like a pair of teenyboppers at an Enrique Iglesias concert. Rather, she jumped and I sort of jiggled.

"He's *sooo* gorgeous!"

"I told you about his mother. Are you okay with that?"

"Ha! I told him I don't do mothers or fathers. If he wanted to see me, it'd be just him and me. He said okay to that."

"Good! Stick to it—trust me, you don't want to meet his mother."

"So when?" she asked excitedly. I knew what she meant.

"Five o'clock tomorrow in San Antonio. Federal Building. I'll pick you up tonight at ten. The whole trip's on me."

I was about to max out my credit card, but who cared? Mission—Saving La Familia was going to succeed, and we were going to make it happen!

"It's been ages since I've been here, Rick," I said, taking his hand as he, in gentlemanly fashion, helped me out of his SUV. Actually, it'd been only about six months since I'd dragged Hugh Goss to *Habanero's*, but my white lie was necessary. The subject of Hugh was still a delicate one.

Now owned by Héctor Rodríguez, *Habanero's* had undergone a transformation from a watering hole and seedy salsa bar for twenty-and thirty-somethings to a pricey dinner club that featured California-style Mexican, Spanish, and Cuban food in its restaurant.

The real drawing card was the cocktail lounge with its room-size dance floor. A variety of Latino bands played everything from Santana to Los Lobos, from Miami Heat to Ricky Martin, from Julio Iglesias and his son to Marc Anthony. One band even played the '40s Latin-swing numbers, like Don Tosti's *Pachuco Boogie*.

And you did not get on the dance floor unless you could move your hips or shake your booty. When I'd brought Hugh Goss here — what a disaster that was! The man could not move below the waist. He was like a talking hand-puppet, an indication that our future estrangement was close at hand, perhaps.

I was dressed to the hilt, I'll have you know. My hair was swept up and lacquered back in a twist. Drop earrings of red-crystal beads matched the Y-style necklace, the tip of the Y nestling strategically in the cleavage visible above the deep-cut, surplice bodice of the black velvet sheath I wore. The dress used to fit me like a glove but now hung a little loosely due to the weight I'd lost after my surgery. Compared to my usual daytime schoolteacher look, I was wearing a ton of makeup. Flora had advised me the night before how to enhance my eyes without a lot of goop. The result was, I must say, fantastic. Glammed up but natural-looking.

Even Rick remarked that he felt he was squiring tonight my wicked twin sister. I rather liked that idea and proceeded to flirt accordingly.

"Hey, *Señor* Ramos," one of *Habanero's* bouncers hailed us at the entrance in fluent Spanish. "Where've you been, man? Haven't seen you here in weeks."

"I've been busy, Raoul," Rick replied, returning the man's greeting in Spanish. They bumped fists, gripped hands, and did their elbow-tapping, macho-male thing. "Dina, Raoul's brother, Pancho, is our roofing foreman."

"*Con mucho gusto*," I said, smiling. Pleased to meet you.

Raoul was a big bruiser of a guy with a shaved head, two gold-stud earrings, and wearing a navy-blue, pin-striped suit that was probably a size 48-extra tall. When he shot me a wide grin, I could see one gold molar. Mr. Rodriguez obviously believed in hefty security. Standing next to him at the entrance door, I noticed his bouncer-buddy was just as big as Raoul and had as little head-hair. Instead, the second bouncer had a trim, black *Van Dyke* beard and mustache. From the bulges in their jackets, it was clear that they were *packing heat*, as Lisa would call it. I wondered if they were ex-Marines or ex-Army Rangers. Raoul took his time giving me a thorough once-over.

"Ah, *Señor* Ramos, your women are getting prettier with the more money you make."

That made me frown. Rick, his right hand firmly clasped around my waist, glanced at me guiltily. Despite his embarrassed look, he looked handsome and debonair in his gray slacks and navy blazer. My knees had practically buckled earlier that evening when he'd picked me up.

After Raoul's off-the-cuff comment, Rick turned back to the Terminator and visibly stiffened.

"Raoul, this is Dina Salazar, my *comprometida*," he said in Spanish. My fiancée.

That single word made all the difference. We weren't engaged but on the brink of being, so what Rick had said was nearly correct for all intents and purposes. All of a sudden, Raoul was rushing to show his respect. When he apologized to me for his disrespectful remark, I dismissed it.

"I've known Rick since we were poor college kids," I told him, taking the crook of Rick's arm. "But we were apart for several years." With that, I'd alluded to our history and at the same time assured the man he was forgiven.

Looking up at my man and returning his frankly adoring

stare, I felt a renewed sense of wonder. There was much about Rick's world that remained a mystery to me. His business, his employees, his love life these past five years. He'd told me a lot about the first two topics but nothing about the last one. Evidently, if Raoul's comment could be taken as fact, Rick hadn't been a total workaholic or a total monk.

To learn that he'd brought other women to *Habanero's* or met them here wasn't shocking to me, but it did stir my little cauldron of simmering jealousy. Nevertheless, I pushed aside all the questions and suspicions that sprang up to burn my mind and heat up my emotions.

"Hope you don't mind, Dina—the *comprometida* thing. I know we're not engaged. It just seemed appropriate."

I shrugged it off. Telling the bouncer we were fiancés seemed a petty thing to object over. We were close to becoming engaged, and we both knew it.

"Not at all."

I was in the mood to have fun!

For two hours, we danced to every ranchera the band tonight, Los Vaqueros, played. We did the salsa, the cumbia, the cha-cha, our version of the Cuban rhumba, Latino-rock, and swing. All the dances we used to do as college kids and the slower ones that the now older, more affluent crowd at *Habanero's* wanted as well. We even remembered how to do the silly macarena from our college days.

My pantie-girdle, black and lacy to match my bra but as sturdy as a bulletproof vest, was holding in all my innards so that I could move freely. Despite my recent appendectomy two weeks ago, I was swiveling my pelvis, bumping and grinding with the best of them.

And so was Rick. Could that man move! His shoulders, soon shed of the sports jacket, rolled like ball bearings, his slim hips swayed and pumped, his nimble feet slid and shuffled. We rocked on that dance floor, and the feeling of moving so well together was liberating. And joyful.

There was a connection between us, like an invisible, gossamer presence of pure love and mutual understanding. Even I, if I'd wanted to for some perverse reason, would never be able to break it. It's difficult to explain, but there it is.

It's what brought us back together. That and a wild leap of faith that this time, we were going to make it work. No more fuck-ups!

Finally, near to collapsing, we left our table by the dance floor and went into the bar, which separated the nightclub from the restaurant area. The bar lounge was cooler and quieter. Given that I'd met several people whom Rick knew — including three single women who gave me angry looks — we wanted to be by ourselves.

We perched on rattan bar stools and ordered two more drinks. The entire bar, nightclub, and restaurant were decorated in a Latin-tropics motif, reminiscent of the Yucatán, Cuba, or Puerto Rico. Nicely done and understated, not Disney-ish.

Our faces were shiny, and drops of sweat clung to the ends of our hair. I began fanning myself with the cocktail menu.

"How're you holding up, *querida*?" Rick pointed to my abdomen while sipping his *Tequila Sunrise*. We looked like we'd just emerged from a sauna.

"Fine, but I think I'm winding down. I'm having fun, but it's been an exhausting week. My insides feel okay, though." Rick reached over and touched my belly. I swatted his hand away. "Don't do that. People'll think I'm pregnant. And they know we're not married."

Rick slid me that rakish, lopsided grin of his. "Would you like to be?"

I sipped my vodka-on-the-rocks. "Which one, pregnant or married?"

"Both," he teased. "I did it the wrong way last time. Maybe

it's not fashionable anymore, but this time let's do it the right way. Marriage first." He bent over to whisper, "You're still on the Pill, aren't you?"

I nodded. Two weeks after my surgery, I went back on birth control. We hadn't resumed our sex life, an unfortunate result which I knew Rick was anxious to correct. By dressing and dancing like a vamp, I was trying to get myself back into the mood and forget about my brush with death and the delicate state of my lower torso. On top of everything, my jealous nature had returned to haunt me. I took a long draw from my vodka drink.

"Rick, did you introduce me as your fiancée to let everyone know you're not available? Especially those three women — boy, did they give me the evil eye!"

"Well, yes. It's the truth, Dina. We're both out of the marriage market . . . Aren't we?" He looked uncertain as if I might be having second thoughts. Learning earlier that I was taking off on the midnight flight to Dallas that same night had unsettled him. He still was uneasy about Lisa and me going without any of the men in my family.

"Well, sure. I'm not looking anymore. I've found my man again. And this time, it better work."

I gave him my best half-lidded gaze and crossed my legs, aware that the skirt of my little black dress had ridden up to my lower thighs. Rick's gaze shifted as he scooted his stool closer to mine. Soon my knee was grazing the crotch of his gray slacks, and his long legs were sandwiching mine, his feet propped up on the rungs of my bar stool.

"Dina, I've missed our lovemaking." Rick was frowning a little. "What did the doctor say?"

"When I feel ready," I said softly, "but he said to take it slow and gentle." Over two weeks without Rick's naked body pressing against mine — believe me, I was more than ready!

Rick was inching in closer. "I can do slow and gentle.

Whatever you like. Whatever you need. Whenever, wherever."

"You badass." I laughed shortly. "Tonight, I feel almost ready, but we don't have time. When I return . . ."

I looked pointedly at his crotch, now being massaged lightly by my knee. He was moving my legs between his so that my knee was brushing back and forth against his hard bulge. We were engaging in foreplay on barstools in a crowded bar.

Boy, was my wicked twin having fun!

"I guess we should go," Rick said, looking disappointed and more than a little worried. He dropped his gaze to my exposed thighs, put his drink down, and slid his hand up the outside of my leg under my dress. My legs were hoseless, and the brush of his hand on my bare thigh was unnerving. It made my skin shiver.

"Yeah, we should go." I didn't budge off the barstool. Unwanted jealous thoughts were crowding my mind, competing with the hot waves of desire I felt as Rick caressed my thigh. "Okay, I just have a question or two to ask you."

Oh God, I knew what I was about to do—I was going to blow the whole evening. I was going to let my jealousy demons out of their cage.

"Yeah?" He suddenly looked anxious.

"Rick, I haven't asked you much about these past five and a half years. That guy, Raoul, he greeted you like you've been a regular here. You brought dates here, didn't you? You picked up women here, didn't you?"

Rick clearly sensed the loaded questions were out to get him in trouble, and he became instantly guarded. His gaze caught mine and something in his expression relaxed. He knew he had to tell me the truth, whatever the consequences might be.

"Yes, to both questions. Look around. A lot of men come

here to meet women, have some fun, maybe get lucky." He sighed and frowned. "Look, Dina, I never said I was a celibate hermit during those years, especially the last three. When I knew you were seeing other men, I thought for sure I'd lost you—so yeah, I went looking."

"Did you bring Anita here?"

"Once, yeah. Those six months or so after Angelina's birth, when I was trying to be a good husband."

"Rick, I need to know everything—" No, you don't, I told myself.

"No, baby, you don't need to know every detail." Rick leaned his forehead against mine. "I know you, Dina. You're a jealous woman. Which I kind of like about you. But you let it take hold of you sometimes. Don't let that part of you come between us." He shot me a wry smile. "That summer when you were in DC with Velásquez, I let jealousy consume me and to get back at you, look what happened. Jealousy's a destructive thing—I don't want it to ruin what we have. Which is pretty damn wonderful."

Rick had switched to Spanish, even before I'd realized it, so it took a few seconds for me to catch up with my translation.

"Those women in there," I probed in Spanish, not letting it go for the life of me. "You dated them, didn't you? Did you sleep with any of them?"

When his gaze flicked downward and he remained silent, I fumed. My *diablito* was cackling, making fun of me. I was losing it.

"Look, Dina, I'm not going to give you specifics about those years. They're over and done with. We found each other again. That's what's important. Someday, after we're married . . .oh, say twenty years afterward. Then I promise you I'll tell you everything that you want to know. By then, you'll laugh and say, in your wiseass way, *I don't believe you. Why would any woman want to screw you, Rick Ramos?* So, until then, I'm saying nothing specifically. And I won't ask you about the men you dated. Including what you did with that *gabacho*, Hugh Goss."

Naturally, he was the wiser of the two of us. He'd won our little, verbal towel-snapping routine. I was still frustrated and vexed, however. Maybe the mix of vodka and painkillers and getting hot and sweaty were all making me a little crazy. And my nervousness over the trip to Texas and all that was about to happen.

"Oh, you're a goat with low-hanging balls," I declared hotly in Spanish.

To which Rick reacted with low, throaty peals of laughter. The bartender, having overheard me, turned his back to us and chortled, his shoulders shaking.

"Where did you hear that?" Rick asked, his lips still twitching with mirth. We were back to English.

"I overheard Roberto call Jesús that."

"Dina, do you know what that means?"

"Not exactly."

"You just said I was over the hill sexually." He leaned toward me. "Let's go to my car, and I'll prove to you I'm not."

With that, he pressed his point, literally and figuratively, by grasping my knee and holding it steady against the bulge in his trousers. The searing challenge in his dark eyes assured me he wasn't bluffing.

"Okay, macho-man, I know you're not. But I've got just enough time" —I glanced at my watch—"to change clothes, grab my bag, and pick up Lisa."

"I should go with you," Rick urged, scooting back. "I don't like you and Lisa risking your necks. Going into cartel territory is not a good idea. I don't care what this DEA dude says. They can kill him as easily as they can kidnap you girls. And if that happens, you know what'll they do to you."

"It's going to be fine. This Joe Torres sounds like he knows what he's doing. He's a federal officer, and he speaks Spanish. And he's an expert on the Mexican drug cartels."

Rick wasn't mollified. His eyes were still flashing panic.

"So, what's the plan for finding your cousin?"

"In her last email, she said to go to this bar. That's where the husband of this woman—Torres's undercover agent—works. He'll make sure we're who we say we are. Then the husband'll tell us where to pick Teresa up. I wrote Teresa and told her to expect two American women, about thirty. One's tallish with auburn hair, and the other one's shorter with dark, curly hair. Joe Torres said he'll be close by, in the car."

"The husband of this undercover agent—he's a guy who works for the Gulf Cartel?"

I shrugged, frowning. The plan was beginning to sound full of holes, like fungus-covered Swiss cheese.

"Teresa says he owns this bar where the Cartel mercenaries go to drink. But she assured me we can trust him. She does, anyway, with her life. Teresa's being extra cautious in case her husband knows she's in Nuevo Laredo and sends someone to find her. The DEA guy seems okay with the plan. Honestly, Rick, what can go wrong?"

That got a big, ironic smile out of him, followed by a loud, masculine snort. We slid off our barstools.

"I'll get our jackets," he said, slapping a bill on the bar.

The cold night air carried a hint of possible rain, and we walked arm-in-arm together, warming ourselves against each other. As we passed Raoul, we noticed he was baring his shoulder holster, and his bouncer-buddy was doing the same. Rick wanted to know if they were having problems. Raoul indicated the long, low-riding, black *Lincoln* parked along the curb. It was a late model, and the windows on the curbside were down. A mob mobile. We used to call them *cholo* cruisers.

"Héctor don't like no *cholos* or gang bangers in here," Raoul said. "We turned them away, and they're pissed off. I'm calling the cops." He had his walkie-talkie handy and switched it on. "Hey, Jorge, call in a black-and-white. We got trouble."

We left the parking lot right away. At last glance, the *cholo* cruiser was thundering down the street, its speed picking up. I sighed. What was it about Latino males? The poor ones went out of their ways looking for danger and excitement. Did the richer ones, like Rick, find danger and excitement in other ways? Like chasing women?

I voiced my thoughts, stupidly so, apparently. Boy, Rick's mood all of a sudden changed.

"Yeah, well, Latinas seem to go out of their way looking for danger, too. I could name two that I know." His tone was harsh and cross.

"I have to do this, you know that," I snapped impatiently, "I promised my grandmother."

Rick sighed and sat there in the driver's seat, looking very weary and forlorn. And remote. He kept shaking his head.

By now, my heart was racing like a runaway horse's, and I wanted to appease him, reassure him so he wouldn't worry.

"There's no need to be upset or angry over this. It'll be okay, you'll see. I'll be back in three or four days, in time for Christmas. Joe Torres says Teresa and her son will have to stay in San Antonio for a day or so to be debriefed. Interrogated, he meant, I suppose. Anyway, I promised you I'd join you at your family's on *La Noche Buena,* and I mean to keep my promise."

"Yeah, *chica,* if you aren't the sex slave of a Cartel honcho by then. Or thrown in some ditch by the Rio Grande."

I clapped my mouth shut as he drove in silence. The tension was thick enough to spread on bread. So he was angry and worried. What could I do about it?

My mind was made up, the tickets were bought, and Lisa

was ready. Rick was clearly making a big deal about my adventure to Texas and Mexico, and it was all over nothing. Macho males, especially overly protective, Latino ones, could be very trying.

When we pulled up in front of Flora's house, his mood had morphed into something altogether different.

"Dina," Rick said gruffly, staring ahead at the windshield, "I need to tell you something."

"You told me you didn't want me to hear that you've slept with those women at *Habanero's*." I tried to sound flippant.

"No, it's not that—" He flicked his hand dismissively.

I was starting to get frightened. Omigod, this is it! He's breaking up with me all because I'm going to help rescue my cousin in Mexico!

How could he do this to me?

"I've been wanting to tell you this for some time. I had to wait until you and Angelina warmed up to each other. Y'know, bonded together. I think maybe you have—at the hospital, I could tell you and Angie kind of clicked."

"Yeah, at least, we've started to."

"And you have no qualms about someday being her stepmother?"

"Maybe a few, Rick, to be honest. But we'll work it out. She's your flesh-and-blood daughter, and I'm determined to be a good mother to her. God knows she needs one."

"Yeah." Rick grew quiet for a long, uncomfortable moment. Then he looked me square in the face. He didn't touch me though I'd made a motion to caress his face. His expression looked so mournful, so sad.

"I have to tell you this. I can't let it go any longer."

Oh, shit, I thought. This is something bad. His expression scared me.

"She's not my daughter, Dina. Not my biological daughter."

I sat there. What was he saying?

"You were right all along. Years ago you warned me, you told me. Anita set me up. I was her meal ticket. Money — that's all she ever wanted from me."

What was he saying? Angelina — not his daughter?

"She was already pregnant when I met her at that party. She'd heard I had a steady job — my father had a roofing business. She needed a home and money — her family had kicked her out. She didn't look pregnant, so how was I to know? My cousin — all he knew was she and her sister were easy lays. When she told me in September, she was pregnant by me, I told my father. I was out of my mind for fear of losing you, but he said I had to quit school, work full-time. Y'know, be a man. Be responsible. Marry her and give the baby legitimacy. Papa had already put the business in my name — what could I do?"

He wrenched his gaze away from my stricken face and rested his forehead on his hands, both gripping the steering wheel hard.

"I supported Anita for the two years of our marriage," he went on quickly, his voice cracking with suppressed fury. "I gave her a twenty-five-thousand-dollar settlement when I divorced her. That was all of my money at the time. I got a good lawyer, so she couldn't get the business my father had spent his life building. Where all that money went — well, I've got a good idea where it went. In her veins or up her nose. Anyway, before I took custody of Angelina, I washed my hands of her. Her family, too."

Rick was speaking so fast, I could barely follow what he was saying. I sat there, frozen.

"Child Protective Services got into the picture and ran some tests on Angelina. She was two at the time. They wanted to make sure her body was clear of drugs. I told them to run a paternity test as well. I don't know why I did that — maybe

I felt it in my gut, y'know, that she didn't have any Ramos traits. The paternity test showed I wasn't her father. Her biological father, anyway. I don't know who her real father is, and it doesn't matter. It didn't matter to me then and doesn't matter to me now. But I thought you should know. My family knows. In case it's ever brought up."

We sat in the dark, alone with our thoughts. So much for our romantic evening, I thought. I removed my hand from the back of his head where I'd been stroking the nape of his neck. He raised his head and pinned me with a heart-rending, pleading stare.

"You drop this bombshell on me tonight?" I was so astonished, my voice hissed out in a whisper. But that was just on the surface. Below, I was numb.

"Dina, you had to know the truth before we went any further." Rick's tone was somber and foreboding.

"Sure, I should've known about this two months ago." *Before I fell back in love with you, you asshole.*

"I didn't know how you'd take it. I wanted to wait to see if there was a chance the three of us could be a family. Is there, Dina? Is there still a chance? Knowing Angelina's not my biological daughter?"

He raised my fallen hand to his lips and kissed my palm. I snatched it away like he'd burned me with a cigarette tip.

"All those years we were apart, all the pain and suffering you put me through," I muttered breathily, shaking my head in wonderment, "the loneliness, feeling like my world had caved in, like what was the point of it all—and for nothing! To marry a worthless woman who tricked you into raising *her* child!"

The absurdity of it all blew my mind apart. All I knew was I wanted to be away from him, to be on some plane hurtling through the night sky, taking me somewhere—far away from Rick Ramos and his dirty, little secrets!

I jerked the car door handle, but Rick stopped me before I

could get out. I glanced at his face and was shocked to see tears streaming down his cheeks.

"What upsets you the most? The fact that Angelina's not my real daughter? She *is* in every possible way. Dina, baby, I love that little girl. I always will." He grabbed hold of one of my shoulders and roughly turned me to face him. "Or is it because Anita tricked me and stole me away from you?"

"Both," I growled. I wrenched myself free. "How could you do this—not tell me this before? You tricked me into falling for you again! You just needed a mother for Angelina—a cook, a housekeeper. That's why you came back to me!"

"No. That's not true!"

"Don't touch me."

His eyes were wide with panic. I knew, somewhere in the back of my mind, I should feel sorry for him. But I didn't. I could feel nothing but icy numbness. He tried to restrain me, but I shook off his grip again.

"What does this mean?" he asked in full fear mode.

I seized my little clutch purse and scampered out of his car. I could not escape fast enough. Before I slammed his car door shut, I leaned over.

"What does it mean? It means leave me alone!"

Even as I was stalking up the front walk on my three-inch heels, trying to keep from stumbling, I was asking myself, why did he have to ruin things? Why did he have to tell me? Do I really hate him for telling me the truth? For letting this whole mess happen in the first place? Do I really mean, leave me alone forever?

I honestly didn't know.

CHAPTER TWENTY-THREE

Lisa Luna — "Never accept a drink from a stranger in a bar." Well, duh, I told her in reply. One of my college friends had been roofied one time, and we spread the word to every female we knew for four years. Word-of-mouth is just as good as social media, in my opinion!

I felt like I hadn't slept in days, all foggy-headed and sick to my stomach. And I'd made the mistake of confiding in Lisa Rick's bombshell about Angelina. She wouldn't let go of it, harped on the topic during the flight and afterward, like chewing on a juicy bone. I knew she meant well, but it chafed me to hear her trying to find a solution to what was for me a strictly emotional dilemma.

"Man, are you in a foul mood," she griped, struggling to keep up to my long, sneakered strides.

Why Lisa wanted to change clothes at the hotel in San Antonio was beyond me. She was dressed for our meeting with Joe Torres as if she was interviewing for a job at the Federal Building.

"I didn't sleep all night," I explained curtly, "and I don't want to hear anymore. Please, just drop it, Lisa. Nothing can be done. He lied by omission, should've told me from the beginning that Angelina wasn't his real daughter."

For hours — from the three-and-a-half-hour flight to Dallas, during our two-hour wait at the Dallas-Fort Worth airport to catch the Express jet to San Antonio to the time spent at the hotel in San Antonio, Lisa had been playing relationship counselor.

"Define real. Okay, okay, so she's not his biological daughter, but you're making a big mistake. Big mistake. You would've done the same thing, Dina. Yeah, you would've, I know you. You would've waited to see how things were going to work out before dropping the big bomb."

I picked up the pace and stubbornly remained silent. My strides became longer and more determined. I fumed. I cried. Well, inwardly, anyway. I hadn't shed a tear—no, not me, brother. You wouldn't catch me weeping over Rick. Oh no, not anymore. Not sneaky, underhanded Rick Ramos! I'd rather get hit by . . .a truck!

I stopped just in time on the sidewalk as a brown *UPS* truck zoomed by. Shit, Dina, pay attention. How could I rescue my cousin and give Rick the silent treatment if I lay flattened on some street in San Antonio?

But Lisa was probably right. If I'd been Rick in the same situation, I'd have been just as sneaky—maybe *cautious* was a better word—about popping out with the *big, ugly secret*. Why scare off a potential mommy substitute too soon? Wait until there's an emotional connection, then break the ugly news. "We've gone three blocks already, Lisa. I don't see any Federal building. Over there's a bank."

I was scanning the four corners of the intersection, scrutinizing the buildings. It was already dusk, and people were scurrying home at the end of a long day. Shoppers and businesspeople thronged the downtown commercial area. Below the bridge we'd just crossed over meandered the renowned River Walk of San Antonio. We'd passed the Alamo and its park and were heading toward the center of downtown.

"What did the concierge say? Three blocks from our hotel?"

Lisa, huffing and puffing, caught up to me on her high

heels and looked around.

"I didn't ask the concierge. I asked that cute bellman, and he said, *tres, uh, kiyays* and pointed this way. That's three streets, right?"

"Right, but do you see a Federal Building?" My leaden brain finally picked up on what she'd said. "He said, *treice* or *tres*?"

We scanned the intersection again while Lisa frowned and thought. It was ten to two and our appointment time with Joe Torres, the DEA agent, was at two o'clock. I didn't want to be late and risk the chance of his changing his mind to help us. We didn't have a prayer of rescuing Teresa and her son without his expertise and contacts.

"Now that I'm hearing the two words — I think he said tresay. I wasn't concentrating too hard on what he was saying — he had the nicest hair. It fairly gleamed — "

"Oh, for Pete's sake, Lisa! If he said *treice*, that's thirteen! We can't walk thirteen blocks, especially you in those heels. It'll be dark soon, and we'll be late. Mr. Torres'll think we're a bunch of flakes."

I edged my way into heavily trafficked Commerce Street, spied a yellow cab, and flagged it down.

"Sorry," Lisa murmured guiltily. "I gotta learn Spanish. Everyone around here seems to speak it."

"Yep," I said, sliding into the cab, "we're in Old Mexico. Least, it was up to eighteen-forty-eight. Boundaries — *las fronteras* — were set at the end of the War with Mexico."

"Okay, I'm at a disadvantage here," Lisa admitted, "from now on, Dina, you do the talking."

But Lisa soon forgot her pledge.

"I'm a private investigator," she chirped while pumping Joe Torres's hand, "well, part-time PI. But I'm very interested in your work. Whatever I can learn from you, I'd appreciate it, Agent Torres."

"Call me Joe."

Lisa agreed with me later that our DEA contact was either a youthful fifty or a prematurely graying forty. He was a little shorter than I, probably five-eight, slim of build, and darker-skinned than both Lisa and me. Except for his dark, thick mustache, he was still the clean-shaven professional Rick and I had met in LA. I could tell he was surprised by Lisa's appearance, maybe because she looked younger than he expected her to look.

He'd been waiting for us in the tiled lobby of the Federal Building on Houston Avenue, where the security guard confiscated Lisa's *Mace* canister and my tiny tube of pepper spray.

"Sorry about the"—I flicked a forefinger toward the uniformed guard—"we brought it on the plane in our check-in bags . . .with airline permission, of course. Thought we might need some protection in Nuevo Laredo."

Agent Torres smiled pleasantly and waved his hand dismissively.

"No problem, Miss Salazar. You'll get those back when you leave the building. It's just a precaution. These days we take lots of precautions. Don't worry, that's what we're here for, to give you protection on this . . .mission of ours."

He smiled pointedly at Lisa and led us to an elevator, where we ascended five floors. All the while, Lisa questioned him about his work, his training. Joe Torres used to be a Texas Ranger and, before that, was in Army Intelligence. He'd been working undercover for the DEA for fourteen years and had just finished a job in Mexicali, Mexico, and one in the Mexican border town of Reynosa. He knew the Mexican state of Tamaulipas like the back of his hand. I was surprised. To me, Joe Torres looked like a Los Angeles businessman in his dress shirt, brown-and-gray tie, and brown-tweed sports coat.

"My mother was born in Ciudad Victoria, the capital city

of Tamaulipas. She thinks I have a government desk job. If she only knew . . .But why give her grief when it's not necessary? Lies of omission are sometimes the kindest ones."

I looked at him, my dulled, sleep-deprived brain suddenly sparking to what he said.

"That's what I do best, girls, is lie. You have to be a good liar to do undercover work. Are you a good liar, Miss Luna? Miss Salazar?"

He flashed both of us a benign grin, but I could tell he wasn't joking. He was deadly serious. Lisa nodded her head enthusiastically.

"Dina's an even better liar than I. She had her grandmother believing that Dina was just her career name and that—"

"Lisa, I don't think he wants details," I interrupted abruptly. My upset stomach—from lack of food and sleep—was making me feel woozy and cotton-mouthed all at the same time. I leaned against the elevator wall and closed my eyes.

"Are you okay, Miss Salazar?" Agent Torres inquired,

"She needs to eat something. And get a good night's sleep," Lisa supplied, sidling next to me and cupping my arm. "You see, Joe, she broke off her engagement last night, and she didn't sleep on the plane. So she's kind of messed up."

Oh, great! Lisa was now telling the world about my personal problems. Maybe it was a good thing she couldn't speak Spanish, or she'd be announcing my newly single status in Mexico.

Agent Torres swept us past an antechamber of sorts and into a DEA conference room, sat us down, and minutes later was plying me with snacks and a can of cold *Pepsi*.

Another agent had joined us, Mike Medina. He was a tall, husky *Texican* or *Tejano* with sandy hair and big brown eyes. Younger than Joe, he wore a plaid red and blue shirt, tan cords, and a navy windbreaker. He spoke with a Texan's drawl. Based on their ring fingers, Joe was married, but Mike wasn't. Lisa immediately shifted her attention to the younger bachelor.

"As I was saying, we're both good liars. And I've done stakeouts and undercover surveillance for my uncle's security firm," Lisa was telling Agent Medina, who in turn nodded and smiled, pretending to look impressed, I suspected.

The soft drink and crackers were reviving me, thank goodness. The fog in my mind was lifting, and I no longer felt like death warmed over.

"The reason I asked, Miss Luna —" Joe began.

"Lisa, please. And Dina," she interjected.

Both men nodded.

"Lisa. Dina. I asked about lying to find out if you're able and willing to go into a potentially dangerous situation. Stay calm, cool, collected. Lie through your teeth, play the role to the hilt — and not get yourselves killed in the process. Can you do this?"

Joe Torres looked us both square in the eye. I nodded. Lisa did, too.

"Our chief wanted us to assess you both before we took the next step. You see, in Nuevo Laredo, trouble finds you. You've already heard the news reports about the spate of violence down there — the shootings, the kidnappings, Americans disappearing, murdered. There's a drug war going on between the two major rival cartels in the states of Chihuahua and Tamaulipas. This poor border town, Nuevo Laredo, has grown into a city, one with all the problems you find in any city. But the border towns in Mexico have the additional problems of poor, desperate people emigrating or trying to. Waiting for a chance to cross into *el norte*. On top of that, you have the NAFTA factories that pay just enough to whet the appetites of Mexican consumers. The stores down there are overflowing, but too few people have enough money to satisfy their wants. They're like kids looking into a candy store but without the coins to buy anything."

Joe paused, then darted a glance at Mike.

"To add insult to injury," Mike continued, "you have the cartels smuggling millions of dollars of contraband across the borders each day. Their thugs are highly paid mercenaries, paid ten to fifteen thousand a month compared to a Mexican army salary of seven hundred. These Gulf Cartel commandos in Tamaulipas drive around in new cars, wearing black uniforms and *Rolex* watches, wielding automatics, using military hardware stolen from the Mexican army. They throw their weight and money around like Mafia hoods of the nineteen twenties. Well, the situation is volatile, to say the least."

Agent Medina signaled Joe Torres, who disappeared from sight without a word. "Young *gringos* and *gringuitas* go down at night, go clubbing at the *discotecas* and bars, and then vanish."

Agent Medina leveled us a significant look. Maybe he, too, was expecting somewhat older women and now was worried that we were too young and green, too silly and immature.

"God only knows what kind of hell those young women wake up to after being slipped a Roofie—a drug—in their drinks."

My thoughts fixated on the young women kidnapped after being drugged. *That* got my full-alert attention! Oh yeah, I knew about those date-rage drugs firsthand—well, almost firsthand. That happened to one of my college roommates.

Lisa slid me a look of concern...like uh-oh. Funny, though, I wasn't afraid. Maybe my sleep-deprived brain was just too zonked out to register fear. In fact, I was impatient to go down there and get it over with. Bring Teresa and her son home.

"Despite the State Department warnings," Agent Medina continued, "young Americans keep crossing into Nuevo Laredo. Since last summer, over thirty US citizens have been kidnapped for ransom or sex slavery. Or killed. This all happened in Nuevo Laredo. Last month, there was a clash between local police and gang members on the Gateway to the Americas Bridge, which connects the town to Laredo, Texas. Even as far north as Dallas, these cartel triggermen have been involved in gangland slayings. Lately, these commandos've been out of control."

"I guess you're trying to scare us," Lisa grumbled.

"You bet. Yeah, we want you to be apprehensive and watchful yet be able to play the part of two *gringas* down there on a little Christmas shopping trip. A little carefree but not careless."

"We're young," Lisa piped in, "but not stupid. And Dina speaks Spanish really well."

"I'm not fluent," I hedged, "but good enough to get by."

"Well, don't worry about that," Mike said, "the Mexicans will spot you as *gringas* a mile away. You dress, carry yourselves like Americans. They'll expect you to speak Chicano Spanish."

I smiled at Mike. I hadn't heard the word, *Chicano*, in a long time. Joe entered the conference room, followed by a young man carrying a box of sandwiches and four cups of *Starbucks* coffee drinks. Lattes, they were, according to Joe. The four of us dug in. My depression was vanishing, and I was now ravenous. Maybe hearing about the dangers we faced in Nuevo Laredo had something to do with it.

"Not exactly gourmet, but we splurge on business lunches," Joe quipped sarcastically, unwrapping his ham-and-cheese on rye and commencing to eat. Mike chose his but held it while he stared at Lisa and me. He clearly wanted our total concentration.

"We'll all be wearing wires, so we'll be monitoring you when you go into that bar. When you make your contact with that guy—the husband of our undercover agent—we'll be able to hear every word that's said. From what you've told Joe, the guy will recognize you, especially you, Dina. You described yourself to your cousin, right?"

I nodded and fingered a lock of my hair—meaning, the color of it. Reddish-brown.

"He'll give you, I assume, the address where we are to pick up your cousin and her son. We'll get them, whatever luggage they have—we're taking two cars—and cross back into the US. We've got their papers, their visas, under the names Teresa and Alejandro Gómez. Not Vargas. Hope that's all right."

I nodded vigorously this time, overcome with rapture at two things, the men's efficiency and the taste of my tuna salad on whole-wheat sandwich. A sip of latte added to my bliss.

"Thank you *sooo* much," I mumbled, my mouth full.

"We'll need you to do one more thing for us," Agent Medina added.

Despite nearly swooning over the flavor of my tuna salad—even the chopped cucumbers and pickles were crunchy—I caught the uneasy look he exchanged with Joe Torres.

"Sure, anything," Lisa chimed in between bites of food. She'd chosen a roast beef on sourdough.

"We need you, one of you, to plant a bug inside that bar before you leave—under a table or counter. Under a bar stool, perhaps. Anywhere but the bathroom."

"A bug?" I was thinking crunchy beetles—maybe as a result of watching too many episodes of the *Fear Factor* TV show. Lisa's eyes were bugging out—sorry, the pun. My head was leaden, my mind still giddy from loss of sleep.

"A listening device. One of our standard electronic ones. Has a transmitting radius of five miles. The DEA's setting up a receiving post in Laredo. We're trying to intercept drug shipments. This and the additional information Teresa Vargas can give us. Anyway, this bar might turn up something.

We've never been inside this bar, but our agent says it's frequented by Cartel commandos. It's called *Los Huevos*. A rough dive, unfortunately."

"On Calle Campeche," I added. "Teresa's last email was yesterday. She said to go there and ask for Oscar de la Hoya."

"The Mexican-American boxer? The ex-lightweight champ?"

I shrugged. "I don't know. That's the code thingie. Or whatever, the thing I'm supposed to say to the bartender. I'm supposed to ask for Oscar de la Hoya."

I broke off at their reaction. To my growing uneasiness— my taste buds stopped enjoying that wonderful tuna salad— the two DEA agents excused themselves and left the conference room. Lisa and I sat at that long table with sixteen captain's chairs and continued to eat and sip our coffee in silence. When they returned a few minutes later, Joe Torres was just snapping shut his cell phone.

"Is something wrong?" I asked them.

Jeez, do birds fly and bees sting? Of course, something was wrong! Were they going to change their minds and not help me, after all? I put my sandwich down, feeling kind of sick all of a sudden.

The two men sat down again, their countenances having undergone an even more sobering change than before they left. I had a feeling our little excursion into a Mexican border town wasn't going to be a picnic. Their attitudes no longer carried a cavalier, swashbuckling trace. No more *been there, done that.*

"Girls, now's your chance to back out. We can try and bring out your cousin, ourselves."

Lisa and I swapped a brief look.

"Heck, no. We've come this far—" Lisa began.

"What's the glitch?" I inquired. What had I said that got them so spooked?

"Dina. Lisa," Joe said, bending over, his hands folded and

resting calmly on the table, "we're walking into—no, we're sending the two of you, young American civilians, into the tiger's den. *Los Huevos* is a hangout for Gulf Cartel commandos. They call themselves the Zetas. They're ex-soldiers from an elite force in the Mexican army who've transferred all their military mystique—the honor, valor, loyalty—to a drug trafficker. They're ruthless, totally cynical, disciplined fighters. They eat young women like you for breakfast. Your little squirt of pepper spray or *Mace* will be like poking a vicious, man-eating tiger with a stick."

"We'll use our wits then," I assured them. No way was I backing out now. Teresa and the agent's husband were expecting Lisa and me. They weren't going to trust anyone else.

"Look, we have to do this. They're expecting us—two young, Mexican-American women, one tall with reddish hair who speaks Spanish. Anyone else and this guy—Oscar de la Hoya or whatever his name—will clam up. If you guys go in there, those thugs will be alerted and the whole plan'll fall apart. We have to go down there and get my cousin out. If anything happens to her or her son, my family"—I was thinking, Grandma Gómez—"will blame me. I can't let anything bad happen to her. She's family. *Es mi familia*," I added in Spanish.

I turned to Lisa with a question in my look—as in, are you with me? She nodded without hesitation.

"Absolutely, I'm going, too. You can't scare us, Joe."

I wiped my mouth with a paper napkin and stood up, feeling revived and committed.

"Look, what *is* the problem? You already knew about the bar, this *Los Huevos* place. Why the change in attitude?"

Joe Torres shook his head. "Something's wrong. Our agent's husband is Matteo. The agreed-upon code was *Where's the soccer stadium?* You were to ask Matteo that question. He was going to draw a sketch of a map of how to get there, to the soccer stadium. Which is close by. You'd be in and out of that place in two minutes, tops. You see, on the back of this map would be the address of where to pick up Teresa Vargas and her son. They're not staying at the agent's house. That would've been too dangerous for the woman and her family. This was your cousin's last email to you?"

I nodded my head. Suddenly I had a pounding headache on top of my leaden fogginess.

"Why did your cousin change it at the last minute?" Joe Torres asked, his voice strident with tension. "I tried calling our agent down there. She's not answering. Something's wrong."

Lisa and I stared at Agent Torres, his hands clenched together. Then at Agent Medina. He was chewing his bottom lip and rubbing the side of his face. They weren't exactly the picture of cool, calm, and collected. They looked like nervous wrecks.

"Well, I don't know. That's what Teresa said in her email yesterday—Friday. I checked it at about six PM. Ask the bartender for Oscar de la Hoya. Let's go. We're ready to go now."

Joe and Mike appeared startled, two seconds before leaning back and barking short, ironic laughs. Mike indicated that we should sit down.

"We're not going down there now. It'll be dark by the time we get there. Are you serious? Even we don't go into Nuevo Laredo after dark."

The landscape between San Antonio and Laredo, Texas, surprised me. I guess I expected miles and miles of desert and cactus, sagebrush, saguaros lifting their arms to a blue, cloudless sky. Instead, there were farms and green orchards of mesquite trees, from small clumps to thirty-foot, fanlike shrubs. Their feathery branches waved in the breeze under gray, cloudy skies. A norther, according to Joe, was sweeping down from the icy midwest, making us shiver in our lightweight jackets.

Well, so much for preconceptions, I thought, rechecking my cell phone. It was Sunday morning, and we were two hours ahead of California time. I'd had ten messages in the intervening thirty-four hours since Lisa and I left California. Six were from Rick, ordering me—not begging me—to return his calls. Ha! Some nerve!

The other four were from various members of my family—two in Spanish from Grandma Gómez. She was worried, thought I was already in Mexico with cousin Teresa. I decided I'd call everyone back after we returned to San Antonio when I had good news to report.

My thoughts kept returning to Rick and his bombshell Friday night in the tension of our two-hour journey down to Laredo. Lies of omission were the kindest ones, Joe Torres had said, because they were meant to protect. Weren't long-held secrets like lies of omission? Was Rick's secret that he'd purposely withheld from me—his lie of omission—meant to protect Angelina?

Not meant to harm me or trick me, was it? It was meant to protect Angelina. His little girl.

Well, *no me diga.* I actually had an insight in the middle of all this. The realization—that Rick hadn't revealed his secret to me at the beginning of our renewed romance in order to protect his little girl from losing a new mommy—hit me with the impact of a ton of bricks. Somehow, knowing this made me feel a lot less angry with him.

Rick Ramos was not trying to deceive me. He was hoping I'd learn to love the little girl as much as he did. But did I? Enough to forgive and accept the latest of Rick's secrets?

The hours flew by on Interstate 35. I remained deep in thought while Lisa kept a steady flow of conversation going with Joe Torres. Lucky for Mike, who was following us in the second car, flying with us at 70 mph, the legal speed limit of this section of highway.

Finally, we entered the Texas town of Laredo. Once we passed all the American hotels, restaurants, and fast-food franchises and approached the border, it began to look like Mexico. Bordertown Mexico. US Border Patrol vehicles, white with broad, green stripes down the sides, were everywhere.

Our border crossing was International Bridge No. 1 — there being two other bridges, I'd learned. We crossed over the Rio Grande, a wide, murky brown river, just before noon in one of five lanes of traffic going south. Joe paid our bridge fees, two dollars per car, and we found ourselves traveling down Avenida Guerrero, the main thoroughfare which stretches for nearly a mile, going south.

Boy, did we know we were instantly in Mexico. The *Rio Bravo del Norte* — Mexico's name for the Rio Grande — was behind us as Joe expertly turned right, left, taking streets that skirted the downtown, tourist shopping area. We passed pedestrians risking their ankles on choppy cement sidewalks, a few tropical juice bars and cafes, and outdoor barbeque stands advertising *cabrito* or roast goat or lamb, Joe said — and *carnitas* wrapped in tortillas. A peach-colored church fronted a tree-shaded plaza. A canary-yellow storefront was spilling out women laden with grocery bags. Another storefront was painted a bright parrot-green.

Lots of men were lounging around outside and at open-air cafes. It was Sunday, after all, typically a day of rest for the Mexican male. Not so for the Mexican woman. She was probably at home preparing a batch of tamales and wiping snotty noses. But, despite the third-world look of things, there was a kind of dusty beauty here. People moved at a languid pace, so different from the States, where hustle-bustle rhythms ruled. There were Christmas decorations draped here and there, tiny lights wrapped around trees and store windows painted with *Navidad* scenes.

It all whirred by as we sat in Joe's car. People looked normal, I supposed, anticipating and preparing for Christmas celebrations. *La Noche Buena* was three days away — Wednesday. How strange it was, knowing that underneath the ordinary life here in Nuevo Laredo, another darker world existed.

Joe pointed out the marquee of a dilapidated movie theater we were passing in his car. The feature movie was *El Masacre en La Calle* — Massacre in the Street. Agent Torres threw us an ironic grin and shook his head.

"Why show a movie like that when they have the real thing in their town?" he asked rhetorically. Lisa and I exchanged glances of unease.

The crowds thinned as we moved to the left of Avenida Guerrero, going southeast of downtown. When we came to Calle Campeche, I stiffened. I could see Lisa tense up, too. Even Joe sat up straighter in his seat, alert and watchful.

Lisa and I were wired. A sparkly Christmas tree pin holding an actual miniature microphone was on my knit shirt collar, hanging over the collar of my jeans jacket. A battery was taped to my midriff above my girdle. Lisa had a similar contraption. Only her mike was in the cloth flower attached to her blazer lapel. Joe Torres had an earpiece receiver, as did Mike Medina. Both cars were nondescript *Ford* sedans. Joe's was dark blue, and Mike's was white. They, of course, carried Texas license plates.

We bumped along an uneven road, partly paved, partly graveled, passed a newer cinema house and *el Catedral del Espiritu Santo*. The cathedral raised my hopes a little. How bad could things get when there was a cathedral nearby?

Teresa, where are you? I wondered. Why couldn't we have just met her at the bus station? Or at the very cathedral we just passed?

Good grief, what kind of man was her husband, this Pedro

Vargas, that he would put a reward on her head? What kind of world had my cousin lived in all these years? Everything here looked so normal—a typical Mexican commercial town, but still poor, sleepy, and rundown by American standards.

And where were these murderous cartel thugs? Had they all slithered under rocks as daylight broke, venturing out at night like vampires? I voiced my question to Agent Torres.

"Oh, the majority of the cartel commandos live near Matamoros, about two hundred and fifty of them. Maybe more that we don't know about. A small contingent is here, maybe fifty or so, another one in Reynosa. They move around, go where they're needed to protect the drug shipments. The Gulf cartel's boss is currently in a Mexican prison, but the cartel members are still loyal to him and his second-in-command. Could be why Pedro Vargas made his move two months ago after your uncle, Roberto Martínez, died and took command of the Juárez Cartel. Vargas saw his chance to take over some territory while the Gulf cartel kingpin was in prison."

"Yes, that'd make sense," I said as if I knew what I was talking about. So far, none of it made sense. What I knew about Mexican drug cartels, you could put in a shot glass, but I had a feeling I was about to find out a heck of a lot more.

"In fact, an FBI memo came out last week, warning all US federal law enforcement agents to watch their backs. The Cartel is plotting to kidnap and murder any American agents they can get their hands on. They know we're putting pressure on the Mexican government to do something about these drug lords and their armies. A small gang within the Gulf Cartel has valid visas and passports, allowing them legal entry into the States. This splinter group has made some payback killings in the Dallas area. I'd say their ruthlessness is second only to Middle East terrorists, so don't be fooled by their youth"—he glanced over at Lisa, who sat in the front passenger's seat—"or good looks."

Joe turned a corner and braked to a stop at the curb. Mike pulled in behind him. Down the street at the next corner was a stucco building, two stories high, painted in two shades of bright blue—peacock blue with royal blue trim. The windows were painted over and covered with rusted metal shutters. A wrought iron door blocked a painted front door, also in royal blue. I wondered if this was someone's symbolic creed, as in true blue for loyalty. Or someone's inside joke.

Probably not. Other stucco buildings in this sports neighborhood—I could see the roof of a sports stadium a couple of blocks away—were garishly painted. It seemed to be a trademark in this town.

There were two new, black *Chevy Suburbans* parked at the corner, angled so that the corner entrance was blocked by the strategic positioning of these long vehicles. A military maneuver, perhaps?

The scar on my belly, encased tightly within my panty girdle, started to throb for some strange reason. A subtle reminder of my mortality? My heart began to race in syncopation. From all appearances, this Oscar guy—the bartender?—wouldn't be the only one we'd find inside *Los Huevos*.

"*Huevos* means eggs, doesn't it?" Lisa asked, checking out the blue building as I was doing. She was fishing into the pocket of her blazer, probably to reassure herself that her *Mace* can was still there. Her tiger tickler, as Joe had warned.

"Mexican slang, it means—" Joe Torres paused, "something else. Male testicles. Girls, there's going to be a lot of testosterone pumping in there. Be extra careful what you say and do. Don't antagonize them. And don't flirt with them. These are killers, not college boys."

For once in her life, Lisa didn't look too happy to hear about the overflow of testosterone.

"All right, let's double-check our equipment," Joe ordered. "Everything in place—cloth flower, Lisa, firmly secured.

Christmas tree pin, Dina. Check your battery packs, see if they've come loose."

"Heck, no. I'm strapped in as tight as Dina's girdle," Lisa blurted, then slapped her hand over her mouth.

Ha! Like I cared if Joe Torres knew I was wearing a girdle.

"She had an appendectomy two weeks ago," Lisa went on to explain.

"You should be home recuperating, Dina." Joe Torres blew out some air, mumbled something in Spanish, shook his head some more.

"I'm fine, Joe," I said. Inside, I was a pulsating mess.

"All right, girls, you have two minutes. *Two*. You're tourists who got off the beaten track on your way to the soccer stadium. You talk to Oscar, get what you need, plant the bug, then get the friggin' hell outa there. You're not out in five. We go in. Then things'll get a mite complicated. Anybody ask you, your Uncle Joe's outside. Mike's a friend. If you can, plant the bug, Dina. It's in your pocket? If you can't, it's okay. All right, got all that?"

We nodded. I felt the two-inch-square electronic device with my fingers. It was in the lower left pocket of my jeans jacket.

All of a sudden, I wanted to weep. Oh dear God . . .

I started to pray.

"Okay, Dina, we can do this," Lisa reassured me. "You do the talking, remember."

I clambered out of Joe's car after Lisa, then heard the wheels of another car brake to a stop behind us. A dirty white cab had pulled up beside Mike's big, white sedan. Two men were getting out. A tall one and a shorter one. In a flash, Agent Medina was out of his car and pointing a gun at them. The two men raised their arms. All this was done in seconds of silence.

Shit!

Lisa, gazing at the bright blue building on the corner, just two doors down, was straightening her shoulders, tugging at the shoulder strap of her purse, oblivious to the scene in the street behind us.

"Those *Suburbans* look like trouble to me."

I shook her arm. "Yeah, well, now we've got double trouble."

"Huh?" She turned around and looked where I was jerking my thumb. "Damn!"

CHAPTER TWENTY-FOUR

Frank Salazar, Jr. — "The best fights are the ones you never have." One day, my very wise and smart older brother Frank dropped this pearl of common sense on the family doofuses, Roberto and Jesús, who promptly ignored it over the years.

Grandma Gómez — "I spit on all the evil men in this world."

There was nothing we could do about the confrontation outside in the street, so I squared my shoulders, threw an exasperated glower at Rick and Jesús, then nudged Lisa forward.

"C'mon, let's get this over with," I mumbled, making the sign of the cross.

"Why the heck did Rick show up—and who's the other guy?"

"My brother-in-law, the one who served time in a federal prison for computer fraud." I urged her along the broken sidewalk.

"Why is he dressed like that? He looks like the Unabomber."

"Because he always dresses weirdly. He's a punk rocker wannabe at heart. Or maybe just a punk. Rick—" I huffed. "I have no clue why *he's* here."

But I did know why and I was both flattered and ticked off. Not wanting to deal with either emotion at the present moment, I pulled Lisa along. We had a job to do.

Mission—Saving La Familia had just begun.

The wrought iron security door appeared locked, but when I gave it a jiggle, it opened. The front door, a distressed and scarred royal blue, was slightly ajar. I noticed the small sign on the wall next to the door, with scrolled lettering in white, *Los Huevos*, on a black field. It was framed in wood and attached to the place like an afterthought.

Peculiar. As if there was no need to advertise the name of this place. As if everyone knew what it was—the hangout of the Gulf Cartel's men. The Zetas.

There was no one in the streets nearby, except for the DEA agents, Joe and Mike, and our two unwelcomed intruders. A glance back indicated that Joe was examining Jesús's ID while speaking with Rick. Mike had lowered his gun. No doubt it was obvious the two knew where to find us. I'd told Rick where we were going, of course, Friday night, and evidently, the cabbie knew the place, probably thought the two Americans were cartel men or drug smugglers. What—coming to *Los Huevos* to do business? He'd probably met other crazy *norteamericanos* before and figured—it's their funeral.

I could've smacked my forehead. Rick had insisted on knowing the details. He'd dropped everything at work, probably left Angelina with his mother and yanked Jesús along. Must've caught the first flight after we'd left.

All for me.

Because he was worried. Because he cared.

"Here goes," I whispered to Lisa and shoved the door open.

It took a moment or two to adjust my eyes to the interior gloom. We stood there side by side, like two lost waifs, blinking and squinting against the dim fluorescent lighting, the smoke, and the dark-painted walls.

The noise was a cacophony of electronic bleeps and squeals from the standing video arcade games along one near wall, the gangsta rap in Spanish from the speakers on the far wall, and the deep laughter of the men.

The men.

Joe was right. The place was pulsating with testosterone.

At first glance, there seemed to be eight to ten men in the large room, all wearing black shirts and trousers, all young and muscular. Their heads ranged from shaved to buzz cuts to cropped. Some heads were bald but covered with tattoos. Dark eyes turned our way—dark, malevolent eyes devoid of innocent curiosity. Two men, closest to us and standing in front of arcade games, had already drawn their pistols.

Joe was right. These men were not college boys.

We froze.

Someone growled something in rapid Mexican—like don't scare the shit out of these pretty broads, only the word he used for *broads* was vulgar. Lisa grabbed my arm so hard, it hurt.

I located the long, U-shaped bar. Behind it was a dark-haired man of short stature in his mid to late forties. He wore a trim mustache and short beard, fusing together Kung-fu style. Bulging biceps and forearms showed through the stretched, short-sleeved t-shirt he wore. On the front of his tee was the emblem of *Los Dos Laredos*, the local baseball team. From my research, I learned that Los Dos Laredos was the only professional baseball team with two home stadiums in two different countries.

A little tidbit of trivia, which, of course, did us no good at the moment. Still, that shirt made him seem a little less threatening.

The bartender was staring at us, as were all the other men in the place. A few by the pool tables in back to the left of the bar were slapping American bills down on one table and guffawing at each other, eyeing Lisa and me every once in a while as they tossed down drinks. Smoke swirled around their faces.

So this is what these commandos — these cartel thugs — did on their day off? And waited for *estúpidas* to show up to amuse them?

My throat was so constricted, I couldn't speak. Lisa pushed me in front of her in the direction of the bar.

I put on my most innocent, bungling, lost-tourist face and walked up to the bar. A sideways glance, and I nearly fled the joint. There were guns — *Uzi*-type guns — stacked like umbrellas against the wall behind the two pool tables. Maybe four or five. The men I mindlessly smiled at wore pistols in holsters, either strapped to their shoulders or fastened to their belts. Like *banditos* with *bandoleras*. I imagined knives were hidden in scabbards on their calves as well.

"We-we're looking for the *Parque de fútbol*," I squeaked hoarsely in Spanish at the bartender.

The man leveled narrowed eyes on me. "*Norteamericanas?*"

"*Sí*," I said, striving to rid my voice of its nervous quiver.

After all, we weren't supposed to know who these men were or what kind of place this was. Nevertheless, we weren't blind, either. Lisa leaned into me.

"Wrong code," she whispered, "ask about the boxer."

Shit! I'd forgotten, in my throat-constricting nervousness, and had confused the two different codes. Teresa gave me a new one on Friday.

"*Estoy buscando* Oscar de la Hoya."

There. I'd gotten out the code words. Maybe I'd rushed it but in my anxiety to hurry and get out of there, I figured the husband of Joe Torres's undercover agent was inside, would jump in and help.

"No beer, no answers," the bartender said in Spanish, crossing his arms over his muscular chest.

Two men lounging at the bar were nudging each other and snickering. One opened the side of his mouth, revealing a large, pointed, gold canine, kinda like a lopsided vampire. Maybe he was saving up to get the other tooth done. He slid down the bar while the others near the pool tables watched, predatory expressions on their young, saturnine faces.

I hesitated. We had only five minutes — no time to drink a beer. As if I wanted to drink anything in this den of thieves and murderers, anyway.

"Order something!" the bartender snarled.

"Okay, okay," I said, jumping in my skin. "Uh, *dos Carta Blancas.*"

He turned away and, while Gold Tooth slunk into a barstool close to where I was standing, Lisa scooted up beside me.

"Oh, uh, we don't have time . . .we have to get to the soccer stadium. Uncle Joe wants to see it, remember?"

I glanced at her, surprised at how calm she sounded.

"I, too, speak English," Gold Tooth said in a heavy Spanish accent. "I practice with you," he added, pointing to Lisa's cloth flower on her lapel.

The guy was eyeing Lisa's curvaceous bosom. He wasn't bad looking, but his face was pock-marked, and his smile was smarmy rather than friendly. Yet, Lisa cozied up to him and plopped herself down on the stool next to him. She smiled and flicked her dark hair over her shoulder.

"Sure, let's practice." I noticed her right hand sneak into her blazer pocket.

Ohh nooo, Lisa. No *Mace*, not now, I thought. We'd have our throats cut or heads riddled with bullet holes before she'd get off the first squirt. Gold Tooth was playing with us. I hoped Lisa knew. I grabbed her arm to remind her. Leave it alone.

The muscular bartender smacked two bottles of beer on the wooden counter, and when I paid him in US dollars, he pointed to a framed photograph on the wall next to his cash register. The colored picture showed the bartender and the former lightweight boxing champ at a much younger age.

"That's Oscar and me," he informed me curtly. His Spanish had a trace of an English accent. "I used to be one of his sparring partners in my youth. I own this joint."

I looked at him intently then. This was the husband? Our contact? Soon this would all be over. Teresa would no longer have to fear for her life or her son's.

First, we had to survive *Los Huevos*.

Lisa was chatting up Gold Tooth while his friend at the bar, a stocky guy with a buzz cut, a diamond stud in one ear, and a snake tattoo on his neck, kept staring at me. The head of the snake peered out above his black tee collar. It seemed to bob its head over the guy's Adam's apple. Yew, creepy!

I took a sip of my beer. It was cold and tasty. It was the beer that Rick and I usually ordered in Mexican restaurants.

Rick! He and Jesús were outside with Joe and Mike, waiting for us, probably chomping at the bit. If Lisa and I didn't get our *culos* out of this friggin', scary place, the guys would be storming in here like gangbusters.

And they'd all die.

So would Lisa and me. After these *matones* had their fun—

The bar counter was the ideal place to plant Joe's DEA bug, but Lisa's new friend was too close. Surely, he'd see me.

"Why are y'all wearing black?" Lisa asked coyly, laying on her Texas drawl. Gold Tooth was stroking her shoulder.

"Our *patrón* likes black. So you want to see the soccer *estadio*? I can show you now—me and Cip, we will take you there."

The bartender widened his eyes, then looked at me in silent warning. I leaned over to Lisa and elbowed her.

"No need to get too friendly," I said softly in her ear.

"Don't be such a bitch," she snapped loudly. Gold Tooth liked that. He leaned back and chortled. His canine sparkled in the light of the bar. "Go sit at the table and leave us alone," she ordered me angrily, then whipped her head back around, her hair flouncing out and slapping me in the face.

I stared at the back of her bouncy curls. Jeez, what on earth was she doing? It took a moment, but I finally caught on.

"Well!" I grabbed my beer and turned away.

"Here, take this." The bartender pushed the cardboard coaster my way. On the top was the logo of another brand of beer. The intense look he gave me captured my attention, so I took the coaster and bottle of beer to a nearby table.

I began to panic. We were taking too long, but I figured we had to wait until the bartender felt it was safe to pass me Teresa's address.

"You want to be my bitch for today?" Gold Tooth was asking Lisa, his arm slithering around the backrest of her stool.

I didn't hear Lisa's reply, for the blood was rushing in my head. I took another sip of beer to quiet my nerves. Oh damn, we were blowing it. We were sitting among the cartel's kidnappers, rapists, extortionists, murderers . . . and we were blowing it!

My gaze fastened on the logo coaster, but at the same time, my peripheral vision took in something else. Three black-uniformed guys were approaching my table, one of them Snake Man. His belt buckle was a huge, silver disk with a snake embossed on it, and his belt and boots were dyed-green snakeskin. What was with this guy and snakes? Even his face was now taking on a reptilian appearance. He gave me the shivers.

I dug into my left jacket pocket and touched the tiny canister of pepper spray. Ohh nooo, mustn't get these guys pissed off. My fingertips grazed the square-shaped high-tech device Joe had given me. The transmitter I was supposed to plant.

The table. Of course.

But the three cartel guys were approaching.

"Eh, *chinga tu madre—*"

One of them, Snake Man, had shoved the guy next to him. Instantly, the three whipped out knives and were angling them upward from belt level, switchblade fashion. Growing up in a latino barrio with two older brothers, I knew this was the weapon of choice for minor, petty skirmishes.

Rapid Spanish fired out of their mouths—mostly Mexican slang, dirty cussing, and macho threats.

Shit, they were fighting over me!

The bartender shot out something I couldn't understand, trying to calm the thugs down. So while these testosterone-pumping dirtbags were wrangling over who was going to take me upstairs and bang my brains out, I swiveled in my seat. Facing the front door, I quickly took out the DEA bug and peeled off the paper covering the special adhesive on its back. Joe Torres had told us the glue was so strong that it was used to stick tiles on the outside of the space shuttle.

While the dirtbags distracted everyone, I set upon one part of my mission.

My hand shaking a little, I carefully pressed the square metal device against the underside of the wooden table, about a foot from the table's edge. That done, I stuffed the paper square into my pocket and turned back around just as Snake Man strode up. He'd apparently won the Mexican standoff. How I didn't know, but the other two guys were backing down, still watchful, still brandishing their knives. Finally, they sheathed them and turned away, muttering oaths under their breaths.

"Wanta dance?" Snake Man asked in Spanish, stabbing his knife into the top of the wooden table. He did it so hard, the hilt and handle wobbled a little.

Huh? I looked around, glanced over at Lisa, who was throwing me scared, ready-to-bolt looks. The room full of cartel thugs had grown quiet—all except for the blaring gangsta rap. They were watching, waiting to see what I'd do. And if I refused his kind invitation?

"Can I finish my beer first?"

That polite request—issued in a quivering but respectful voice—must've thrown Snake Man for a loop because he looked confused for a second or two. He did what I took for a smirking shrug, then sat down at the table. He was peering at my bottle of beer, his head bent back as if he were looking down his nose at me. The snake's head on his neck moved. It seemed to stare at me. Even its forked tongue appeared to move.

"Want some X?" He pronounced it *equis*.

I knew exactly what he was referring to—the drug commonly known as Ecstasy, or X. The rager drug, meant to enhance sexual pleasure. Meant to obliterate inhibitions.

Oh sure, anytime, lover boy.

And if I refused? I kept glancing at the knife still vibrating on the tabletop.

"Uh, well, as much I would like to, my uncle is outside, waiting in his car. He brought us here." I pointed to the street.

Snake Man stared at me in utter disbelief, like who would be dumb enough to bring his niece to a cartel hangout?

"And my boyfriend and my brother. They're all outside, waiting for us. I am so sorry, but we have to go. If they were not here, I would be happy to dance with you. And, uh, other stuff."

I stood up to leave, for I could tell Snake Man wasn't buying any of it. Strangely, I had enough presence of mind to snatch up the coaster. I pocketed it and took another swig of beer, hoping to distract him. If Snake Man noticed, he gave no indication.

"Lisa," I called out, "we have to go."

Snake Man and Gold Tooth were now standing, also, daring us to make a beeline for the front door. Lisa's head rotated back and forth between Gold Tooth, Snake Man, and me. She was at a loss for words . . .of all times!

Now what, I thought. What the fuck do we do *now*?

The bartender hissed a harsh warning in Spanish — we were American tourists, the federales were patrolling Nuevo Laredo's streets, Diego was due back this afternoon. His warnings made the men pause — I didn't care who the hell Diego was, but if his showing up helped Lisa and me get out of this hellhole, I knew I'd be eternally grateful to him.

But they didn't pause for long. Gold Tooth went after Lisa. Snake Man lunged for me, clapped a hand on my wrist. The four of us stared at each other. Snake Man's right hand settled on the handle of his knife.

Bam! The front door slammed open.

Rick in a black leather jacket and Jesús in his Unabomber outfit stood inside the door. Rick's hands were hidden in the pockets of his coat, his face a mixture of fear and fury. Jesús advanced, calling out to Lisa — acting as though she'd kept him waiting outside a beauty salon.

"Lisa, c'mon, girl! We gotta go!"

"Dina, we're leaving!" Rick jumped in, speaking in Spanish. "Your uncle and his friend are mad that you're taking so long!"

Rick moved to my side, yanked me away from Snake Man while Lisa pulled herself loose from Gold Tooth. All this was done in a matter of seconds but long enough for Snake Man and Gold Tooth to react. Their hands went to their pistols. Their guns whipped out and pointed in the direction of the four of us, now huddled by the front door. Gold Tooth was blocking Lisa's escape.

"Who are these assholes?" Snake Man snarled in Spanish.

"Our boyfriends," I blurted out, hugging Rick at the waist. Well, if we were going to die, I would die holding onto this man I loved with all my heart, even though I was still mad as hell at him. I wanted to squeeze my eyes shut against the shooting that I was sure would follow, but I was as mesmerized as the others. The scene was something out of a French farce. Or the western movie, *The Magnificent Seven.*

Lisa was too stunned to speak. Jesús froze like a statue and stared at the guns.

"Uncle Joe's tired of waiting—c'mon," Rick hissed the last between clenched teeth as he put his body in front of mine and simultaneously edged us to the door. Snake Man's gun swiveled in our direction.

Suddenly, Jesús, his face half hidden by his black, cropped beard, his shades, and the hood of his navy blue sweatshirt, curled up one hand by his shoulder. He dragged one foot as he hunched over and hobbled across to Lisa. Then he grabbed her arm, his face screwed up in a goofy grimace. He began to mumble crazy nonsense in a silly, high-pitched tone of voice.

What was this act—Quasimodo? Even Lisa gawked with her mouth open.

"What is this? Who is this *freak*?" Gold Tooth exclaimed in his halting English. He turned to the bartender, who said something in Spanish that I couldn't make out, but they both broke out laughing. Clearly, the bartender was trying to defuse the situation with nasty humor.

Then Snake Man began to laugh, a harsh, ugly laugh. The gesture he made with his hands was a sexual insult, but Jesús ignored him, pretending to be a love-smitten cripple—or a hallucinating schizophrenic. I wasn't sure.

Rick pushed me out the door and into Joe Torres's car before I could say or do anything. Jesús and Lisa, I was happy to see, were right behind us. Jesús dropped the crippled act, grabbed Lisa's hand, and dashed to Mike's car.

"We're splitting up," Joe cut into my dazed mind, my thoughts a jumble. I was in the back seat, loaded with questions but still stunned by our narrow escape. Rick was riding shotgun, slamming his door shut even as Joe sped away down the street.

I looked back to see Mike's white sedan peel away from the curb, Snake Man appearing outside the blue door. He stood there, arms akimbo, still holding his pistol, staring after the two cars, a look on his face which meant more trouble.

"Did you get the address?" Agent Torres asked.

"I don't know," I breathed, still dazed.

"What d'ya mean, you don't know? What about the bug?"

Joe was staring at me in the rear-view mirror, incredulous. Rick had wheeled around in his seat, his face lined with concern.

I took a deep breath and flipped over the coaster now in my hand. The bartender had written a three-digit number on the solid white backing, followed by two two-digit numbers. I read them aloud. Agent Torres punched them into his international cell phone, then handed it to me.

"Here, your cousin's expecting to hear *your* voice."

"I planted that bug, Joe," I croaked hoarsely, "under a table."

"Good girl," he said. Lisa and I nearly became the sex slaves of two horrible beasts, and all he said was *good girl*?

The two cars were speeding toward Avenida Guerrero. Rick looked behind us.

"One of those black *Suburban's* following us."

The cell phone in my hand continued to ring. My God, where are you, Teresa, I wondered. Please, please . . .

Joe spun around a corner, taking a left turn sharply. Mike's sedan turned right, practically on two tires. Rick and I both watched as the black *Suburban* followed Mike's car.

"Damn good thing," Torres said. "We wouldn't be able to get your cousin with that *pendejo* following us. Hope they make it to the bridge in time. The federales are there today in their pickup trucks. We made sure of that."

Lisa and Jesús! Agent Medina!

"Joe, what's going to happen to—" I began.

A woman's voice broke in and said, "*Diga.*"

I switched to Spanish. "Is Teresa there? This is her cousin, Dina, from California. We're here in town. We have to pick her up right now. *Right now.*" My voice carried a strident urgency and began to shake. I felt on the verge of tears again and struggled to compose myself. A moment later, a different woman's voice came on. A softer, younger voice.

"*Prima, oh gracias a Dios! Estás aquí en Nuevo Laredo?*"

Of course, I was here in town. I wanted to shout hysterically. Six of us just risked our lives to come here and find you. I told her we were coming to pick her and her son up and take them to the States. She started weeping but still managed to give me the address, which I wrote down on that coaster. She gave me directions from the Plaza Juárez and the *Cadillac Bar*. After that, we hung up, for she had lots to do, she said.

"Joe, do you know where the Plaza Juárez and the *Cadillac Bar* are? She said Americans know those two places in downtown Nuevo Laredo."

"Sure. The *Cadillac Bar*'s a great place to eat," Joe said, taking the coaster I handed him. "Next time you come to Nuevo Laredo, go there. Have a ribeye. Good steaks."

Ha! The next time I came to Nuevo—was he joking?

"Thanks all the same. The closest I'm getting to a Mexican border town is San Antonio. Joe, it was really creepy and scary in that bar."

"Yeah, we could tell. That's why we sent in your boyfriends—thought they'd bolster your cover. I was afraid one of those thugs would recognize Mike and me. We've been here so much—never there at their hangout, though. You girls are something else, you know?"

Rick gave Agent Torres a hard, angry look. "They could've been killed."

"Yeah, I know, but they insisted. It wouldn't have worked

otherwise. This guy, Oscar? Or whatever his name is. That wasn't our agent's husband, y'know. He's homesick. She called me while you were in there, said we could trust their son. What's your take on him, Dina, the bartender? Do you think he'd make a good CI? Confidential informant?"

"I don't know, Joe. I think he was helping us as a personal favor."

Who knew? Maybe he wanted to save us Americans. Or maybe he got paid off.

"That's fine. You girls did really well. And don't worry about Mike and your friends. Mike's an expert at shaking a tail. He'll take them downtown in the thick of traffic and shoppers, head to the bridge. That asshole'll think twice before firing at 'em. They won't shoot, not with federales at the bridge."

Firing? Shooting? I didn't like the sound of that. Lisa and Jesús!

Omigod, they were serving as decoys so that we could go get Teresa and her son. Maybe that'd been part of Joe's plan all along—a decoy car.

In the distance, we heard two popping sounds, loud enough to make the three of us jump in our seats and look around. Even Torres looked shocked.

"Damn! That sonuvabitch's shooting at 'em."

Rick looked back at me, and our gazes met.

Lisa. Jesús. Agent Medina.

Tears began to trickle down my cheeks. Rick smiled at me and handed me his handkerchief. *Dios!* What American male under fifty carried a handkerchief? Maybe a contractor who was always getting his hands dirty? One whose dream was to become an architect?

A man with more heart than brains?

"Thanks," I muttered between hitches in my breathing. "Why, Rick? Why did you come? You and Jesús—you're crazy lunatics."

"Not any crazier than two schoolteachers I know," he rasped gently. "Jesús was handy and willing. Y'know, Dina, whatever you have to go through, I'm there for you. Wholeheartedly. What else can I say?"

I sniffed and wiped my nose. We stared at each other for a long moment before he turned his attention back to the road.

Several minutes later, we found ourselves on the city's northwest side, passing the bus station. Another turn, and we were on Calle González. Halfway down the block of what I'd guess were middle-class bungalows made of stucco and wood—stood Teresa and her son, Alejandro.

My cousins.

The men jumped out and hurriedly stowed their four suitcases in the trunk while I stepped out to greet them.

No introductions had to be made. We embraced and then stared at each other. By now, I was crying so hard that I couldn't speak, anyway.

Teresa resembled my sister, Pet, a little, was close to her in age—had the same dark, curly hair cut short. Her face was round and pretty like *Abuelita's*, and her figure was petite like Grandma's side of the family. She was dressed in a smart, chocolate-brown pantsuit and wore tan heels that matched her large tan purse. She gave me a speculative look, as though she expected me to look different. She hadn't yet met the Spanish-American side of our family, the tall, fair ones—*los rubios*, as Grandma Gómez called us.

Next, I embraced her son, Alex. He was a handsome boy with a cap of dark curls—no longer dark blond, I noticed—much lighter skinned than his mother and had deep blue eyes. In fact, he looked like an American prep school kid in his navy blazer, gray slacks, and red tie. From what I'd learned about Teresa Vargas, I don't know what I expected, certainly not braceros. She was university-educated and was accustomed to money, having left a walled-and-gated hacienda and a household of servants.

However, her face and eyes reflected a mingling of the anxiety and fear she'd felt daily for the past two months. She smiled widely at me, obviously relieved, but there remained still a nervous twitching and glancing about her. As though she expected danger to come driving up and blasting us with bullets. I felt the same way. We wouldn't feel safe until we'd crossed the border.

Before we left, Teresa turned and gave her protector—a small, plump, gray-haired woman in her seventies—a long, tight hug. They spoke softly, confidentially in Spanish while Joe, Rick, and I waited and watched. Both women were weeping, and even young Alex was sniffing back tears. Rick approached the boy and introduced himself in Spanish, shaking his hand.

I thanked the elderly woman and hugged her — she and her husband and son had risked their lives to give my cousin sanctuary. Overcome with curiosity about these people—and Teresa's entire ordeal—I nevertheless bit back my questions. Joe Torres finally stepped forward, hugged the elderly woman, and spoke to her as if he'd known her all of his life. Heck, maybe he had. Then the DEA agent introduced himself to Teresa and her son. Teresa smiled and held out the lapel of her suit jacket.

Ah, another suit full of cartel secrets, I surmised.

We'd learn the entire story soon enough.

Right now, we had to get out of Nuevo Laredo. Get out of Mexico. Get out of Gulf Cartel territory.

Strange, but it no longer seemed like a foreign country to me. It was my cousin's home—was *Abuelita's* and my mother's birth country—and someday, maybe, Teresa and her son would return.

After Teresa hugged her elderly friend for the last time, the

DEA agent got us situated in the back seat, then he and Rick climbed in.

Rick smiled at me, glanced over at Alex and Teresa, nodded a warm welcome. He was thinking what I was, I was certain—how difficult it must be for them to leave their native country, to flee it. Rick cast the seven-year-old boy a sympathetic look as if he wondered whether the boy would miss his father, drug lord or not.

I wondered, too, whether Alex missed his grandfather, my uncle, Roberto Martínez. Had he been the kind of man his grandson loved and would miss? Knowing Grandma Gómez's surface hardness, I wondered about that.

What had happened to both Teresa and her son in their journey to emigration? And how much would they be sacrificing in order to be free in *el norte*? Certainly, the United States was not a perfect country. Would they be happy there? All these questions had once swirled about in my mind. Now all I could focus on was crossing the border. Getting them to safety.

Joe informed us that we'd be crossing the border at the *Puente Solidaridad*, 38 km to the northwest. This new bridge enabled motorists in a hurry to bypass both Nuevo Laredo and Laredo. Joe had their papers ready. In three hours, we'd be back in San Antonio, Texas. Home of the Alamo.

I looked over at my cousins, took Alex's left hand in my right. His other hand clutched tightly his mother's. I couldn't speak. I was so filled with emotion.

Gratitude. Relief. Pride. Love.

From the shimmer in Teresa's dark eyes, I knew she felt the same. Our tears flowed freely.

At the *Puente Solidaridad*, we stopped. Two Mexican customs officials, wearing khaki-colored uniforms, approached the car. Joe Torres handed over three American passports, then asked for Rick's and mine. Five American passports in all.

We waited silently while one of the officials peered into the car, first the front seat, then the back. His dark-eyed gaze roved slowly over the three of us, and then he barked something in Spanish at the other man, who was stamping the five passports matter-of-factly. The official at Joe's window pulled a paper out of his pants pocket and unfolded it. It looked like a flyer of some kind.

He took a glance at it, then bent over and looked long and hard at Teresa and her son. The official came over with the passports and was about to hand them to Joe Torres when the one scrutinizing us halted him. A stream of rapid Spanish ensued as if they were arguing among themselves.

My heart began to race. Dammit, they were going to prevent us from crossing.

Teresa covered her mouth to hide a sob. Alex clutched his mother's arm and squeezed his eyes shut. Rick looked back at me, his mouth open in alarm.

"Just a minute," Joe Torres interrupted the two customs officials in Spanish, "there's no need to question them. They're my niece and her son. Here, take this."

The DEA agent held out his hand, palm down, his thumb holding in place a folded American bill. The man questioning the identities of Teresa and her son stepped up and clasped Joe Torres's hand as though shaking it. The money was exchanged, the passports materialized in Joe's hands, and he was waved forward.

American customs agents in white shirts greeted us, and Joe produced his DEA card. He'd been here before, obviously, and they knew him. We were waved through. When the front wheels of Joe's car touched American soil on the northern side of the bridge, there was an audible, collective sigh.

We were home!

CHAPTER TWENTY-FIVE

Grandma Gomez — "*Si guiere cambiar el pasado, hay que perdonar.*" If you want to change the past, you have to forgive. This basically means, only by forgiving can one change the past. I scoffed at her words at the time — that it was possible to change the past simply by forgiving the people who hurt you. Now, I think it might be.

"Are we okay, Dina? You and me?"

I looked up at Rick's handsome face. He was gazing at the *luminarias* lining the walkways on San Antonio's River Walk. We were standing at the crest of Selena's bridge, so-called by the locals, because one of the movie scenes about the Tejano singer's life was filmed right on that bridge. The Christmas decor and Tivoli-lights wrapped around riverbank trees made the night scene a sparkling Disneyland of color. It was magical and romantic.

Rick's arm was around my waist. Mine was around his, my hand clutching his leather jacket as if, in a puff of smoke, he'd disappear.

"Yes," I said, "you know I love you. I always will."

I paused as a river barge full of tourists passed under us. I knew what I had to say must be phrased carefully. He had to understand. I had to make him understand.

"So you're going to marry me? Someday?" I took so long to reply that Rick shifted his gaze to my face. Clearly, he was worried.

"Yes, I think so." I turned my body into his so that we could snuggle a bit. I shook my head in wonderment—we were so close to being shot to death that very day. Now here we were in relative safety, enjoying each other in this magnificent setting. It seemed surreal.

"Dina . . ."

"No, hear me out, Rick, please. These past three months have been . . .tumultuous—yes, that's the word. Tumultuous. You came back into my life after nearly six years of trying to forget you. Trying to hate you. I warmed back up to you, tried to forgive and forget what happened. The forgiving began to happen, and then I tried to warm up to Angelina. Thinking she was part of you, your flesh and blood, despite what I knew and felt about her mother. And just when I was beginning to love her—after my appendectomy—and she begins to like me, I think—wham, bang! Friday night happens. We go from hot and sexy to—" I shook my head again in awe—"to cold reality. More than cold. Like being dunked in ice water. I came out numb, not knowing what to think or what to feel."

With my right hand, I stroked the front of his leather jacket. I wished I could touch his skin to soften or warm the effects of my next words. He was looking intently at me, boring a hole into my head as though he were trying to read my mind. Rick's thoughtful frown deepened.

"I need time, is what I'm trying to say. You've had years to adjust to the knowledge that Angelina's not your biological daughter. I've had two days. She's grown on you, and you've learned to love her." I tried to appease him with a smile. "Please, just give me time."

"You mean, before or after our wedding?" Rick was resorting to his ironic self as a shield.

"Before," I said decisively, my hand moving under the front of his jacket. My fingers snagged the waistband of his dark jeans and tugged him closer. "I need a long engagement."

His frown morphed into confusion.

"How long? Dina, the developer gave me the chance to buy one of those two-story homes I'm building for half-market value. I told him yes. The house'll be finished in six to eight months. I don't want to move into it without you."

I smiled at his practical bent of mind. I liked that about him. Rick Ramos would be a good provider. He was already a great father and a wonderful friend to my family and me. Could I trust him as a husband? Would he be faithful? Would he love me as I grew older and maybe fatter, as my hair turned gray, as our lovemaking grew stale? Would he grow tired of me? *Dios*, marriage was such a gamble! Motherhood, too. You gave so much of yourself —

Scary decisions lay before me.

"How long?" I repeated.

I raised up and smacked him on the lips. "As long as it takes me to feel right about the three of us. As long as it takes me to know, I can be a good mother to Angelina despite everything. She deserves the best, especially after what she's been through."

"You are the best," Rick murmured into my hair. When he leaned away, I could see he was smiling. "We make a good team, *querida*. I've never doubted it."

I said, "I think so, too." And I meant it.

He bent his head to kiss me.

People are like sandwiches. It's all about what they're made of.

"Hey, hey, get a room," Lisa called, jogging up the steeply arched bridge, Jesús in tow.

Rick and I gaped at the two. Well, mainly at Jesús. They'd apparently been shopping. Or rather, Lisa'd been shopping for Jesús. Lisa was a miracle worker. Even Our Lady of Guadalupe's miracle paled by comparison.

"Look at him, *el tejano*," Rick said, chortling.

Jesús was wearing blue denim jeans with a matching western shirt, cinched at the neck with a black bola tie and silver clip. On his head, a black Stetson was angled jauntily. On his feet were pointy-toed, lizard-skin boots the pale-gold color of a Texas sunset. His hair and mustache had been trimmed, and his beard shaved off. I could actually see most of his face, and I was surprised to see that he wasn't bad-looking. Lisa urged him to strike a cowboy pose, thumbs hooked into his belt, the silver buckle being the size of a dish.

"This all is for rescuing us from that horrible place," Lisa gushed. "Don't you think this look suits Jesús? He looks like a real Texican."

Jesús puffed out his chest and grinned proudly.

"Wait til Connie sees me in this. Hey—" He held out his hand. In his palm lay a mushed bullet. "Look at this. Nine millimeter. This sucker went through Mike's trunk and flattened against a metal gun box. He gave it to me—as a souvenir."

Lisa burst in, "The other bullet missed, probably ricocheted off the road. Last look we had of your boyfriend, the snake dude"—she looked at me, laughing—"he was being chased by a pickup full of federales. Mike said they'd stop him, collect a payoff and let him go on his way. But the main thing, we got away."

"Man, let me tell you, Mike was sweating bullets, himself. He kept saying it's the closest call he's had in a long time. Wish I'd had a gun." Jesús was now drawling, sounding more Texan than California Chicano. "Man, I sure'd liked to've gotten off a couple rounds into that *Suburban*. Mike wouldn't let me have his gun."

Gee, I wonder why.

"Yeah, too bad that jerkoff didn't crash into the Rio Grande," Lisa added. "He rammed his *Suburban* into the back of Mike's car, almost ran us off the road. Mike had to drive across a plaza, actually missed a few trees and benches but not by much. We had angry Mexicans running after us and that *Suburban*. We told Mike he needed to get a *Hummer*. The Army-issue kind."

I had a feeling by the time their story was repeated back in California, Jesús would've captured the cartel thug, trussed him up, and single-handedly tossed him over to the federales. After emptying Mike's gun into the thug's car, of course. Lisa's version would have them dashing across the bridge just as the *Suburban* flew into the Rio Grande. Actually, I think I was going to like their versions better.

We'd heard the gist of their getaway and border crossing over dinner. Agents Joe Torres and Mike Medina had treated us all in the hotel's dining room earlier that evening, but Rick and I knew it gave Lisa and Jesús great pleasure in repeating their hair-raising, bullets-flying car-chase.

That might become the high point of their lives.

Now, US Marshals were guarding Teresa and her son's room while they rested. The next day, Teresa faced a full day of interrogations. She wanted me to remain at her side for moral support while Lisa and a marshal stayed with Alex in the hotel. Rick and Jesús had to fly home in the morning, although Jesús had begged to stay. He was really getting into his Lone Ranger role.

"You've got some story to tell your kids and grandkids," Rick told Jesús and Lisa. "In fact, we all do. What I don't get— Jesús, how did you come up with that comedy routine? The one you pulled in that bar, the one that broke the tension and gave us an out?"

Jesús doubled over, cackling.

"That? Dude, that's an old Jerry Lewis number from *The Nutty Professor*. I don't know, man. It's the first thing that popped into my head. Didn't know if it'd work—sometimes, the only thing a guy can do is play the fool. 'Specially when you're outgunned. Y'know?"

Rick and Jesús grinned and shook hands, bumping arms, compadre-style. I began to see my brother-in-law in a new light. Maybe he wasn't such a loser, after all. Rick saw something in the guy I hadn't seen before — perhaps cleverness, satire, a Mexican male's take on mainstream America. I didn't know what it was, but if Rick could learn to like Jesús, so could I, I figured.

"We're off to the movies," Lisa said. "Want to come?"

Rick and I looked at each other. He blinked once and began to rub one hand along his thigh. I lowered my eyelids. Lisa's and my room at the Marriott River Walk was vacant and would be available, it seemed, for the next few hours. That alone was an inspiring thought.

"It's up to Dina," he said, glancing at me.

"I'm not in the mood for a movie," I said, grinning up at Rick.

He looked relieved and grateful.

"We'll just hang out on the River Walk," Rick said. His hand, planted firmly at my waist, slithered down and dug into one of my back jeans' pockets, pressing against my rump.

"Yeah, I bet," Lisa crowed, smirking.

"Catch ya later," Jesús drawled, winking.

They moved on down the bridge. We watched them leave, Lisa already talking up a storm and taking charge of the situation. Jesús was going in one direction when Lisa grabbed his arm and hauled him off in the other.

Rick thrust me against his body as a family of five started to climb the bridge.

"Are you up for it?"

"Oh, yes," I replied.

Time to take off that darned girdle!

I sat in one of the observation rooms in the Federal building, Mike Medina and another DEA agent at my side. We were seated on padded, metal chairs behind a one-way, security glass window. There was a small speaker on the wall with a control-volume knob. Mike turned up the volume as several more federal officers entered the room.

We'd just returned from a ten-minute coffee break, during which I had a chance to speak to Teresa in confidence. Earlier that morning, she'd recounted her experiences on the run after fleeing her husband's country compound.

She'd gone to Juárez with Alex, ostensibly to go Christmas shopping. From there, she and her son had escaped their bodyguards through the back door of a large department store. Carlota's son, Jaime, had hidden them in the back of a rental van and had driven them to Monterrey. Since no one knew she'd been secretly meeting Jaime in the city, passing letters to him to give to his mother or mail to California, neither her father nor her husband suspected his involvement. As far as they knew, Teresa had no other family except her mother's and her step-grandmother, whom she never knew.

For months she'd planned their run. She had hidden caches of money, a wig, clothes for her and her son, and luggage at the house of her beautician, a woman for whom she'd already done many favors. Through this woman, she'd contacted an old university friend with whom Teresa had worked in the Red Cross and in the Foundation for Cancer Treatment and who now lived in Monterrey. Teresa had once given the woman a large sum of money so that her husband could receive the best possible treatment for his prostate cancer. The woman, whom Teresa refused to name, was more than happy to return the favor and give them refuge.

Joe Torres's undercover man had transported them to Nuevo Laredo, where Joe's elderly aunt and her husband lived. The ones who'd given Teresa and her son final sanctuary. His aunt was the undercover agent, though not officially connected to the DEA — Joe thought it prudent to give that impression — and it was the youngest son who tended bar at *Los Huevos.*

"I have so many more questions, *prima,*" I told her in Spanish during our coffee break.

"Maybe the officers will ask questions that will answer some of yours," she said, blowing the steam from her cup. "By the way, I liked your friends, Lisa and Jesús. The strange-acting one is married to your sister, no? Well, he is also very brave. I heard what he did inside that horrible tavern, such courage! But I especially like your *novio,* Enrique Ramos. He is *muy caballero.*"

"*Sí,* that's what everyone calls him. *Un caballero.*"

At that point, Joe Torres had called us back inside the interrogation and observation rooms. I squeezed Teresa's hand in encouragement.

Now, Teresa Martínez Vargas was sitting at the head of a table with seating for six, flanked by Joe on one side and an ICE official on the other. Two FBI agents were also present.

The Immigration and Customs Enforcement agent silently took notes while Joe Torres resumed his questioning, his tone relaxed and respectful. I could tell Teresa liked and trusted the man, whose avuncular demeanor seemed to inspire trust and confidence. I liked him, and Teresa knew that, too.

She also knew I was in the adjacent room, watching the whole proceeding. Joe felt I might've been an emotional distraction and wanted the interview of my cousin to wrap up in one or two days. Tomorrow, Tuesday, was Christmas Eve, and everyone wanted to go home. Teresa was assured that Alex was safe in Lisa's care, under the competent guard of two US Marshals. Her son was watching Spanish-language movies in their hotel room down the hall from ours, and soon we'd be joining them for a lunch break.

As people were settling in again, my thoughts returned to early that morning. I'd said goodbye to Rick and Jesús at the door of their yellow cab, having kissed and hugged them both.

I'd most likely miss celebrating *La Noche Buena* with Rick and his family, but Joe Torres had assured me that if all went well — if Teresa was truthful and open, that is — the four of us would be on our way back to California by Wednesday morning. Christmas Day. Lisa said she didn't mind, for her uncle, Leo, and his family celebrated the holidays with a big Christmas dinner, and she'd be back in time for that. I'd already spoken to Mama, Pop, and *Abuelita*. They'd delay their festivities until I returned with my two cousins.

I knew Teresa and Alex were anxious to meet the family in Salinas. Teresa kept mentioning how Grandma Gómez had inspired her, how Grandma's leaving her husband, one of the founders of the early Juárez Cartel, had given Teresa the courage to leave hers. How Grandma's letters had encouraged her to do what was right, especially after Roberto Martínez's and his wife's sudden deaths.

My attention sharpened as Joe renewed his line of questioning in Spanish. There were translators in the Interrogation Room, so I assumed all of the federal officers present in both rooms understood the language.

"*Señora* Vargas, tell us about your father. Roberto Martínez, *el jefe* of the Juárez Cartel until his death on September thirtieth of this year."

Teresa looked at the glass as though she were seeing me.

She'd be talking about my uncle. My mother's long-lost brother. The brother she never knew, except through photos and letters from Teresa and Grandma's sister, Consuelo.

"He was a kind man, my father," Teresa began.

Her Spanish was cultivated, her pronunciation was clear, easy for me to understand. I noticed that she ignored the raised eyebrows and sardonic smiles of the two FBI agents in the room. "I did not know that he was *un jefe del cartel* until I was about five or six, when he was made *caudillo de la charreada de Juárez —*"

I translated as best I could in my mind. Honorable Master of the City of Juárez Rodeo.

"He had great power then, but in my little girl's mind, I thought it was because he was in charge of the rodeo and all the festivities, like a Chairman of the Board. At the end of the rodeo, my brother and I — my brother, Juan, emigrated to Spain as soon as he finished *el colegio*. He studied at the University of Salamanca and is now an oncologist in Madrid. He flew home for Papa's funeral in October. He is now back in Madrid, and soon I hope my son and I will join him there."

Joe Torres exchanged a quick look with one of the FBI men, then nodded, encouraging Teresa to continue.

"I think he was aware of my father's business and wanted no part of it. Anyway, Juan and I were then six and eight at the time of the Juárez rodeo. We went to the stables and cow pens to say goodbye to our favorite horses and bulls. It was then that we saw the boxes of sugar being loaded into the cattle trucks that were leaving for *el norte*. Men with guns were guarding the loading of these boxes of sugar and animals. We thought it strange, and like children, we asked — what if the animals urinate on the sugar? Won't it be spoiled? The guards laughed and chased us off. Not before we saw the specially built panels on those trucks. Underneath the floor, on the sides. Naturally, we figured out it wasn't sugar hidden inside those cattle trucks. They were smuggling cocaine and other drugs. Maybe heroin, I really didn't know for sure at the time.

"Later, those trucks were replaced by refrigerated trucks carrying perishables like melons and strawberries. Anyway, after that, my brother changed grew quiet and moody. Years later, he told me he was moving to Spain and never coming back. I think it broke my father's heart."

I flicked a glance at the federal officials inside the observation room. One wrote something on a thick yellow pad of paper. I wondered if Juan Martínez in Madrid would be contacted to verify Teresa's story.

"Growing up, I never asked my father about his business. We had a house in *el campo*—a walled hacienda with servants, a *finca* with cattle and horses nearby. Most of the time, I lived with my mother and Juan in Juárez, where I attended school and where we had a house. My mother's close friend owned a beauty salon, and she was the one who helped arrange secret meetings with cousin Jaime." Teresa paused to take a drink of water.

"I went to the University of Mexico in Guadalajara and received a diploma in Journalism. Of course, I knew what my father was, what he did by then, but my mother's rule was to never inquire. It was not to be our concern. My mother died a violent death with my father, so as it turned out, my father's business should have been her concern."

Teresa's voice hitched, and she paused to recover her composure.

"When did you return to your father's hacienda, the headquarters of his drug smuggling operation?" Agent Torres asked.

Teresa looked down at her hands, laced together tightly on the table, the only indication that she was a little nervous. Amazingly so, she remained primarily calm and dry-eyed except for the moment she spoke of her mother. I would've been balling my head off by now, I knew, if I were in her place. She'd obviously prepared herself for this ordeal, and she knew it'd soon be over. Her strength astounded me.

"When I discovered I was pregnant shortly after I finished my studies. Pedro Vargas is not my son's father. An American student at the university, whom I fell in love with, is

Alejandro's father."

I leaned closer to the window, intrigued. Was there no end to the secrets in my family? The artichoke layers kept peeling off!

"I returned home—I did not tell the American that I was expecting his child. He was there for only the spring and summer before going back to Pennsylvania for medical school. I suppose I was ashamed and embarrassed. Recently, my grandmother in California—Dolores Martínez Gómez—found him through Lisa Luna's uncle. He is a pediatrician in Pittsburgh, and he wrote several emails to me before we fled the hacienda. My son is looking forward to meeting him. His name is Alex O'Connell." She paused to take a deep breath. "After that, we hope to join my brother and his family in Madrid."

More furious writing by the feds in front of me and behind me. I sat back, amazed.

Well, Grandma Gómez, the clever little witch that she was, had enlisted Leo Luna's help at the same time that Lisa and I were trying to arrange for Teresa and her son's emigration to the States. I had to marvel at my grandmother's resourcefulness. So if Grandma Gómez had gotten Leo Luna to help find this physician in Pennsylvania, why rope *me* into this family intrigue?

Boy, Grandma had a lot of explaining to do!

Then it dawned on me. One rebellious, somewhat estranged granddaughter looking for another rebellious, also estranged granddaughter. The poetic justice of this situation began to make sense to me.

Poetic justice or cosmic retribution?

The other fact hit home—Alex's fair hair and blue eyes, explainable now in light of Teresa's revelation. So his true father was an American! Further impetus for Teresa to visit the States on her way to Spain.

"If you knew about your father's true business affairs at this time, why did you consent to marry your father's accountant—the Juárez Cartel's accountant, Pedro Vargas?" The ICE officer was bending forward, his brows furrowed. He was as fluent in Spanish as Joe Torres.

"He was not the Cartel's accountant at the time. He worked for the Bank of Mexico, and he seemed like a decent enough man. Pedro was educated, I needed to legitimize my child, the boy's father was a poor medical student in another country, I was feeling lost and lonely, my father pressured me into the marriage—all of these reasons. It seemed best at the time. I did not know then how ruthless a man Pedro Vargas was, how he was biding his time, had planned to use our marriage as a means of entering the Cartel. I did not dream that he would then plot to take over Papa's role in the business. When *Papá* died, he was in excellent health. So was my mother. I suspected Pedro had them killed, but, of course, I could never prove this. Not in court. Then I overheard Pedro speak to the head of Cartel security. He made comments that made me realize who had ordered the murders." Teresa paused and heaved a shudder of repulsion.

"That was when Pedro's true nature became apparent. Even if I could have proved in a court of law that my parents were murdered by his orders, there was nothing to be done. My hands were tied, all the voices silenced. No one cared as long as business continued." Teresa sighed, shaking her head.

"For months before their murder, I had been planning my escape but only in a general way, putting away money, that sort of thing. I knew one day I would have to leave. So I had kept in secret contact with a few close university friends, all the while pretending to be totally uninterested in my father's and husband's drug operation. But I picked up bits of information here and there, read invoices that were left on my father's desk, shipment schedules, truck routes, Pedro's computer when I had the chance. I memorized names, both Mexican and American, the couriers, receivers, distributors. You see, I knew I would need help—leverage, as you say in English. I never took the risk of making photocopies of documents—that would have been foolhardy, gentlemen. I have no doubt at all that Pedro would have me killed if he had found such copies, so I took photos of those documents on my cell phone, took notes, and then deleted the photos. I also kept a written journal of those notes and stored it."

The federal officers in the observation room were practically falling out of their chairs. *This* was what they were genuinely interested in. Not Teresa's personal life.

"So where's the rest of the information, *Señora* Vargas? These names, schedules, truck routes—we saw copies of what you sent to your cousin. Agent Torres said there was more."

"I brought four suits with me. All handmade, lined with interfacing. That interfacing is my journal of notes, an excellent way to conceal things, is it not, *Señor* Torres?"

"Yes, indeed. Can you have that fabric for us by tomorrow?" Joe Torres was bent over, his elbows nearly raking grooves in the table.

"Oh yes, if cousin Dina will help me rip open all those seams. I have dots of data, too, from the Organization. Did I mention, gentlemen, I am an accomplished seamstress?" Teresa smiled sweetly at the DEA agent and the other men at the table.

Joe's chin rose off his folded hands, his mouth hanging open.

"Dots of data?" he asked, not understanding.

"This suit I am wearing, that you complimented me on, that you thought was a couturier's creation. Merino wool, the finest Spanish merino wool, it is made of. I bought the wool and satin and made those suits, myself. I could not risk anyone seeing what I was doing."

Joe was frowning, getting restless at my cousin's getting sidetracked. I knew, however, that she was leading up to some revelation.

"Instead of writing with fabric ink on the interfacing this time, which would've taken too many hours and I was running out of time, I took the dots from Pedro's study. Pedro had a habit of storing information on these tiny microchips, making copies of them on flats of plastic boards. These dots are the size of a large period on a printed page, using—I would have to estimate—thirty-six point sized word-processor print. Just before I left with my son, I took several flats of these dots and glued them to the interfacing of these four suits."

At this point, all the men at the table were leaning forward, openly intrigued.

Teresa looked from face to face, appeared relieved that they were interested.

"Normally, the adhesive that the Organization uses can be seen with an ultraviolet-black light. I used regular fabric glue to adhere these dots to the interfacing. Pedro had these dots placed on the trucks used for transporting items manufactured by maquiladoras. Especially the electronics factories. As I understood it, if a shipment box contained a data dot on the outside—not easily detected, of course—that box contained the Organization's contraband. That way, boxes could be separated after they entered the United States. Anyway, I hope these data dots will be useful. I had no way of reading them, but I am certain your computers can. It's the least I could do for all your help."

Joe Torres, the ICE officer, and the two FBI agents sat back, staring at Teresa as if she were Joan of Arc incarnate or Einstein revealing his Theory of Relativity for the first time.

There were looks of frank admiration on all the agents' faces.

Teresa gazed through the glass in my direction and gave me a thumbs-up gesture. She smiled widely.

"*Las nietas de Abuela Gómez no son estúpidas,*" she added for my benefit. The granddaughters of Grandma Gómez are not stupid.

No, indeed, we're not, I thought. I sat there, watching her, admiring her—no, in awe of her.

My Mexican cousin.

Smiling, I gave her a double thumbs-up in return.

CHAPTER TWENTY-SIX

"Amor vincit omnia." Love conquers all. Where this *buen dicho* originated — it was Latin, so probably one of the Roman historians — I couldn't tell you, but I sincerely hoped this was true.

My niece's traditional *quinceañera* displayed all the glitz and pomp of a wedding ceremony. First, Frank's eldest was blessed at church by the parish priest, then Amelia, a pretty fifteen-year-old, was feted at a reception. She was dressed in a billowing, frothy white gown, decorated with a pale pink satin sash, and on her feet, she wore pale pink heels to match. A sparkly rhinestone tiara crowned her upswept coif, and rhinestones glittered from her ears and wrists. It was her day to shine!

Amelia danced with her proud father in the rented hall in Salinas, decorated in pink, white, and silver. After a few turns around the dance floor, moving smoothly to a *paso doble,* other couples joined them.

Rick took my hand and, without a word, led me into a fluid series of two steps. The navy suit he was wearing accentuated his tall, well-built frame but didn't impede his sexy movements. Not that he needed a suit to enhance his good looks, but it did give him added panache. A debonair quality to his masculinity.

Kind of a taller, younger Benjamin Bratt in a tux. I thought so, anyway.

"All this is thanks to you, Rick, you know that. Frank and

Isabel would never've been able to afford such a fiesta. Look at all the *damas* and *chambelanes*, dressed to kill. And the food, my God, such a spread—the *cabritos al pastor*, the *enchiladas con mole*, the *gorditas de pollo*—"

Not to mention the honeyed ham and platters of fresh fruit, shrimp, and *dulces*.

"My favorite's the *gordita de nopales* with that great *pico de gallo*. You made those, didn't you? Aha, I knew that was your dish. Never thought cactus could taste so good. And hey, I just gave Frank and Roberto a lot of work. Your brothers do good tile work. Even Jesús works his tail off for me. I haven't given them a thing."

As usual, Rick was being modest, another trait he had that I admired. I looked over at Jesús, holding court in one corner, surrounded by a multitude of little nieces, nephews, and second and third cousins as he told and retold our encounter with the Gulf Cartel's commandos in Nuevo Laredo. No doubt embellishing each one's part in the drama. At one point, he stood up and acted the role of Snake Man, his hand on a make-believe gun, grimacing and snarling—although not quite as menacing as the real thing. Creeps! Every time I remembered Snake Man and Gold Tooth and that horrible little bar in Nuevo Laredo, I shivered. Damn, we were lucky to get out alive!

The children were saucer-eyed, the little boys in their new suits imitating the posture of Jesús in full cowboy mode, gunning down Snake Man. We noted that Jesús was apparently omitting his Jerry Lewis comedic bit as the crippled, blathering fool. Still wearing his Texas garb, Jesús was now outgunning every Cartel thug in *Los Huevos*.

"Jesús is maybe embroidering the story a bit," Rick suggested an amused glint in his eyes. "Ya think?"

I pointed to two children on the dance floor, hand-in-hand, kind of skipping in rhythm to the fast *pasodoble* beat. Seven-year-old Alex was sporting a black-and-silver Mariachi suit and clasping the hand of Angelina, resplendent in a long, pink taffeta creation. She was swishing and swirling cheerfully, her dark sausage-curls bouncing up and down as she skipped along, beaming at her taller, handsome dancing partner.

"Angelina looks so pretty," I told Rick. "I'm glad she likes the dress I bought her."

"I've never seen her so happy. Think she's got a thing for Teresa's boy. He's a real heartbreaker, that kid. Polite, stoical, bright. How's he adapting to American life?"

The music switched to a slower rhythm, and the hired dee-jay, a teenaged cousin by marriage, bowed formally, then took Frank's place at Amelia's side. Rick and I continued to hold each other, our feet and hips making their own adjustment to the change in beat.

"Fine, I think. He's been studying English for over a year and Teresa has him in an ELD class at school. But oh, Rick, look at the genes he's got. Teresa's one of the brightest women I know — and look at the boy's father. A physician. Good-looking, too."

We glanced over at the linen-draped table where Teresa sat with Alex's father, a sandy-haired, blue-eyed Irish-American who was at present in deep conversation with Pop and Mama. That Dr. O'Connell was also holding hands with a radiant Teresa, dressed like a model in one of her infamous suits, did not escape us. Grandma Gómez, sitting at the same round table, was watching Rick and me dancing. Her face lit up when she caught my eye. We nodded at each other respectfully.

A few days after we returned from Texas, Teresa told Grandma Gómez that her father had been planning a trip to California to finally visit his mother. I doubted that this was true, but Teresa knew that hearing this would make Grandma feel better. Grandma had wept, along with Mama. To think that he was at long last forgiving his mother for abandoning him as a baby—well, afterward Pop told me Grandma seemed a lot more at peace.

At another table nearby sat Flora and her new husband, Steve. Yeah, that was another interesting story. After discovering that her long-lost love in Spain was happily married, fat and balding, she'd returned to the States and renewed her romance with the trust-fund kid. They'd eloped to Vegas and were now occupying her house near the Alameda. Steve was whispering in her ear, making her erupt with laughter. Needless to say, I was no longer living in Flora's house.

Hey, whatever floats your boat—that was my new philosophy. To each his own. People might think I was short a fuse or two for taking back Rick, considering everything. But they wouldn't know the entire story.

I'd learned there were layers and layers of truth to everything. People were complex, and so were their needs. So were their stories and their secrets. Sometimes it took a long while for people to reveal themselves. Down and deep personal truths were funny that way.

Rick turned me about. Another table came into view. Lisa Luna and her cop-boyfriend, Tyler, were chatting with my sisters, all decked out in their finest. Lisa made a tiny wave when she saw me, and behind her hand, she pointed in Tyler's direction. Then she made an O with her thumb and forefinger as if to say, Boy, is he worth it! I wondered how long it'd be before his control freak of a mother started interfering. Oh well, until then.

I was living in an apartment, had gone back to teaching, of course, after my Christmas break. Teresa was now working freelance with *Univision*, the Spanish-language television channel, and studying English at night. She and Dr. O'Connell, the boy's father, were getting reacquainted via email and occasional visits. The boy and his namesake had hit it off immediately. Funny, how that is. The power of genes? In a few months, Teresa and Alex would be leaving for Madrid and the home of her brother, Juan Martinez.

Agents Joe Torres and Mike Medina? Joe emailed me once to say briefly that they were fine and their continued investigations of both the Juárez and Gulf cartels were paying off. He said they were learning a lot from that bug I'd planted in *Los Huevos* and the other information Teresa had smuggled out of the hacienda. I decided to leave it at that. For my part, I was done with all that. Teresa and her son had new identities and would soon have a new home with Dr. O'Connell or Juan Martinez. That's all I cared about.

"Yeah, that Alex has good genes," I repeated, tearing my gaze away from the boy and Angelina dancing shyly together.

"We've got good genes, too," Rick said. "Wouldn't hurt to put those good genes to work — to make the next generation, I mean. Eventually, I mean."

"All in good time, *Señor* Ramos. All in good time."

That was no white lie.

The End

ABOUT THE AUTHOR

Donna Del Oro lives in Northern California, is bicultural, and loves her Hispanic heritage. She is the author of the Delphi Bloodline series (Athena's Secrets, Athena's Fears, Athena's Dilemma), Born to Sing, Dreaming and Scheming in Los Angeles, and Sonya's Midlife Crisis.

Made in the USA
Las Vegas, NV
01 August 2023

75517134R00223